SMILE

PLAID FOUL

BOOK I

DNIAS DIRK

authorHOUSE®

AuthorHouse™ UK
1663 Liberty Drive
Bloomington, IN 47403 USA
www.authorhouse.co.uk
Phone: 0800.197.4150

Published by AuthorHouse 07/16/2018

ISBN: 978-1-5462-9235-7 (sc)
ISBN: 978-1-5462-9234-0 (e)

Print information available on the last page.

This book is printed on acid-free paper.

Dedication

'For things that perceive pain and for the possibility of ineluctable pain of artificial intelligence.'

I wish to dedicate 'Smile' to several people, animals and things. In general terms, the tips have come from members of staff at the Jobcentre in Pollokshaws, Glasgow, my brother Peter, who advised me against not starting drinking, my sister Joanna who offered to pay for a writing course, and internet research, rather than having been gleaned from private novel reading. The inspiration for the characters has come from people I have met, including the former Special Adjudicator Sir Kenneth Forbes, a woman whose name I do not know, whom I encountered in court, my father Dr Brian Donaldson, my late grandmother Jean Donaldson, as well as famous names like Ben Afflek and Ronan Keating. The inspiration for the ideas has come from the most painful personal experiences as well as formal education and training, including law, legal practice and criminal justice, as well as Citizens Advice. In general, the people who gave me support were employed within the Jobcentre in Pollokshaws Glasgow: Wendy, Heather and Lorraine, as well as my parents and my Auntie Ann.

I have no patron exactly and thus I am unable to express my gratitude to the same for the inspiration.

I disbelieve there is anyone, even a curious thug, who seriously wishes to claim the honour of the book dedication. I have no spouse or partner and no children. The people who are most important to my project are my parents: Dr Brian and Eileen Donaldson. My inspiration has come from the writers I have read, originally William Diehl, as well as Mark Billingham, Stephen Leather, Tami Hoag, Jesse Kellerman and Michael Crichton, and of course Ian Rankin, and many others.

I wrote originally for my mother; however, I did not write this book for any person in particular. I simply wanted to bring a segmental conclusion to over ten years of craft, in terms of publication and in terms of financial return.

The book is not about a person in particular and is not written in their memory. The people whom I admire are my father, Tony Blair, Steve Davis, Tim Bendzko and Tom Odell.

The people who tirelessly support the themes of my book are the mentally ill and the torture victims, as well as children and adults with nothing, as well as creatures in pain.

I was encouraged to become a writer by my Auntie Ann. She offered to fund a writing course.

The people who contributed to my overall writing career are members of staff at the Pollokshaws Jobcentre in Glasgow. They did so by taking an interest in my writing and offering suggestions, as well as paying me my benefit throughout the majority of my writing journey.

I did not promise anyone I would dedicate my first book to them. I dedicate my writing to my Auntie Ann, my mother and father, my friend Karen Kelly who has taken the trouble to read parts of my writing, and to my friend Tina/Ms Moore/mate/babe who has availed me of so many friends and acquaintances and fun nights out, as well as allowing me to be part of her family, to Sandy who said: 'All the little things', to the man I fell in love with James, and who was the muse for one of my character's amatorial break-down, even if only for a short while (he likes Pink Floyd), to the other James, just in case he thought or felt I'd been unfair on him, to Shepherd, Paul, Thomas, Brendon, Ginty, Paula (you know who you are) my parents' cats Alexander and Sergei (Sergei has gone missing and is presumed dead) and to Glen's Vodka and Pall Mall cigarettes.

In terms of my personality and character, I do not mind who you are as long as you can demonstrate courtesy, are kind, and respect pain.

In terms of reflecting my relationship with the recipients of my dedication, my mother thinks I try to be too clever, use too many words, my father does not read novels because they are not important enough, while my Auntie Ann is effortlessly better-read than I am.

The themes of the book are justice, pain and disfigurement. My adversaries, including Frank Mosson, Tony Blair, Gordan Brown and David Cameron and tergiversators, including Kenneth Hill and David Sievewright, and my torturers whose names I will conceal contributed to the themes.

I wish to dedicate the themes to all sentient things that have suffered.

I have selected the following quotation. 'Life is a waste of time, time is a waste of life but get wasted all of the time and you'll have the time of your life.'

Acknowledgements

The editor at AuthorHouse advised: 'You might want to add a dedication page and an acknowledgments page, although these are optional.'

The present writer politely suggests an acknowledgements page presents the author with the opportunity to appreciate more sincerely people who have assisted with the project.

In some ways this might be the elementary section. So many of the manque assaults have been embarked upon and the author is merely trying to better appreciate the people who have helped and to be more *ad hominem* in terms of their help. In other ways, it can be the arduous section. The author is trying to explicate more personally who helped, why they helped, how they helped, which help they gave, and when and where specifically they helped and how that would matter in terms of the fulfillment of the work.

It is made harder for the present writer, since four almost invisible years have elapsed since the topic of acknowledgments was taken on board The old quotes coming from family and friends, as well as those that were anthropomorphic, are out of time and out of touch. Unfortunately, none are entwined within the present project. I have written 'Smile' through a splintered lens of disenfranchisement. In a sense, I have crossed the Rubicon. I have written to a length and to a degree where old references are defunct and new conceits are less ennobling.

I will, however, give my favourite quote and perhaps relegate the earlier quotes to the end; they belong to an earlier stage of the writing journey.

'You like? Twenty bucks and you can
kiss 'em!' (Roadhouse, 1989.)

In terms of the actual writing of the book, I blandish my forays that I did that alone. In terms of producing the book, I owe my gratitude to the tireless staff at AuthorHouse. In particular I would like to thank Alex Ceniza for taking the trouble to understand me as a person, as well as the project itself. I would also like to thank my Senior Publishing Consultant JM Morris for exhorting me at junctures where my sense of commitment might have been waning. I would like to thank the editing team at Authorhouse for flagging up my schoolboy errata. I would especially like to thank Dorothy Lee for her direct help, for all the responsible advice and insider information she has dispensed. She has always reverted to me and has never once exacerbated the strain of life-writing.

Within the family, I would like to thank my Auntie Ann for encouraging my dream. She has never forgotten my birthday or Christmas. She has enthroned so many long hours knitting me a gallimaufry of outstanding jumpers, ranging from the risible to the ingenious. I would also like to thank her son, my late cousin, Ken MacTaggart. He afforded me so much time over the telephone toward his demise, was perhaps the only person in my life who could truly empathise with my disordered thoughts and lacerated feelings. He was liked by everyone and is sorely missed. He became a true friend, rather than a distant cousin. I would like to thank Frank Burns for the botanical references.

Finally, I would like to thank my parents Brian and Eileen for not mollycoddling my intussusception. They have ensured that writing did not surmount identity.

Contents

Part D Data Analysis; Processing the Information

SEVENTH INTERLUDE: The End of Jack Dorcha

Part E Conclusions and Recommendations; Deductions

PART A

Introduction: The Preludes

1966...

2pm...

Outer Hebrides, Lewis...

Aboard the Sunseeker Manhattan 50...

(i) The Boat

The very, very small elite group of biggest Scottish multi-millionaires cruised through the boisterous turbulence of the loch. The sun above them was blazing like Titan's fiery wheel in the sky. It was a-dazzle with splendour and it was an altogether soul-swelling experience to Olivia McLean. Her eyes were brown, sloe and milk chocolate. Her bony arms paraded her self-renunciation, her feeling of hard-earned satisfaction. Her perfect posture exhibited all her aerobic exercises. Her graceful build exhibited she could be impressive and perceive pride. Her sculptured cheekbones showed what could be done with money and instil confidence. Her round chin gave away the young woman in her and her feeling of desirability. Her vigorous constitution showed that softer could be harder and feel stronger. Her curving ears showed that natural talent could breed satisfaction. Her big and voluminous eyelashes had been promoted to winged eyelashes, they were plucked and shaped. They made her eyes look big and bright. The sun added sheen to collagen-inflated lips, parading her youthful vanity and feeling of confidence.

Between gaps in the sea-formation, and the headlands, lances of its molten-gold beams splashed against the vitreous elements of the Sunseeker Manhattan 50.

James Bennet, Ealdahach Wren, Jaeger White, Aiden Fields and Peter Reid were in the full beam master cabin.

Peter Reid had small eyes. He half-chuckled to himself. He tapped his pug nose making no more impression than his thin lips, reassuring of years of boring meticulous pharmaceutical control and his present feeling of exiguous appreciation. He raised his entire forehead 'I have to say,' he said, 'I'm surprised, the vessel's private en-suite facilities are most sanitary.'

Aiden Fields popped out of the guest cabin, which was meant for those all important VIP'S. His eyes were blue- glacial blue. They were protruding eyes, revealing his very sensitive but very approachable personality and exposing his feeling of worry and stress. His swollen lips exposed years of promoting tough fabrics, persecutory complexes and familial unrest, as well as his present feeling of tentativeness. 'Yes,' he said, 'And, I must admit, 'the leather upholstery does smell of heaven.'

Ealdahach Wren's eyes were silver- like silver lightning. He blinked owlishly. 'You do realise,' he said, 'there already is and will be for the human being, as our immediate species, if and when it becomes too evolved, not just the capacity for pain but the experience of infinite multi-universal agony.'

'Even if there were,' said Peter Reid, 'chemicals can fix that.'

Ealdahach waved his head. 'No Peter, no James,' he said, 'the only possible escape would be a superior intelligence committing a non-organic shutdown.'

James Bennet had green eyes. He smiled complaisantly. 'You're always thinking ahead, Ealdahach.'

'He's always dreaming,' said Peter Reid.

'Anyway,' said James Bennet, ' the vessel has other extras, you know.'

'Oh, yes?' said Aiden Fields.

'Yes,' smiled James Bennet. 'The heating is incredible.'

'The machines will overheat,' said Ealdahach Wren, 'They won't be able to cool down. They will burn in eternal agony.'

'You really need your head read, E,' said Peter Reid.

James Bennet searched for a useful distraction. 'There is also,' he said, 'the individual generator, the hydraulic passesrelle and the twin 800hp diesel engines.'

Ealdahach Wren waved his head. 'Yes,' he said, 'your mechanical engineering, James is one of the progenitors to artificial pain.'

Peter Reid sighed with exasperation. 'Where do you get this from E?' he said. 'Alcohol? Drugs?'

'No,' said Ealdahach Wren, 'from the abysmal depths from my sleep, from the unlimited bounds of my imagination.'

'That's hardly empirical research,' said Peter Reid.

'Your chemicals, Peter,' said Ealdahach Wren, 'can cause indescribable torment, but non-organic intelligences will suffer what our friend Aiden might call hell.'

Aiden Fields frowned. 'What has my religion got to do with this?'

'Your religion,' said Ealdahach Wren, 'recounts historic torture, man's inhumanity to man, reflects present pain and prophesizes future non-biological pain.'

Jaeger wrinkled his turnip nose scarred by rosacea and alcohol. 'Aiden doesn't need patronised, E,' said Jaeger White. 'He gets the real world.'

Aiden Fields gawked slightly. 'I suppose so.'

'Yes, Jaeger,' said Peter Reid, 'and what is the real world?'

'The real world, Peter,' said Jaeger White, 'involves being fed and watered.'

James Bennet smiled kindly. 'Yes, I agree,' he said. 'At the same time, Aiden understands traditional ideas.'

Jaeger White's eyes crossed in exasperation. He pouted his cracked lips, revealing years spent working outdoors with livestock and the hardiness of his inner feelings.

'Can the bloody man not speak for himself?' said Jaeger White.

Aiden Fields frowned again.

'Anyway,' said Peter Reid, 'you can't prove any of your outlandish theories.'

'Imagination, Peter,' said Ealdahach, 'is more important that knowledge.'

'Seriously, it is belief E,' said Peter Reid.

Aiden Fields gawped. 'I accept belief.'

James Bennet nodded respectfully. 'Of course, Aiden,' he said.

'I prefer something more earthly,' said Jaeger White.

'Yes, more terrene, more sublunary,' said Ealdahach Wren

'I thought you did mechanical engineering,' said Peter Reid.

'Yes, Peter,' said Ealdahach Wren, 'but I also do fairness.'

James Bennet nodded politely. 'Yes, your son, Ealdahach.'

'Of course,' said Ealdahach Wren.

'Ewald?' said James Bennet.

'Yes, indeed,' said Ealdahach, 'he is a lawyer.'

Peter Reid sniffed. 'A lawyer, really? My son is a doctor.'

'Yes, Peter,' said James Bennet, 'that would be your son Taylor.'

'Of course, James,' said Peter Reid. 'He is a consultant.'

'Most impressive,' said James Bennet.

'Yes, James,' said Peter Reid. He expanded a fraction. 'I understand your son would be working with cars.'

James Bennet smiled happily. 'Yes,' he said. 'He's working with Jarrod.'

Peter Reid furrowed his brows. 'Who?' he said.

'My son,' said Aiden Fields.

'Obviously,' said Jaeger White, 'Jarrod is also very political.'

'He is?' said Peter Reid.

'Yes,' said Aiden Fields, 'he believes in Irish Republicanism.'

'He sounds naïve,' said Peter Reid.

'Not necessarily,' said Ealdahach Wren, 'Sometimes the lawyers help the doctors.'

Peter Reid scowled. 'Meaning?'

'My son could keep your son, Peter out of jail,' said Ealdahach Wren. 'He could also defend his reputation.'

'My son's reputation needs no defence,' said Peter Reid.

'Perhaps not yet,' said James Bennet. Searching for another distraction to break the tension, he said: 'What do you think of the dining space, Jaeger.'

Jaeger White nodded authoritatively. 'It is very satisfactory.'

'What are you cooking for us, Jaeger?' said Peter Reid.

Jaeger White huffed slightly. 'My best smoked salmon of course.'

'Sounds delicious,' said Aiden Fields.

Jaeger White nodded firmly at Aiden Fields. 'It is followed by a choice of premium beef, lamb or steak.'

'I agree with Aiden,' said James Bennet. 'It sounds irresistible.'

'Only if the animals,' said Ealdahach Wren, 'were put out of pain properly.'

Jaeger White sighed.

Peter Reid frowned.

James Bennet smiled.

Aiden Fields shrugged.

Atop deck, the sun was still streaming, creating rejuvenated pockets of re-directed light. Olivia McLean flashed fever from her almond-shaped eyes. She snuggled against Jack Dorcha. 'You like boats, Jack,' she said.

Her father stood there: Lewis McLean. 'Careful darling,' he said, 'Mr Dorcha is a most persuasive man.'

Olivia shrugged. Her lips protruded a little.

Jack Dorcha's eyes were brown; cat and upward slanting; chips of emerald ice. They were predatory flinty eyes glared unblinking, split lips boasting the number of mouth-smacks he had sustained, and re-affirming the proving the anger of his feelings; his wavy, saddle, boxer's nose evidencing the injury and nasal fracture, with a nasal bump/hump. It was not a genetic family trait. His face was distorted and white with rage. 'You think I can't resist your child, Lewis?'

Lewis McLean had brown milk chocolate eyes but his angry gaze sliced Jack Dorcha. 'Put it this way,' he said, 'you either resist her or you won't be able to resist me.'

Jack Dorcha's brows knitted together. 'I do have them, you know?'

Frank Sharp's gunmetal eyes fired deck-wise from Jack Dorcha in derision. 'How is Scott by the way?'

'He's always learning,' said Jack Dorcha.

Frank Sharp smiled tolerantly at Olivia. 'Ask him what a boat is, Olivia?'

The cabin crew funnelled out from below deck.

'A boat is just a thing of transport,' said Jaeger White.

'Quite,' said Peter Reid.

'Also', said Ealdahach Wren, 'a means to hurt innocent sea creatures.'

Peter Reid loured. 'How?'

'Many a majestic nervous system has been harpooned,' said Ealdahach Wren.

Frank Sharp shook his head. 'There are no harpoons on board here, E.'

'No,' said James Bennet. 'How is Hugh?'

Frank leaned back slightly. 'He continues to master the piano.'

'Does he?' said Peter Reid haughtily. 'Does he master stitches?'

'No,' said Aiden Fields, 'I do that.'

James Bennet chuckled. 'Yes, your textiles. As long as he plays fairly.'

Jack Dorcha waved his head with disinterest.

Olivia McLean smiled diplomatically. 'Go on, then,' said Olivia, 'what is a boat?'

Jack rotated his head. 'Well, it's a small vessel.'

Olivia smiled. 'A small vessel?'

'At least,' said Frank Sharp.

'Yes,' said Peter Reid, 'it requires more.'

'So?' said Olivia McLean.

'Well,' said Jack Dorcha, 'a boat is specifically designed for navigating in near-shore areas or inland waterways.'

'So,' said Olivia McLean, 'a ship would be a bigger vessel.'

'Quite,' said Peter Reid.'

'Of course,' said James Bennet, 'there is a thin line.'

'Yes,' said Ealdahach Wren, 'a boat assumes no little amount of water, a ship represents a threat to life.'

Jack Dorcha's head slanted. 'There are quite a few differences which set both of them apart.'

'Really?' said Olivia McLean.

'As I say,' said Lewis McLean, 'Careful, darling.'

James Bennet interjected. 'Apart from recreational purposes, boats have also served an integral purpose in the commercial world.'

'Really, Mr Bennet? said Olivia McLean.

'Yes,' said James Bennet, 'by allowing active transportation of both passengers and cargo,'

'Certainly wherever short distances are concerned,' said Peter Reid.

Olivia McLean flashed her toothpaste smile again. 'And what different types of boats do you get?'

Frank Sharp lowered. 'Boats can be classified in to three main sections.'

Olivia simulated enthusiasm. 'They can?'

'Yes,' said Frank Sharp, 'The first main section are unpowered or man-powered boats.'

Olivia McLean gawked. 'Like rafts?'

'Of course,' said Peter Reid. 'And gondolas, kayaks etc.'

Olivia McLean nodded. 'And the second?'

James Bennet smiled at Olivia McLean. 'Sail boats, I think, Olivia.'

'And the third?' said Olivia McLean

'Motorboats,' said Frank Sharp. 'Engine-powered.'

'That is,' said Jack Dorcha, 'if you're comparing boats in terms of propulsion.'

'Oh, yes,' said Olivia McLean.

'Yes,' said Jack Dorcha, 'For instance, there are a vast range of boats: fishing boats, bass boats, bow-rider boats, catamaran boats, cuddy houseboats cabins boats, centre console boats, dinghy boats, houseboats, trawler boats, cabin cruiser boats, game boats, motor yacht boats, personal watercraft boats, runabout boats, jet boats, wake-board/ski boats, banana boats, life boats...'

Frank Sharp sneered. 'Perhaps Jack does know something.'

Jack Dorcha levelled him with his eyes. 'I know a lot more than that.'

Olivia McLean smiled ingenuously. 'Are there any other types of boats?'

'Many,' said Jack Dorcha.

Frank Sharp stared at Jack Dorcha derisively. 'Really?'

'Yes,' said Jack Dorcha. 'There are hydrofoil boats, cigarette boats, cuddy boats, tug boats, high speed crafts, bumper boats, pilot boats, fire boats, well boats... The list extends.'

'You're boring her, Jack,' said Lewis McLean.

Olivia frowned. 'No, he's not, dad.'

'Then she's patronising you,' said Frank Sharp.

'What kind of boat is this?' said Olivia McLean.

Jack Dorcha huffed. 'The best of fleet.'

'What is that?' said Aiden Fields.

'A sail-boat?' said Olivia McLean.

'No,' said Jack Dorcha, 'it's not a mono-hull sail-boat.'

'A catamaran?' said Olivia McLean.

'No,' said Peter Reid, 'it's a motorboat.'

'Yes,' said Jack Dorcha, 'it is a gulet or luxury yacht.'

Frank Sharp snorted. 'But not an ocean-liner.'

'But big enough,' said James Bennet.

Suddenly, there was an announcement. 'The salmon is ready,' said Jaeger White.

'Ah!' said James Bennet, 'perfect.'

Peter Reid grumbled. ''We'll see,' he said.

'About bloody time,' said Frank Sharp

They all gathered round the above-deck dining table and sat down.

'What d'you think, darling?' said Lewis McLean.

'It's simply scrummy, Dad,' said Olivia McLean.

James Bennet smiled benevolently. 'Isn't it just?

'Except for...' said Frank Sharp.

'Not yet,' said Peter Reid.

Jack Dorcha gawped. 'What?'

Aiden Fields gulped.

'Nothing,' said Ealdahach Wren, 'as long as the meal is peaceful.'

'Forget peaceful,' said Jack Dorcha, 'I'll open the Glenfiddich 50.'

'Can I dad?' said Olivia McLean.

'No,' said Lewis McLean.

'One glass won't hurt the girl,' said Jaeger White.

'Really, Lewis,' said Jack Dorcha, 'you must stop being so protective.'

Lewis McLean grinned contentedly. 'Accepted, Jack.'

Jack Dorcha popped the cork. It made Aiden Fields recoil. He poured whiskey into everyone's glasses. He took a great swig.

'I decided,' said Jaeger White, 'We would have the lamb first, then the beef.'

'Eh?' said Jack Dorcha.

'Why don't you just serve them both together,' said Jack Dorcha.

'No,' said Jaeger White, 'I prefer to cod my customers.'

Olivia McLean gawped. 'But we just had salmon.'

'Yes, darling,' said Lewis McLean. 'He means bait.'

'So?' said Olivia McLean.

'The best things come to those who wait,' said Lewis McLean.

'Quite,' said Jaeger White.

1995...

1:30 pm...

Glasgow...

Queen Street...

The office...

(2) The Office

One woman directed a wolf whistle at the young man, while another blew him a kiss as he stepped out of the Lamborghini Aventador with his elderly sour-faced client to an abrupt gust of chilling wind. Queen Street was otherwise desolate and the grumbling sky was low and grey, muffling the cold hard ground. There was the piercing countertenor shrieking of agitated seagulls above. The ribbon-like pestiferous inner city Glasgow air tasted of lemony milk. It made the lawyer want to pee. He disentangled his groin as he ambled. The lawyer presumed a subordinative arm around his client's cloaked shoulder. The client shivered. He brushed his arm off. The exorbitant slick tires of the Aventador reeked of buried rubber that ponged like putrefying vegetable matter. Andrew McLean did his arrogant best to ignore the introversive genus locus.

The lawyer modulated his youthful voice. 'Please, Mr Sharp, 'step into the office. All will be revealed.'

Hugh Sharp glanced at his lawyer haughtily and snorted with derision. 'If only you had weaved the enchantment in court.' Hugh Sharp tugged his cloak tightly to his breast in the freezing wind. He steadied himself. He hoisted his cane in upwards clutches. He hobbled with his adroit lawyer into the office. He glowered at the young man. 'This better be impressive, son.'

Andrew McLean escorted his client into the firm. They walked across the gangway into the elevator.

'It is a steep climb, Sir.'

'No more steep than your fees.'

They ascended three floors. The young man lead him into his own office. He ushered the old man down.

Andrew McLean's deep blue eyes betrayed a knowledge of abuse. The parts around his eyes showed that he knew how to take a shot. 'Coffee, Mr Sharp?'

Having ensconced himself in a luxurious chair, Hugh Sharp re-appraised the young man with brown eyes which were in contrast to his multifarious boyish experiences; incongruous with his lust for love; his concupiscence; and his hold over life. They had seen so many things but had retained their dark awareness. His eye areas themselves were etched with signs of a hard life. They communicated that he was not that vital any more, but not that finished. He waved his head. 'No, I don't think so.'

Andrew McLean pushed out his gleaming mouth. 'Really? It's Kopi luwak.'

Hugh Sharp tottered his head. 'Yes, I do know it.'

Andrew McLean smiled. 'Then you'll know it's the world's most expensive coffee.'

'Correct.'

'In fact, the main factor of its high price-'

Hugh Sharp grunted. 'Yes, I know. It is the uncommon method.'

'You do know?'

'Of course. It has been produced from the coffee beans which have been digested by a certain Indonesian cat-like animal called the palm civet or also civet cat.'

'So will you have a cup?'

Hugh Sharp waved his head. 'No, I wont.'

'Tea?'

Hugh Sharp spluttered. 'Certainly not. I have never drunk tea in my life. Agatha and I never indulged it. Benjamin was warned not to drink it.'

'Agatha is your wife?'

'Yes, she died in a fire.'

'And Ben, is he your son?'

'Yes, he plays piano.'

'What about tea?'

'Tea is for the pusillanimous. Stronger men enjoy harder flavours.'

Andrew McLean smirked. 'Sunny D is quite challenging.'

Hugh Sharp groaned. 'I don't want fruit juice. You expect me to drink lemon squash after the morning I've just had.'

'A glass of cold water?'

Hugh Sharp sighed. 'As a suitable accompaniment perhaps, providing it is cold and fresh.' 'No, I am sure I will require something far stronger.'

'We keep some very nice whiskey in the conference room cupboard- for special clients.'

Hugh Sharp nodded vaguely with interest. 'Is it the Isabella's Islay?'

Andrew McLean's fine-looking face contorted. 'The what?'

Hugh Sharp frowned. 'No, I didn't think so. The Macallan M?'

Andrew McLean gawked. 'Sorry?'

'Me too.'

'No, but we do have a very nice one.'

'Which is?'

'The Johnnie Walker Whisky JW.'

Hugh Sharp loured. 'Yes, that would seem somewhat more approximate to your station. Very well, make sure the glass is pristine.'

'I will rinse it myself.'

'I don't want you to rinse it, I expect you to open it up.'

'I'm afraid our glasses have all been christened.'

'Then you will make sure at least that I enjoy a proper quaich.'

'You mean a whiskey glass?'

'No, I mean a quaich.'

Hugh Sharp's searing dark eyes looked daggers at Andrew McLean. Hugh Sharp picked up his quaich, sipped, and squinched. 'So, young man, what on earth was that supposed to be?'

'The Johnnie Walker.'

Hugh Sharp shook his head. 'No, I mean the performance.'

'You mean my address.'

'Your feeble address.'

Andrew McLean glared indignantly. 'I saved you from prison, Mr Sharp.'

'You cost me a fortune.'

'It is called Controlled Representation.'

Mr Sharp scowled. 'Controlled representation?'

'Yes, it is the only kind that is permitted.'

'It was two very bad things. It was slow, painfully so, and it was stupid, infuriatingly so.'

'The court requires clear address.'

'Yes.'

'In what way?'

'You were supposed to tell the court, not be told by it.'

Andrew waved his head apprehensively. 'No, Mr Sharp if I had done that, the judge would have expelled me from the court, he would also have put you away.'

Hugh Sharp sneered. 'I thought you were reckoned to be the best young lawyer in the country.'

Andrew McLean glared indignantly. 'Of course I am. I got the best results in the country.'

'Then the standard is indubitably too low.'

Andrew McLean beamed. 'It is beyond reasonable doubt.'

Hugh Sharp barracked. 'There is no way you can claim that now. It's not even on the balance of probabilities.'

'I trust, Mr Sharp that you do not wish to defame your own legal representative.'

Hugh Sharp grumbled. 'Not exactly, no.'

'Good.'

'I wish to kill you instead.' Hugh Sharp glowered at Andrew McLean as he twitched his cane.'

'You're going to bludgeon with that?'

'No, I may shoot you.'

Andrew McLean's bright young eyes glinted. 'Why?'

'You're supposed to make me money, not cost me a fortune.'

Hugh Sharp blew his petty cash box to pieces with his cane.

Andrew McLean grimaced. 'It was an extremely difficult case.'

Hugh Sharp scoffed. 'What was so difficult about it?'

'You kept large sums of money without declaring them.'

'That money was owed. My bitter rival knows it's his fault.'

'So?'

'You can't just hide it from the tax authorities.'

'Why not?'

'It's the law.'

Hugh Sharp gasped. 'What about the other side?'

Andrew McLean sighed. 'I argued the other side.'

'Most ineptly.'

Andrew McLean shook his head

'No, I argued the best way I could.'

'How?'

'I argued you were of the firm belief that you had declared your gains, that your financial representatives; that is to say, your firm of accountants was to blame, not you.'

Hugh Sharp goggled. 'What would that have amounted to?'

'Ignorance of fact.'

'That's not what I instructed you to do.'

'I know.'

'I told you to explain to the court that I didn't know what the law was.'

'I know you did.'

'So why didn't you?'

'Because that wouldn't have worked.'

'Why not?'

'Ignorance of the law is no excuse, Mr Sharp.'

'What's that supposed to mean?'

'It means you can't just say that you didn't know what the law was and are therefore not to blame.'

'Why not?'

'I don't know.'

'Why don't you know?'

'I didn't make the law, I only advise, assist-'

'That's probably the problem; you are just an assistant, not even an associate, never mind a Senior Partner.'

'The Senior Partners didn't want to represent you, they said I could.'

'Your first-class means fuck all.'

'I did my best.'

'Your best was no where near good enough. What you've done is fucked up completely.'

'I told the judge your side.'

'Yes, but you didn't win.'

'He said he would take care of it.'

'Yes, but he's imposed a massive fine.'

'It's better than jail.'

'I'd rather go to jail rich than keep my liberty poor.'

'Surely not. And you're hardly poor.'

'I'm a lot worse off than I was.'

'Then perhaps you should have declared your gains.'

'You're supposed to defend me, not edify me.'

'I did defend you. I stopped you going to prison.'

'Why would I have gone to prison.'

'Obtaining pecuniary advantages by deception is a serious offence. You could have gotten years.'

'Only your way I've gotten nothing.'

'Mr Sharp, I'm a lawyer, not a miracle worker.'

'I certainly won't be paying you any fees.'

'I'm afraid you'll have to do that.'

Hugh Sharp sneered. 'Or you'll take me back to that parcel of land and lose again.'

'Or I'll lose my job, my employers expect paid.'

'You deserve to lose your job, you're terrible at it. You've made a complete botch-up of my case.'

'I saved you from jail Mr Sharp.'

'You lost me thousands and thousands of pounds.'

'You couldn't have spent that in jail.'

'I didn't need to be going there in the first place.'

'That's not the way the law sees it.'

After they had finished their conversation, the abrupt gust of chilling wind had become a squall of immediate frozenness.

Andrew McLean shivered. Hugh Sharp braced the conditions. The grumbling sky had become a rumbling sky. Hugh Sharp's taxi arrived. The lawyer waved off his client.

'Good journey,' said Andrew McLean.

'I will get you soon,' said Hugh Sharp.

1995...

9 pm...

Glasgow...

Hyndland...

(3) The Brother's Visit

Later that day Andrew McLean entered his Lamborghini Aventador and sped towards his brother's house in Hyndland. He rapped on the door.

'Andrew?' his brother said.

'Hello, brother. Who are you at the moment?'

'Chase.'

'Very well. You look terrible.'

'I feel worse.'

'Come in.'

The older brother escorted him to the living room. 'Are you driving home?'

'Why?'

'I just wondered if you could use a whiskey.'

'I suppose I could leave the car here and pick it up tomorrow.'

The older brother shrugged. 'It's up to you.'

Andrew scraped his head with his nails. 'Okay, yes, I'll do that. Is it the Isabella's Islay?'

'The what?'

'Apparently it's the most expensive whiskey there is.'

'I see. I only have McKendricks or Glenfiddich.'

'I'll have McKendricks.'

They sat down together at the conservatory table.

'So?' said Chase.

'I was threatened.'

'Threatened?'

'Yes.'

'By whom?'

'A client.'

'Which client?'

'Hugh Sharp.'

'Is that the one with the mansion in Aberdeen and all the money?'

'Yes, the man's mad.'

'Mad how?'

'He plans to kill me.'

'Why?'

'He thinks I botched his case.'

'Which case was this?'

'The capital gains case.'

'And what happened?'

'I kept him out of jail, he received a fine instead.'

'And he wasn't happy with this?'

'No.'

'Was he guilty?'

'As hell.'

'You mean he didn't declare his capital gains.'

'No.'

'You've done nothing wrong then.'

'That's what I thought.'

'How does he plan to kill you?'

'He blew our petty cash box to bits.'

'What with?'

'His cane.'

'I don't follow.'

'He has a gun cane.'

'Is it legal?'

'I presume he has the license. Anyway, we went to the Court of Session. The judge decided the capital gains were irregular and that he had not paid tax on them.'

Twenty-three years ago...

1995...

10 pm...

Glasgow...

Bearsden...

Westbourne Crescent...

(4) The Nephew

The inexplicably blighting mid-summer night empyreans were Stygian, nocturnally irradiated by the incidental sodium-vapour lamps and through the chatoyant constellation of microscopic chinks in the suspiciously drawn curtains and meticulously aligned blinds which illuminated the detached houses of the plush prosperous crescent. The indigo rain fulminated like sandbags on the serpentine pavements. A four-year old boy in his sodden school uniform staggered in the high wind towards his uncle's house, his young heart pounding in his young fragile chest. He knew he had been here before; he knew at one point he had gone here. It had been a journey. He had been sick in the car. He had had to breathe outside the window. How he had wished he had had had to have had arrived sooner. Everything was different; alien; in the pitch dark and without his daddy's car. The musty smell of mushroom flared in Nicholas's gooey nostrils made ever more rank by the eddying rain.

'Try this,' mummy had said one Sunday evening, as she placed a small bowl in front of him as he was watching

He had grimaced. 'What is it?' he had said.

'It's a fungus.'

'What's that?'

'It's a very powerful plant.'

Nicholas had frowned. 'It doesn't look like a plant.'

'No, it's been squished, jumbled-up and cooked.'

His eyes had swelled. 'What does it do?'

'It gives you weird and wonderful dreams.'

He had gasped. 'What will I dream of?'

'I imagine you will dream of a meadow.'

'A meadow?'

'Yes, a leana.'

'What's that?'

'It's a Scottish word for meadow.'

He had nodded.

'And you will be looking for someone.'

'Who?'

'Joanne.'

'Why?'

'She has been captured.'

'By who?'

'By whom. The knife-man.'

'Why?'

'The king ordered him to.'

'Why?'

'She refused to marry him.'

'Why wouldn't she marry him?'

'He was too old and ugly.'

'So what will the knife-man do?'

'He will try to save her.'

'How?'

'By killing the king instead.'

'What happens?'

'The knife-man kills the king and you and Joanne get married.'

Nick reached his uncle's front door and knocked. He waited a few moments. His uncle opened the door, squeezing his tired eyes, tilting back slightly.

Sweat pouring down his face, Nick puffed. 'Uncle Chase!' he said.

The uncle groaned. 'Nicholas?'

'Mummy's gone.'

The uncle massaged his forehead. 'Gone?'

Nick sniffed. 'Yes.'

'Where?'

Nick shrugged, as a tear strolled down his cheek. 'I don't know.'

The uncle glanced at his watch. 'Why don't you know?'

'Mummy never said.'

The uncle nodded his head. 'What about your daddy?'

'He didn't come home.'

The uncle swallowed. 'Do you know why not?'

'No.'

The uncle nodded intently. 'Why not?'

'He didn't say.'

The uncle nodded again. 'How did you get here?'

'I ran.'

The uncle gaped. 'You ran?'

Nick bobbed his rain-lashed head. 'Yes.'

'All the way from Hyndland to Bearsden?'

'Yes.'

Nick pursed his lips with respect. 'You must be cream-crackered.'

Nick nodded sorrily.

'And you're soaking wet,' said Uncle Chase.

'Yes.'

The uncle took his nephew by the shoulder and lead him indoors.

The uncle reposed his nephew by the fire, fetched a large warm white towel from the heating rail in the bathroom, rubbed his head, instructed him to dab his school clothes. 'Wait a minute, Nicholas,' he said. When he returned he brought his a can of coke and a Mars bar. 'So, Nick,' he said, 'tell me again, what happened?'

'I came home from school.'

'Yes, and?'

'The door was locked.'

'The front or the back door?'

'Both.'

'So?'

'I climbed through the window.'

'Which window?'

'The window at the side of the house.'

'I see. And then?'

'I looked for mummy.'

'You did?'

'Yes, everywhere- even in the cupboards.'

'And you couldn't find her?'

'No.'

'So?'

'I waited.'

'For how long?'

'Forever.'

'And?'

'Mummy's always there when I come back from school.'

'So what did you do?'

'I waited for daddy.'

'When does your daddy usually come home?'

'About eight o'clock.'

'So?'

'I climbed back out of the window.'

'You did?'

'Yes.'

'And?'

'I ran to you.'

Uncle Chase smiled. 'I see.'

'When will they be back,' uncle Chase.

Uncle Chase smiled nervously. 'We need to be patient.'

Nick nodded.

'Uncle Chase?' said Nick.

'Yes?'

'Why are you bleeding?'

'I took a nick from the Glasgow Smiler.'

'Nick's eyes crossed with confusion. 'You took me from the Glasgow Smiler?'

'No, not Nick as in you but nick as in a small cut or notch.'

'I see. Why's it on your face?'

Uncle Chase shrugged. 'That's what he does.'

'Why?'

'He likes to refigure people.'

'What does "refigure" mean, Uncle Chase?'

'It means to make a person look the way they deserve to look.'

'Is it sore?'

'Not half.'

'I feel sore.'

'Yes, I can see that, Nicholas.'

'I want mummy back.'

Uncle Chase sighed. 'Yes, me too.'

'We just have to be patient.'

A tear strolled down Uncle Chase's cheek. 'Yes.'

1995...

Ireland...

Dublin...

Rathnew...

Grafton Cottage...

(5) Rathnew 1995; Jarrod Field's Injury

The large ancient cottage shuddered like a barn of loose corrugated iron as the rampageous wind threatened to swallow up the entire building. Munitions of rain fulminated off the roof tops and the various curtilage, rinsing all the windows. The pre-historic lights guttered and perished. Catherine Fields fetched candles and lit them up. Sean was crying. 'Love me for a reason' was playing. They could taste the Guinness and the cakes. The smell of chocolate pervaded the room.

Albert Bennet clapped his hands. 'Speech, speech!'

Lewis McLean smiled. 'Yes, why not.'

'Confession, I think you mean,' said Scott Dorcha.

'Yes,' said Glasson Dorcha. 'Your people have so much to say.'

'Very well, Albert, Lewis, Scott,'' said Jarrod Fields. 'As you know, it's my birthday.'

Jane squeaked. 'How old are you again, Mr Fields?' said Jane.

'He's thirty-eight,' said her mother Judith.

'Why are you as old as that?' said Richie.

'It's called nature, son,' said Doctor Taylor Reid.

'I agree,' said Ben, 'Talent comes from within.'

'Indeed, son,' said Hugh Sharp.

'There is also nurture,' said David.

'Quite, son,' said Ewald Wren.

'There is both,' said Susie.

'Correct darling,' said Susanna.

'The way you've been behaving,' said Judith, 'I thought it was Christmas.

'Yes,' said Jarrod, 'Given it's past afternoon, I am now officially thirty-eight.'

'So?' said Hugh Sharp.'

Jarrod Fields opened up his arms. 'I would like to offer my greatest thanks to my wife first, Catherine.'

Catherine winked at her husband. 'You can thank me all you like but you still have to pay the bills.'

Albert Bennet chuckled.

'May I also thank my two boys Michael and Sean.'

'There's something I have to tell you dad,' said Michael Fields.

'Yes,' said Sean Fields, 'he's been very bad.'

Hugh Sharp gulped.

'It will have to wait, daddy has to make his speech. May I also thank Lewis and of course his brilliant son Andrew.'

'Thank you, Jarrod,' said Lewis McLean. 'Your boys are a credit to you.'

'A credit he thinks,' said Hugh Sharp.

'How old are the boys, Jarrod?' said Judith White.

Jarrod turned to Michael. 'You're fourteen, aren't you, son.'

'Old enough to know when someone's doing the wrong thing.'

'The wrong thing,' said Sean.

'Two years younger than my daughter,' said Judith White.

'How old is your daughter, Judith,' said Ewald Wren.

'Same as my grandson Richie,' said Jean Reid, 'Seven.'

'Same age as my daughter,' said Andrew McLean. 'You're seven as well aren't you?'

'Yes, dad,' said Susie.

'How old is your son, Ewald?' said Lewis McLean.

'David?' said Ewald Wren.

'I'm four,' said David.

'I'm older than you,' said Sean, 'I'm five.'

'How old is your boy, Hugh?'

'He's not a boy, he's a master musician.'

'So how old then?'

'Seven.'

'How old is your grandson Jean?' said Judith White.

'He's seven,' said Jean Reid.

Ewald Wren left the room to visit the bathroom.

Later Sean flailed on the floor, his small hands splaying in his father's blood.

2003...

Ireland...

Dublin...

Rathnew...

Grafton Cottage...

(6) Rathnew 2003; Orientation

The early eventide precipitation was plumping from the desolate Rathnew sky like a giant airstrike of aqueous missiles, resiling from the battered roof tops, splattering on to the hybrid curtilage, comprising flora and stone, causing the big old cottage to shudder like a buttery full of hangdog cows. Inside the cottage, the gigantic open log-fire combusted, lank chromatic beams slurping upwards into the giant vent, emitting a minacious whistle. The youths were all together attempting the art of jamming. Susie was frantically jotting notes down onto a notepad, trying to recollect the words of a song. Ben was proudly playing the piano, Jane was unselfconsciously singing, Sean was strumming the guitar, knocking back a can of draught Guinness. Alexander and Martin were echoing Jane's lines.

Catherine Fields, Ewald Wren, Lewis McLean, Chase McLean, Hugh Sharp, Albert Bennet, Judith White, Jean Reid and Scott Dorcha were all in the huge kitchen, milling around the refectory table. It was Chinese.

Lewis McLean grabbed both of Catherine Fields's hands. 'Your reception has been simply flawless, Catherine.'

'Thank you, Lewis,' said Catherine. 'I'm so sorry about your son.'

Lewis smiled wistfully. 'Me too. I'm sorry about your husband.'

'How long has he been missing now, Catherine?' said Judith White.

'Who?' said Jean Reid. 'Jarrod or Andrew?'

'Jarrod has been missing for eight years,' said Catherine, 'He was presumed dead after seven.'

'Searching for a distraction, Albert Bennet said, 'Perhaps we should join the youngsters.'

'How old are your boys now, Catherine?' said Judith White.

'Michael's twenty-two and Sean is thirteen,' said Catherine. 'How old is your daughter now, Judith?'

'Jane's fifteen.'

'That's the same age as my niece,' said Chase. 'She's fifteen as well.'

'Susie?' said Albert Bennet.

'Yes,' said Chase McLean.

'She's certainly grown up,' said Lewis McLean.

'You mean she no longer makes wild accusations,' said Hugh Sharp.

'Let's not get into this, Hugh,' said Albert Bennet.

'How old is your son, Mr Sharp?' said Chase McLean.

'He's fifteen,' said Hugh Sharp, 'Becoming more accomplished every day.'

'I can hear that,' said Ewald Wren, 'Is that him on the piano?'

'Yes, he's dumbing down,' said Hugh Sharp.

'That would be your daughter singing, Judith,' said Jean Reid.

'Yes,' said Judith White, 'she's come out of her shell somewhat.'

'Who's playing the guitar?' said Albert Bennet.

'That would be my son, Sean,' said Catherine.

'And the caterwauling?' said Hugh Sharp.

'That would be my nephew, Alexander,' said Albert Bennet.

'How old is he?' said Ewald Wren.

'He's six.'

'And who is the other one?' said Jean Reid.

'That's my son, Martin,' said Ewald Wren.

'What are they playing?'

'I think it's *'All the things she said',*' said Chase McLean.

'What is that?' said Jean Reid.

'It's a song about a girl liking a girl,' said Chase McLean, 'It's number one at the moment. Susie sings it at home.'

'So does Jane,' said Judith White.

'Sounds positively disgusting,' said Jean Reid.

'I don't know,' said Albert Bennet. 'I gather it's becoming more received.'

'What do you think, Ewald?' said Catherine.

'I must confess,' said Ewald Wren, 'I have never especially liked homosexuality.'

'Me neither,' said Scott Dorcha, 'It's far too weak.'

'I agree, Mr Dorcha,' said Jean Reid.

Scott Dorcha nodded sternly at Jean Reid who returned the nod.

'Why Ewald,' said Lewis McLean,' have you never especially liked homosexuality.'

'It was the law of Scotland for so long,' said Ewald Wren. 'Men used to go to prison for it.'

'As they should,' said Jean Reid.

'No, mother,' said Doctor Taylor Reid, 'Gone are the days when we can confuse orientation with illness.'

'Exactly, Doctor,' said Chase McLean. 'I think law has been too intractable for too long.'

Scott Dorcha grimaced. 'Are you gay, Chase?'

'And not ashamed, Scott,' said Chase McLean.

'If you don't mind me saying, Chase,' said Albert Bennet, 'You have the pride of a gay person.'

'Not at all and thank you, Albert,' said Chase McLean.

Judith White's facial expression wrinkled. 'They do say to love the person, if not the condition.'

'It's hardly a condition, Judith,' said Lewis McLean.

'I don't know,' said Hugh Sharp. 'What do you think Doctor Taylor?'

Doctor Taylor Reid coughed importantly. 'There are a number of factors.'

'Yes,' said Jean Reid, 'You were clearly too soft on your son, Lewis.'

'Or your mother was too hard on him,' said Judith White.

'I assure you ladies,' said Chase Mc Clean, 'My mother and father gave me first-class understanding.'

'A boy needs it drummed out of him,' said Jean Reid.

Jean Reid caught Scott Dorcha's glance. 'I agree, Mrs Reid. 'I made it abundantly clear to my son Glasson what was acceptable.'

Jean Reid nodded self-righteously at Scott Dorcha. 'Of course.'

'What about genetics?' said Albert Bennet. 'I believe they play a part.'

'They are clearly inferior,' said Hugh Sharp.

Lewis McLean edified Hugh Sharp with his honest eyes. 'I assure you, Hugh,' said Lewis McLean, 'my son does not suffer from inferior genetics.'

'Doctor Taylor?' said Judith White. 'Is gayness to do with nature or nurture?'

'Nurture obviously,' said Jean Reid.

'Both are factors,' said Doctor Taylor Reid, 'The way you were born and the way you were brought up.'

'And what are the other factors?' said Albert Bennet.

'There is also the order of the births,' said Doctor Taylor Reid.

'What d'you mean?' said Judith White.

'A later order male fetus stands more chance of being gay,' said Doctor Taylor.

Ewald Wren regarded Doctor Taylor Reid quizzically. 'How do you conclude that?'

'More estrogen is being produced in the womb,' said Doctor Taylor.

'And what does that do?' said Judith White.

'What it does, Judith,' said Doctor Taylor Reid, 'is it predisposes the male fetus to more feminine orientation

Chase McLean nodded. 'And vice-versa.'

'Tell me Chase,' said Judith White, 'Can you tell if a person is gay, Chase?'

'I once felt I could,' said Chase McLean.

Albert Bennet stuck a finger out. 'And why would it be once?'

Chase coggled his head. 'Because the feelings are rampant at that stage.'

'That's right,' said Doctor Taylor Reid, 'Emotional beliefs are very powerful at an earlier hormonal stage.

'And what about now?' said Albert Bennet.

'To be honest, Albert,' said Chase McLean. 'When the senses aren't on fire, it can be difficult to tell.'

Lewis McLean smiled understandingly. 'My son has had a lot of ignorance to contend with.'

'Incidentally, Chase,' said Albert Bennet, 'could you work out if any of the children were gay?'

'Careful, Albert,' said Catherine Fields.

'Yes, children and sexuality don't mix,' said Judith White.

'No,' said Jean Reid, 'Albert's asking a relevant education point.' She glared at Chase McLean.

'Yes, Mrs Reid,' said Chase McLean.

'How perceptive are you, Mr McLean?' said Jean Reid.

'It would probably take the statement,' said Chase McLean.

Scott Dorcha stuck his nose up at Chase McLean. 'So, no then,' he said.

Hugh Sharp sneered. 'What about you, Doctor Taylor?' he said.

'Yes, I've watched them a bit,' said Doctor Taylor Reid.

'And what are your conclusions?' said Judith White.

Doctor Taylor Reid faced Albert Bennet. 'I rather think your nephew's gay.'

Hugh Sharp huffed. 'It wouldn't surprise me.'

'Really Doctor?' said Albert Bennet.

'Yes, Albert,' said Doctor Taylor Reid.

'That's funny,' said Albert Bennet, 'because Alexander seems to respond more to feminine things.'

'Such as?' said Judith White.

'Despite his analytical mind,' said Albert Bennet, 'he seems to like music and dancing and singing.'

'The heterosexual males can be accommodating as well,' said Hugh Sharp.

'I'm not quite sure these things are to be accommodated,' said Lewis McLean.

'So Doctor?' said Albert Bennet, 'what makes you say that, Doctor?'

'Actually something my son said,' Doctor Taylor Reid.

'Richie?' said Catherine.

'Yes, Catherine' said Doctor Taylor Reid. 'He and Martin were exploring each other in the shower.'

'But that's pedophilia,' said Judith White. 'Your son's a monster.'

'No,' said Doctor Taylor, 'I mean Alexander and Martin.'

'And that makes it okay,' said Jean Reid.

'It's within parameters,' said Doctor Taylor Reid.

An instinct of turpitude stung Ewald Wren's conscience. 'Really, Doctor,' he said, 'How do you know that?'

'My son overheard them,' said Doctor Reid.

'What were they doing showering together?' said Scott Dorcha.

'They'd been playing out in the garden together,' said Catherine Fields. 'They were both caked with mud, so I sent them to get washed.'

'Quite right,' said Judith White. 'They couldn't be tramping mud all over the place.'

'So, sorry about this Ewald,' said Albert Bennet, 'could Martin be gay as well?'

'Absurd,' said Ewald Wren, 'and you're not offending me, Doctor. I know Martin likes the females.'

'How do you know that?' said Judith White.

Hugh Sharp intercommunicated. 'You wish to impugn, Judith the orientation of the son of a judge.'

'How does he know?' said Catherine Fields

'The man knows his own son,' said Jean Reid.

Scott Dorcha faced Doctor Taylor Reid. 'What about your son?' he said.

'Yes,' said Doctor Taylor Reid. 'What about him?'

'I'll ask. Is he gay?' said Scott Dorcha.

Doctor Taylor Reid grimaced. 'No, he's coming from a very different direction- he's a homophobe.'

'As he should be,' said Jean Reid.

'And why is he a homophobe?' said Chase McLean.

'Because we did not believe in weakness,' said Jean Reid, 'Especially disgusting sexual concepts.'

'You did have a child,' said Lewis McLean.

'As a concept yes, not as a pleasure,' said Jean Reid.

'What about Hugh's son?' said Albert Bennet.

'My son is as straight as the lines of a piano score,' said Hugh Sharp.

'Ben?' said Catherine Fields.

'Yes, that's right, Catherine,' said Doctor Taylor Reid, 'I'm pretty sure he's heterosexual.'

Hugh Sharp nodded his obvious approval. 'Of course he is.'

'What makes you so sure, Doctor?' said Lewis McLean.

'He responds to Jane completely and seeks solidarity in the other males,' said Doctor Taylor Reid.

'What about Catherine's boy, Doctor?' said Chase McLean.

'Who?' said Scott Dorcha.

'Sean,' said Judith White.

'Again,' said Doctor Taylor Reid, 'I'm pretty sure he's straight.'

'And why would that be?' said Albert Bennet.

'He seems to be very open-minded,' said Doctor Taylor Reid, 'but he puts his attention to Jane rather than one of the boys.'

Catherine smiled her approval. 'And what about Michael?'

Doctor Taylor Reid smiled. 'I think he's straight as well.'

'What makes you think he's straight?' said Judith White.

'What does straight mean?' said Jean Reid.

'It means heterosexual,' said Judith White.

'He has special attention for Jane and none of the boys,' said Doctor Taylor Reid.

'And what about the girls?' said Lewis McLean.

'Who?' said Scott Dorcha.

'Susie and Jane,' said Catherine Fields.

'I think Susie and Jane might...'

Ewald Wren left the room to visit the bathroom.

(7) The Weather-Worn Man

Catherine Fields saw her moment. 'Speaking of the unspeakable, we need answers.'

'We do, Catherine?' said Lewis McLean.

'Yes,' said Catherine, 'It is the anniversary of my husband's death.'

'Yes, Catherine,' said Hugh Sharp, 'Most unfortunate night. Poor man died in a pool of his own blood.'

'Yes most, frightful scene,' said Jean Reid.

'It really was very messy,' said Judith White.'

'I want answers,' said Catherine Fields, 'I want to know what happened to my husband.'

'He died, didn't he?' said Hugh Sharp.

'Yes,' said Catherine but his body was never recovered. My sons, Mickey and Sean also want answers.'

'My daughter Jane wants answers as well,' said Judith White.

'My niece Susie wants answers,' said Chase McLean.

'Yes, she does,' said Lewis McLean.

'Your nephew wants answers,' said Hugh Sharp.

'There is nothing to say,' said Albert Bennet.

'We all want answers,' said Jean Reid.

'For instance?' said Albert Bennet.

'They still want to know who did it,' said Catherine Fields.

'Jane still wants to know,' said Judith White.

'I'm sure your daughter,' said Hugh Sharp, 'would never have come to any real harm.'

'I think my niece wants to know as well,' said Chase McLean.

'Yes, I think my granddaughter does,' said Lewis McLean.

'All I can say,' said Catherine Fields is that my son wouldn't have done it.'

'Glasson wants to know,' said Scott Dorcha, 'why he still feels like a girl.'

'Perhaps we should go through,' said Albert Bennet, 'and not dwell on the past.'

True enough, Susie was busy trying to remember all the words to 'Love me for a reason' and feeding them to Jane. Richie was swigging beer attempting to sing Ben was playing the piano, Jane was dancing. Sean was strumming the guitar, while Alexander and Martin were screeching at the top of their lungs.

'You look like a girl,' said Martin.

'You look like two girls,' said Alexander.

Ewald Wren frowned. 'We never judge a person on appearance, Martin.'

'But you are a judge, daddy,' said Martin.

'Yes,' said Chase McLean, 'we never judge a book by its cover.'

'I am a fair person, son,' said Ewald Wren. 'I don't give people unnecessary bad description. Now, apologize to Alexander.'

Albert Bennet nodded. 'Thank you, Ewald. Tell Martin, you're sorry, Alex.'

'So this is your nephew?' said Hugh Sharp.

'Indeed it is. Hugh,' said Albert Bennet. 'And this your son?'

'Of course.'

'So what are the answers?' said Catherine.

It was then that a bearded figure entered the room. Catherine Fields fainted.

PART B

Literature Review; The Suspects

CHAPTER ONE

The Glasgow Smiler

Glasson Dorcha aka 'The Glasgow Smiler' was in the capacious furnished basement of his luxury town-house mansion. Its value exceeded one million pounds. Of course he could have afforded more when he purchased it but he had fallen head over heels in love with the the place. It had been beautiful to him. It started with a thick high stone perimeter wall with elegant tan oaken gates with engraved copperplate edges. Through there was a gently rising sweeping expansive garden with a large beautiful tree with a paved driveway leading to a huge stone-built edifice. He had lived here for over a decade. There were giant posters of beautiful woman, including all around the brick walls. There were also pictures of handsome men. It accommodated a massive novelty fridge freezer containing salmon, lamb, and beef, a cooker, a drinks cabinet, and an array of boxes containing various chemicals and pharmaceuticals; electronics; and textiles. He was reclining on a setae, an occasional table by its side holding a quaich of Mccallan with four ice cubes. He was listening to 'Rise like a phoenix' by Conchita Wurst. He liked Eurovision music and he specifically identified with this song. The singer was a woman but he thought he looked beautiful. He was doing methylenedioxymethamphetamine; ecstasy. It was also known as Adam, XTC, go, disco biscuit, crystal, X or hug drug. He had a whole cabinet full of recreational drugs. He switched off you tube, climbed out of his seat and stood naked, gazing in to his full-length mirror. He was singing to himself; crooning. He had a high scary voice. No, he didn't look quite the way he used to; he was older, far less pretty, much heavier. He was not happy twenty years ago either, but with the ecstasy surging through his senses he could *feel* as beautiful as before, as anyone else. He peered at his tiny shrivelled penis and smiled wistfully. He glared at his ghastly beard and bathetic tears pricked his eyes. Physically, he was a man. Indeed he had been raised as a boy.

In his intense state, he thought about his dad. His name was Scot Dorcha. He remembered they had been in the kitchen. His father had clutched him by the neck. "*Where's my fuckin' coke, Glasson*"?' he had said.

Glasson had blinked with feigned innocence, as he gulped. 'I don't know.'

His father had looked daggers at him. 'Don't you even dare try to fuckin' lie to me!'

Glasson shivered. 'I'm not fuckin' lying.'

His father had glowered. 'Of course you fuckin' are. You and your ugly wee fucking boy-whore snorted the whole lot, didn't you?'

'He's not a whore,' he had protested.

His father sneered. 'No? What is it you do exactly then? I can't imagine you study together.'

Glasson had shrugged. 'We- we communicate.'

His father had scoffed. 'Communicate? What maggot-faggot gay diseases?'

Glasson sniffed. 'No, love.'

'You mean he shags your miserable girl's arse.'

Glasson didn't answer this.

'I'm not angry with you son. I just need to know if there's any left.'

Glasson nodded sadly. He pulled a pouch out from his shirt pocket.

His father took the pouch, pulled Glasson to his chest. 'Good boy,' he said. 'You know your dad loves you, whatever you are.'

Glasson smiled sadly. 'I know dad.'

'Now, let's get this thing wired up.'

'I'll make the tea.'

'Good. Is he still giving us it?'

'Yes,' he said, 'it would be here tomorrow.'

'Good. So you fucked up his sleep.'

'Yes, he hasn't slept for years.'

'What about his mother?'

'His mother was doing everything.'

'What is everything?'

'She was living in the fast lane.'

'What about his dad?'

'He knew about it but he didn't say.'

'His father killed my father.'

'Yes, I know dad.'

'Take me through what you've done so far.'

'I poured the kettle of boiling water slowly over his head.'

'Remind me what happened, son?'

'He squealed and then he whimpered.'

'Good, what happened next?'

'We got him to swallow the staples.'

'Was the switch flicked?'

'Yes.'

'And then what next?'

'He swallowed the giant pain pill, he was opened up, raped and tortured and branded.'

'Good.'

Suddenly, his daddy's face changed. He clutched his chest. He collapsed to the ground. He writhed in agony for a few seconds.

'*Dad*?'

'I'm okay, son.'

Glasson was panting, tears of astonishment pricking his blood-shot eyes.

He left the family house. He knew he could have gone to college or university. He went abroad to be with his boyfriend. If he couldn't enjoy his cock, he could enjoy his arse.

He remembered being in the old warehouse with his father.

'*Glasson*,' his father had said, 'you confuse me.'

'Confused Daddy?' It was more echolalia than a question.

'Aye. You're a boy but you fuck about like a girl.'

'I am a girl.'

'No, you're a boy.'

This time his answer was more definite. 'No, I'm a girl.'

'You're taking the piss.'

Glasson shook his head unaffectedly. 'No.'

'How the hell do you know that?'

'What's that?'

'How do you fucking know you're a girl?'

Glasson shrugged. 'Because I fucking do.'

'This isn't on, son. I don't mind you being handsome-'

'Then why didn't you call me Kenny?'

'You're trying to be clever, son. Anyway, it's your mother's fault- but-'

'Pretty.'

'What?'

'Pretty.'

'No, handsome.'

'No, pretty.'

'Son, I am one of the biggest cunts in Glasgow, Glasson.'

'Why are you a cunt, daddy?'

'I control people with money.'

'Glasson, it's impossible for me to have a gay son.'

'I'm not gay.'

'That's what I expect to hear.'

'I fancy boys.'

His father smacked him in the mouth.

'So you are fucking gay!'

Glasson trembled. 'No, daddy.'

'Are you ripping the pish?'

'No.'

His daddy rubbed his forehead. 'A transsexual. Fuck!'

By reason of his thoughts and feelings, he knew he was a

woman. He was recording his sounds. He intended to use them. He intended to teach all the families a lesson. He intended to teach them what it was like to be ugly, to be rejected.

He sat down at the Steinway. He sang as he played.

Verse 1:

Smile
Smile
Take a look at yourself
Just now

Smile
Just smile
Be thankful for the looks
You have
They can look so bad
They can look like
A hulk in the dark

Your smile will break your heart
Your smile will break your heart

Plaid Foul

Verse 2:

Mush
Mush
Mushrooms have power
To slight

Mush
Mushrooms
They can blind your eyes

They can hurt
Like a knife in the heart

Dnias Dirk

Your smile will break your heart
Your smile will break your heart

Plaid Foul

Chorus:

Smile
And the look you were looking for
Becomes a kind of dinosaur
With fangs and claws and open pores
The vision of an eyesore
You're looking like a child

Smile
And the yes you were pining for
Becomes a mass of general nos
From boys and girls and older folks
You're feeling like a fright

Verse 3:

Knife
Knife
Feel the sharpness within
Tonight

Knife
Just knife
Be fearful of
The slit
So sad

It can cut so bad
It can feel like
A stab in the sack

Your smile will break your heart
Your smile will break your heart

Plaid Foul

Chorus:

Smile
And the look you were looking for
Becomes a kind of dinosaur
With fangs and claws and open pores
The vision of an eyesore
You're looking like a child

Smile
And the yes you were pining for
Becomes a mass of general nos
From boys and girls and older folks
You're feeling like a fright

Verse 4:

Smiles, mushrooms and knives
Can engender a paradise

Or crush your mind

The difference
Will be clear
In a while
It's the Glasgow smile

Chorus:

Smile
And the look you were looking for
Becomes a kind of dinosaur
With fangs and claws and open pores
The vision of an eyesore
You're looking like a child

Smile
And the yes you were pining for
Becomes a mass of general nos
From boys and girls and older folks
You're feeling like a fright

Once he had finished playing, he moved away from the piano seat and sat down on a chair. He lit a cigar. He remembered his lawyer's advice.

'So what happens?' he had said.

'You can get a fine or prison if you take, carry, make or sell drugs or psychoactive substances.'

'What are the penalties?'

'The penalties depend on the drug and the amount you have and whether you're also dealing or producing the drug.'

'What else?'

'It's also to do with the type or class of drug.'

'For example?'

'If it's a class A drug- for example: crack cocaine; cocaine; ecstasy; (MDMA); heroin; LSD; magic mushrooms; methadone; methamphetamine (crystal meth)- for possession you can get up to seven years in prison, an unlimited fine or both. For supply and production, you can get up to life in prison, an unlimited fine or both.'

'And if it's a class B drug?'

'Well, if it's amphetamines, barbiturates, cannabis, codeine, ketamine, methylphenidate (Ritalin), synthetic cannabinoids, synthetic cathinones (e.g. mephedrone, methoxetamine, in terms of possession you can get up to five years in prison, an unlimited fine or both.'

'And in terms of supply and production?'

'You can get up to fourteen years in prison, an unlimited fine or both.'

'And if it's a class C drug?'

'Well, if it's anabolic steroids, benzodiazepines (diazepam), gamma *hydroxybutyrate* (GHB), gamma-butyrolactone (GBL), piperazines (BZP), khat-'

'Possession?'

'Up to two years in prison, an unlimited fine or both (except anabolic steroids- it's not an offence to possess them for personal use).'

'Supply and production?'

'Up to fourteen years in prison, an unlimited fine or both.'

Having remembered his lawyer's advice, he knew he was going to get the judge. Aside from what the judge's father had done, the judge had put him away. A breach of the Misuse of Drugs Act. He was going to teach the old man what it felt like to look like a monster. He was going to get all of them. If their forefathers hadn't done what they had done his father would have been very different; less angry, able to love him properly. Despite the way his father had treated him- like a cockroach- he had still loved him.

CHAPTER TWO

The Farewell Bash

Prima Facie I had a lot to learn. Apparently, I had been given far too much. Apparently I was 'unavailingly self-centred', 'flatulently pompous', 'gallingly conceited', 'spuriously intelligent', 'loathsomely edacious', 'financially merciless', 'emotionally redundant', 'physically hideous', 'sexually invisible', 'existentially unworthy'...

My eyes were silver. It was a symbol of inner power; of inner wisdom.

It depended on the lighting of the room; sometimes they could be grey. My eyes were very rare. I was creative, inspired and a genius. They could be a sign of witchcraft or royalty or a combination of the two. They should perhaps have been beady given that I had lead a clean life, but as a result of senescence they were rheumy. Still, I felt it important to make it clear to Belay that this unconstructive description was totally unnecessary. As for Belay, his eyes were heavy. According to Belay, my morbidly obese ego was crying out for a lobotomy in life; a test in pain; an exposure to non-descriptive models. He was at pains to stress that if I resisted I would suffer unimaginable discomfort. I countered that I was an extremely successful academic and that I would nor profit from his defunct commination. I appended that if he continued to go about his business in that way, he would inevitably sustain the condign penalty or a suitable amercement; a mulct. He retorted that I was in no way a man of justice but rather a man of greed, survival and revenge, who had had far too many privileges redound to him, and far too many opportunities granted to him, as compared to others, including himself. I questioned Belay on how he had made it this far. He replied that he was considerably better. I begged to differ. I declared that I was the fair man, that he was the bully. He rasped that he was entirely sick of me and that he wanted me as far away from the judiciary as possible. I would have respected him if it had been said with good intention but it had been uttered so brutally that I took exception. In short, Belay was a man who would tell you exactly what he thought of you. I ventured to question him on these points. I took the opportunity to remind him that he had enjoyed considerable wealth himself, that he had exerted massive social influence, that it was hardly my fault that he was homosexual and that he did not have an immediate family. In addition, I said it was not my fault that he imbibed copious amounts of alcohol, that he presumed to take narcotics, that he had been abused. He talked about being bullied as a child, about being sleep-deprived his whole adolescence, about having been rejected by the males he had fallen in love with, about his head having been electrically stapled, about having writhed in agony ripping his hair out, about having boiling water poured slowly over his head, being fucked with the electric shock pen, being slipped an agonizing drug, opened up, rendered temporarily blind. I sighed that he was mentally ill, that I might have to section him, that he necessitated care and treatment. I explained to him that I had worked hard my whole life, that I had always turned up- that my attendances had been perfect, that I was naturally exceptionally clever, that I had never indulged in brutalizing vices, that I was still doing it; working. He warned me that this was going to be crap later. He presaged that by the time a person realizes they have been rejected, as I would be by his employer, he would then be rejected by the others he presently assumed, that he would eventually reject himself, that I would probably become an alcoholic, stumble in to drugs, abuse my pension, rant and proclaim, use up parts of my brain rendering people like me objects of conceptual disgust.

Despite Belay's denunciation of me, I am prepared to admit that I did smoke. I was ten when I stole my first fly puff. I was in primary six. I was behind the bike sheds of Doolin Primary School. My friend Patrick gave it to me. He found it lying irresistibly in the corner of the back-room of his dad's shop. It was 1950.

'Wally,' Paddy had said- my name's Ewald but he used to call me Wally- 'Look what I've got.'

'What is it?' I had said.

'It's called a cigarette.'

'Where did you get it from?'

'I found it in dad's shop.'

'Where?'

'Liking beside a box on the floor in the back room.

'You did?'

'Yes.'

'What does it do?'

'It makes you dizzy.'

'Is it legal?'

'Yes, James Dean does it. So does Humphrey Boart.'

Sure enough I felt dizzy. For once in my life I felt cool. I felt glamorous. I was fourteen when I started officially. It was 1954. In the 1950's smoking was the epitome of cool and glamour. Hollywood icons such as James Dean and Humphrey Boart were never without one. By the late 1950s around half the population of industrialized nations smoked. In the United Kingdom up to 80 per cent of adults were hooked. Smoking had become as natural to me as breathing.

Despite my early fraternization with weed, I had never once imbibed alcohol. My father told me never to drink. He warned me that it was many a man's ruin. He said I would end up poor, unsuccessful and alone. I decided to follow his advice. Indeed, I was 77 before I was broken. It was at a place called Fall's Hall. It was an Aberdeenshire mansion. I did it as an academic exercise to prove I could be one of the people I was probing.

And I certainly had never ingested magic mushrooms. To me, mushrooms had been things your devoted wife might serve her uxorious husband along with fillet steak and champ. I had certainly never expected my daughter to have tried them. To be honest, I had never even suspected she had existed. As for the common mushroom, it is known as *Agaricus campestris* (or *Psalliota campestris*). A true mushroom is never large in size; its cap very seldom exceeds four, at most five inches. The mushroom was to become important to me since it was how my daughter had died.

As a child, I had come across mushrooms. They had grown wild under the oaks of the meadows of Doolin.

I had to find myself as an old man at seventy undergoing experiences I didn't think I had had to understand.

I recall that within an alien vision I saw the man.

'You lost Ewald,' he had said. 'You weren't good enough. She was mine.'

I also saw the woman I had fallen in love with.

'I'm so sorry, Ewald,' she had said. 'I am betrothed to another.'

Back to mushrooms, I had never once in my life played the field or explored the meadow. I had never indulged in a series of sexual relationships without committing myself to anyone. I had had only one sexual encounter out with marriage. It was 1962. I had fallen in love with an Irish woman called Alainn. I had married Adrian as soon as she would allow me. I was a happily married man with four very challenging children. My eldest was David. My youngest was Lilly. The two in the middle were Melissa and Martin, Melissa was the second born, Martin the third. Later it was my job to stay out of the ring.

I was to find myself in the deeply invidious position of being the highest suspect in a double murder-hunt. I had a mushroom knife held against my throat. I was confronted by a man who believed his brother and sister-in-law had been murdered. He believed I had done it, that I harboured a big secret. He believed I was far closer to his sister-in-law than I might have imagined. He believed I was active in the killing of his sister-in-law and passive in the killing of his sister-in-law. He seemed to know too much for me to ignore. He issued me with an ultimatum. Either I satisfied him that all those who were involved were probed and castigated or I would be ruined, or face imprisonment; or worse still, I or my immediate family would be forfeited. Left with no choice and steered by my conscience, I subsequently carried out my own private investigation. I became a sleuth.

Anyway, on the night of my leaving do, the illumination in the *Premier Inn* was chatoyant. A glittering mirror ball peppered the capacious hall with variegated streaks of caramel light. Ingenious light-emitting-diodes cast a blinding phantasmagoria of tints about the dance floor. 'Sixty to Zero' by Neil Young was playing:

(*There's a judge in the city/ He goes to work every day/ Spends his life in the Courthouse/ Keeps his perspective that way.*")

The stench of sweat and alcohol suffused the room, plumes of magenta-grey smoke wafted in from outside. My lemon tea tasted like the product of parturition. Guests clutched to their drinks like alpenstocks.

The Inn itself was at Pacific Quay, situated on the banks of the River Clyde to the west of Glasgow city Centre. The SECC and the Hydro were a short walk across Bell's Bridge. Other nearby attractions included the Glasgow Science Centre, the Riverside Museum and the Tall Ship.

I nudged up beside my wife Andrea. The Scot's gin had performed well this year. She was performing badly by comparison. She had started in neutral conversing with a friend outside. She had stepped into first gear with a Caorunn, into second with a Hendrick's, into third with an Edinburgh Gin raspberry, into fourth with the resurgent Greenall's, into fifth with Bombay Sapphire, and was now into sixth with Gordon's.

I gazed at her with concern. 'Everything all right, my dear?'

'Yes, I'm quite fine,' she said.

'It's just you seem a trifle flustered tonight.'

'No, really I'm fine.'

I knew she wasn't. She was fielding the guests as though they were cubs. It was most uncharacteristic of her to appear so agitated; she was usually the personification of equanimity.

Besides Andrea, my children were there. Some of my colleagues, including a couple of judges were present. Belay had refused to turn up.

My youngest son Martin was exercising his vocals. I had witnessed him knocking back cheap pints all night. I had donated him several tolerant facial expressions and had advised him to slow down. He had ignored me as usual. He never used to drink but since I had stopped his Valium, he had taken to getting drunk and losing his temper. My eldest son David was diplomatically trying to assuage his growing ire, which was directed at a friend of mine, a property investor. My eldest daughter Melissa was standing beside two men. One of the men I distinctly remembered was a former client, the other I gathered was an acquaintance of his. Intermittently, she would look on at her brothers, suppressing her contempt for both. My youngest daughter Lily looked as though she had been drinking. She was busy flirting with a trio of boys, sons of my colleagues I guessed.

Martin addressed the investor. 'You seem to be saying an awful lot,' he said.

The man smiled congenially. 'Oh, you know,' son he said. 'I say things but no one really seems to listen.'

'I'm not surprised,' Martin said.

'Excuse me?'

'You're very arrogant.'

'Sorry son, did I say something wrong?'

Martin growled at him. 'Everything about you is wrong. And I'm not your son.'

At that moment I piped in. 'Martin, please!' I said.

My friend peeked at me for guidance. I nodded at him apologetically.

'I'm terribly sorry,' he said.

'But you'll persist anyway.'

'Persist?'

'In showing off.'

'Sorry?'

'You're so sure you've done it all.'

'I-I-'

'Yes, you strut about the place as though you own it, you speak to people as if you know them all, you look like you're above everyone and I suspect you've achieved nothing in your life.'

'Ewald?' my friend said to me.

'Just ignore him,' I whispered, 'He's been' -I gestured with my hand- 'Drinking.'

My friend nodded with understanding.

Martin did not relent. 'You just assume everything,' he said.

'Shut up, Martin!' said David.

'I'll get on to you in a moment.'

'What is it I've assumed?' said my friend

'You have assumed the right to walk over everyone.'

'Grow up, Martin!' said David.'

Melissa looked on again and rolled her eyes.

'And how precisely have I done that?' said my friend.

'You have no manners whatsoever.'

My friend smiled with puzzlement. 'It's called the free market, son.'

'It's called unjustified arrogance.'

My friend peeked at me. 'Just ignore him,' I mouthed. 'My apologies,' he said, bowed and turned away.

'Where are you going?' Martin said.'

'Sorry, son,' I said at last, 'he's out of our league.'

My friend looked back. 'It okay, Ewald,' he said.

'Why're you letting him speak to us like that?' said Martin.

My friend was becoming annoyed. 'Does your boy not know more than this?' he said.

I glowered at my youngest son. 'Yes.'

'Yes?' said Martin. 'Why are you indulging him?'

'Son, not yet.'

My friend bridled. 'Listen to your father!'

Martin looked daggers at my friend. 'He tells me that, not you.'

'Sorry, Ewald,' he said. 'I'll just stay out of this.'

Martin adopted a supercilious tone. 'Please do. And it's Sir. And please leave the hotel.'

'Oh, give it up, Martin,' said David. 'You're just at the beginning.'

'And you're at the end I suppose?' said Martin.

'I have a wife, four children and a job.'

'You have a crap job.'

'And what do you have?'

'I've got the rudimentary concepts.'

'And that's what you think it's about?'

'Of course.'

David sighed.

'Face it bro!' said Martin, 'You couldn't even cut 'the Highers.' You were nowhere near a first class.'

'Well, maybe I didn't need one. Anyway, it's dad's night, not yours.'

David turned his back on his younger brother, Martin wobbled back to the bar.

I turned my attentions back to Andrea. Reassessing her agitated demeanour, I concluded that she needed space. I ventured outside to take in the air. It was cold and dark. A small huddle of smokers acknowledged my exit but considerately afforded me solitude. The evening breeze whipped against my face. I gazed up at the gelid star-studded empyreans. I motioned to light up when a voice echoed in my mind.

It was Belay. 'It's time to go, Ewald,' it said.

'Go, *Belay*?' I had said.

'Yes, you're seventy-five.'

'Excuse, me Belay, I am seventy-seven.'

'So?'

'So you remember "the Act".'

I had frowned. 'Yes.'

The Act to which Belay had adverted was the *Judicial Pensions and Retirement Act 1993*. It was an Act of the UK Parliament which strengthened the mandatory retirement provisions instituted by the *Judicial Pensions Act 1959* for members of the British

Judiciary. While the 1959 Act forbade service past age seventy-five any judges appointed thereunder (*Lord Denning* being the last exempt jurist), the 1993 Act made the ordinary retirement age seventy, and while enabling a minister (presumably the Lord Chancellor) to allow individual judges to remain in office until seventy-five, it expressly forbade persons aged over seventy-five to hold any Judicial post whatsoever. An exception was the post of Lord Chancellor, a political appointee. Schedule 6 contained the Retirement Dates for certain Judicial Offices. Section 38 covered Immigration adjudicators. This applied to myself.

'But I can still do it,' I had said

'The law already said you can't,' Belay had said.

'But surely there must be another reason.'

'Yes, there is.'

'Which is?'

Belay's brow furrowed as his mouth turned grim. 'You are a contemptibly weak bastard, Ewald.'

'How dare you speak to me like that, Belay! I've worked hard my whole life.'

'Fuck you have!'

'I have always thought that you're the rudest man I've ever met. I don't know why I have agreed to work for you all these years.'

'Because I know you've cheated.'

I glared indignantly. 'How exactly may I ask have I cheated?'

'You're a tranquillized academic.'

'A what?'

'A bastard diazepam junkie.'

'What?'

'You might be able to convince your doctor with misconceptions of fairness but not me.'

'So?

'You're not in the same league of a man who has worked hard his whole life.'

'Being a Special Adjudicator is an intensely stressful business, Belay.'

'So is being an employer. And not nearly as stressful as being an appellant.'

'I concede their problems are different.'

'I don't give a flying fuck about your patronizing concession.'

'Have you been on the *spiritus frumenti* again?'

'Sorry?'

'The *usquebaugh*?'

'Yes, so.'

'That is hardly my fault.'

'No, but the executions bloody are!'

'What executions?'

'You forget.'

'There is nothing to remember.'

'Oh, there is- including the life-sustaining instantaneous distractions.'

I waved my head. 'You're losing me.'

'The hypnosis.'

'What hypnosis?'

'Exactly.'

'What are you saying, Belay?'

'People aren't happy.'

'I've done nothing wrong.'

'That's not how they see it.'

'Who?'

'The families.'

I stood my ground. 'Who are they?'

'They're still around.'

'They're not people of justice.'

'Your brand of justice was too ruthless and too short term.'

'In what way?'

'I've just told you.'

'Eh?'

'I'm afraid, *Ewald*, 'it's over.'

'But *Belay*-'

'Yes?'

'You're not married.'

'No, correct.'
'And you don't have children.'
'No.'
'What do you have?'
'Nothing sweetheart.'
'A man never calls another man "sweetheart."'
'He does when he doesn't use.'
'Then for heaven's sake, take it!'
Belay curled his lip. 'Never!'
'Why not?'
'It's too insulting.'
'Why?'
'I employ asylum judges, not cherubs.'
'No, alcoholic aggression is weak,' I said.
'You think?'
I stared at my employer incredulously. 'Of course it is.'
'How many heart attacks have you had?'
'None.'
'So?'
'So you want to avoid a fourth, Belay.'
'How many times have you been tortured?'
'Never.'
'So?'
'I never provoked a man the way you have.'
'Well, we must have something more relaxing.'
I nodded. 'Yes.'
'Who was she?' he said.
'Who?'

CHAPTER THREE

Indelible Memory

At that moment, the evening sky seemed to change. The clouds parted and the moon rose above, shining indigo. The air seemed to warm up slightly. 'The way we were' played from inside. There was the taste of real coffee in my mouth. I pictured Belay's face looking at me, as though he were staring in to my past. My question echoed in my mind's ear: "*Who*?"

'The girl,' Belay had said.

I had squinted. 'My wife?'

'No, the first girl you fancied.'

'I'm not sure who you mea-'

'You were seven weren't you?'

I cricked my neck. 'I was?'

'You were in primary three.'

'You're sure?'

'Yes, it was 1947.'

'So it was, the school had just opened.'

'Do you remember which School it was?'

'Of course, Doolin National School. Yes, it was built in 1946 but it opened the following year in1947.

Belay nodded.

'I'm surprised you know this, Belay,' I said. 'Yes, it was built by Burkes of Galway.'

'Anything else?"

'The Parish Priest was Canon Lydon.'

'Doolin's a coastal village,' said Belay.

'Yes, in County Clare.'

'On the Atlantic coast.'

'Yes, it borders the spa town of Lisdoonvarna.'

'And?'

'It is a noted centre of traditional Irish music, which is played nightly in pubs.'

'Anything else.'

'Yes, it has a harbour and several streets: Fisher Street, Fitz Street and Roadford.'

'So?'

'So?'

'Do you remember the act?'

'Which act?'

'The act of 1947.'

'Wha-'

'You were seven.'

'I was?'

'Seven is an important number to you.'

'It is?'

'Why?'

'You were also beaten by seven years.'

I scratched the back of my head. 'Seven? You mean the National Health Service (Scotland) Act 1947? You mean the act which created a separate NHS for Scotland accountable to the Secretary of Sta- '

'No, I mean "*The Act.*"'

'I don't fol-

'You were playing doctors and nurses.'

'Yes.'

'Do you remember what she said?'

'Kiss and not tell.'

'What was her name?'

I smiled. 'None of your business.'

Belay smirked.

There was a short pause. 'Do you remember your first true love?' said Belay.

My mind spiralled back seventy years. A sensation of recaptured concupiscence welled up within my loins. 'I said...'

'I'm...I'm coming...'

'And do you remember what she said?'

'She said...'

'I'm waiting...I'm waiting...'

I didn't realize at this point that my employer was extracting the urine.

I nodded at Belay respectfully. 'I'm tremendously impressed you know this, Belay.'

'It was the second most pertinent memory I extracted from you.'

'Why?'

Belay slanted. 'The employer of a judge needs to his judge in order to control him.'

'You think you have controlled me?'

'No, I know I have.'

'Yes?'

'Do you remember 1962?'

I smiled again. 'Of course. I was twenty-two.'

'And where were you?'

'Dublin.'

'Where exactly?'

'Rathnew.'

'And what was happening- at that time, I mean?'

'Well, the Irish Republican Army had officially called off its border campaign in Northern Ireland.'

'Anything else?'

'Yes, it was to do with the Congo.'

'And?'

'Aileen was married to Aiden Fields but...'

'But?'

'There was also my friend Patrick and I and another man.'

'Who?'

'His name was Hugh.'

'So not your primary school friend? The one at Doolin.'

'No.'

'Your father was a business services man?'

'Yes.'

'Patrick's father was Aiden Fields?'

'Correct.'

'And he was a textiles man.'

'Yes.'

'In Doolin.'

'Yes, Fisher Street.'

'What did he sell?'

'Groceries- and traditional Irish music.'

'But that's not textiles.'

'No.'

'So?'

'He owned a small shop as well.'

'What exactly did your father do?'

I leaned back, considering. 'Well, he assisted with the designing, constructing and usage of machines. He also helped ships, boats and barges seek shelter from stormy weather and stored them for future use.'

'You mean a port?'

'Yes, a facility for loading and unloading vessels.'

'Your father's name was Ealdahach.'

'Well remembered.'

'So?'

'Various people were leaving Ireland?'

'Which people?'

'The artists.'

'Why?'

'To entertain United Nations troops there.'

'In the Congo?'

'Yes.'

'And?'

'My father was trying to assist the artists.'

'How?'

'By helping them with the development of their paintings.'

'And why were you there?'

'Patrick's father and my father were firm friends.'

'Aiden Fields and Ealdahach Wren?'

'Yes.'

'Why was that?'

'They had shared something very important.'

'What?'

'They had fallen in love with the same woman.'

'Who was she?'

'Irene.'

'Irene who?'

'Irene O' Reilly.'

'So Aiden Fields and Irene had Patrick.'

'Yes.'

'So?'

'My father had to concede his friend had won.'

'What else?'

'My father became more competitive.'

'How?'

'He made himself more intelligent.'

'How?'

'By learning more and more.'

'Why?'

'He vowed that his son i.e. me would never lose his angel of delight to his rival.'

'So?'

'When my friend Patrick's father Aiden Fields asked my father Ealdahach Wren to come over, I also went over.'

'And?'

'Aiden Fields wondered if he would be losing his son.'

'Patrick?'

'Yes.'

'Then what happened?'

'U Thant arrived in Dublin.'

'And?'

'He paid tribute to Irish soldiers who fought in the Congo.'

'So?'

'It was 13 July 1962. I was studying there.'

'In Dublin?'

'Yes.'

'For what?'

'My finals. Beside the river.'

'Which river?'

'The Liffey.'

'And?'

'I met Alainn.'

'You remember her breath?'

I smiled fondly. 'Yes, it was like mint.'

'And her hair- can you remember the smell?'

I smiled fondly again. 'Yes, it was like strawberry.'

Belay smiled wryly. 'And her lips?'

'They tasted like cherry.'

'And d' you remember what she said?'

'She said: "*I'm married, Ewald*".'

'To Aiden Fields.'

'Yes, but she was having sexual relations with other men. My friend Patrick was one of them. He died in the Congo.'

Belay nodded.

'Before he left he said, if he never returned, she was to live her life.'

'Who else was she seeing?'

'An older man.'

'Older?'

'Seven years I think.'

'How old was Alainn?'

'She was twenty-nine.'

'And?'

'The older man was also twenty-nine.'

'And?'

'The older man said I was not welcome here.'

'What in Dublin?'

'Yes.'

'Alainn had a child, didn't she.'

'Yes, Jarrod.'

'Jaro means anger, does it not?'

'Yes.'

'Who was Jarrod's father?'

'That's what I don't know.'

'Let me get this the right way round. Your friend, Ewald was Patrick. You grew up together.'

'Yes.'

'Patrick's father was Aiden Fields.'

'Yes.'

'Your father was Ealdahach Wren.'

'Yes.'

'So what happened?'

'Aiden Fields had sexual intercourse with Patrick's girlfriend Alainn.'

Belay gasped. 'Aiden Fields slept with his own son's girlfriend?'

'Yes.'

'Did your friend Patrick know this?'

'No.'

'Wasn't that a bit perfidious?'

'In the least, yes.'

'What did your friend Patrick's mother, Irene, have to say about this?'

'She was unaware.'

'So you don't know who Jarrod's father was?'

'No.'

'Did Alainn have any other children?'

'Yes, a girl.'

'Who?'

'Susanna.'

'And?'

CHAPTER FOUR

The Retiral

After a protracted silence, I said: 'So?'

Belay's brown eyes had dark circles underneath. Indeed the circles had darkened with each night he had stayed up to fill out appeals. 'So,' he said, 'it's time to go, Ewald.'

'You know I could section you, Belay, for this.'

Belay glared at me. 'At least you know part of the name. And you do know Ewald Wren, I could finish you.'

I peeked innocently. 'Why would you wish to do that?'

'You've run roughshod over too many people's feelings with your egregious arrogance and disgusting indifference.'

'Which people?'

'The staff, the lawyers, the appellants.'

I glared ignominiously. 'How?'

'You're inordinately selfish.'

'In what way?'

'You place your ego above sense and sensibilities.'

I smirked. 'Have you been reading Jane Austin again? I always knew you were a homosexual.'

'No, I've been reading complaints.'

'I'm most sorry, Belay, I have no idea what you're saying.'

'You have a lot to learn, Ewald.'

'About what exactly?'

'The real world.'

'You're forty-five, Belay- barely middle-aged- I'm seventy-seven- a very old man'

'And that's part of the reason I'm retiring you.'

'And what have Ito learn?'

'Pain and suffering; relationships; life.'

'Explain.'

'Very well, you abuse your wife, you neglect your youngest son, you hide behind your oldest son, you glorify your oldest daughter, and you have not the slightest conception of your youngest daughter.'

'You have no basis for these allegations.'

'How long have I known you, Ewald?'

'Many, many years.'

'So you can't refute my factual statements.'

'I *am* more intelligent than you, Belay.'

'You're more academic in your feeling, Ewald, that's all.'

'I do smoke, you know.'

'Exactly.'

'And you drink- copiously in fact.'

'Exactly.'

'And I know you've taken illegal drugs.'

'So?'

'You're a complete hypocrite.'

'But you haven't experienced it yet.'

'What?'

'The other side.'

'What other side?'

'A very painful side. I'm sorry, Ewald, you're far too patronizing.'

'You're far too crass, Belay.'

'I haven't been nearly remonstrative enough. You are totally out of touch, Ewald, you always have been.'

'So?'

'It's really time to go.'

'This isn't over Belay.'

'No, you're right it's not.'

Belay did not so much as show me the door as give me the

final stare to leave. I was left feeling most indignant. *What an ignoramus*, I thought. Up until that point I had considered that my decisions had still been of the standard. I had thought I had so much more to do. I had felt I had had more decisions to make, more social improvements to make, more justice to deliver: more goodness to impart. Still, it seemed I had outlived my professional use.

The music changed. 'The Trial' by Pink Floyd came on.

'(*The evidence before the court is incontrovertible/ There's no need for the jury to retire/* In *all my years of judging I have never heard before/* Of *someone more deserving the full penalty*')

I emerged from my trance. I checked my wristwatch. It was vastly approaching midnight. I went back inside the Inn.

I gazed at Andrea. 'My darling?' I said.

'I'm sorry, Ewald, I really feel I must retire for the evening.'

'Is there anything on your mind?'

'It's- it's nothing Ewald, really.'

I said I would be up shortly.

By and by, the room emptied. The last of the bar staff left. I found myself on my own. I felt the urge for one last smoke. I ventured outside for the final time. I motioned to light up again when suddenly I felt a nick in my throat.

CHAPTER FIVE

Couteau a Champignon-point

An arm swung round my chest, squeezed me backwards, while the other hand held a knife to my throat. Taken from behind, I couldn't see my assailant.

A voice growled: *'Do you remember this?'*

I waggled my head.

The voice said: *'You used it to initiate a blood brother.'*

I gasped.

The voice said: *'Any sudden movements and your will wear the Glasgow Smile.'*

The voice relaxed slightly. 'You are very close to death.'

My own voice squeaked. 'What do I do?'

'You listen.'

I wiggled my head again.

'Now,' the voice said, 'I accept description.'

I squirmed. '2.5,' the voice said.

I was gasping. I nodded.

'It's life with a little something extra. The 2 being what we've experienced and accomplished and the .5 being the next adventure.'

'Feels more like death.'

'Now,' the voice said, 'turn around slowly

I did so, baulking from the knife.

I saw a man with a beard, lowering his knife. His eyes were

hooded. He was of medium build, broad-shouldered, and swarthy face. I placed him in his mid-forties. He coughed importantly. 'In Spain,' he said, 'they call it '*Jubalacion*.'

As I peered into the hoods of his eyes, I said: 'Which is?'

'Optimistic and joyful.'

'You're Part-Spanish?'

'No, just Scottish.'

'So?'

'Do you accept description?' he said again.

He pressed the gun tighter to my temple. 'I'm not sure I quite understand what you're talking about?'

'I'll repeat the question. Do you accept description?'

I tried to be careful. 'Not if it involves anything deleterious.'

The man rattled his head as if he didn't need the word. 'Do you accept description?'

'No, not like that.'

'Do you accept description?'

'As I said, not like that.'

'In which case, you die.'

I sighed. 'I would seriously urge you not to kill me. I have a wife. I have four children.'

'So did another family.'

'Yes. Which family?'

The man ignored me. 'But you didn't accept description.'

'I will accept description if you do not hurt anyone.'

'I will only hurt one person if you accept description.'

'In that case I do not.'

'In which case you die.'

I stood my ground. 'In which case I will die. Goodbye my love, good-bye kids...'

I waited for the rip. I could feel it fulminating in my mind. The man held me by the face and glared at me.

'What's your name?' he said.

'I thought perhaps you knew me.'

'I have never met you before.'

'Why are you detaining me then?'

'I want to know.'

'Yes. What do you want to know?'

'I want to know who you are?'

'My name is 'Wren'.'

'Yes, I thought so, as in the bird.'

'How would you think so?'

'Your name was in the Herald.'

'And?'

'It read that you were having a leaving do.'

'So?'

'Not just yet. Why were you called Wren?'

'I suppose it was better than 'Eagle'.'

'In what sense better?'

'In sense that while the king of the birds is the golden eagle as it outflew other birds, it was beaten by a small bird who had hidden in its plumage.'

'And what's your first name?'

'Ewald?'

'Why Ewald?'

'I guess I was born to be fair.'

'When were you born?'

'I was born in 1940'

'Who was your father?'

'Ealdahach Wren.'

'What did he do?'

'He was a business servicer.'

'What do you do?'

'Nothing any more.'

'What do you mean?'

'I'm retired.'

'Yes, I thought so.'

'Why?'

'No reason. What did you do before?'

'Nothing important.'

'Did you work for the Scottish Parliament?'

Was this knife man patronizing me? *I thought*. Or was he

offering me respect? In the end I settled for the honest answer: 'No.'

'You were not a Scottish Minister, a UK Government Minister or a Member of Scottish Parliament.'

Was the man paranoid schizophrenic? 'No,' I said.

He squeezed his chin. 'Good.' He said it a way that made me feel as though he wished to bring me down. 'Did you work for the Scottish Executive?'

'No, but-'

The man waved a pointer in my face. 'But?'

'I was fair.'

The man nodded as though he had had something important confirmed to him. "Did you work for the Scottish Executive Justice Department.'

'No.'

'Good.' Again it sounded like he was putting me in my place.

'Did you research justice?'

I was feeling embarrassed now. 'Of course I did.'

His expression was inscrutable. 'Were you a Chief Research Officer?'

'No.'

'Good.'

His evaluation was beginning to offend me. 'But if it makes a difference...I was a judge.'

The man did not waver. 'Did you work for the Supreme Courts?'

Was he patronizing me again or offering another chance for respect? 'No,' I said.

He smiled thinly. 'Good,' he said. 'You were not the Lord High Chancellor of Great Britain.'

Do I sound like him? 'No, of course not,' I said.

'Good,' he said again. 'You were not a Lord of Appeal in Ordinary.'

I could see plainly where this was going now. He not only wished to work out what kind of judge I had been but he also wanted to rub my nose in it as well. 'No,' I said.

'Good. Did you work for the High Court of Justiciary?'

I sighed. I wished now that I had. My sunken cheeks flushed for my guests.' 'No.'

'Good. Did you work for the Crown Office?'

This was another veiled compliment. 'No,' I said.

'Good.

If only? 'No.'

'Good. Did you work for the Court of Session?'

'No.'

'So not the Teind Court.'

'No.'

'Nor the Court of Exchequer, nor the court for Trial of Election petitions, nor the Registration Appeal Court, nor the Restrictive Practices Court, nor the Valuation Appeal court?'

'No.'

'You were not an insolvency judge?'

'No. I rather fear it would be easier for me just to tell you.'

'No, I would prefer to work it out- by a process of elimination.'

He waved his head sternly. 'No.'

'You would?'

'Yes. Did you work for the Scottish Executive Justice Department: Courts Group?'

'No.'

'But you were a fair man?'

'Yes, I believe I was.'

'Tell me, did you require the Head of Division (Judicial Appointments and Finance)?'

'Yes, of course.' I said 'of course' since he obviously knew his way around top jobs.

'But you were a judge.'

'Yes.'

He grimaced. 'You were an *asylum judge*, weren't you?'

'Yes.'

At this point, he drew down the knife. He gazed at me wistfully. 'I believe you might have killed my brother.'

I gasped.

FIRST INTERLUDE

Ealdahach Wren Challenges Jack Dorcha

They were still at the dining table. The lamb had not been dished up yet.

'Your drinking, Jack,' said Ealdahach Wren, 'and its consequential thought disorder and emotional distress will lead to pins and needles. You will be asleep in agony.'

Jack Dorcha railed. 'The only pins and needles here,' he said, 'are the things that hold your jerry-built brain together and jag you when you deem to know more.'

'There is room for more kindness,' said James Bennet.

Peter Reid coughed. 'There is room for heaven and hell,' he said.

'Go for him, E,' said Frank Sharp.

'Perhaps the two of you should calm down.' said Lewis McLean.

'I haven't served the lamb yet,' said Jaeger Fields.

'I'm sure it will be beautiful when it arrives,' said Aiden Fields.

Olivia McLean shrunk. 'I'm sure it will.'

'Tell me, E,' said Jack Dorcha, 'how is the business services industry.'

'Fine, before you defalcated most of it.'

'It was all in the contract, E,' said Jack Dorcha.

'That's not what my son says.'

'I have better lawyers than your son Ewald.'

'Unscrupulous you mean.'

'Come, now,' said Jack Dorcha, 'Let's not get greedy. I gave your business services the MOT it desperately needed and made it fit to run.'

'Just so we're clear, Jack, take me through business services.'

'Of course, it's a general term.'

Ealdahach nodded patiently.

'And?'

'It describes work that supports a business but does not produce a tangible commodity.'

'I had a tangible commodity.'

'Perhaps, but not a successful one.'

'Go on.'

'Information technology (IT) is an important business service that supports many other business services such as procurement, shipping and finance.'

'What else?'

'A good business service aligns IT assets with the needs of a company's employees and customers and support business goals, facilitating the ability of the company to be profitable. Documenting the value that an IT company provides to the business often involves an audit of IT infrastructure processes, the creation or updating of an IT service catalogue and/or the provisioning of an employee self-service portal to improve communication.'

'You realise you broke the contract.'

'What are you going to do? Sue me?'

For the first time Ealdahach Wren betrayed signs of malintent. 'It's tempting, although there are other ways of civilising people.'

'Are you threatening me, E?'

'I think your mouth is working for the execution.'

'You mean prosecution.'

Ealdahach Wren smiled stiffly.

CHAPTER SIX

Me; Ewald Wren

'Your brother?' I said.

He glowered at me. 'Yes,' he said.

I exhaled. 'Who was your brother?'

'I believed you would know that?'

'No, I'm afraid I don't.'

The man looked at me distrustfully. 'I'm surprised.'

'Why are you surprised?'

'Judges tend to have very good memories.'

'Yes, but I don't know his name.'

'His name was Andrew McLean.'

I frowned. 'I recall a Lewis McLean. My father knew him. He was a gas and oil exporter.'

'Indeed.'

'So?'

'Well?'

'You're not his son, are you?'

'Yes.'

I gasped.

A vivid sensation of consternation pulsed through the wynds of my retired memory. At once I could perceive a vicious howling noise. I could see people, figures, shadows... I perceived brilliant light of the early afternoon sun streaming through the towering windows of the building. I felt my body leap, as though out of a chair and dash towards the exit. The memory vanished. I trembled. A bead of sweat poured down my face.

The man glowered at me. 'You are remembering something.'

My heart quivered. 'No- no I'm not.'

'But you are responsible.'

I gulped. '"*Responsible?*"'

'Yes.'

I stammered. 'Wha- McLean- who are you?'

'*Chase.*'

'Chase?'

'Yes.'

'That's your first name.'

'Indeed.'

I tripped over my words again. 'It's- it's extremely posh.'

Chase shrugged. 'Perhaps.'

'And what do you do?'

'I write.'

'You do?'

'Yes.'

'What d' you write about?'

'Crime.'

I looked askance at the man. 'Is that when you're not committing it.'

'By that you mean?'

'You've assaulted me.'

'How have I assaulted you?'

'By putting a knife to my throat.'

'So?'

'It creates the necessary fear of life endangerment.'

'So?'

'I didn't even know your brother. What did he do?'

Chase pressed with his shoulders. 'He was a lawyer.'

'What law did he do?'

'Asylum.'

I squeezed my chin. 'How old was he?'

'Twenty-six.'

'What level?'

'Assistant.'

'Yes, that is possible.'

'No, it happened.'

I suspended my disbelief. 'What makes you think I was responsible?'

'I think you wished to survive.'

'What do you mean?'

'I believe you may have wished to keep a secret.'

'What secret?'

'Murders.'

I gazed at Chase quizzically. 'Murders?'

'Executions.'

The words spoken by my employer Belay as he was retiring me came flooding back: '*No, but the bloody executions are*!' They made Chase's word echo. 'Executions?' I said.

'Carried out at your court.'

I tested his knowledge. 'Which court?'

'The Court Service.'

'What makes you think there were executions at the court?'

'An anonymous caller.'

'Yes?'

'He said: "*Weapons...people killed in there...executions... He used her... The judge is retiring...*"'

'" *There*"?'

'In the Court. You were judge at the time.'

'When?'

'9 July 1995.'

'How do you know that?'

'I received the call two weeks ago.'

'So what d' you think the caller meant?'

'I infer he meant my brother was killed.'

'And?'

'That you were the judge.'

'Why?'

'You've retired.'

'So?'
'That makes you the first suspect.'
'There are many judges.'
'But you are an asylum judge who is retiring.'
'Why would I have killed him?'

CHAPTER SEVEN

Drive to Aberdeen Countryside

My captor clutched me fiercely with his left hand front-wise by the neck, his knife held aloft by his right hand. He pulled be backwards out of the Inn, down the stairs in to the car park. The wind was howling and the rain pelting as we ambled in the midnight air. Chase dragged me to a car. It was a BMW.

'Get in,' said case.

I shook my head. 'I'm not going anywhere with you.'

Chase snarled. 'You can either go in the boot or you can drive.'

I groaned. 'You expect me to drive? At this time? In this weather?'

Chase smiled plainly. 'Of course.'

'Well, I can't.'

'Why not?'

'I'm intoxicated.'

'No, you're not, you're sober as a judge.'

I scowled. 'How do you know?'

'Your article in the Herald said you've never had a drink in your life.'

I tried to think quickly. 'Well, I started tonight.'

'No, I don't think so, your cigarette breath is dry.'

'What if I resist?'

'Then this couteau a champignon will enter your face.'

'Come on! It's after midnight and the weather is atrocious.'

'Well, it's either you drive the car or I drive the knife.'

I sighed. 'Alright! Where am I driving to?'

'North.'

'Where exactly?'

'The hills of Aberdeen.'

'But that would take hours.'

'Then we must get started.'

Eventually, I got in the driver's seat and set off.

'Why are we going there?' I said.

'I want to show you the location of the second suspect.'

'The second?'

'Yes, I still think you did it.'

'Then why go there?'

'Where the murders of my brother and his wife are concerned, I'm prepared to be wrong.'

'Who is the second suspect?'

'I don't know.'

As I drove, my heart pounding in my chest, Chase kept the mushroom knife firmly in his right hand. There were times I contemplated making an emergency stop, so as to surprise Chase, and wrest the blade from his grip and drive it into his chest. At seventy-seven I wasn't sure I had the strength.

From time to time in the captive drive, Chase would crack the odd joke. His jokes did nothing to settle my nerves; they only intensified my trepidation.

'You know,' he said, 'It's so fortunate you don't drink. I think the drive has been bracing enough.'

I sighed. 'Yes.'

Chase glanced at me almost respectfully. 'You're quite the speed merchant.'

'Yes?' I said.

'For an old man I mean.'

'I just want to get this over and done with as quickly as possible.'

Later Chase said: 'You're really rather indecisive at times.'

'Yes?'

'For a judge.'

'In what way?'

'You can't decide which lane your in.'

'Do you drive, Chase?'

Chase laughed heartily. 'Not very well, no.'

'Then I think you'll find I'm being responsible as I can as a hostage.'

Later still, Chase said: 'I'm rather surprised you have four children.'

'Yes, your gear stick is so flaccid.'

Was this homosexual banter? 'I am seventy-eight you remember and I only used it to impress my wife.'

SECOND INTERLUDE

Peter Sharp Challenges Jack Dorcha

As the small elite group of multi-millionaires sat at the dining table above deck on the Sunseeker Manhattan 50, Jack Dorcha knocked back another Glenfiddich 50, continuously expanding. He stood up, wobbled and slapped his right thigh. He smiled slightly. His smile seemed to teeter on the edge of a loud cackle; it was a single-edged smile. His sick laughter re-bellowing in the open sea sky. 'Damn!' he said, 'isn't it perfect? It's so good to have all my old friends around me. You know I haven't felt this alive since Scott was born. Beautiful day it was. He looked up at me just as I'm looking up at the sun-drenched sky.' He hiccuped. 'A bit like today,' he said.

Peter Reid glanced at Olivia McLean who was peeking nervously. 'Careful, Jack, you're affected,' he said.

Lewis McLean nodded with gratitude at Peter Reid. 'Yes, please pace yourself, Jack.'

Frank Sharp scoffed. 'You're drunk, Jack- as always.'

'Seriously, Frank, said Jack Dorcha, 'I thought you liked emotion.'

Jaeger White nodded with some self-assurance. 'Clearly, my whiskey works,' he said.

Aiden Fields smiled with disapproval. 'It's working too, well,' he said.

Ealdahach Wren nodded. 'On one hand,' he said, 'whiskey

eases a man's pain; on the other, it causes no little amount of social awkwardness.

'Yes,' said James Bennet, 'and then there's the debilitating hangover.'

Jack Dorcha cackled. 'My mind has never been clearer.'

Ealdahach Wren smiled sadly at Jaeger White. 'Yes, it's definitely kicking in.'

Jack Dorcha's lip curled. 'What's wrong? You all seem wroth with me.'

Frank Sharp grimaced. 'That surprises you, Jack,' he said.

Jack Dorcha cackled again before taking another swipe at his quiach of Glenfiddich 50. 'Christ, Frank,' he said, ''you always make the most powerful sounds.'

Frank Sharp loured. I'm only saying what needs to be said.'

'Oh, yes?' said Jack Dorcha.

'Naturally,' said Frank Sharp.

Jack Dorcha grinned. 'Not a Sharp-' He looked at Aiden Fields- 'Or a flat.'

'Aiden is sober,' said Peter Reid, 'hardly flat.'

Jack Dorcha adjusted his thoughts. 'You did well for yourself, Frank,' said Jack Dorcha.

'We all did,' said James Bennet.

'Except for those left behind,' said Ealdahach Wren.

This time Peter Reid agreed. 'Correct, E.'

Ealdahach Wren nodded.

Jack Dorcha glowered at Frank Sharp. 'Still, Frank,' he said, 'you did so much better because of me.'

'How do you calculate that one, Jack?' said Frank Sharp.

Jack Dorcha laughed sardonically. ''Your quaint Scottish din went global.'

Frank Sharp's bushy brows beetled. 'I could have done that without you.'

Jack Dorcha grinned derisively. 'You believe so.'

'Of course I do,' said Frank Sharp.

Jack Dorcha shook his head. 'Not without electronics and instrument engineering.'

Frank Sharp glared at Jack Dorcha with no impression. 'So you tweaked a few things?'

Jack Dorcha snapped. 'No, Frank, I made it happen.' He exhaled generously. 'You must remember, not every deaf child identifies with the clamour of Scotland.'

Frank Sharp bristled. 'No, I suppose not,' said Frank Sharp.

The rest of the group fell silent.

'Really, Frank,' said Jack Dorcha, 'despite early music, folk music, classical music, pop rock and fusion and jazz, the music of Scotland wasn't everything.'

Frank Sharp railed. 'You don't know it,' he said.

Jack Dorcha shook his head. 'I rather think I do,' he said, 'the accordion, the bagpipes, the fiddle, the guitar, the harp, the tin whistle, the bodhran.'

Frank Sharp loured. 'It's not as simple as that.'

Jack Dorcha lowered. ''No, it's not,' he said, 'The great Highland bagpipe is not everyone's favourite.'

'Did I say it was?'

'No, but you presumed a strangled cat.'

'You're showing your ignorance again.'

'Really. I believe they were introduced to Scotland by the Gaels of Ireland.'

'So?'

'I got people paying for your great Highland bagpipe.'

'I know that.'

'There you go then.'

Frank Sharp waved his head. 'You might have had money, but you've battened off other people's work.'

'But they went for me.'

'Went for you.'

'Yes.'

Jack Dorcha shook his head off entertainingly. ''Of course they would.'

'Why?'

'Because it's so self-indulgent- as well as boringly narrow.'

'You don't understand music.'

'Maybe not to your extent but I knew what could work within reason.'

Frank Sharp bristled. 'They humiliated me.'

'Yes.'

'So?'

'You were good at what you believed in but you were unimaginably self-absorbed.'

'So?'

'They broke in to my house, broke all my instruments, urinated on my property.'

'Of course they would.'

'Why?'

'You were making fortunes out of tribal garbage.'

'I had my face slashed.'

'Of course.'

'Why?'

'You were a man of third-world entertainment that got caught out.'

'So?'

'You needed my money and my connections.'

'Your connections threatened my life.'

'Oh?'

'They said if I didn't deliver I would be made the bum note of the industry.'

'Perhaps they were telling you something.'

'Like what?'

'You weren't as good as you felt you were.'

'So?'

'So, I'm not surprised, not exactly.'

'Tell me, Jack,' have you heard of death music.

Jack Dorcha's grin broke. He lowered his tone. 'Only yours.'

'Would you mind,' said Frank Sharp, 'putting on the stereophonic system, Aiden.'

Aiden nodded quietly. 'Sure.'

The music started.

'What is this?' said Jack Dorcha.

Frank Sharp smirked. 'Tribal garbage.'

Jack Dorcha gulped. 'Yes?'

'Yes, Twinkle Toes.'

'Who sings it?'

'Roy Orbison.'

Jack Dorcha gawked.

Suddenly, there was an announcement. 'The second course is ready,' said Jaeger White.

'Ah!' said James Bennet, 'the lamb.'

'I must admit,' said Peter Reid, 'it smells pretty good.'

Aiden Fields smiled gratefully. 'Doesn't it.'

'Yes,' said Olivia McLean.

'Perfect!' said Frank Sharp.

'Perhaps our host deserves to be served first,' said Lewis McLean.

'Thank you, Lewis,' said Jack Dorcha.

'No, thank you,' said Lewis McLean.'

Frank Sharp smiled portentously at Jack Dorcha. 'I'm sure *it* will make a very satisfactory second course.'

Ealdahach Wren stifled a smirk. 'With all this death music, may the blessed eat in peace.'

Jack Dorcha frowned nervously.

CHAPTER EIGHT

Music Hall; The Disgruntled Client

In the abyssal blackness of the bitter cold wind-swept lashing rain, we arrived. Having steered through the front gates I crawled along the stone-chipped driveway and pulled up outside a giant house.

I bolted up deliberately, looking to be impressed. My eyes inventoried my surroundings.

I surveyed the house. 'So this is it?' I said. 'This is the your second suspect's house?'

'No, it's the third suspect.'

'Third?'

'Yes, I'll explain shortly.'

I adopted a marginally sarcastic tone. 'The search light does lend it an air of mystery.'

'Quite.'

'The bad weather also lends it an air of sinisterness.'

Chase nodded.

'So,' I said, 'you don't know who owns this edifice.'

'No, my brother never said.'

'Your brother? Andrew McLean? The murder victim?'

'Yes.' Chase gave me an exasperated smile. 'My brother was a lawyer. He was not in the habit of giving away his clients' names, although he did tell me a few things.'

'So the owner was your brother's client?'

'Yes, and he was sixty-three.'

'In 1995?'

'Yes.'

'D' you know if he's still alive?'

'He either is, or someone else has taken over.'

'But he would be eighty-five now.'

'Yes.'

'What makes you think your brother was murdered?'

THIRD INTERLUDE

James Bennet Challenges Jack Dorcha

As the small group of elite millionaires made their way through the lamb at the dining table on the Sunseeker Manhattan 50, Olivia McLean's nostrils flared with delight, while her father Lewis McLean beamed at her.

'This really is very good,' said Aiden Fields.

'Good?' said Jack Dorcha. 'It's nothing short of delicious.'

Jaeger White winked at Jack Dorcha. 'It's what I put in it.'

'Did you get any help?' said Frank Sharp.

Jaeger White smiled at Peter Reid. Peter Reid nodded back.

'Just a little,' said Jaeger White.

James Bennet piped up. 'You were saying, Frank, that you were threatened.'

'Indeed,' said Frank Sharp.

'That's curious,' said James Bennet, 'the same thing happened to me.'

'Oh?' said Lewis McLean.

'Yes,' said James Bennet, 'my mechanical engineering plant suffered a fire.'

Olivia McLean gaped. 'You mean it was deliberate?'

'Yes, Olivia,' said James Bennet, 'I believe it was.'

Jack Dorcha gaped. 'Why should anyone wish to blow up your company?'

'Perhaps they felt my mechanical engineering had gone down hill.'

Jack Dorcha frowned. 'Why would they think that?'

'Well, Jack,' said James Bennet, 'ever since you unilaterally changed the design, construction, and use of my machines, bad things seemed to happen.'

Jack Dorcha scowled. 'Such as?'

'Such as the cars wouldn't always run smoothly.'

'Important point, James,' said Peter Reid.

'Yes, Peter,' said James Bennet. 'Unfortunately in addition, my machines would no longer have my original safety features.'

'Safety is often wasted on the foolish,' said Frank Sharp.

'Health and safety always comes first, Frank,' said Lewis McLean.

Aiden Fields nodded. 'I agree.'

'Plus,' said James Bennet, 'some of the break pedals started to malfunction.'

'They often do,' said Jack Dorcha.

'Not the way I designed them,' said James Bennet.

Jack Dorcha coughed imperiously. 'Your team obviously didn't understand my intention.'

'You mean,' said James Bennet, 'your way of saving money and assuming insight into the mechanical engineering industry.'

Jack Dorcha. 'No, I mean, we had to aim higher.'

'Higher meaning that my company would reach the sky.'

'But,' said Jack Dorcha,'your auto-mobiles were the most advanced in the country.' Jack Dorcha lifted his eyes. 'Hell, this boat uses some of the same technology.'

'Yes, and do you see what's happening now?'

'What?'

'Your Manhattan Sunseeker 50 is starting to slow down.'

'That's just the turbulence.'

'No, your pretentious more cost-efficient engine is burning up.'

'Then you must fix it.'

'Yes, it's better when I control the machines, not you.'

'I'm very sorry, James, if you felt I was controlling you.'

Just then, Jaeger White spoke: 'The beef is ready.'

'Great,' said Olivia McLean.

'Yes, it smells heavenly,' said Lewis McLean.

'I do hope you have the engine-room for my premium beef,' said Jaeger White.

CHAPTER NINE

Fall's Hall; The Rivalrous Uncle

I drove across the countryside to another ridiculous house. I looked at the sign on the front gate. 'Fall's Hall,' I said.

Chase smiled satisfactorily. 'Yes, this is the fourth suspect, the bitter rival.'

'Who is he?'

'I don't know.'

'Why don't you know?'

'The disgruntled client never told my brother who he was.'

'And your brother could not tell you?'

'No.'

'Why might he have murdered your brother and/or his wife?'

'I don't know.'

'How would he have done it?'

'No idea.

'Where would he have done it?'

'Perhaps he was at court as well.'

'Why would he be at court?'

'Perhaps he wanted to defend himself.'

I frowned. 'In the asylum division?'

'Perhaps it was informal. Could he be arrested or detained?'

'Not with that evidence.'

'What would happen if the evidence were stronger?'

'He would have legal rights.'

'How could he be detained?'

I squeezed my chin. 'Individuals may be detained for a number of statutory reasons.'

'In which instances?'

'In all cases, an individual may only be detained if there are reasonable grounds for suspecting they have committed or are committing an offence punishable by imprisonment (section 14(1) of the Criminal Procedure (Scotland) Act (1995).'

'And what would happen then?'

'Well, following detention, he would only need to tell the police his name, address and date of birth.'

'Any case law?'

'Yes, of course.'

'So?'

'Well, following the case of Cadder in 2010, the UK Supreme Court held that a detained person is entitled to have a lawyer provide advice ahead of interview by the police.'

'And what does the lawyer have to do?'

'The lawyer must attend at the police station or may provide advice by phone.'

'What does that mean?'

'It means that everyone is entitled to legal advice throughout the interview process and a lawyer is permitted to attend at interview.'

'What else?'

'It is strongly advised that a person exercise his or her right to legal advice if he or she are detained by police.'

'Does the detained person have any entitlements?'

'Yes, they are entitled to reasonable breaks, rest and food, if necessary, during their period of detention.'

'Can the police do anything?'

'Yes, samples such as mouth swabs may be taken only if they are necessary to the investigation of the case.'

'What happens after arrest?'

'Once the period of detention has expired (twelve hours), the police must arrest or release the person.'

'And what if the person is arrested?'

'They will either be kept in custody until the next court day (a Monday if you are arrested on a Friday, Saturday or Sunday), or you will be released and ordered to appear at court on a specified future date.'

'What else?'

'You may also be released while a report is sent to the Procurator Fiscal, who will decide whether to prosecute you.'

'And what then?'

'If they decide to start criminal proceedings, you will be notified and given dates when you must attend court.'

'What else happens if you are arrested?'

'It would be important that the person seek legal advice from a solicitor he knows or they would arrange for the duty solicitor to meet with him.'

'I see.'

Chase stared into my eyes. His voice was conclusive. 'It's time to go back,' he said.

'The hotel?'

''Not quite.'

'What about my wife? My children?'

'I think they will survive without your early morning appearance.'

'So?'

'Thorntonhall.'

I squinted. 'Thorntonhall?'

'Yes, it's a village.'

'Yes, I know that.'

'It's in South Lanarkshire?'

'Of course. It lies just east of the boundary with East Renfrewshire, close to Waterfoot and Jackton. It is west of East Kilbride, and North of Eaglesham.'

'Yes.'

'It's a very affluent area.'

'Yes, you will see where the client's son lives.'

'Am I expected to drive all the way there?'

'Would you rather stay here.'
'Well no.'
'Let's get in, then.'
I deferred to the logic.

CHAPTER TEN

Thorntonhall; The Talented Son

As I hit the gas southwards from the Aberdeenshire countryside towards South Lanarkshire, dawn was breaking. It caused me to squint. I put down the sun visor. The sun was rising slowly above the dismal horizon.

Chase seemed to have awoke from a snooze. 'Ah!' he said.. 'At last some light.'

I glanced quizzically at Chase. I smiled tolerantly as I nodded. 'Yes,' I said.

'And the rain's gone.'

'Yes.'

'And the wind's died down.'

'Yes.'

'You're still annoyed with me.'

'Not at all.'

'No?'

'No, I relish being forced at knife-point. I love being forced to drive for five hours to an unwanted destination, being persuaded to drive sideways to another unwanted destination, and then being reasoned with to drive to a third unwanted destination.'

Chase gazed sarcastically. 'You do?'

'No.'

'Why not?'

'It's unfair.'

'Is it?'

'Yes.'

'Good, we'll be needing some of that.'

'And what is that?'

'That thing in your hand.'

'You mean the ceateau a champignon.'

'No, I mean the other hand.'

'It's medicinal.'

'You're a drug-abuser, aren't you?'

'It's just a bit of coke.'

'You mean cocaine?'

'It's been a hard night.'

'You know I could almost feel sorry for you.'

'Why?'

'It's so weak.'

'I think you'll find it's the opposite.'

'How?'

'Look out, Ewok!'

I jolted. A massive lorry came out of nowhere. I swerved to avoid it. I was trembling.

'You see?'

'Just as well I did.'

'With my weakness.'

'With my own alert reactions.'

Eventually, the car arrived outside a detached house.

'What d'you think?'

'What am I supposed to think?'

'This is the fifth suspect- the son.'

'Who is he?'

'I don't know his name.'

'Why might the owner of this property have killed your brother and his wife?'

I frowned. 'I don't even know if he is the owner. He could be the occupant, the tenant or mortgagee- the squatter even.'

'How would a man just occupy this property? I take it's a good property.'

'Of course it is.'

'You think so?'

'Yes, it's very upper-middle class.'

'So?'

'Either his co-habitant occupies, tenants, mortgages or owns the property or someone else does.'

'And?'

'Has let him stay.'

'Or?'

'He rents the property from a commercial landlord.'

'Which would mean?'

'He doesn't own the property but he rents it.'

'Why might he have killed your brother and/or his wife?'

'I don't know.'

Although Chase kept the mushroom knife in his hand, there was no real need for an enforcement weapon.

'The sixth suspect also lives here,' said Chase.

'Who?'

'The overshadowed fiancée.'

'Why might she have killed your brother and/or his wife?'

'I don't know.'

'Why are they suspected then?'

'Because of her close relationship with the talented son. 'Now, Ewok,' said Chase, 'We go to Hyndland, to the seventh suspect.'

'I'm tired, Chase,' I said, 'I have to go back home.'

'You'll be home once we're done.'

CHAPTER ELEVEN

Hyndland; The Aggrieved Mother

We drove from Thortonhall village in South Lanarkshire, which lay just east of the boundary with East Renfrewshire, close to Waterfoot and Jackton; west of East Kilbride, and North of Eaglesham towards Hyndland.

'As you'll know,' said Chase, 'it's a residential area in the West End of the City of Glasgow.'

'Yes,' I said. 'It borders the Broomhill, Dowanhill, Kelvinside and the Partickhill areas. It's very middle-class.'

'Indeed it is populated mainly by professionals many employed at the nereby university of Glasgow and young bourgeois bohemians including a number of noted authors, poets, actors and footballers.'

'Who owns this property?'

'My niece's friend's mother? The seventh suspect.'

'How do you know of her?'

'The police told me of her.'

'They did?'

'Yes, in 1995.'

'What happened?'

'After my brother and Susanna went missing, they said my niece had a friend.'

'Your niece is Susie.'

'Yes.'

'And the friend?'

'They just said the friend.'

'And the friend's mother?'

'And what happened?'

'They wanted to take Susie away.'

'Why?'

'There was no one to look after her.'

'And what happened?'

'I said she would come with me.'

'And did she?'

'Yes, I took her to my house.'

'Then what?'

'We played cluedo.'

'And?'

'She won.'

'What about your nephew Nicholas?'

'He arrived later.'

'How?'

'He raced all the way over to my house.'

'And?'

'After I had rubbed him down, I gave him a can of coke. Nicholas and Susie played cluedo.'

'So?'

'I was trying to work out what had happened to their parents.'

'And what had happened?'

'They had gone missing.'

'So?'

'I tried to re-assure them they would be fine.'

'I see. Why might your niece's friend's mother have killed your brother and/or his wife?'

'I don't know.'

'What do you know?'

'I think he was being blackmailed by the disgruntled client.'

'Why?'

'I think the disgruntled client knew his secret.'

'What was his secret?'

'I don't know.'

'Why d' you think he had one?'

'Something my brother said.'

'Which was?'

'My brother said: "*This money is owed. My bitter rival knows it's his fault.*"'

'How would he have done it?'

'I don't know."

'And what if it went to court, Ewok?'

'There is the Sheriif Court.'

'And?'

'Sheriff Courts are the busiest courts in Scotland.'

'Why is that?'

'Due to its territorial scope, Glasgow Sheriff Court is one of the busiest courts in Europe.

'What does it deal with?'

'It deals with civil matters but the business of a Sheriff Court is mainly criminal cases.'

'What if the matters are more minor?'

'More minor matters will be heard before a Sheriff who will describe the outcome of a trial.'

'What if the matters are more serious?'

'More serious matters will be tried before a jury.'

'And what do the jury do?'

'The jury return a verdict.'

'And when do they return a verdict?'

'After they have heard all the evidence and submissions in a case.'

'And what about sentence?'

'The Sheriff passes sentence on anyone who pleads guilty or who is convicted after trial.'

'What is the maximum sentence afforded to the Sheriff?'

'The maximum sentence afforded to the Sheriff Court is five years custody.'

'And what if it gets worse?'

'If a Sheriff feels the offence merits a higher sentence, they can remit the case to the High Court, where there is no limit on a custodial sentence.'

'What else?'

'Sheriff Courts in Glasgow or Edinburgh also have dedicated drugs courts and domestic abuse courts which specialise in dealing with these types of crimes.'

'And?'

'Specialist prosecutors deal with these cases and those courts run on a frequent basis. There are also dedicated Sheriffs to deal with such matters.'

Chase nodded his head. 'We will now visit my niece's house.'

'Who is she?'

'The seventh suspect.'

I swabbed my brow. 'Where does she live?'

'Keppochill.'

I sighed. 'We're certainly moving down the property ladder.'

CHAPTER TWELVE

Keppochill; The Battered Niece

I climbed in to the car resignedly. Chase entered the passenger seat. The rain had stopped completely and the wind had died down. The sun was now glaring through the windscreen. A rainbow painted the sky above.

'Isn't it pretty,' he said.

'I suppose so,' I said.

Chase burst in to song. '"Somewhere over the rainbow, way up high..."'

Without thinking and remembering my daughter Melissa when she was a toddler, I added

I added: '"There's a land that I dreamt of..."'

'Once in a lullaby.'

I shook my head, suddenly realising myself. I was driving the car of a man who had held me at knife-point. 'Why are we singing Judy Garland?'

'It's relaxing.'

'It's regressive.'

'Now, we're going to go from the richest part of Glasgow to the poorest.'

'Where?'

'Keppochill.'

'Where?

'Where?'

'My niece's house. The eighth suspect.'

'Susie McLean?'

'Yes.'

'And?'

'After my brother and Susanna went missing I was asked what my feelings were?'

'By whom?'

'Social Services.'

'And what happened?'

'I took Susie and Nicholas in.'

I winced at the first divulgence. Despite my academic propensity, I had never gotten my head round sexual proclivity. Having had gotten married early and whose only concupiscence had ever been related to my wife, and having had four children I was loath to embrace gayness. I also had to apply the *Homosexual Offences Act*, which even at the time he had considered to be overtly mean, he had understood gayness to be unacceptable. But he had kept up with social and legal changes. He could see that it had become very common indeed.

I choked as I said, 'Did you have a partner?'

'No.'

'Did you smoke?'

'Yes, why?'

'The adoption agencies don't generally accept smokers.'

'No, I suppose not.'

'Did you drink?'

'Yes, heavily.'

'So you felt guilty?'

'Yes.'

'Did you have mental health problems?'

'Yes, I was in the psychiatric hospital.'

'What was your diagnosis?'

'Paranoid Schizophrenia.'

'Do you still have it?'

'Sometimes.'

'What about now?'

'I don't know, maybe.'

'So you felt no use?'

'No.'

'How old was Nicholas?'

'Four.'

'And you were twenty-five?'

'Yes.'

'How old was Susie?'

'Nine.'

'I see. You were telling me about the Sheriff Court.'

'Yes.'

'Take me through the higher court.'

''Well, the most serious of all crimes are dealt with in the High Court of Justiciary.'

'And what do they include?'

'These include murder, rape, serious sexual offences, high value drug cases and firearms.'

'And what does the High Court do?'

'It sits permanently in Glasgow and Edinburgh.'

'What else does it do?'

'It also travels on circuit, sitting at cities such as Perth, Aberdeen, Livingston and Paisley.'

'And what happens?'

'All trials in the High Court are heard before a jury.'

'And what can the high court do?'

'The sentencing powers of a High Court Judge is unlimited and people can be given Orders for Lifelong Restrictions (OLR) which effectively means they will always be subject to control by authorities. To date, no-one placed on an ORL has been released from custody.'

'I see.'

'Why might your niece have killed your brother and his wife?'

'I don't know.'

'Yes.'

'Who was the father?'

'Taylor Reid.'

'Yes.'

'You will drive to his house.'

'Where is it?'

'Hyndland.'

'We've just driven from Hyndland.'

'Yes, now it's time to go back.'

'What are we supposed to work out?'

'You will need reference points for your investigation and punishment.'

Chase smiled thinly. 'We will now go to the father of the husband's house.'

'Must we?'

'Yes, he's the ninth suspect.'

FOURTH INTERLUDE

Peter Reid Challenges Jack Dorcha

Having finished the premium beef prepared and cooked by Jaeger White, the elite group of Scottish multi-millionaires splintered from the table.

Frank Sharp grunted. 'I need a fag.'

Jaeger White bridled. 'Is that all my slavery gets?'

Aiden Fields peeked at Lewis McLean and cowered.

James Bennet nodded fairly at Frank Sharp. 'We always did have a fag, Frank.'

Jack Dorcha loured at Lewis McLean. 'What about you?'

Lewis McLean smiled tolerantly. 'I don't smoke. I never have done.'

Frank Sharp snorted. 'Are we supposed to believe that?'

'No, Mr Sharp,' said Olivia McLean. 'Dad doesn't.'

Ealdahach Wren nodded hurriedly. 'As he shouldn't. Smoking causes lung cancer.'

Frank Sharp glared defiantly. 'That has never been proven.'

'I'm afraid it has,' said Peter Reid.

'You export chemicals, Peter,' said Jack Dorcha, 'You don't understand them.'

'No, I understand them, Jack, 'You don't.'

'Oh, yes, my friend,' said Jack Dorcha, 'In what way?'

'They cause malignant tumours,' said Peter Reid.

'The only tumour here is you, Peter,' said Jack Dorcha.

Peter Reid dimmed his head. 'And circulatory diseases.'

Aiden Fields smiled timidly. 'I felt there was something in the wind.'

Lewis McLean gasped at Aiden. 'It is the wind of understanding, Aiden.'

Peter Reid lifted his eyes from Lewis McLean and stared at Jack Dorcha. 'They also cause respiratory illnesses.'

Olivia McLlean gasped. 'I'm finding it hard to breath.'

'That's just the heat, darling,' said Lewis McLean.

'And they cause mental and behavioural disorders,' said Peter Reid.

'I wonder who the mad one is,' said Frank Sharp.

James Bennet shrugged. 'Perhaps no madder than you, Frank.'

Peter Reid continued his glare at Jack Dorcha. 'And they cause digestive system illnesses.'

Jaeger White snarled. 'There's nothing wrong with my food.'

Peter Reid tightened his mouth. 'They also cause diseases of the nervous system and sense organs.'

'Yes,' said Ealdahach Wren, 'they can cause the most pain.'

'Plus, there are accidents, Jack,' said Peter Reid.

James Bennet nodded. 'Everyone has them.'

Peter Reid nodded firmly. 'And they cause genital and urinary organ disease.'

Olivia McLean shivered. 'I feel I need to pee.'

'Yes, darling,' said Lewis McLean. 'You go to the cabin.'

Olivia McLean toddled off.

Peter Reid glowered at Jack Dorcha. 'And they cause nutritional and metabolic diseases, infectious and parasitic diseases.'

Jack Dorcha scowled at Peter Reid. 'The only disease is you.'

Peter Reid gnarled. 'If you keep speaking to me like that, Jack, 'I'll give you a major health problem.'

'You've never really thought chemicals through, Peter.'

'I have spent my life doing chemicals. You don't really smoke, Jack, do you?'

'I don't see that I need to.'

'And you never really smoked much cocaine.'

'Only occasional of course.'

'And you never ingested insecticide.'

'I stamp on the dangerous insects.'

'And your brain never suffocated.'

'No, Peter. I sense you are threatening me.'

'Not yet. I know men who lost everything to chemicals they didn't understand.'

'I did understand them, I just avoided the obvious bad ones.'

'You do realise how disappointing that is to them.'

'Then they should have avoided them.'

'Or the pushers shouldn't have gotten greedy.'

'You deserve sprayed for your assumption. You see what this is? This is a can of wasp spray. This would suffocate your brain.'

'And then what?'

'You get paranoid schizophrenia.'

'And then what?'

'You have alarm bells ringing in the ears.'

'And then what?'

'The brain goes up high.'

'And then what?'

'The brain starves.'

'Then what?'

'You get bi-polar.'

'They're obviously too weak.'

'Or they were unlucky.'

'Since you have dismissed pharmaceuticals, perhaps it time you experienced their power, or rather their ability to remove power.'

'You wouldn't really apply that to my brain.'

'No, Peter,' said Ealdahach Wren, 'Jack may be a brute, but he has feelings.'

'Listen to E,' said Jack Dorcha. 'You know he's usually right.'

'Yes,' said James Bennet, 'that wouldn't be fair.'

'He's not really going to do it, dad?' said Olivia McLean.

Peter Reid stepped closer to Jack Dorcha and stood right up to him. He glared at him with unflinching eyes. He held the insecticide aloft. Jack Dorcha was trembling. Peter Reid stuck the nozzle against Jack Dorcha's nose.

For the first time Frank Sharp twitched.

'No, Jack,' said James Bennet.

Peter Reid peeked at James Bennet. He swung his pointer onto the trigger.

'If you do this Jack,' said Ealdahach Wren, 'the man's brain will be finished.'

Peter Reid was tapping the trigger.

Jack Dorcha waved his head slowly in fear.

Peter Reid tightened his stare.

Lewis Bennet exhaled strenuously.

'No, Jack seriously.'

Peter Reid glanced at Lewis Bennet. Lewis Bennet nodded. Peter Reid nodded.

Suddenly, Peter Reid removed the can of wasp spray from the nostrils of Jack Dorcha. He swung the can outwards to the right. He depressed the trigger and cast a furious continuous river of mist out over the side of the Sunseeker. Jack Dorcha stood gaping. A tear leaked from Jack Dorcha's left eye and strolled down his cheek. Jack Dorcha swallowed piteously. 'Thank you, Peter,' he said.

Peter Reid smiled thinly. 'Don't thank me, Jack. Thank the responsible customer.'

CHAPTER THIRTEEN

Hyndland; The Arrogant Doctor

The streets were quiet. Hence I drove slowly; plodded tortoise-like.

'You know,' I said, 'there almost seems to be more felines around here than humans.'

'Yes,' said Chase, 'the area is known for its cat over-population.'

I was forgetting myself. 'I like cats,' I said.

'What kind are they?'

'Selfish.'

Chase smirked. 'What are their names?'

'Lilly named them. Volkova and Katina.'

'They sound Russian.'

'Indeed.'

'They also sound like lesbians.'

I grimaced. 'What?'

'*All the things she said*?'

'Pardon?'

'*All about us*?'

I shook my head.

'I thought not.'

'What d' you mean?'

'It sounds like your daughter either sings for herself or the girls.'

I scowled. 'My youngest daughter barely likes boys.'

Chase smiled smugly. I chose to ignore this. 'And the tenements, they are largely red-sandstone. And if you look, many of them are fronted by communal city gardens.'

Chase exhaled with boredom. 'Yes.'

'And they are embellished with ornate doorway carvings and stained glass windows.'

'Quite,' said Chase. I believe they were built in the late Victorian and Edwardian eras.'

'Yes,' I said, 'it looks like it.'

Abruptly, Chase exclaimed. 'Here!' he said. 'Stop right here!'

I pulled up outside the house Chase was pointing at.

Chase exhaled. 'Perfect. This is the tenth suspect.'

I groaned. 'It's only a few blocks away from where we were before.'

'Mrs Judith White's house was quite different.'

I tipped my head. 'It does lend a certain character to the area.'

'Many of these town houses,' said Chase, 'had been split into multiple apartments.'

'To cater to modern urban living.'

'Indeed.'

'Yes,' I said, 'This particular one though has remained an individual property.'

Chase lifted his head. 'So what d'you think?'

I gave the town house a *coup d'oeil*. 'Yes, it's quite impressive-all in all.'

Chase arched his brows. 'Quite?'

I nodded surely. 'Yes, it almost rivals my own.'

'Newton Mearns has better houses?'

I shook my head. 'Not entirely.'

Chase lifted his head disingenuously. 'Judges get paid more than doctors?'

'Usually.'

'Even Leads?'

I turned to look at Chase. 'Was he a Lead?'

Chase waved his head. 'Who knows?'

'Your brother never said.'

'No.'

I nodded. 'Even if he was, he wouldn't have out-earned a highly qualified judge.'

'Spoiled then?'

'Clever.'

'In what way?

I shrugged. 'We judges have to catch the doctors out.'

'What about a bad judge?'

'We are fair, not bad.'

'And is this before the doctor treats you or after he had put you to sleep.'

I gave this a moment's thought. 'Medicine might survive law but law regulates its survival.'

'Good shout.'

'Why might have Doctor Reid have killed your brother and/or his wife?'

'I'm not sure.'

'But?'

'He might have wished to get them back.'

'For what?'

'Who knows? Tell me, Ewok, what role does the jury play?'

'The origin of the Scottish Jury is somewhat obscure.'

'But?'

'It is thought to have developed around the same time, albeit in a different form to the English Jury system. It is believed that is was formerly established in the 11th and 12th century following after the Norman style of Government.'

'And?'

'Every person who is registered on the electoral role and is aged between 18 and 65 years is eligible to serve on a jury.'

'And?'

'A citation to attend will be sent to their home and they must attend court at the allocated time.'

'How many people does it take to have a jury?'

'Fifteen members make up a jury.'

'And then what?'

'There must be a majority of eight jurors in favour of a guilty verdict to convict an accused. If members of a jury require to be excused for a good reason after commencement of the trial, their number cannot reach below eleven. There must be a majority of those left in favour of a guilty in order for such a verdict to stand.'

'And how is a jury selected?'

'Selection of the jury is as simple as placing their names in a glass bowl or vase and selecting them at random. The juror will be assigned a seat within the jury box and must keep that seat throughout the trial.'

'And what happens?'

'Jurors will be told at the start of the trial that they must decide their verdict according to the evidence. They also swear an oath to do just that.'

'I see,' said Chase. 'We will visit the eleventh suspect.'

CHAPTER FOURTEEN

Lower Whitecraigs; The Bitter and Twisted Grandmother

We passed Whitecraigs railway station. It served the Whitecraigs and Davieland areas of the towns of Giffnock and Newton Mearns, East Renfrewshire, Greater Glasgow, Scotland.

'You know the station is managed by Abellio Scot rail,' said Chase.

'Yes,' I said, 'It lies on the Neilston branch of the Cathcart Circle.'

'Indeed. The line here forms the boundary which separates Newton Mearns and Giffnock across Ayr Road.'

'Yes, the station was originally opened as part of the Lanarkshire and Ayrshire Railway on the first of May 1903. In some timetables the station was known as Whitecraigs for Rouken Glen.'

Chase pointed at a house. 'Stop here,' he said.

I pulled up outside the house.

'Fancy, isn't it?' said Chase.

'Yes, it's very well-to-do.'

'This is the eleventh suspect.'

'Why might the husband's grandmother have killed your brother and/or his wife?'

'I don't know.'

Chase squeezed his chin. 'What happens in a trial, Ewok?'

'Evidence is lead first by the crown.'

'What does that mean?'

'It means that each witness is given their 'evidence in chief', the defence, if they so wish, are entitled to cross each crown witness.'

'And then what?'

'Once all crown witnesses have been lead, the crown will close their case. As part of the crown case, a joint minute may be read.'

'What is that?'

'That is simply a written agreement of evidence between the crown and defence.'

'Then what?'

'The jury must accept what is written in that document as proved facts.'

'Then?'

'After close of the crown case, the defence may, if they wish, lead evidence of their own.'

'And?'

'There is no duty on the defence to lead any evidence or prove anything.'

'So the onus of proof lies with the crown throughout the trial.'

'Exactly. They must approve the charges against the accused by way of corroborated evidence.'

'You mean evidence from more than one source.'

'Yes.'

'For example?'

'For example, this could be eye witnesses.'

'What would that be?'

'That would be direct evidence.'

'And?'

'There is also circumstantial evidence or a mixture of both. The crown must prove the case beyond a reasonable doubt.'

'And what is a reasonable doubt?'

'A reasonable doubt is not a fanciful or hypothetical doubt but something that would make you hesitate in considering something important in your own affairs. The crown witnesses must be accepted by the jury to be both credible and reliable.'

Chase squeezed his chin again. 'We must visit the twelfth suspect.'

FIFTH INTERLUDE

Aiden Fields Challenges Jack Dorcha

Peter Reid had emptied the full tin of wasp spray.

Lewis bowed his head at Peter Reid. 'Well done, Peter.'

Peter Reid was hobbling back.

Jaeger Fields levelled at the group. 'You are best to return to your seats gentleman.'

'Yes,' said James Bennet, 'I think that would be the best thing to do.'

'Yes,' said Ealdahach Wren. 'Sitting is often more comfortable than standing.'

'It can also be limiting to the man,' said Lewis McLean.

'The man was nowhere near,' said Frank Sharp.

Jack Dorcha was trembling. 'I need a drink.'

'Please, Jack' said Aiden Fields, 'Let me help.'

'I'll fetch one,' said Olivia McLean.

'No, darling,' said Lewis McLean, 'He may fetch his own.'

'You're too weak, Aiden,'

'I made you look good,' said Aiden Fields.

'Perhaps I've outgrown your textiles.'

'My cloths and fabrics were expertly woven.'

'Yes, but without me you would have been a nudist.'

'I gave you that beach.'

'You may have supplied the sand, but I gave you the warm ocean.'

CHAPTER FIFTEEN

Sound Technology

Chase unlocked the garage door. He pulled up the shutter. I was treated to a parade of the most expensive high-tech looking equipment. Chase walked forwards to one of the work benches. He picked up a device and pushed a button.

'What does that do?'

'You'll see.'

I nodded tentaively. 'What is all this?'

'This is how you're going to do it,' said Chase.

'Do what exactly?'

'Probe all the suspects.'

'Why am I to probe all the suspects?'

Chase groaned. 'Because I need to be crystal clear who killed my brother and his wife.'

'And if I don't?'

'As I said before, I will kill you and all the members of your immediate family.'

'And I could easily contact the police. In fact I have a phone, I could do that just now.'

'No. There are two reasons you shouldn't. For one, I could finish you in court. Secondly, I have the knife.'

I bristled with ignominy. 'You have nothing on me, Chase.'

Chase loured at me. 'I have buckets on you.'

'The buckets are empty.'

'No, they're coming to the brim.'

'In what way?'

'I know you were the presiding judge at the time my brother was in court. I know you used her-'

I breathed laboriously. 'You don't even know who she might have been.'

'Oh, I really think she was the hired help.'

I gawked. 'The what?'

'The intended assassin.'

I hunched my shoulders. 'In which case, you don't know.'

Chase grit his teeth. 'I know that people were killed there. I know the court used weapons. I know you were the judge who was retiring.'

I wiped my brow. 'How? You can't prove your anonymous caller?'

Chase gave me an unamused stare. 'That's where you're wrong.'

'Wrong?'

'Yes.'

'How?'

'That's what I'm about to teach you. Come over here just a second.' Chase moved towards the devices, crouched down and picked one up.'

'What is that?'

'It's a listening device.'

'A listening device?'

'Or a covert listening device.'

'What does it do?'

'What does it do? What it did that evening was transmit the telephone call and the voice of the anonymous caller to a recorder.'

I furrowed my brows. 'Really?'

'Yes, it contains a clear voice recording of the caller.'

I shrugged. 'I see. Very well, then, let me listen to it.'

'Certainly.' Chase pushed a button. The tape rolled. A voice sounded. It was low and angry: *'Chase. Weapons...people killed in there...executions... He used her... The judge is retiring...'* After a short burst the sound recording fell silent.

I exhaled with exasperation. 'That could be anyone, talking about anything. Hell, it could be you, Chase as the voice, talking to yourself.'

'Except its all locked in to the device.'

'What d'you mean?'

'The device has recorded the precise date and time of the call and the origin of the call.'

'What origin?'

'The call came from a number in Glasgow.'

'You mean the anonymous caller didn't even bother to hide the source.'

'Yes, he did but the device penetrates concealed numbers.'

'So what was the number?'

'The number came from the court.'

'Well, that's ludicrous. If the court were responsible for foul play, why would it wish to implicate itself?'

'I think there was a party to the court that didn't agree.'

'For those recorded statements you just showed to me to get accepted, you would have to prove they came from a reliable source.'

'The reliable source is the court. And no, all I have to prove is that the statements were made.'

'As I said, that could be anyone.'

'Yes, anyone from the court.'

'What is the point in these devices?'

'They serve a very important point.'

'Which is?'

'They gather information about suspects. They are used in all sorts of contexts: surveillance, espionage, police investigations...'

'Tell me about surveillance.'

'There is surveillance, audio surveillance devices, hidden audio surveillance, listening audio surveillance, audio surveillance equipment, surveillance equipment, covert listening devices, eavesdropping equipment, mobile listening devices, spy equipment, wireless listening devices, bugging equipment...'

'Tell me more.'

'Your mobile phone can be tapped. Your location, text messages, and even voice conversations can easily be recorded and sent to others without your knowledge.'

'What else?'

'There is light technology which allows your phone to appear as if it is turning off when it fact it stays on and the microphone can be used to monitor any sounds within hearing distance of your cell phone.'

'What about audio surveillance?'

'Audio surveillance provides provides the ability to monitor a room of telephone conversation which can either be recorded in situ or transmitted to a receiver /recorder away from the environment.'

'Tell me about room monitoring.'

'There are several different options.'

'Which are?'

'There are portable systems. Portable recording or transmitting systems are ideal for meetings or negotiations which take place in a situation without your direct control. A recording briefcase, pen transmitter, or calculator transmitter etc. provide a superb means of achieving excellent results. This type of device can accompany you into a room and be operated at your discretion to transmit or record a conversation.'

'What else?'

'There are static systems.'

'Which are?'

'If there is a requirement to listen to and/or record a conversation at which you are not present, the most effective method is to install a radio transmitting device.'

'What are the alternatives?'

'There is (one) a battery operated transmitter for regular access or short-term use. It is relatively inexpensive and can be easily concealed. Practical lengths of transmission time vary according to the type of device and battery chosen.'

'And two?'

'For long-term use where regular access is inconvenient or

impossible, a mains electricity device is recommended. This type of equipment is easy to install and can be left to operate indefinitely.'

'Under what circumstances is audio surveillance used?'

'It is used (one) when the requirement is to record the conversation to which you are party, e,g. to provide evidence of a verbal contract and (two) when it is necessary to listen to and/or record a conversation in surroundings that you cannot be present, e.g. to prove conspiracy.

'And how do they work?'

'It's usually done with a radio transmitter and a microphone. It's commonly known as a bug or a wire.'

'Tell me about the radio transmitter.'

'In general, the easily hidden devices that listen to room or telephone conversations. Sometimes they are disguised as pens, calculators, electrical or telephone sockets etc. The conversation is invisibly transmitted over the air waves to a radio receiver.'

'I see.'

I scratched my head. 'Go on, what is a bug?'

'It can be used to eavesdrop but it is also possible to remotely activate the microphone of cellular phones, even when a call is not being made.'

'But you weren't eavesdropping, seemingly the call was being made to you.'

'That's correct.'

'So?'

'I used the listening device for a separate purpose.'

'Which was?'

'To record the call that was being made to me.'

'Why would you do that?'

'I was getting other calls beforehand.'

'What other calls?'

'Voices telling me my brother had his wife had been killed.'

'So who was making these other calls?'

'I don't know.'

'Why not?'

'I hadn't anticipated the need to trace them.'

'I see. What else does this bug do?'

'It's used to listen to conversations in the vicinity of the phone.'

'But you never used one that way.'

'No, I just recorded the telephone call- the one I just showed you.'

'What would be the advantage of a bug?'

'The advantage would be you can hear private conversations, including confessions without being in the room.'

'What would be examples?'

Chase crouched down again and lifted up another device. 'There's this thing here.'

'What is that?'

'It's called Q-Phone Pro.'

'What does it do?'

'It listens to cell phone-'

'You mean mobile phone-'

'Yes, mobile phone conversations. It also receives copies of text messages. It calls in to bug the room conversation.'

'Anything else?'

Chase set the Q-Phone Pro down again. He crouched down and picked up another device.'

'What is that?'

'B-Bug.'

'What does it do?'

'It listens in on any room conversations with no distance limit.'

'I see. And with these devices how do you activate the microphone?'

'It is called a wire tap.'

I nodded. 'Which is?'

'These devices connect between the telephone line to be monitored and a tape recorder. When the phone line is in use the recorder will activate and record both sides of the conversation. When the telephone line is not in use, the recorder's switch off to conserve tape and battery life.'

'I see. What else?'

'There is a telephone transmitter.'

'Which is?'

'A telephone transmitter is a small device which is connected to the telephone line or hidden inside a telephone socket, double adaptor or in the actual telephone itself. This device will transmit both sides of the conversation whenever the telephone is used. This can be monitored by a receiver located some distance away to record the conversation.'

'In that case, the detective would have to access the building first.'

'Yes, that's correct, but as I say, mobile phone (cell phone) microphones can be activated remotely, without any need for physical access.'

'Isn't that illegal?'

'This roving bug feature has been used by law enforcement agencies and intelligence services to listen in on nereby conversations.'

'What else is available- if you're trying to detect voice without physical access?'

'There are also automobile computer systems.'

I nodded again. 'And those are?'

'Well, to give an example, in 2003, the FBI obtained a court order to surreptitiously listen in on conversation in a car through the car's built-in emergency and tracking security system.'

'I see. And the other thing you mentioned- a wire. What is that?'

Chase

'It surprises me sometimes that you don't know these things, you were a judge.'

'Yes, but the evidence I administered was largely testimony, personal account, not technologically extracted.'

'Then it was a very naïve court.'

I shook my head with indignation. 'The asylum division is not a naïve court, Chase.'

'No?'

'No, it understands the worst crimes in humanity.'

'Then it would have understood the murder of my brother and his wife.'

'No, it did not understand that.'

'Why not?'

'Because it didn't need to, it wasn't responsible.'

''So you say.'

'So you claim. Tell me, Chase, what is a wire?'

'Put simply, a wire is a device that is hidden or concealed under a person's clothes.'

'What does it do?'

'It covertly listens to the person wearing the wire.'

'And when are they used- typically I mean?'

'Typically? Wires are typically used in police sting operations.'

'And these gather information about suspects.'

'Correct. Furthermore, the act of 'wearing a wire' refers to a person knowingly recording the conversations or transmitting the contents of a conversation to a listening post.'

'And how is it done?'

'Usually some sort of device is attached to the body in an inconspicuous way, such as taping a microphone wire to their chest. 'Wearing a wire' by undercover agents is typical plot element in gangster and police related movies and television shows.'

'I'm not interested in that.'

'Well, I am.'

'Why?'

'I'm a crime fiction writer.'

'And what does the wire do?'

'The wire device transmits to a remote location where law enforcement agents monitor what is being said.'

'I see. And what other ways can you track sound?'

Chase squeezed his mouth. He eyeballed another device. He crouched down again on the floor and picked it up. 'There's also this thing here.'

'What is it?'

'It's a laser microphone.'

'It is?'

'Yes, you can get audio from optical sources.'

'How does that work?'

'A laser microphone can be used to reconstruct audio from a laser beam shot onto an object, in a room or a window. A laser microphone is a surveillance device that uses a laser beam to detect sound vibrations in a distant object.'

'So it can be used to eavesdrop with minimal risk of exposure.'

'Where is the object typically?'

'The object is typically inside a room where a conversation is taking place. It can be anything that can vibrate; for example, a picture on a wall.'

'How far has this technology gone?'

'Researchers have also prototyped a method for reconstructing audio from video of thin objects that can pick up sound vibrations, such as houseplant or a bag of potato chips.'

I smiled with some appreciation. 'Extraordinary. So you wouldn't have to enter the building first?'

'No.'

'What if you were able to enter the building first without being detected?'

'In that case there are voice recorders.'

'What would be examples?'

Chase squeezed his face again. 'I'll just show you.' He lead me to a work bench. 'This is the desk top calculator with hidden voice recorder.'

'I see. And what's that?'

'This is the encryption charger voice recorder.'

'And that?'

'This is the magnetic voice recorder. There is the mobile phone recorder and voice recorder. There is the U-350 flash drive recorder. There is the USB car charger. There is the USB voice recorder. There is the voice pen recorder. There is the voice recorder 8GB.

'Which of these voice recorders are the best?'

'The best one is Zoom H1. The tiny H1 recorder has a special double x/y microphone arrangement, which means both mics are equidistant from the sound source, making for a pitch-clear recording. It comes with a 2Gb memory which you can update to 32Gb.'

'What else?'

'There are also microphones and amplifier. There is a range of microphones and amplifiers that can be used with voice recorders to achieve covert usage.'

'What else?'

'What other ways are there to detect private speech and conversations?'

'You can make devices for listening through walls.'

'How?'

'Well, the first step is to figure out where the voices meet the wall best. If you know people are speaking on the couch and that the couch is the back of the room, you want to use the spot on the wall that best corresponds to the back of the room.'

'And the second step?'

'You take a clean wine glass and press it to the wall. The cone shape shape pulls sound and channel it through the handle. You use a thin stemmed glass for best results.'

'And the third step?'

'You place an earplug in your free ear to block out ambient noise.'

'And the fourth step?'

'You put on a stethoscope and place the round, metal end to the wall. A stethoscope should work as a listening device since it is designed to hear the heartbeat from within the thick chest cavity.'

'I see. What if the sound itself is outwith your hearing range?'

'You can get analogue to digital converters that will record audio at very wide ranges. A very good microphone ADC will sample 192kHz which gives you a Nyquist limit (upper frequency) of 96kHz. You need a really good microphone as well. A phantom powered ribbon microphone would be best but it would be expensive as well, but you can hire professional audio equipment.'

'I see. How would you detect a voice or voices in a room or

a private conversation conversation without having planted a device in the room first?'

'You can detect sound waves. The American intelligence agencies have used lasers to detect conversations. From a distance outside, they would shine a small, invisible laser spot on a window of a building where secret conversations were being held. The reflected light off the window would be distorted due to the subtle vibrations of the glass.'

'What else is there?'

'There is a sound amplifier listening and observing device.'

'How does it work?'

'It has a directional microphone. It is powerful enough to monitor conversations up to one hundred metres away. It also has a built-in digital recording chip for recording for 12s, playback or copying. The sound amplifier listening and observing device enables you not only to hear sounds of any volume over one hundred metres and even record them, but also to follow objects optically with no need of using extra monoculars. With this sound amplifier listening device at hand, even the faintest singing of birds can be detected. The built-in digital recording chip can be used for recording 12s, playback or copy the file onto a standard audio tape for preservation. Designed with a powerful optical zoom finder function with a magnification of 8x, you are able to follow objects optically with no need of of using extra monoculars. It's lightweight and runs on a nine volt battery. It is easy to carry from place to place. This high-quality sound amplifier listening and observing device is definitely a surprise for every opera-lover, bird watcher, animal observer etc.'

'What about actually seeing things?'

'It is a common misconception that spy cameras are the pinnacle of electronic surveillance equipment. There is no doubt that gathering evidence on video can provide great evidence that if obtained correctly, is difficult to defend against, however where camera can fall is by virtue of the fact that their placement can often prove more difficult than voice recording equipment or remote listening equipment. Covert recorders and listening devices generally do not require such carefully thought out placement, because when they are positioned on top, underneath or even inside other objects, they are by design more adaptable as a spy device and the spy camera.'

'What if you go up market?'

'Devices designed and built for intelligence services are still more expensive and difficult to find. Some of the more sophisticated bugs have a 'burst' transmission. A device about the size of a fingernail can record several hours of ordinary conversation and then transmit it to a remote receiver in a burst.'

I nodded respectfully at Chase. 'You certainly know how to obtain private information.'

Chase picked up a device. It was the one he first picked up.

'What is that?'

'It's a voice recorder.'

'And?'

'Just listen.'

He pushed a button, then a second button. After a few seconds he pushed a third button. There was a slight crackling sound. There was a voice: 'What does that do?' There was a second voice. 'You'll see.' Chase pushed a fourth button. The sound stopped.

I swallowed nervously. 'You just recorded our conversation.'

Chase smiled patiently. 'Yes. You see?'

I exhaled deeply. 'Yes.'

CHAPTER SIXTEEN

The Ultimatum

'Do you understand, *Ewok*?'

'*Ewald*!'

'So?'

'*Chase*?'

'Obviously.'

'What have you understood?'

'You're ready to slit my throat.'

'Yes.'

'And?'

'I obviously have to do something for you in order for you to spare my life.'

'Not quite.'

I gawked. 'No?'

'No, you have to do something for me or I will kill you and your whole family.'

'But I trusted you with my family details.'

'That is of no concern to me.'

'So?'

'You must investigate everyone who might have killed my brother and his wife.'

'Investigate?'

'Yes.'

'That is not the criminal law of Scotland.'

'No?'

'Of course not.'

'Enlighten me.'

'In terms of the investigation of crime, most crimes are reported by an individual to the police.'

'You were a judge.'

'Yes, but that comes later.'

'So?'

'You would require to report these alleged crimes to the police.'

'Then what?'

'The police would attend the place where the incidents took place.'

'I believe they took place in the court.'

'Then they would attend the court.'

'And then what?'

'They would take statements to any witnesses to events and seize any potentially relevant evidence.'

'But I don't know who the witnesses were.'

'Why not?'

'I wasn't there. What if I did have witnesses?'

'As I said, they would seize any potentially relevant evidence.'

'Such as?'

'Such as weapons, documents, and even bodily fluids or tissues.'

'I believe there were weapons involved but it was twenty-two years ago.'

'Then it would be impossible for the police to believe there is sufficient evidence to form a case.'

'What if they believed there was sufficient evidence?'

'They would send a report to the Procurator Fiscal.'

'What would the Procurator Fiscal do?'

'The Procurator Fiscal acts on the authority of the Lord Advocate-'

'Who?'

'One of two law officers who head up the Crown Office and Procurator Fiscal Service in Scotland.'

'And?'

'In turn, Procurator Fiscal Deputes act on behalf of the Procurator Fiscal.'

'Meaning?'

'When a police report is received by a Procurator Fiscal or their Depute, they will consider whether there is enough evidence to prosecute the individual.'

'What if there isn't?'

'In that case, they might ask the police to investigate matters further or decide not to take matters further.'

'And if there is?'

'Where there is enough evidence, the Procurator Fiscal Depute will then decide in which court the prosecution should take.'

'And where would the prosecution take place?'

'The least serious matters may be dealt with by way of Fiscal Fine and not have to go to court.'

'Go on!'

'Generally speaking, the least serious crimes requiring prosecution, such as minor road traffic offences, will be dealt with by the Justice of the Peace Court (formerly the District Court). More serious crimes will be prosecuted in the Sheriff Court and the most serious crimes (murder, rape etc.) will be prosecuted in the High Court.'

'So, the killings of my brother and his wife would go to the High Court.'

'Yes, assuming the aforesaid.'

'They deserve it.'

'So?'

'Allow me to summarize. I believe you killed my brother. I suspect you killed my brother because he knew you had killed people or had had people killed. He knew this because he had represented at your Court on numerous occasions. I suspect he was going to expose you.'

'You can't prove that.'

'I have the statement: "*They killed people in there*".'

'And?'

'I consider that you may also have killed him because you were in love with his wife Susanna and jealous of his marriage.'

'You can't prove that either.'

'I have your wife's statement: *"I can't believe Ewald would do that to me. I can't believe he would cheat on me."*'

'So?'

'You will start with the nephew.'

'This is the nephew of the rival of your brother's client? The only link to your brother's client?'

'Exactly.'

'And apparently the nephew resides at an unlikely mansion called Fall's Hall in Aberdeen.'

'Correct.'

'Why couldn't you just chase up the file and prove your brother was to attend the Court Service and extract the details from there?'

Chase huffed. 'I did.'

'And?'

'It's not there.'

'What do you mean?'

'It wasn't even available through Box-set.'

'How would you know about Box-set?'

'I asked the current Senior partner of my brother's law firm.'

'In which case you can't prove your brother's client was even attending court.'

'I still believe what my brother told me. And I also believe what the anonymous caller was saying.'

'So?'

'I also want you to investigate my sister-in-law's family and their friends.'

'Surely you would make a more realistic detective than me.'

'I write crime fiction, I wasn't a judge.'

'You wish to turn me into a sleuth.'

'If you like.'

'I don't.'

'I don't see you have any choice, unless you want you and your family to die, or be finished in court.'

'Incidentally, how would proving that your niece was responsible for your brother and his wife's deaths help you or your nephew Nicholas?'

'My nephew deserves to know the truth- and he deserves justice. Plus, if Susie is innocent, I will have made it up to her as well; I will have proved I am not useless.'

I was feeling more and more indignant. 'Who are you, Chase, may I ask, as the most contemptible man I've ever met- homosexual, heavy-smoker, alcoholic, mentally ill, belligerent- to accuse a retired judge of either committing two murders or being an accessory.'

'I'm not as weak as you think.'

'No?'

'No.'

'But you are.'

'How so?'

'You're an academic, Ewok.'

'You think so?'

'Yes. I think you were using.'

'Drugs?'

'No, tranquillizers.'

'What makes you say that?'

'It would take a very cool customer to make judge.'

'Or a very hard worker.'

'Or a man who had cheated all his life.'

'I was not and am not on drugs.'

'Tranquillizers I said. And you seem relatively unperturbed by a gun pressed at your temple.'

'You have shaken me.'

'And, as you know, I will do much more. And if you had not killed my brother yourself, your Valium would have made you indifferent to telling someone else to do so.'

'This is totally fanciful. I could have you fined for this.'

'For what?'

'Defaming me.'

'I suspect defamation would be the lesser evil of exposure.'

'I could also jail you.'

'For what?'

'For threatening my life and the lives of my family.'

'But you've retired.'

'I still have my contacts.'

'Who?'

'Belay.'

'Who is?'

'A very serious man- a man far more commanding than yourself- who employs judges. And anyway, your only evidence is your brother's statements and an anonymous phone call.'

'So?'

'You wouldn't be able to prove them anyway.'

'I don't need to do that.'

'You would if you wanted a court to take you seriously.'

'It could be done with argument.'

'You define?'

'Of course.'

'Even if you don't kill me now, how do you know I'll go through with the investigation?'

'I'll just find you again and kill you.'

'But I would have time to call the police.'

'And I would have the opportunity to argue that you have committed a double-murder or have been an accessory to both.'

'With insufficient evidence.'

'With enough reasoning to support a charge.'

'But if I have no knowledge of either committing or inciting a double-murder, the prosecution would have nothing to work with.'

'So?'

'How could the claims gather momentum?'

'You've already just had a mental aberration.'

'I have.'

'Yes.'

'When?'

'When I said: "I believe you may have been responsible for my brother's death."'

'So?'

'I sense clear insight is only a matter of time.'

'What makes you say so?'

'A man who has retired has more time to think and more time to remember and more time to *feel* the past.'

'You know this, do you?'

'Yes.'

'Because you are an alcoholic. What jury would afford such a man credence.'

'A new jury which would have fresh evidence.'

'But I don't drink. I never have.'

'So?'

'Alcohol could bring nothing to any recognizance of guilt. Furthermore, you are very possibly a man of diminished responsibility; you may well even be permanently insane. Your threatening me and you have not been involuntary intoxicated; there has been neither fraud, nor coercion. And what of this female you brother alluded to?'

'I suspect she was no less guilty than a tranquillized judge.'

'How do you know even if I had been tranquillized that it was not involuntary?'

'Was it?'

'I was not on tranquillizers full stop.'

'Why mention the excuse?'

'I didn't, you did. And you mean the defence?'

'You are still aware of the fact I'm retired.'

'I wasn't asking you to penalize the guilty parties, I was insisting that you probed and castigated them.'

'But I am retired.'

'As I said, it's: "Life 2.5."'

'It is life-'

'With a little something extra.'

'The 2 being?'

'The 2 being what we've experienced and accomplished-'

'And the .5?'

'Being the next adventure.'

'You know you're forcing me to look into and punish these suspected murders.'

'So?'

'That in itself is a very serious crime.'

'No more serious than those I could expose you in respect of. In other words, you will either die now, your family will die later, or you will be penalized by *Her Majesty's Advocate*.'

'I want a two-week turnaround.'

'You expect me to probe all the suspects in two weeks.'

'Precisely.'

'Then we really have to understand murder and how it works.'

Chase nodded assertively. 'Yes.'

'But first we must get out of Rathnew.'

'Quite acceptable.'

'We must drive back to Dublin, then to Larne. We then take the P&O ferry service back to Cairn Ryan. It will take two hours and twenty-six minutes. We then stop off somewhere we can discuss murder detection.'

'Sounds fine.'

CHAPTER SEVENTEEN

Murder Questions

Chase and I arrived back in Scotland.

'Where will we go now?' said Chase.

'Where do you live?'

'I'm not telling you that.'

'Okay, so where do we go?'

'We deserve a break. Let's go to the hottest straightest bar in Glasgow.'

I grimaced. 'I'm seventy-seven, Chase. I don't know what that is.'

Chase up-sided his head. 'I don't know what that is either.' He stuck a finger in the air. 'We'll ask someone, drive to the City Centre of Glasgow.'

'What do I do with the car?'

'You park it somewhere convenient.'

'You don't drive, do you?'

'Not well, no.'

We arrived outside Cosmo.

The bouncer was shaking his head. 'I can't let you in.'

'May I ask why not?' I said.

The bouncer shrugged. 'I think he feels you're too old.'

Chase tilted his head. 'I think that would be a breach of the law, would it not be, Ewok.'

'I think you'll find it's the licence holder's discretion whom he admits and serves.'

'Ewok?'

'The man's correct. There is no automatic right to enter a public house, unless you are an officer of the law, it would be a question of taking one's business elsewhere or reporting matters to the licensing board.'

'Where else can we go?' said Chase.

'There's the blue dragon.'

'What is that?'

'It's just around the corner.'

We walked towards the Blue Dragon. 'Go on then,' said Chase. 'Why do people commit murder? They say it's all about love, lust, lucre and loathing.'

I coggled my head. 'Those are certainly four motives.'

'There are more?'

'Of course. There are a plurality of reasons why someone would kill someone. However, they usually fall into three categories?'

'Oh yes? What would they be?'

'Survival, greed and revenge.'

'Why would that be?'

'They represent the three most instinctive reasons for extreme behaviour. As a human being, you are constantly trying to survive, get more out of life and beat the other human beings that stand in your way.'

'I see. And unusually what categories to the reasons fall in to.'

'Selflessness and mental health. The rest are random.'

'Let's start with survival, then.'

'Very well. A person may kill another person in order to keep a secret. If the secret were to be divulged the person could suffer harm. They could be imprisoned, killed or even worse. You get people who are afraid of their own safety. There is also the hostile witness.

'Survival.'

There are people who kill for organs. There are also people who kill someone to climb a transplant list.'

'What about greed?'

'There is obsession. Some people are so obsessed by someone or something that they commit murder. It could be an obsession with a another person or a thing that they consider paramount. Some people are obsessed by God or by an evil spirit and so commit murder. 'Yes. There is sexual jealousy. There is perversion. There is fantasy. There is also love and money. There are also property disputes. There are political motives. There is also ego. Some people have such a high ego stake that they are prepared to kill someone because of it. There is also status. Some people value their status so highly they will kill for it. There is power. Some people commit murder in order to advance themselves within the executive or the judiciary. There is freedom. It is only by killing someone that they may achieve the release they desire. There are organised crime, gangs and drug deals. There is cause. They will kill a person for the cause or for getting in the way of the cause. There is also autobiographical and film rights.'

'What about revenge?'

'There is frustration. Some people are so angry with a person or an event that they are driven to kill. There are personal vendettas and class-conflicts. There is domestic violence. There are transient emotions. Sometimes some people feel moved to commit murder because of short-term feelings. There is also rivalry. There is humiliation. There is honour. There is a crime of passion. There is mob contract. There is murder-for-hire.'

'And what about the unusual motives?'

'There are selfless reasons why a person might commit murder. There is the urge to protect. Some people kill someone to protect a loved one from harm. Some people feel sorry for someone so kill them. They kill them out of pity. It can also be done out of empathy or sympathy.'

'And the mental health reasons?'

'There are psychotic or mentally disordered motives. There are also cases where voices take over. These voices cause the person to commit murder. There is also longer-term mental instability. This can be alcohol or drug-induced.'

'What are the random motives?'

'There is ignorance. Some people commit murder when they have a mistaken view of the victim. It could also be that they don't know any better. This leads on to a lack of intelligence. Some people's capacity for understanding and ability to perceive and comprehend meaning is so low that they kill someone.'

'What else?'

'There is the extreme vandal. Such a person may kill a person in the course of committing mass destruction. There is also sport. Some people kill for fun.'

'And not necessarily out of greed.'

'Exactly. There is also warfare, terrorism and insurrection.'

'Those could fit into all three categories.'

'Feasibly. There is also the controlling influence and freedom. Some people commit murder to escape a person or situation. And that again would not necessarily be greed.'

'No.'

'How do you know all this?'

'I was a judge, Chase. Having talked about motives for murder and why people are killed, we have to consider the methods for murder and how people are killed.'

'And how are people killed? The top tenth method is drowning.'

'I thought it would have been more popular than that.'

'No, murders involving drowning are so rare. They are sometimes so outlandish.'

'For example, driving a car in to a lake or using a bathtub.'

'And what about the ninth?'

'Narcotics.'

'For example?'

'Someone purposefully slipping their spouse an overdose of pain medication, to a hospital worker intentionally over-medicating a patient. Drug dealers can supply drugs to a person who later suffers a fatal overdose.

'And the eighth?'

'Fire.'

'For example?'

'Gasoline to start a house fire. There is also the accidental, the result of arson incidents.

'And the seventh?'

'Asphyxiation.'

'Which means?'

'Something interferes with oxygenation of the cells. This can be caused by gas, such as carbon monoxide, or it can involve a more physical action, including locking a victim in a car trunk, or tying a plastic bag around his or her neck. The neck can also be compressed.'

'And the sixth?'

'Strangulation.'

'For example?'

'Strangling and choking.'

'And the fifth?'

'Blunt objects.'

'For example?'

'Clubs, hammers, baseball bats or even firewood or broom handles, possibly even a golf club.'

'And the fourth?'

'Personal weapons.'

'Which are?'

'The hands, fists, feet or even a head butt- also pushing.'

'And the third?'

'Other weapons or weapons not stated.'

'Which are?'

'Presumably motor vehicles.'

'And the second?'

'Knives or cutting instruments.'

'Such as?'

'Knives, razors etc.'

'And the first?'

'Firearms.'

'Such as?'

'Handguns, shotguns, rifles. There is one more: poison.'

'Typically?'

'Slipping their loved one poison with his or her dinner.'

'And where do people commit murder.'

'Land or sea.'

'When would a person commit murder?'

'It could happen at any point, any day or night, any week, any month, any year. But the murderer has to overcome a lot of powerful neural wiring.'

'What do you mean?'

'The human brain is coded for compassion, for guilt, for a kind of empathic pain that causes the person inflicting harm to feel a degree of suffering that is in many ways as intense as what the victim is experiencing.'

'So what happens?'

'Somehow that all gets decoupled.'

'How does it get decoupled?'

'It's to do with regions in the brain.'

'Which regions?'

'There is the activity in the orbitofrontal cortex (OFC), a region of the fore-brain that has long been known to be involved with moral sensitivity, moral judgements and making choices about how to behave. The nearby temporoparietal junction (TPJ) also takes on some of this moral load, processing the sense of agency- the act of doing something deliberately and therefore owning the responsibility for it. It makes an enormous difference in how you later reckon with what you've done. The OFC and TPJ are not alone in this moral processing. A region known as the fusiform gyrus is more active when subjects imagined themselves killing civilians, while there is greater activity in the lingual gyrus when subjects kill soldiers- they feel justified in killing. In all of us its clear that murder's neural roots and moral roots are deeply entangled.'

'Having just explained when murders take place, we have to consider the types of people who commit murder, who kills people.'

'Am I right in saying that the spouse is almost always the one who committed the murder?'

'Not really. In terms of family current or past, immediate family or not, 9.4 per cent of murders are committed by the husband, wife, common law husband, common law wife, mother, father son, daughter, brother, sister, in-law, stepfather, stepmother, stepson, or stepdaughter. 1.8 per cent of murders are committed by other family members. In terms of former family or other relationships you get, 4.2 per cent are the boyfriend, girlfriend, ex-husband or ex-wife. In terms of non-family, no emotional relationship murders, 14 per cent Acquaintance murder (this is a very broad category that includes everything from prostitute and johns to taxi cab drivers and their fares) 3.1 per cent friend, 5.2 per cent other known, 11 per cent stranger murder, 39 per cent unknown relationship (note these murders are very likely to involve gang fights to others where there is no direct relationship between the victim and the criminal. In terms of drug-related murders, 0.086 per cent of the total.

Chase bowed his head at me respectfully. 'I'm impressed, Ewok.' You certainly understand why people commit murder, how people commit murder, when they commit murder, and which people commit murder.'

I smiled accommodatingly. I was becoming sensitive to Chase's affirmation. 'I'm quite competent, Chase.'

'Yes, but you neglected to mention *where* people get murdered.'

'Am I being murdered here tonight?'

Chase shook his head. 'No, not tonight.'

'In which case, we can put the streets down on our list.'

Chase smiled wryly at me.

PART C

Data Collection; Investigating the Suspects

CHAPTER EIGHTEEN

Day One; 7: 36 am; Rude Awakening

There was a ferocious bang. It re-bellowed like thunder in my lechatelierite skull. I snapped conscious like a knee-severed tree-branch. I sat bolted upright in bed, my back squared away by the bedstead. The bedroom window was smashed to smithereens. There were shards of glass strewn all over the plush carpet. As I daubed my cob-webbed eyes, I glanced over at Andrea. She squirmed with overwhelming exhaustion on the mattress and moaned quietly. There was a buzz buzz.

'*Ewok*!' a voice growled.

I trembled. 'Yes, Ewald.'

'This is your first day,' the voice snarled.

I groaned. 'I've just woken up. My mind's still bouncing.'

'You heard the alarm then.'

'It's the only thing I could hear. What in God's name did you do?'

'I fired a bullet through your master bedroom window.'

I gaped. 'Why?'

'I had to make sure you were up.'

I modulated painfully. 'Do you plan to pay for that?'

The voice was direct. 'No, I plan to make you pay if you don't do as I tell you.'

I yawned in agony. I'm really not in the mood.'

'Why not? Are there mushrooms in your brain?'

'No, of course not.'

'Is a dirk embedded in your heart?'

'No.'

'Well, in which case, you are fit to investigate the only link to the second suspect.'

'Who?'

'The nephew of the bitter rival of the disgruntled client.'

I squinted. 'Seriously, I can't.'

'Seriously, you will.'

'You think?'

'Of course.'

'So?'

'You better get ready.'

'Or what?'

'You and your family will be forfeited if you do not ascertain who killed my nephew's parents, my brother and his wife.'

I grumbled. 'Yes, I remember. I'll get started.'

'Good. Now, all we know, Ewok is that he is gay.'

I stuck out my tongue. I had never liked homosexuals. Perversely, my late employer had been one. 'So?'

'You will enlist your youngest daughter.'

I scratched my head. 'Why?'

'She is capable of unravelling him.'

My post-dawn face wrinkled. 'How?'

'Your daughter is bi-sexual.'

'How would you possibly imagine that?'

'I know more than you think. Now, get ready.'

'Yes.'

I was sitting at the oval breakfast table which was overspread with a floral tablecloth in the kitchen plodding my way through a chunky bowl of Asda porridge. I found Asda porridge to be superior to the leading brand. I was gulping a large mug of Gold

Blend, pulling on a Pall Mall cigarette. I had managed to keep up with the most advanced tobacco in terms of choice and design. I was retro-aspecting. Having slept over at the Inn two nights ago after Chase had finally exited my farewell bash, we left the following morning around ten. When we arrived home, Andrea had gone straight back to bed. She had slept throughout the day, throughout the night and was still sleeping now. Surprisingly, the gun shot had not broken her sleep as it had mine. She was still sleeping off the various gins and the mammoth endeavour surrounding the leaving do. David would be at his own home with my daughter-in-law and grandchildren. Melissa would have been back with her boyfriend. The morning after the farewell bash, we arranged a taxi for Martin to take him back to his flea-pit. The gun shot through the window had roused Lilly. I had explained to her what had happened.

It seemed I had been left with no choice. Either I satisfied Chase that all those involved in the suspected killings of his nephew's parents, his brother and his brother's wife, were investigated and punished or I, and more importantly, my whole family would be forfeited. He had warned me that if I presumed to contact the police, they would have to find him, and in the event they tried to, he would kill us all.

So I would start with the nephew. He was the only link to the third suspect. All I knew was that he resided at a mansion named Fall's Hall in Aberdeen. I left the breakfast table and went to the laptop on the kitchen surface. I googled the address but got no joy. I realised I would have to get directions.

Lilly appeared in the kitchen. 'I'm ready dad.'

I smiled contentedly. 'Yes.'

We drove north. As we approached Aberdeen, I realised I would have to pose a few questions. I pulled up outside a rundown-looking rural pub. I stepped in to the pub. A mob of eyes fixed on me. I walked towards the landlord.

'Excuse me, landlord,' I said. 'You wouldn't happen to have heard of a country house in these parts called Fall's Hall.'

'Certainly,' he said.

The landlord curled me with his finger aside and fed me the information. In return, I handed the landlord a twenty-pound note for a round for his customers. I stepped out of the pub to no little applause, climbed back into the car and navigated the country roads. Eventually, Lilly and I found ourselves outside a pair of front gates.

Lilly squealed. 'This is the place, dad.'

'Yes, Lill, I think it is,' I said.

'It's utterly amazing.'

'They obviously have money.'

'More than we have.'

I glanced reprovingly at my daughter. '*We*?'

'Yes, dad.'

I frowned slightly. 'We must not draw attention to ourselves.'

'Why not?'

'I need to investigate.'

'And dad?'

'I can't do that if I just drive straight into the house.'

'So?'

'I'll park the car farther along.'

'Sure dad.'

'Now we'll both get out and take our time.'

'Can we go inside.'

'No, Lill, because I need to work out the nephew.'

'To see if he did it.'

'Yes.'

'Okay then, so what do we do.'

'We'll walk together.'

Lilly nodded.

Having parked the car farther up the private road so as to avoid notice, my daughter and I disembarked. We ambled together back to the front gates. As we approached the calcified gates, they suddenly swung open. Lilly gaped. I scratched my head. We made our way along and over over the crunching chips of the serpentine driveway. No one greeted us. Together we reached the outside of the edifice. Lilly cocked an ear. I glanced at my daughter and did the same. There were two voices sounding. One came from inside the house and one came from beyond the garden. One voice was a young high impassioned voice; the other was an old low vacant voice.

The younger voice sounded:

Is there life beyond the waterfall?
Or is it just a dream?
Is there life beyond the waterfall?
Is it what it seems?
Live life to the max or not at all!
Find a love supreme!
And live beyond! - Beyond! - Beyond the waterfall!
Beyond the waterfall.
Beyond the waterfall...

The older voice sounded:

With a knife
The mushroom can be opened
And the poison then awoken
Causing pain, nightmares or homicide

With a slice
The life that you've been living
Becomes so unforgiving
That you contemplate suicide

Lilly goggled. She mopped her brow. 'What is that dad?'

I gaped. I stammered. 'It- it almost sounds like harmony.'

Lilly nodded firmly. 'And madness.'

'Yes,' I said, 'and madness.'

'So?'

'So you follow the younger voice and I will follow the older voice.'

Lilly smiled firmly. 'Let's do that.'

Lilly skipped across the garden, penetrated a gap in the hedge and vanished. I ambled farther towards the house.

My mobile rang. 'Lill?'

'Yes, dad. I'm squelching up the embankments.'
'Good. I've tracked the older voice to a window.'
'What should I do?'
'Make yourself comfortable and listen to the younger voice.'
'What are you going to do?'
'I'm going to listen to the older voice. Good luck, Lill!'
'Good luck, dad!'

CHAPTER NINETEEN

Day One; 4 pm; Surveilling the Nephew

As I perched outside the window where the older voice came from, I remembered the way the McLaren 1P LM had swerved up outside the entrance to the house. The beast had glinted like a giant collection of knives in the flames of the moon.

My mobile rang. 'I've spotted the nephew.'

'Good, Lill,' I said. 'Keep observing.'

'Will do, dad.'

Brackish lachrymosity promenaded like a mellifluous duet of emancipated pink calf-lovers in sensuous bitter-sweet ripples of tough/tender caresses and quasi-erogenous tingles from both of Alexander's liquid eyes, which were youthful, ingenuous and exuberant cobalt blue, all the way down the dacumen esplanade of his swarthy but ruddy cheeks, dribbling glorious globules of tart vinegar on his not ungracious gustatory tongue, as he mindlessly meandered the vast curtilage and sprawling gardens of the ancient mansion, like a poor lost soul, waiting for someone deeply special to manifest in the gloaming. He heard

'The glory of love' in his mind. He heard: *'like a knight in shining armour from a long time ago...'*

'Why Does It Always Rain on Me?' by Travis, which was from

their 1999 album 'The Man Who?' was playing on his MP3-player. He didn't especially recall lying when he was seventeen. He might well have lead poor sweet Jenny down the garden path towards a hostile goose that would have wildly hissed at her some years hitherto but that was merely because he harboured no wish at all to dent her perfect sensibilities, and that was also a different story.

The notoriously unforgiving north-east Scottish climate, a mixture of mouldy pea soup and out-of-date Scotch broth, came lashing like the vicious whips of a giant comet of ice daggers. The helpless debile earth recoiled violently from its incessant merciless blows. As the clouds devapourised, giant pails plummeted implacably like an apoplectic metal worker's dense hammering blocks from the utterly dismal bubble-like hibernal October sky, a sky that re-bellowed; echoed the stentorian thunder in Alexander's quivering heart. The cheerless cosseted firmament fronted redoubtably onto the once most purposeful but now thoroughly object-less demesne of Uncle Albert's large and stately house: Fall's Hall.

The big old house, the sacred mansion was empty these days; desolate; had been for so many, many years. It could no longer hold a candle to its erstwhile chatoyant incandescence. Alexander could feel it wailing for more people. Its suppressed *genus loci* yowled like a night-wolf through the defining moments of the decades for a blessed felicity it once remembered having known...

It was once upon a time quite a place- quite a decorated shed. It once effortlessly provoked the most spellbound of peripatetic cerebral phenomena. As the track finished, Alexander could hear echoes of the past such as '*will she come tumbling down*?', '*what if there's a fire*?' and '*lions, tigers and bears, oh my*!' This would have been as incorrigibly silly but laudably adventuresome fun-loving kid relations had the best places of all to play hide and seek in, among other popular children's games; eliciting the most thrilled of frolicsome locution, as such relations fearsomely essayed to outwit the designated child-catcher of the day; inciting the most abandoned of frenetic actions, as ruthless dyed-in-the wool huntsmen and women, dead eyes, vitally chased after petrified foxes on nervous horses with their ferocious dogs; and inspiring the most reverential of fitting awe, as serendipitous adult relations furtively sipped the finest flutes of vintage champagne and dreamed of their ultimate legacy which would one day delapse.

Despite the barely repairable ravages of time, the requirement to be dazzled up, and the hit and miss vicissitudes of heritable proprietorship, it was still a place of prodigious dimension, with high-ceilinged vertical inside partitions and titanic upper covering. It was still a place of imposing, if somewhat uncombed, exterior. But it was now a place of arrantly bedraggled garden, with fruits- coul blush apples, quince and brambles- and vegetables- asparagus, sorrel, Jerusalem artichokes and scallions- which were seldom, if ever, eaten and flowers- peonies, rudbeckias, dahlias and zesters- that were never picked unless a sophisticated lady should come by, which in view of Alexander's more than ambiguous sexual orientation and Uncle Albert's chronic dipsomania, was very rare. Then again, it was still a place of bountiful acre, where the most blessed of free-range hens roamed free, just like the large, natural, channelled and sinuous river which surged by. And, still, above all, a place of breathtaking waterfall, where fluttering hearts, young and old, like the fleet crystal-clear waters of the fall catapulted themselves theatrically and conclusively into the cold dispassionate void of invariable rebuffs: the Bennets may have been devilishly handsome but they had a deep-seated sensitivity which was all too often overlooked; still a place of tributaries of local lakes, Dee and Don river, north-east sea and Atlantic Ocean.

Miniscule twinkles of gritty but moribund day-star, sweet and carroty, waltzed like the orange beaks of life-long mating swans on the fading mottled river's epidermis.

Alexander was giggling through the streaming tears. He sniggered gleefully at the ones who imbibed alcohol and who smoked, who took drugs and hadn't done the things he had done. They were obviously just very lazy and incorrigibly selfish, with no concern for others, with a Schadenfreude for the various triumphant nervous systems that were in a state of desuetude worse than his own. His mercuriality betrayed a tear. He smiled at the squirrel that halted in the glade and then ran up the tree. He peered timidly at his rippling reflection in the cold river. He looked at his gold watch.

So, torrential was the rain and so picturesque the spectacle that it momentarily sidetracked Alexander from the agreeably coherent and impressively eloquent epilogue of his sopping and bespattered legal tome: *Stair Memorial Encyclopedia. It's so beautiful,* he thought. *Like a young dream. Like a young lover's dream.* Alexander whispered at first. Like a holy man. Like a man of the cloth. Indeed, like his jealously treasured and achingly missed father might have done. Like a religious tradesman. Like his father would once have whispered to him: his son, a sweet child with petite azure eyes and winsome smile; an unconditionally adoring child. *Once we have laid the carpet my good boy, we must tack it,* he once would have said. There would forever be magic in humble, even thread-bare carpets. Even in the wee old town-house in the backward forgotten city. Supernaturally weaved into the unravel-able fabric of their close-knit father-to-son enchantment.

And then he uttered. From the jade zenith of the earthy ridged embankment, which enclosed the dead zone, like Moses upon the mountaintop to God. 'Oh, Dad! Why did you go? Why did you go so soon? Why did you have to fly off that cliff? Could you not have turned? Were you going to fast, Dad? Were you distracted? Were you trying to impress Mum with your speed?

His innocent and ingenuous tears glinted like spikes of ice in the diminishing luminosity of the dying day-star. These were the tears of the forever loving but alas forever lovelorn. In the softest lowest voice, he despairingly essayed to smoothly and sentimentally croon his faithful old ballad, 'Beyond the Waterfall', which he had stoutly composed on the pint-sized black-lacquered baby grand in the commodious front room of the once stunning secluded north east of Scotland mansion. It was supposed to be a duet but then there was nobody else to sing with. It went:

First verse:

'Look at me! I am so cold.
Look at you! You are so bold.
Look at us! Our hearts are gold.
Look beyond! A chance untold...

Second verse:

Must I now, jump the cliff?
Is your mind, so adrift?
Maybe so: to feel the lift,
So, then: our souls eclipse...
(Da, da da, da da da, da da da...)

Chorus:

Is there life beyond the waterfall?
Or is it just a dream?
Is there life beyond the waterfall?
Is it what it seems?
Live life to the max or not at all!
Find a love supreme!
And live beyond! - Beyond! - Beyond the waterfall!
Beyond the waterfall.
Beyond the waterfall...

Third verse:

What is left for me to feel?
I'm still here. I am your deal?
You are here? A grape to peel.
What is left? Something unreal...
(Da, da da, da da da, da da da...)

Chorus:

Is there life beyond the waterfall?
Or is it just a dream?
Is there life beyond the waterfall?
Is it what it seems?

Live life to the max or not at all!
Find a love supreme!
And live beyond! - Beyond! - Beyond the waterfall!
Beyond the waterfall.
Beyond the waterfall...'
(Da, da da, da da da, da da da...)

After an acoustic delay line, caused by the reflection of sound waves from the dimming sundown river's surface, of his somewhat saccharine refrain, which was hopefully not a derry; that was to say, a meaningless chorus, reverberated within the miserable gloaming, Alexander breathed laboriously. He had hoped one day his slushy descant would be published, like his long-lost love...

Notwithstanding the deeply absorbing and signal history of the place, the grounds, now, were used only for a self-indulgent attention-grabbing sojourn. They were used to watch and to wonder- and to believe.

The giant pails turned into gargantuan baths, swelling the old faithful river and loading down the fall of the waters; they engorged far-off lakes, contributed to the great north-east sea and then meshed with the prodigious Atlantic Ocean.

Alexander re-mounted the outcrop on the earthy ridge, as the dead zone, the slow-moving waters, in his cold-weather lagging, clutching a small thin flat container with a narrow neck, with very warm tea inside, he considered the stasis in his life with his usual dysthymia; which was his tendency to be despondent.

He was alone- so very alone. How he longed to be de-isolated! He didn't even possess a solitary companion, never mind a fancy piece.

And so, it was him and *just* him: the rain, the river and the waters of the fall. And the lakes and the seas. The Dee and Don rivers. The great north-eastern sea. The Atlantic Ocean.

At least for the present juncture. He would of course repair to University, when the festive season had terminated, for his final year. He studied the law: the system of rules of the independent legal system of Scotland, regulating the actions of its more than five million members and which it enforced by the imposition of various penalties, which were calibrated in terms of severity. He studied at Aberdeen University. It was one of the toughest universities to gain entry to, unless you had a peerless finesse for high bands.

He had a plethora of acquaintances there but so very few *bone fide* friends. They just didn't seem to notice him. Not even a fleeting look in his soft quiet direction. Perhaps he *was* different. Perhaps his social skills were uniquely egregious. Was he secretly a demaphobe? Perhaps his feelings, his romantic desires were an insuperable obstacle. Perhaps they were a barrier to love and to hope and to happiness. He was so confused, so sad, so lonely.

Would *they* come one day? He had to say 'they'; for even the merest notion of *gayness*, of homosexuality, its mere presence in the mind, was a most discomfiting, even life-disaffirming, thing. Indeed, it was once thought to be a mental illness. It was certainly a most challenging social, political and emotional thing. Perhaps 'they' would come one day by the fall. See the evanescing pulchritude and the deep, deep sadness, and him.

All he really had was his dear uncle Albert and his money. A kind old man and almost a quarter of a million, resting disingenuously in his bank account. A potentially mesmerizing garden, if a skilled gardener were hired, a massive house, a ridiculous but gleaming BMW but still a heavy heart.

The heavy rain turned his encyclopedia, its infinite inherent dryness, into a mushy soup.

It was Saturday evening. For many, the inception of relaxation, of enjoyment, of long-awaited emancipation and attendant dispossession, of things said and done which would later be rued upon.

As he cerebrated in the dying suffocated winter sun, which put music to the stillness's of the fall, he considered. There had to be a point. A beginning; an end.

Waterfalls started with rivers and rivers started with rain, ice and snow. And these started with vapour.

But what would he start with? The egg and the sperm may have been a reasonable scientific exegesis of well-written existential and ontological inceptions but oh how it seemed to him that his life had been on the back burner for so many years. He was already twenty-one. His once petite, azure and sparkling eyes were dimming, his formerly winsome smile was cracking, his short dark cropped hair was thinning just a bit and his *Weltanschauung* was mouldering like a cadaver, becoming ever more cynical. He had only his legal education for impulsion; only exam pressure and intellectual achievement for motivation.

As he sat on the earthy ridge, clutching his small long-necked bottle, which was cooling, he watched the last of the sun wink cheekily off the waters. Like a pop star's swan song to a number one fan.

He somewhat despairingly and adolescently hacked at his already scarred white-bobbled wrists with a cheap plastic razor. Is suicide unlawful he wondered? An attempt which was discovered by a doctor and a mental health officer, which made them think you had a mental disorder could *de jure* lead to detention. And there would be no *Human Rights* get-out. And just about everything else was? Rape, torture, murder- even breaching the peace. Thoughts were legal, though. The Human Rights Act said so. So, too, statements, unless, of course. they were defamatory; tantamount to calumny. Law regulated the actions of the members of a particular country or community and which it could enforce by the imposition of penalties. And so, for that reason it was sound. We simply couldn't have de-ordination. But it didn't exactly breed happiness. *I need love,* he thought. *I need you, whoever and wherever you are.* Someone prepossessing, someone smart, someone funny, someone kind. Was that legal? He supposed that homosexuality had been legalized some tens of years ago; it was longer quite the degeneracy it had been. Not that it was the male body which he insolubly desiderated, more the twinkling eyes, the winsome smile, the earth-shattering touch.

He peered down onto the darkening cracking mirror of the river's surface. He wasn't that ugly, was he? And not too much of a dandy? Jenny had always said he was sweet looking. Most charming.

Uncle Albert said he was a nice-looking lad. Doris had repeatedly said that he would be a heartbreaker someday. One or two girls at University said he had lovely eyes and a nice smile. But nobody else said it.

Nothing changes but the waters of time, *he thought.* Time never stands still, not even for a second. But my life stands still-years at a time and then suddenly I move on to the next stage, just when I thought I understood. When the new dawn has broken, I'll still be sleeping. Only when the sun finally sets will I awaken; then it's too late, the world's an empty space, just like my heart without you, you whom I've never met, never known to have loved. And what good is love in the darkness? No one watches you cry alone, sees the pain in those forgotten eyes. To step out in to the light requires an inner strength quite beyond some of us. And so, we wait and wait and wait until the sun comes down and we react; try in vain to save the world; save our love.

He stuck out his pouty lips, which shielded years of parental bereavement and his present melancholy, and said, as he madly and forlornly exhorted the burbling early black crepuscular twilight waters, 'So, to reverse this, you must come, my love. You must come, now. Tonight. This very night. When I'm here. Here to receive you. We could watch the waters of the fall plunge into infinite impenetrable darkness together. We might lock eyes. We might behold in wonder nothing but the burgeoning seeds of the blossoming souls within us. We might touch hands. Feel the awesome blue dynamic equilibrium flow between our fingertips. We might, then, finally...*kiss*; de-osculate. Our hearts might shimmer. And our minds might at last be free. Our bodies might quiver with delight. We could sleep beneath the branches of the oaks, beneath the stars, like Rihanna's 'Diamonds', and awake to a glorious invigorating new dawn. And we could watch the rivers glisten in the fresh dazzling light of the new sun.'

He then studied the crop of mushrooms around him. He said: 'Mushrooms killed the reckless. You must never attempt to eat them. Still, I wish I could share the secret they conceal with someone.'

CHAPTER TWENTY

Day One: 4: 30 pm; Frolicking with the Nephew

My daughter Lilly told me about the subsequent events later. She raced towards the nephew. The nephew clocked her. She leapt up in to his arms. The nephew caught her. She gazed at him doe-eyed. He had brown round eyes.

'Alexander, we live in a fantasy land together,' she said. Her eyes rounded, she twisted her pierced lips, announcing her rebellion and her feeling of adventure. 'You're the tin man,' she said.

'I'm what?' said Alexander.

She burst into song. '"*If only I had a heart...*"'

'If only what?' said Alexander.

'I'm Dorothy.'

Alexander took a step back. 'You are?'

'Yes, I understand you.'

'You do?'

'Yes, you were doing the Wizard of Oz.'

Alexander gawked slightly. 'I was?'

'Yes, you were.'

'How?'

Lilly burst into song again. 'It was just like "Somewhere over the rainbow..."'

'I wasn't aware of that.'

Lily beamed. 'Well, you do now.'

'Who are you?'

'I'm the judge's daughter.'

Alexander squinted. 'Who?'

'Lilly Wren.'

'Where did you come from?'

'I came from Kansas. You're from Oz.'

'America? But you are Scottish.'

'We both are.'

'So?'

'You're gay.'

Alexander glared indignantly. 'I never said that.'

'No, but your feelings prove it.'

'How?'

'Do you fancy me?'

Alexander coggled his head. 'Well no.'

'There you go then.'

'Yes, you're crazy.'

'No more crazy than you are.'

Lilly waved her arms about enthusiastically. 'So, throw away that tea?'

Alexander looked at his flask. 'Why?'

'You have to feel something.'

'What exactly?'

'Excitement.'

'Why?'

'That's what you want.'

'Who says?'

'It's obvious.'

'How?'

'I listened to you.'

'How?'

'I was above the waterfall, sitting on that thing-thingamajig.'

Alexander gazed up. 'You mean the outcrop.'

'Yes, exactly.'

'So?'
'My dad is investigating you.'
'Why?'
'He wants to know if you did it.'
'Did what?'
Kill the witch of the east?'
'Who?'
'The woman my dad's enemy thinks killed her.'
'I can assure you I didn't, whoever she was.'
'Who is your dad?'
'Maxwell.'
'How old is he?'
'He's dead.'
'How old are you?'
'Twenty. How old are you?'
'Sixteen.'
'So?'
'Let's go in to your house. My dad's standing outside.'
'Who?'
'The judge.'
'Who?'
'Ewald Wren.'
'What's he doing there?'
'He's investigating.'
'Who?'
'The older voice.'
'Why?'
'I don't know.'
'I can't really let people in.'
'Why not?'
'It's not fair on my uncle.'
'Why not?'
'He's very easily disturbed.'
'Why?'
'He's in his eighties.'
Lilly smiled openly. 'In that case, we should do it now.'

'What now?'

'Have fun!'

'What fun?'

'Here, hold this!'

Alexander took hold and grimaced. 'It's a cigarette.'

'Yes, I know.'

'So, suck it in and breath out.'

'I don't smoke.'

'No?'

'You shouldn't smoke either.'

'No, but it will help you.'

'How will it help me?'

'It has a line.'

'A what?'

'You know, coke.'

'You can't put coke into a cigarette.'

Lilly rolled up her eyes. 'Shows how much you know. Anyway, puff this.'

Alexander shook his head. 'I told you, I don't smoke.

'Then we'll have to try something else.' Lilly lifted a small bottle out from her purse. 'Drink this.'

'What is it?'

'A measure.'

'A measure of what?'

'Spirits.'

Alexander opened his hands slightly. 'I don't drink.'

Lilly pushed up her lower jaw. 'Okay, well smell this.'

'What is it?'

'Poppers.'

'What does that do?'

'It makes you feel orgasmic.'

Alexander waved his head. 'You shouldn't know a word like that.'

'Then you must have thought about it.'

'About what?'

'Another guy.'

'Who says?'

'My dad told me.'

'How would he know?'

Lilly shrugged.

'So?'

'I'm trying to be your friend.'

'You're too young, Lilly.'

'You're not that old either, Alexander.'

'Yes, but I understand what you don't understand.'

'Which is?'

'Same-sex.'

'I don't know what you mean.'

'My brother's coming.'

'Who?'

'Martin.'

'He feels the way you do.'

Lilly watched his eyes bristle. Alexander shed a tear. He rubbed his crimsoning eyes. Lightning struck, bright flashes appeared in the sky, and the baths turned into swimming pools. He dismounted the outcrop on the earthy ridge for a final time, cast the last drops of his plastic cup of tea into the swallowing famished river. Lilly kissed him gently on the cheek before skipping away.

'Where are you going?' said Alexander.

'Back to my dad?'

'Be careful.'

Lilly waved back.

The mobile rang.

'Dad!' she said.

'Lill! What did you work out.'

'He doesn't do anything he thinks is wrong.'

I exhaled. 'Yes, Lill.'

I rang Chase.

'*Ewok*!'

'Chase.'

'So?'

'I have driven all the way up to the mansion Falls' Hall in Aberdeen with my son Martin and my daughter Lilly.

'And?'

'My daughter discovered the nephew.'

'What's his name?'

'Alexander.'

'Alexander who?'

'I don't know.'

'And?'

'My daughter watched him and then she conversed with him.'

'What was he doing?'

'He was communing with nature. He enjoys freedom.'

'And?'

'He is an academic but a hopeless romantic.'

'And?'

I stuck out my tongue. 'He is homosexual.'

'I sense you have a problem with that.'

'It was the law at one point.'

'What was the law?'

'The Homosexual Offences Act.'

'So?'

'It has always felt to me to be so very unnatural.'

'Says who?'

'The Church.'

'You believe in the church as well, Ewok?!'

'Ewald.'

'So?'

'I believed in the canon law.'

'But not Scot's law.'

'I believe in both.'

'But?'

'I think social norms have become too permissive.'

'And?'

I could sense anger in Chase's tone. 'I forget, Chase you're a homosexual as well.'

'And not in the least bit ashamed.'

'No?'

'Not in the least.'

'May I ask why?'

'It is the least of man's crimes.'

'Yes?'

'Anything else?'

'He lost his father.'

'How do you know?'

'He stated, '" Oh, Dad! Why did you go? Why did you go so soon?"'

'Who was his dad?'

'Maxwell.'

'And why did he say that?'

'The father seems to have had flown off a cliff.'

'How do you know?'

'According to Lilly, he said: "Why did you have to fly off that cliff? Could you not have turned? Were you going to fast, Dad? Were you distracted? Were you trying to impress Mum with your speed"?'

'And?'

'He lost his mum as well.'

'Who's she?'

'He didn't say.'

'And?'

'He's a loner.'

'How young is he?'

'Twenty.'

'So?'

'He wouldn't even have been born in 1995, so we can rule him out.'

'Anything else?'

'He emoted that he wished to meet someone.'

'Who?'

'A lover, I believe.'

'Which lover?'

'I don't know, anyone.'

'Was he drunk?'

'No.'

'Can you be sure?'

'Yes, according to Lilly he drank tea.'

'Just tea?'

'Yes, from a flask.'

'Anything else?'

'No.'

'Send him off to meet him.'

'Why?'

'I want to know what else we can get out of him.

CHAPTER TWENTY-ONE

Day One; 5 pm; Martin Tells Alexander a Story

The entire daedal vault of the north east of Scotland sky, a sky of imperishable granite rock which was suffocated by the Gestapo of atmospheric phenomenon, cracked violently in serrated lacerations from the true east of its most extreme dimension to the true west of its most extreme dimension, shearing the obtuse unlettered clouds apart, unimpeachably launching the earth's own satellite, its fabulous moon, into a brand new helter-skelter orbit and laying down the hissing sun, its electric amber rays turning in to bombs of water. The apoplectic heaven's opened. Solid giant anvils of water plunged downwards, swamping and imbruing Alexander's head. Martin bustled across the garden, jinked adroitly between the gap in the hedge row and swaggered towards the nephew. Martin sashayed up to Alexander. Alexander beamed at the slim handsome young man approaching him. Martin tossed his head back. He smiled provocatively at Alexander. 'Hello, Alexander,' he said, 'how are you?'

Alexander tingled. He furrowed his brows. 'Who are you? And how do you know my name?'

'My sister told me.'

Alexander squinted. 'Who?'

'Lilly.'

Alexander coggled his deep-sea ocean-blue eyes. 'And what's your name?'

'Martin.'

Alexander opened up his arms. 'And what is it I can do for you, Martin?'

Martin glared at Alexander. 'You can take this for a start.'

Alexander waved his head. 'I'm not taking anything.'

'No?'

'No.'

Martin stretched out a claw, clutched Alexander's perfectly symmetrical feminine jaw with his young clean fresh strong hand, put both hands around his cranium, barrelled in to his eyes and propelled a mountain mint tongue into the abyss of Alexander's throat. 'Sniff this, Alexander.'

Alexander inhaled. He lapsed into a trance. Martin ogled Alexander. He beamed at him as he danced around him, loosening his jeans. Martin stuffed a sizeable tablet of MDMA into Alexander's mouth; shuttered it with his right hand, smacked his back and made him swallow.

Alexander squeaked. He trembled. 'What will that do to me?'

Martin smiled congenially. 'It will make you enjoy my story.'

Alexander loured at Martin. 'Am I to live after that assault?'

Martin nodded defiantly. 'You will do much more than that. You will thrive.'

Alexander shifted his head for a moment, ardour and concupiscence filling every youthful cranny in his ingenuous brain.

Alexander teetered. 'Okay, what's it about?'

Martin intoned. 'Sniff this. It's about love, Alexander.' Martin left Alexander alone to feel his youthful good looks.'

Thirty seconds passed...

Alexander gasped. 'What was that?'

'You were popped.'

Alexander stuttered. 'It- it was amazing.'

'It's not quite over yet.'

'No?'

'No, you'll feel love shortly.'

Alexander nodded tentatively. 'Love?'

Martin stared through Alexander. 'Gay love!'

Alexander blushed. Tears cascaded from his blue-water eyes.

'You see, Alexander, I might not have a place like this but I do understand feelings.'

Alexander sobbed as he nodded.

'Now, Alexander, let me tell you a story.'

Alexander wiped away delicious tears from his eyes with his hands. 'Yes, very well then.'

Martin sucked in the sodden air and exhaled dramatically. 'My head began to stir and...'

Alexander wiggled his head. 'And?'

'My eyelids quivered...'

Alexander grinned as a paroxysm of ecstasy swept through his body. 'When was this?'

'It was as warm rays of sunlight filtered through my bedroom blinds.'

Alexander beamed broadly with happiness. 'You're a poet.'

Martin tipped his head to the right. 'Just as figurative as you are.'

'So?'

'And so shadowed, I lay in the corner, while the sun busily painted the room with golden light.'

Alexander nodded eagerly. 'Yes, and then what happened?'

'I watched with interest...'

'Yes?'

'As various patterns and images began to form.'

'Then?'

'I saw shadows- dancing shadows- and in this disco of light I saw: bars.'

'Why bars?'

'Listen.'

'Yes, okay.'

'My mind seemed to float...'

Alexander nodded.

'Resting safely, I watched passively as familiar shining waters rocked my floating cradle.'

Alexander nodded again.

'I heard familiar voices- soft and gentle echoes of childhood long ago.'

'Who are you quoting?'

'I'm not quoting anyone.'

'This is your own story.'

Martin smiled as he nodded. ' I was now smiling. Still drifting, my bright sparkling eyes caught sight of those familiar waving shadows as they sailed passed me on their bikes.'

'Did you cycle here?'

'No, I came in my dad's car. Anyway, I looked up and beamed brightly into my blue skies of childhood.'

'Did this actually happen?'

'Yes, it's all true. There, I found other shadows, legacies of childhood bobbing up and down, free and alive.'

'So?'

'So, floating, sailing, dancing through soft pillowed clouds, I knew I had been here before.'

'You were dreaming about your childhood.'

'Indeed. But how different was my present muddled adolescent world where two years of loving my dream-boy had finally brought a painful harvest of disillusionment.'

'You knew you were gay?'

'Since the age of fifteen, yes.'

'That's approximately when I knew. As an only child, I found this countryside to be a very lonely place for a sixteen-year old boy...'

Martin stiffened his mouth in agreement. 'Susceptible in your spirit to the cruel black skies above you.'

'Very much so.'

'And so?'

'I grew heavily to rely on my own imagination.'

'Where do you live?'

'I live in Newton Mearns.' It is a house: large, white and built from stone…'

'And?'

'Outside my back garden boundaries- way beyond the tall imprisoning hedges- stretch fields and trees as far as the eye could reach.'

As the feelings of ecstasy coursing through Alexander's veins, he gazed at Martin with fascination. 'What did this mean to you?'

'These trees had been to me a refuge.'

'What happened there?'

'There I had poured out the secrets of my heart's love, feeling…'

'Feeling?'

'Safe and secure in their hidden leafy depths, and…'

'And?'

'I was assured of their sympathy, as they listened to my helpless cries.'

'Did these monarchs of the forest know everything?'

Martin smiled at the help. 'Yes, quite.'

'What happened to you?'

'I no longer needed them. The constant burning flame of love which had knifed my heart and crippled my mind had at last burned out.'

'Then?'

'Back came the blue skies of childhood and already the cold lonely skies of adolescence were forgotten. I know longer needed to love him.'

'Who was he? Your dream-boy?'

'His name was Craig.'

'That's a really nice name.'

'I always thought so. Anyway, I felt free and alive, accepting life's bitter taste. Perhaps it was nobler to kill this love than to sacrifice myself once more to the painful trauma of heartache now past. This realisation that I could live once again like a child, un-imprisoned by this love-desire and moreover that at last I was safe in my sleep meant I was finally over the love that never was.'

'That was indeed fortunate.'

'It didn't take long for those summer weeks to pass. At school, I could concentrate and warmly welcomed each new day. I became much more involved and people began to like me more.'

'Yes?'

'I was more confident and slowly began to like myself.'

'Yes, of course.'

'Instead of wallowing in self-pity in the comfort of my den, I made an effort to get out.'

Alexander nodded his head.

'Time passed...'

'Yes?'

'The school term was already old and not once had I seen him. There was to be a school disco and it had been a long time since I had been to one. Everyone I knew was going and so I felt I ought to go. That wasn't quite right.'

'No?'

'I actually wanted to go.'

'You felt better about yourself.'

'Yes, there was a new self-confidence telling me to go. It was to be a long walk to the disco but I decided it would do me good.'

Alexander nodded. 'In a sense, you were returning to the fold of the society you knew.'

'Yes...'

'I sense perhaps not.'

'Everyone was there and yet something was missing. I could not be sure what it was but something was not as it should have been.'

Alexander wondered thoughtfully. 'Were you prepared to accept this society without him, your dream-boy? Why should you be so deprived? Indeed bereft?'

Martin smiled sombrely. 'My eyes fell sleepy as they wandered around the large illuminated dance-hall. The music had suddenly become slow and tiring.'

Alexander waved his hand outwards. 'Or was it the light?'

Martin shifted his head back and forth. 'I watched with interest as various patterns and images began to form.'

'Really?'

'Yes, I saw colours- waltzing colours.'

'So?'

'My childhood shadows I had loved and understood, but this sudden blinding kaleidoscope of colour simply reminded me again of my lost love, making me feel old and tired. In the oceans of multi-coloured light pouring from the ceiling I saw, once more, bars. My mind seemed to sink...'

'Oh, no! Then?'

'For me the bars became a spider's web, a web of bright shining golden strands of his hair.'

'He was blond. You mean where you remained trapped?'

'Yes, his livid burning eyes seemed to cripple my mind, while his sharp icy claws knifed my aching heart.'

'What did you do?'

'I looked up and trembled yet again beneath the black skies of adolescence.'

'You had returned.'

'Yes. No longer above the clouds of a long-ago childhood, I would live eternally beneath a dark venomous sky...'

'Incapable of uprooting your desire to love him.'

'I had always loved him. As I opened my eyes to this dream world, I saw what I would see.'

'And?'

'There he was, but sadly-'

'You grasped the knowledge-'

'Yes, with someone else.'

'Who?'

'A girl.'

'For two years, they had been together and for two years I had suffered.'

'Knowing that you could not have him- your dream-boy.'

'Each day in the history of my life had been knifed by the same deadly weapon.'

'What about your future- would he kill that, too?'

'As midnight struck and the town bells echoed in the night sky, I waited patiently by the main road.'

'Which road?'

'Capelrig Road.'

'And what was the name of the secondary school?'

'Eastwood High School. Anyway, the wind was rapidly becoming higher and making an eerie whistling sound. I could hear his footsteps as they made their way along the side of the road. The clouds were now banking black above the roads and hills. Lightning began to illuminate the dark sky, while cars hurtled past me. With my hand, I quickly covered the shiny buckle on my belt, in which for a moment I saw the menace of my frightening face lit up by a sudden sheet of brightness.'

'And then what happened?'

'I began to laugh.'

Alexander smiled curiously. 'Then?'

'My sinister laugh seemed to echo as a wave of thunder shook the black skies above.'

'Then?'

'Then the rain came lashing, the earth bouncing from it...'

'Recoiling from its blows?'

'Yes, and with it I could hear those footsteps, quickening.'

'And?'

'As my lost love approached, all my energy for revenge welled up within my sick soul and I brandished the gleaming blade...'

'The gleaming blade?'

'It was a mushroom knife.'

'And?'

'I crazily drove it into his heart.'

'And?'

'As he lay dead, I suddenly realised that I too was dead and longed again to with him.'

'Craig?'

'So?'

'With a sudden burst of energy, I pulled the bloodied weapon from his torn heart and found oblivion as the blade entered my own.'

Alexander clapped. A tear strolled down his cheek. 'That was very beautiful.'

'Thank you.'

'Your welcome.'

'Did you actually kill Craig?'

'Not quite, no. And obviously I didn't kill myself. I thought about it, felt like doing it.'

'So how did it actually end?'

'I came out to him but he rejected me.'

'That must have been very painful.'

'Agony, yes. How do you feel?'

'Lovely actually.'

'It's taken affect then. What do you do, Alexander?'

'I'm a third-year law student.'

'Snap.'

'Which university do you go to?'

'Glasgow.'

'I presume you go to Aberdeen?'

'Yes.'

'Do you have a boyfriend?'

'No.'

'Do you want to be mine?'

Alexander beamed. 'Yes- yes I do.'

Martin smiled back. 'Okay, but I must ask a few things first.'

'Fire away!'

'What does your uncle do?'

'He's retired now.'

'What did he do before?'

'Mechanical engineering.'

Martin peered beyond the hedge row. 'How did he afford a house like that?'

'His father owned his own Mechanical Engineering company.'

'Who?'

'James Bennet.'

'And?'

'It was successful.'

'Very.'

'And did your uncle know a man called Andrew McLean?'

Alexander cast his mind back through the emotional intensity. 'Yes he did, Mr McLean was a lawyer himself, I mean a practising one.'

'Was?'

Alexander swayed his head. 'Apparently he went missing.'

'When?'

'1995.'

'And how did your uncle know Mr McLean?'

'He had a friend Jarrod Fields. My uncle worked with him. Jarrod Field's sister was Susanna McLean. Susanna McLean was Andrew McLean's wife. My uncle knew Andrew McLean through his colleague.'

'How did your uncle and Andrew McLean get on.'

'I sensed my uncle was wary of him.'

'Why?'

'He seemed to know something important.'

'Any idea what?'

'No, no idea.'

'Do you think your uncle could have killed Andrew McLean?'

'My uncle's very gentle, Martin. I can't see it.'

'What if he did?'

'I would know, Martin. He would have told me.'

'Does your uncle love you?'

'He took me in when I was a small boy, after my parents died.'

'That's not what I asked.'

Alexander shrugged. 'He has always told me that he loves me.'

Martin smiled contentedly. 'Do you fancy me, Alexander?'

'Yes, very much. Do you fancy me?'

'I think your gorgeous.'

'So?'

'Shall we fuck?'

Alexander gazed at Martin quizzically. 'Out here in the freezing pelting rain.'

'Yes.'

'I think it's better that we kiss.'

Martin smiled. He brought his lips to Alexander's. They kissed slowly and tenderly. Gradually, their tongues entwined. Martin groped Alexander's crotch. Alexander became hard immediately. Their mouths were together for more than a minute. When it was over, Alexander said: 'I love you, Martin.'

Martin smiled. 'I love you, too, Alexander.'

'So what next?'

'I have to go back.'

Alexander sniffed. 'Please don't go.'

'I have to see my father and sister.'

'You could stay over if you wanted to, all of you, I mean. I'm sure my uncle wouldn't mind.'

'That's not what you said to my sister.'

'That's different, she was only a young girl.'

'No, I think it's best if you go back in, and my family get going.'

'Back to Newton Mearns?'

'No, I live in the west end of Glasgow.'

'To be near the University.'

'Exactly.'

'Where exactly?'

'Whiteinch.'

'Where is that?'

'Next to Partick.'

'As in Partick Thistle.'

'Yes.'

'Do you support them?'

'No, I support Aberdeen.'

Alexander smiled wryly. 'As a Glaswegian.'

'Yes, Aberdeen we were the best when I was growing up.'

'Yes, I support them, too. That's something else we have in common. When will I see you again? Why were you here in the first place.'

'My father's a judge, at least he was. He wants to know who killed Andrew McLean and his wife.'

'I see. It wasn't me. I wasn't even born in 1995. I really can't see it was my uncle.'

Martin nodded satisfactorily. 'It's goodbye then.'

'When will I see you again?'

'I know where you live, I will surprise you.'

'You promise.'

Martin kissed his index and middle finger together and touched Alexander's lips with them. 'I promise.'

'When will this aphrodisiac wear off.'

'A couple of hours max.'

'So it's goodbye, then.'

'For now. Let me go first.'

'Of course. Bye Martin!'

'Bye Alexander!'

And with that, Martin tailed back along the embankment, jinked through the gap in the hedge row, hop-skipped across the garden and returned to Lilly and I.

'So, son,' I said, 'what happened?'

'He couldn't have done it.'

'I told dad that,' said Lilly.

'He doesn't think his uncle could have done it either.'

'Why not?'

'He said he's too timid.'

'And?'

'He's very nice.'

Lilly smiled knowingly at Martin. 'You fancy him, Martin.'

I grimaced. 'No, he doesn't, Lill.'

'No, dad, he does.'

'Why would you fancy a spoiled princess?' I said.

Martin glowered at his dad. 'Maybe the spoiled princess is a very nice young man.'

I scoffed. 'He's sucking you in.'

'No, he's not, it's you who sucked me in.'

I glared at Martin. 'I've told you before, Martin, you have to control that unearned temper of yours.'

Martin railed. 'My temper, if I have one, comes from your upper-middle class business-class bigotry.'

I scowled at my son. 'No, Martin,' I said, 'it comes from hard work. It comes from being clever. You see, son, you want everything immediately. You want fun and feelings immediately. You're nowhere near.'

Lilly swithered her head. 'I'm sorry, dad. I agree with Martin.'

I smiled gently at my daughter. 'Yes, you would, Lill.' Now, Martin, the reason I made it is that I was far more clever than you are and I worked hard. And Martin, there is an awful lot more going on than you understand.'

'Such as?'

'Such as you would understand nothing of.'

'I understand your colossal greed, your opprobrious assumptions, your shameful bullying, and your ill-sighted judgements.'

'Yes, perhaps, but you don't understand everything. I have a man waiting to kill me, a man waiting to kill you and your sister and the rest of the whole family.'

'So?'

'So what we'll do is we'll wait for the nephew to re-enter the house and double-check if there's more concerning the uncle.'

Eventually, we saw Alexander repairing to the mansion and walk inside.

CHAPTER TWENTY-TWO

Day One; 17: 26 pm; The Rivalrous Uncle

Albert Bennet lounged in his Chieftain's Chair. His cheeks and his eyes were sunken. It was a chair created by Finn Juhl. It was a space filled with symbols inspired by weapons. It was exhibited in 1949, at a Copenhagen design fair. The chair was named by the media after King Frederick IX sat in it during the exhibition. Later it was renamed the Chieftain's by Finn Juhl. It was made from teak and walnut and was upholstered in leather. Albert clutched a Macallan 55 in his thin veined palsied hand. It was a hand made much more the steadier by snifters of the usquebaugh. It imparted a soft smooth taste, normally associated with its more expensive siblings and a fine aroma that Macallan whiskeys were known for.

The front door creaked. Albert stirred in his chair. He laid the Macallan strenuously down on the occasional table. He peered at the picture on the wall of his younger brother with his wife and his nephew. They all looked so happy. His brother had been old, sixty-three when he sired his nephew. Albert wheezed. He was eighty-four. He knew he was eighty-four since he had enjoyed his birthday recently. It was only the other day. His nephew Alexander had given him a...a present. Yes, the Macallan itself.

Albert motioned to rise, phantom discomfort mobilizing. He

picked up his system cane, which was neatly by his seat, clambered to his feet and hobbled out of the sitting room into the foyer. He met Alexander in the hallway. Alexander dusted off the rain from his attire. He was still grinning from the MDMA Martin had given him.

Despite his stupor, Albert glared at his nephew. 'You look unusually pleased with yourself, Alex.'

Alexander enthused. 'Indeed I am Uncle.'

'Oh? Why would that be?'

'I've met someone.'

'You have?'

'Who?'

'Martin.'

'Who's Martin?'

'The judge's son.'

'Who?'

'Sir Wren.'

Albert squinted. 'Not Ewald Wren.'

Alexander's eyes popped. 'How could you possibly know that, uncle?'

'My father, your grandfather James Bennet, knew his father Ealdahach Wren.'

'Who?'

'He was a uniquely successful Business Services entrepreneur.'

Alexander gasped. 'You never miss a trick, uncle.'

Albert shook his head. 'Hardly, Alex. But I have to ask, have you been drinking?'

Alexander gulped. 'No.'

Albert smiled grimly. 'It's just you seem a bit animated.'

'Yes, he had that affect on me.'

'Wren?'

'No, Martin.'

Albert nodded. 'Where were you?'

'By the waterfall.'

'And what were you doing?'

'I was communing with nature.'

Albert cast his nephew a look of incertitude. 'You mean bargaining with the gods'

Alexander struggled to temper the MDMA. He exhaled exuberantly. 'What's it all about, uncle Albert? Eh?'

Albert was compelled to concede of his own intoxication. 'Survival mostly, Alex.'

'Why survival?'

'I don't have the money I used to have.'

Alexander had always sensed within the depths of his beholden subconscious that something was not quite as it seemed. He knew virtually nothing of his Uncle's financial affairs save that money seemed to be haemorrhaging from a once abundant account. 'Why don't you have it?'

'I was forced to spend it.'

'What on?'

'Us.'

'But we have nothing new.'

'Yes, but I had to preserve the old.'

'I don't understand.'

'It's to do with an old friend.'

'You've been helping him.'

'Something like that.'

'Is he ill?'

'Yes, he has a disorder of the mind. Still, he beats me. He seems to think his son can beat you.'

'Who is he?'

'Who?'

'The man that beats you.'

Albert rubbed his forehead. 'No one in particular. All I might say is that he is as dangerous and as poisonous as the mushrooms in the surrounding lands of which I warned you when you first came here.'

'What about his son?'

'Who's son?'

'The one the man thinks can beat me.'

'I don't know his name.'

'But?'

'I believe he resides at Thorntonhall.'

'Where is that?'

'South Lanarkshire.'

'Where exactly?'

'He mentioned Park Drive.' Albert tipped his head. 'Anyway, in terms of survival, when presented with a catastrophe, some people come through it.'

Alexander brought his young blue eyes to his uncle's grey eyes. 'But?'

Albert could not detect any alcohol. 'Some people don't. They go under.'

Alexander was still enthusing. 'Why is that? Were they not good enough?'

Albert shook his senescent head. 'No, they were just as able, strong or brave.'

Alexander shrugged. 'But?'

Albert sighed. 'It happens in every upheaval. Some people survive, others don't.'

'Why is that?'

'They have other qualities. Survivors tend to call that quality 'gumption."

'Where does that come from?'

Albert chuckled. "Gone with the Wind."

'The film?'

'Yes, and the book.'

'So?'

'You will need that quality to survive.'

Alexander waggled his head assumptively. 'Yes. What will you do if the money runs out altogether?'

Albert shrugged his tired elderly hunched shoulders helplessly. 'The only thing I could do: sell up.'

Alexander smiled wistfully. 'I would help you.'

Albert shook his head with benignant defiance. He coughed meaningfully again before pronouncing. 'No, Alex, that money's yours.'

'It is?'

'Yes, yours and yours alone.'

'What d' you think I should do with it?'

'As you please.'

'You're sure.'

'Absolutely. My father, your grandfather, wanted you to have your father's share.'

'Why?'

'My father, your grandfather liked you very much.'

'Why?'

'You reminded him of his son.'

'In what way?'

'You are a very good person, Alex- just like his son was.'

'In what way was my father good?'

'He worked so very hard and was always kind to people. You're very much like him.'

Alexander's young petite azure eyes twinkled. 'In what way?'

'You see the person, the human being; you see the soul. You can also spot the localised drama. You see the good things, not the status. He would be proud of you.'

Alexander's deep blue eyes pricked with tears. He sniffed. 'He would?'

'Yes, for studying so hard, mugging up all the time, burning the candle at both ends; and for working when you didn't have to.'

Alexander shrugged. 'It's just a few grades, uncle.'

Albert waved his head. 'It's more than that. It was six, son. Six A's. And, no, it's more than that. You're clever. Exceptionally clever. And you apply yourself. Night and day. I- I just lounge in my Chieftain's indulging my pernicious vice. Either just that or I observe the ducks and the drakes in the old river pond and gorge on my confounded whiskey.'

Alexander smiled fairly. 'You deserve your whiskey, Uncle Albert.'

Uncle Albert's eyes smiled with diffident surprise. 'I do?'

'Yes.'

He gave his nephew a soft enquiring glance. 'But I thought

you despised alcohol, Alex. I thought you regarded it as the devil incarnate.'

'I- I mean I do.'

'So?'

'So perhaps my dad had been drinking that day and that's why he and mum went over the edge.'

Uncle Albert gulped. 'Yes, perhaps. You remember everything, don't you?'

'I think so.'

'What day is it today?'

'It's the anniversary of my parents' death.'

'How do you feel?'

'Ecstatic because of Martin.'

'That's good. How old am I Alex?'

'You're eighty-four.'

'I am?'

'Yes, don't you remember?'

'I- um...'

'Your birthday was last week.'

'It was?'

'Yes.'

'So it was, you're right. We had pheasant.'

'That's right. I bought eighty-four candles.'

'That's right, it went on fire.'

Alexander smiled complaisantly. 'Yes.'

'And you must be in your twenties now.'

'Just twenty.'

'And how old would your father have been today?'

'My father would have been seventy-seven.'

'What was his name?'

'Maxwell.'

'And your mother?'

'Camille.'

'And your old would your mother have been?'

'Sixty-seven.'

'And how old were you when they died?'

'Five.'

'And how old was I?'

'Sixty-eight.'

'How long have you lived with me?'

'Fifteen years.'

Albert smiled contentedly. 'Yes, you remember everything.'

Alexander shrugged. 'Only the things that matter.'

'So,' said Albert, 'the waters of the fall?'

'Yes.'

'Did you encounter Wren?'

'No, I just watched the river flow past.'

'And?'

'It provided the perfect setting.'

'For what?'

Alexander couldn't contain his felicity. 'Martin.'

Albert smiled fairly. 'You like him.'

Alexander shook his head. 'No, I love him.'

'Yes, go on.'

Alexander gazed in to the air. 'The waterfall was for a lucky person, someone who deserved it, for a different person, for someone who would meet someone.'

'And tonight you did.'

'Finally.'

Albert rattled his brain. 'I think I can go one better for you, Alex.'

'What d'you mean?'

'I think I can create an even luckier person.'

Alexander waved his head. 'It wouldn't be possible.'

'Why wouldn't it be possible?'

'I am as happy as I can be. I saw the light flicker, the sun fade, the waters shimmer and the moon rise. What did you see, uncle?'

'As I was reclining in my Chieftain's, I saw quite an engrossing documentary about squawking birds- on the new channel.'

'And what did you think of them?'

'I thought they worked mightily hard- just to cling onto life.'

Alexander smiled humanely. 'They deserved to live?'

'Yes, I think so. And you do, too, Alex. You're living tonight.' The lenitive Glenlivet whistled through Albert's spry but senescent sensibilities like a cool zephyr through a flailing clay and lubricated his now largely disregarded tongue. He coughed purposefully before saying, 'When your need for companionship has been structured by employment.'

'You have a way of speaking, Uncle.'

Albert winked. 'You have a way of learning.'

'So?'

'So, when the cravings for love and romantic affection; the concupiscence even; have deferred to the constrictions of a brutal company, it will provide not only merited opportunity for pneumatic fulfilment but insoluble equanimity.'

'You mean I have to get a job first before felicity will come my way.'

'No, felicity has already fallen upon you, and yes I promise it will grow higher, but it takes more to appreciate the felicity. And when you do, your heart will have the chance to sing. Then, it will sing. Like a storm-whipped brook. But for now-'

'For now?'

'You must relax. You must let your batteries recharge. You just let your mind unwind. You've worked hard this semester. So very hard. You've passed all your exams. Each and every single one of them. Not one A has passed you by. You have a knack for seventy plus percent. Even if they did change it to sixty five. Funny that! I've always thought of an 'A' as being seventy. They must have thought too much was being asked. And when you are ready, you will study again. You will learn all the things that will sustain you in later life. You have money now but one day it may go and you will need a profession.'

Alexander smiled kindly at his pleasantly and benignly drunk Uncle and said, 'Do you miss the business?'

Albert removed his small single-framed eyeglasses, which corrected his ailing vision, removed a small neatly folded handkerchief from his pocket, rubbed the lens and his eyes and said, 'No, not really. And it was never mine to miss.'

'But it was your father's.'

'Yes.'

'And you were a part of it.'

'Yes, Alex, a long time ago.'

'What was he like?'

'He was a very astute man.'

'Astute?'

'He knew everything about Mechanical Engineering. He knew how to transport a discerning family.'

'Yes?'

'He could raise more money than a sharp gangster could rob from a bank in one of his more gainful raids.'

Alexander slanted his head. 'How?'

'Why, through hard work, of course; through discipline. Through blood, sweat and tears. Through brains. But *me*- I'm just a fool. Just a tired drunken old fool, quite desipient.'

Alexander had often heard his uncle use the word. It was an obsolete word for foolish. He smiled gently and kindly. 'I don't think you are.'

'I worried today, Alex.'

CHAPTER TWENTY-THREE

To Err is Human

'Why are you worried, Uncle?'

'We had the installers in today. He said the heating would come on, but it didn't.'

'Alex, I'm really not sharp enough to follow this instruction manual. I just used to flick the switch and the boiler came on.'

'Let's have a look, uncle.'

Albert handed the instruction manual to his nephew.

'No worries, Uncle' said Alexander, 'I'll follow it for you.'

'You will?'

'Of course.'

'Let's go through to the kitchen.'

'Yes, okay.'

They moved through to the kitchen. Alexander picked up the manual that was lying on top of the kitchen surface.'

'The name uncle of the boiler is Salus.'

'I thought that was a dance.'

'I think you mean Salsa.'

'Yes, Alex, so I do.'

'So, controlling Salus involves a programmable thermostat with plug in RF boiler control.'

Albert palmed his head. 'Ah, that's our first clue.'

Alexander nodded enthusiastically. 'Yes, I think it is.'

'I think the model number could become important later.'

'In what sense?'

'In the legal sense.'

'If the boiler malfunctioned we couldn't sue.'

'Why not?'

'Under Scot's law, you can't sue for primary economic loss.'

'But?'

'But we could sue in delict, say if the boiler had been manufactured negligently and the boiler injured us.'

'So?'

'We should note the model number for future legal reference.'

'Okay, go on Alex.'

'The first thing we do is scan the manual: product compliance, safety information, what is a programmable room thermostat? ... an explanation for householders.'

'Yes, what is that?'

'You could get your money back if the machine was defective.'

'And?'

'I'm still scanning: introduction, integral RF boiler control, installation, powering up the ST6020 for the first time, Wall Mounting Guidelines, RF Transmission, Mounting the Black plate, Mounting the RF Integral Boiler Control to the boiler, RF Communication, Testing the ST620 RF communication, Additional Information, SERVICE and CONTROL functions, 3. USER CONTROLS, Integral RF Boiler Control, ST620 Overview, USER CONTROL FUNCTION SUMMARY ST620; 4 BASIC OPERATION; Reviewing the Set Temperature, Manual override, RF Boiler Control; 5 ADVANCED FUNCTIONS, Menu Screen Overview, ADVANCED FUNCTIONS IN DETAIL, PROGRAM FUNCTION, Changing the Default Time and Temperature Program, How to access the PROGRAM menu, HOLIDAY FUNCTION, Cancelling Holiday Override Mode, FROST (Protection) Function, SLEEP Function, TIME Function, Radio Controlled Clock, LANGUAGE Function; 6 Service Function, HEAT or COOL, CONTROL (PMW) Menu; 7. USEFUL INFORMATION, BATTERY STATUS, OFF MODE, BACKLIGHT, SLIDE SWITCH, RESET BUTTON, RF COMMUNICATION, ENERGY TIP, MAINTENANCE;

8. TECHNICAL SPECIFICATION, Clock, Programming, Temperature, Control, Memory Backup, Radio Frequency (RF) Settings; ST620WBC Warranty.'

'So?'

'This is going to take time.'

Albert smiled with embarrassment. 'No, Alex, I've just realised how desipient I've been.'

'What d'you mean, uncle?'

'I've taken the plug out.'

'Why?'

'I was putting on the washing machine.'

'So?'

'I'm pretty sure now the boiler does work. Try me, Alex, put that adapter back into the socket.'

'Very well.'

The lights came on immediately.

'Yes, I thought so,' said Albert.

Alexander blushed. 'I thought it was more complicated than that.'

'Yes, the radiators would require bleeding. There will be air blocks. I have my radiator key in the shed.'

'So?'

'It just shows that mistakes can be made, accidents can happen, that to err his human.'

'Yes.'

'It also shows that corrections are more straightforward than we thought.'

Uncle Albert glanced at him with no little appreciation. 'Thank you, Alex.'

Alexander bowed his head. 'You're welcome.'

Albert tilted his head. 'I miss Doris.' He scratched the back of his sparse hoary head. 'Anyway, she kept this old place going. And me, of course. She always kept me going.' He sighed with humble appreciation. 'Wonderful woman she was- a true gem. She was good in the kitchen, good in the garden and so especially good with people. But, then, you know all that already.'

Alexander sighed. 'Perhaps we will be happy one day.'

'Felicity has already betided you and it will get better. And when it does,

'No, felicity has already fallen upon you, and yes I promise it will grow higher, but your heart will have the chance to sing. Like a storm-whipped brook.'

Alexander smiled kindly at his pleasantly and benignly drunk Uncle and said, 'Do you miss the business?'

Albert removed his small single-framed eyeglasses, which corrected his ailing vision, removed a small neatly folded handkerchief from his pocket, rubbed the lens and his eyes and said, 'No, not really. And it was never mine to miss.'

'But it was your father's.'

'Yes.'

'And you were a part of it.'

'Yes, Alex, a long time ago.'

'What was he like?'

'He was a very astute man.'

'Astute?'

'Yes, like his own father.'

'Grandpa James?'

'Yes. Your father knew everything about Mechanical Engineering. He knew how to transport a discerning family.'

'Yes?'

'He knew how to make more than a sharp gangster could rob from a bank in one of his more gainful raids.'

Alexander slanted his head. 'How?'

'Why, through hard work, of course; through discipline. Through blood, sweat and tears. Through brains. But *me*- I'm just a fool. Just a tired drunken old fool, quite desipient.'

Alexander had often heard his uncle use the word. It was an obsolete word for foolish. He smiled gently and kindly. 'I don't think you are.'

Uncle Albert glanced at him with no little appreciation. 'Thank you, Alex.'

Alexander bowed his head. 'You're welcome.'

'And so?'

'And so I study Scot's law.'

'And?'

'It means that promises are honoured.'

'And what did you make of 'The Games?', son.'

Alexander squinted. '"*The Games*?"' he said.

'Yes, you know, 'The Commonwealth?"

Alexander gazed at his uncle quizzically. 'That was four years ago, Uncle.'

Albert peered. 'It was?'

'Yes, your birthday was last week.'

'And how do feel now about the referendum?'

'That was a long time ago.'

'So?.

'I still felt we wanted to become ourselves.'

'And?'

'I felt that something got in the way.'

'And what got in the way son?'

'I don't know.'

'But you did vote.'

'Yes, you remember don't you.'

'I- um...'

'We drove to the polling station.'

'We did?'

'Yes.'

'We made you pop that old bit of paper in the ballot box.'

'Not quite.'

'No?'

'No, I asked the man what I should do.'

'You didn't mind me cajoling you into voting.'

'No, I am Scottish, Uncle.'

'You are.'

'And how did you feel about the "no thanks".'

'I feel the people of Scotland must have felt more was out there for them, within the UK.'

Alexander felt a sudden pang of desperate straits. As his uncle made his way onto the first rung of the centuries-old narrow and winding stairwell, Alexander said, 'What if I fail the degree?'

Albert gave a thoughtful puzzled look; almost worried. 'You won't. You won't, son. You'll make sure that you don't. I'll make sure that you don't.'

'How?'

'Well, when the Christmas period is over, I'll take you back to your halls. I'll drive you there myself.' Albert scratched the back of his silver head self-doubtingly. 'But, then, you can already do that. I'll make sure you have your new books and fresh implements.'

Alexander smiled gently. 'Thank you, uncle.'

'You welcome, Alex.'

'What if my mind caves in? What if it heaves to all the pressure?'

'Then you call me. I'll pay your phone bill for now.'

'What if a question comes up that I can't answer?'

'Then you speak to your tutor. I'll speak to your tutor for you. I don't mind.'

'And say what?'

'That you have a mental issue; an intellectual point. One that needs answering.'

Alexander quivered. 'I feel under pressure.'

'I think that's normal. But it would take a catastrophe, the very bursting of our river's banks, to stand anywhere near between you and your qualification.'

'And then what do I do?'

'You'll cross that bridge when you come to it.'

'You're very kind uncle.'

'You think so?'

'Oh, yes.'

'I'm so very glad you like me- not everyone does.'

'Who doesn't like you?'

'Just someone.'

'Which someone?'

'Someone who doesn't even like their up-and-coming daughter in law.'

'Who is she?'

'Jane I believe.'

'No, idea.'

'Good night, uncle!'

'Good night, nephew! Oh, and Alex?'

Alexander's eyes widened slightly with surprise. 'Yes?'

'I know you took something.'

'What makes you say that?'

'You've never been quite as open as you have been tonight. Now, I don't know what it was, but drugs can be dangerous.'

'It was involuntary.'

Albert nodded. 'In that case your legal credibility is still there.'

Alexander's strong caffeine-winged dreams came flying: thoughts, images and sensations re-contextualising and re-interpreting every twist and turn within the stretched, zigzag and undulating country roads of his convoluted heart. He dreamed of his mum and dad, of Uncle Albert, of late Aunt Doris, of long-gone Jenny, of someone still to be met...

I mobiled Chase.

'*Ewok*!'

'I used the laser microphone.'

'Good.'

'Where did you aim it?'

'At the front door. The hallway.'

'And?'

'I have heard the conversation between the nephew and his uncle.'

'Who is he?'

'Albert.'

'And?'

'He is very complaisant, although he imbibes copiously.'

'So?'

'That would explain the delirious singing we heard when we arrived.'

'What else?'

'He knows of my father.'

'Who?'

'Ealdahach Wren.'

'Did you know his father?'

'I remember my father spoke of him.'

'Who is he?'

'He was James Bennet.'

'Who?'

'A uniquely successful Business Services entrepreneur.'

'What else?'

'The uncle's been losing a lot of money.'

'How?'

'I don't know.'

'Anything else?'

'The uncle's wife died.'

'Who?'

'Doris.'

'How?'

'I don't know.'

'I see. Tomorrow you are to visit the talented son of the disgruntled client.'

'Why?'

'I want to know if he might have killed my brother and his wife.'

I sighed with exasperation. 'Yes, Chase.'

'Anything else?'

'It is the anniversary of the nephew's parent's death.'

'So?'

'I'm glad my son made him happy, even if it was immorally.'

Martin, Lilly and I abandoned the freezing deluge, jumped into the car and drove home.

CHAPTER TWENTY-FOUR

Day Two; 7: 15 am; Glasgow, Throntonhall; Son of Suburbia

There was another ferocious bang. I wakened instantaneously. After the last time when the mobile went buzz buzz, this time it sat on the bedroom carpet, neglected and alone, with a soft muted '**vzzzzzt**.'

'*Ewok*!'

'Chase.'

'You will look into the son.'

I daubed my fuggy eyes. 'Yes, how did you wake me up this time.'

'I shot your daughter's bedroom window.'

Andrea wriggled on the mattress. 'What was that, Ewald?'

'Nothing, dear. Stay sleeping. I gaped. 'Why?'

'Your master bedroom window is still in pieces. You really have to fix it.'

I glazed with infuriation. 'Yes, I may just possibly have to check on her first.'

'So Ewok, the son of my brother's disgruntled client.'

'Yes, immediately on to it.'

'Good. We have more to uncover.'

I sat once again at the breakfast table.

'Why did my window shatter, dad?' said Lilly.

'I suspect the hinges have being playing up.'

'But there's glass all over my bedroom.'

'Yes, we'll tidy it up at some point.'

'I have blood all over my soles, dad.'

I nodded frantically. 'Yes, I know. You need elastoplast.'

'I need bandages.'

'Yes, I'll get them.'

I drove from my house in Newton Mearns to Thorntonhall. I pulled up outside the house. This was the house of the son of the disgruntled client, the second suspect.

I had learned that he had a son and had an address. It was Park Drive in Thornton hall. I knew Bearsden, Milingavie, Newton Mearns, and Giffnock to be the most affluent areas in Glasgow. I also knew Park Drive to be the most affluent street in Glasgow. This made sense since the associate was richer than the mansioned uncle. Accordingly, having driven all the way to the ancient mansion in the Aberdeenshire countryside, I had driven back to the relevant drive. I felt comparatively dowdy in my Mercedes. I parked it round the corner to avoid attention. I ambled to the front gates. I gave the house a *coup d'oeil.* It had a bravura, which would have been residual given the father's housing potential. The flair was thus adulterated. It had artistic skill. But it had been thinned out.

There were factors which mitigated in favour of its decency. I considered that there were sturdy basic units of hereditary, finer specific sequences of DNA or RNA that had occupied fixed position loci on stronger chromosomes. I had no idea what the father did, if he was still alive, and if he had been blackmailing the nephew's uncle.

A young man stood in the garden. I would have put him in his late twenties. He was tall, dark and handsome, with a strong jaw and broad shoulders. There was another man in the garden.

'What's this, Ben?' the man said.

I could tell he was one of the chronically inebriated and

jealous. He was making a crapulent lurch toward the pillar-box in the morning as Ben picked up his milk, '*Another* modification?'

Ben was one of those peculiar characters who was forever 'doing things'; getting people in. He was compulsive about it, obsessive, almost neurotic. Tradesmen of all denominations: plumbers, electricians, builders- landscape gardeners even. It was a desperate- forlorn really- essay to claw back some ground on his father's much sought-after opulence. He was carrying his smart phone and looking around for independent electrical contractors. Scottish Hydro had inspected the electrics and failed them. There was no earth in the house. This meant that if the electrics defaulted the pipes could go live and deliver an electric shock; that is if the pipes were touched or if a light switch was pressed. Alternatively, if an engineer was working on the boiler and someone flicked one of the switches, the engineer could be electrocuted. He keyed the words Electricians and Electrical Contractors in Glasgow.

The building was to its credit endowed with an early-blooming garden: a drastically over-planted area of ground; a plot of ground where plants such as fruits and vegetables were grown and flowers ran wild like the wind. Wild like his music. The garden had decent distance end to end if hardly prodigious: it was verdant and tumbling and periodically maintained by a reasonably competent but more essentially cost efficient horticulturist named Jim. Ben's design criteria were rigorous to the point of being unachievable. 'But Mr Sharp!' Jim had once protested, 'If we install any more plants, we're going to have a problem with elephants.' Ben had spangled his ferret-eyes, turned up his straight Grecian nose, pouted his full lips and said, 'No elephant is bigger than my family.' The garden also contained a vibrant fish-pond, once covered with a net in case the young child should take a freak and horrifying tumble. A serpentine chipped driveway, relayed every few years, when the big cheques came in. A roofed pillared portico. And well-proportioned walls. Skilful, elegant, but still a far cry from his father's stunning secluded north-west of Scotland mansion.

From the interior, however, things were more anarchic than ever. Fiancée and father, Ben, had shown no respect for the established laws of music. Not for the first time. He showed vehement antipathy towards the influence, the control, the manipulation, the oppression almost. He had had far too much of it as a child. *I must forgive mother*! he would think. *Relent*! These blasted laws had once been scrupulously and exasperatingly taught by her. By Agatha as she was called. She had been a very accomplished concert pianist, of all professionals. They had also been taught by his father. He was still around. Was that a blessing or a trial? He had been a conductor, marking time and signalling. And also a composer and a performer. Quite the finished article. The insufferable waywardness had resulted in a musical composition which was haplessly simplistic, insipid and intractable. Simply not sterling enough to pique the curiosity of the gigantic publishing companies which dealt *inter alia* in the sale and distribution of great classical music.

Fiancé and mother, Jane, had also shown no respect for established rules of cooking. Not that she knew any. *Do I know some*? she would have thought with a tumble-dryer for a head. *I surely know some*. Her own mother could knit, darn and sew but strangely she couldn't cook. Nobody's mother was perfect. Ben's certainly wasn't. Jane had burned water again. She had turned the six class-A free range eggs into pebbles and the crinkle-cut chips into pastels.

And eight-year old daughter, Anne, had derogated from authority. Particularly her dad. She obstinately refused to tidy her room despite requests *ad nauseam*. Moreover, they were in the throes of de-energization; in the middle of a deeply disordering power cut.

Suddenly, a natural electrical discharge of very short duration and high voltage between a cloud and the ground occurred, accompanied by a bright flash. It lit up Ben's face like Blackpool in a period of illuminations. His dark brown incandescent eyes and big white ghoulish grin. In the polished metal of the large specially engraved placard screwed into the fascia of the piano, which bore the family name. And then came a loud crashing noise, which echoed the stentorian thunder in his mind, due to the expansion of rapidly heated air.

Where the freak is it? he thought. He bayed like a Tasmanian wolf in the maddening darkness. He jumped out of the piano stool and clumped like a ravenous carnivorous Mesozoic creature towards the mirror, in an attempt to admire his fine figure of fury. All he could see were the faint lineaments of a warped and livid countenance. In a funk of a darker blue than the most sunless evening Clyde, he powerfully drove a clenched fist straight into the glass, which cracked instantly. He cackled as he twisted his knuckles and his peepers and glared at the leaking blood. He ripped the mirror from the catches and hurled it onto the cold hard floorboards, which sent shards of broken glass sailing into the far flung corners of the room. He pounced onto the mirror and heard a satisfying crackling noise beneath the balls of his feet.

Ann, who was cowering like a new born kitten, and with piggy eyes peeked at her father from behind the living room door, rubbed her thin lips, her level of self-esteem ever present and her anxiety mounting. 'Mum! Mum!', she cried, before fleeing through the shadowy hallway into the cooling kitchen. 'Father's losing it again!'

Jane simpered like a toothless tigress, her plump lips as always misrepresenting her physical self-esteem and her exasperation. 'Oh, dear!' she said. 'Just wait here, Ann.' Jane dashed from the kitchen to the living room.

'*Ben*?' said Jane.

'*Where the hell is it*?' said Ben.

'Where is what, dearest?' said Jane.

'The old score.'

Jane gawked. 'The what, my darling?'

'The music sheet.'

Jane squinted. 'The music sheet?'

'The piece my mother and I wrote.'

'Oh, that- yes, what was it called again?'

"If only'.'

'Yes, I remember.'

'You do?'

'Yes, you sang it to me when you proposed.'

'I did?'

'Yes.'

'When was that?'

'It was years ago, honey.'

'How many?'

'Fifteen.'

'Fifteen?'

'Yes, we were sixteen.'

Ben's hands were akimbo as he was panting. 'So?'

'I don't know, my sugar cube, maybe we lost it when we moved.'

Ben stomped his feet. 'What!'

'Please don't raise your voice, sweetness, Ann's in the kitchen.'

'And?'

'She's only twelve.'

'So?'

'So it's probably somewhere in the house.'

Ben glowered. 'Did you throw it out?'

'No, of course I wouldn't.'

'No?'

'I keep all your music.'

'You do?'

'I always have.'

'Where is it then?'

Jane scratched her head. 'I have to think, Ben. Are you that sure you need it right now?'

'Yes.'

'Why?'

'It's my best chance.'

'Best chance of what?'

'Best chance of escaping it.'

'Escaping it?'

'Yes.'

'What?'

'Obscurity.'

'Why?'

'It's the best song I have.'

Jane wiggled her head. 'Are you missing your mother, dearest?'

'A bit.'

'I'm sure she's looking down on you.'

'She always did.'

'I think you deserve a lie down, honey.'

'You didn't give it to her?'

'You know I never knew your mother, sweetheart.'

'No, I mean "her"'

'I'm not following you, my darling.'

'The girl you never talk about.'

'I'm not sure what you mean.'

'You said you were very close.'

'When?'

'When I first met you.'

'Yes, honey. So?'

'You said she understood you in a way I could never understand you.'

'I don't remember my gorgeous.'

'I do though. You picked mushrooms together, right?'

'I have never even tried mushroom soup.'

'No?'

'No. Anyway, that's the girls for you.'

'Girls?'

'Yes, we're different.'

'But she sounded very important to you.'

'She might have been once.'

'Would I have been good enough for her?'

'Yes, I think so my love.'

'So?'

'So, she's gone.'

'When?'

'When what?'

'When was she gone?'

'I don't know, twenty-two ago.'

'You were nine.'

'Yes.'

'There's something you're not telling me. There's something you've always not told me.'

'She was put under a lot of pressure, dearest.'

'What pressure?'

'The sort of pressure you're under now.'

'Where is she?'

'She writes now, Ben, I gather, I don't know.'

'How do you know she writes?'

'I read her latest novel.'

'What novel?'

"*Shadows of Flames*."

'What was it about?'

'It was about living up to your childhood mistake.'

'She's sounds wet.'

'She's pretty strong, dear.'

'So?'

'So she's moved on.'

'But you think I should be doing better for you.'

'No, my love. You've done more than enough.'

'Why have you always been reticent about her.'

'I know honey, you feel threatened.'

'Was she beautiful?'

'I believe she could have been.'

'How?'

'Under different circumstances.'

'Why wasn't she?'

'She was disfigured, my sweetness.'

'Where is she now?'

'According to her book, she lives in the east side of Glasgow.'

'Where exactly?'

'Keppochhill.'

'Which is?'

'A very deprived area of Glasgow.'

'Where?'

'I don't know. You put me in Thornton hill, I think she was put in the third most poor area in the country.'

'After what?'

'Ferguslie.'

'Where is that?'

'Paisley.'

'I see.'

'A very poor area.'

'Well, not Thorntanhall drive, honey.'

'No. You know my father was disgraced, Jane.'

Jane smiled painfully. 'Yes, I remember.'

'You know that his lawyer made a botch of his case?'

Jane sighed. 'A bit like my mother's.'

Ben shook his head. 'That was completely different, Jane. My father paid his lawyer and your mother was also paid by my father.'

Jane gulped. 'I think she deserved a trifle more, sweetheart.'

'You realise I could have shot him that day.'

Jane gawped. 'Who?'

'My father's lawyer.'

'How?'

'With my father's cane gun.'

'But of course you wouldn't have done that.'

'Well, no.'

'There you go then.'

'My father said: "My son is beneath the age of criminal responsibility. He could do legally what I would have to do furtively."'

'I know you're both innocent, honey.'

Ben brushed Jane aside and raced into the lounge. He hefted up the shattered mirror from the floorboards and launched it like a NASA space shuttle against one of the living room windows. It made a short, high-pitched and slightly ringing sound as it clinked. He stomped out of the lounge, along the hallway and up the stairs. He de-predated the medium-sized suburban house, turned it upside down, like a rabid dog looking for an old bone in a pitch-black garden. He had the infernal writer's block again and his publisher was going spare. 'One more week, Sharp,' his publisher had said, 'Or the deal's off.'

Where was his frigging juvenilia? Those unripe but at least distinctive works produced in his tortured youth before a mature style had developed, which would hopefully breathe some much needed fire into his stagnating imagination? It was nigh impossible to compose utterly bewitching power ballads, his music of choice, when a fiancé, an eight year old daughter, and an exorbitant mortgage were involved. Things which only nailed you like once dearly beloved Christ to a cross and stultified your desperate creative enterprise.

He tried every single room, both upstairs and down, every conceivable storage space; every cubbyhole. Finally, he checked the hall cupboard. He came across an assault course of obstacles. It was a stack of mangled cardboard and a sea of coats and blazers underneath which he found an old box, which was secured with masking tape. He strenuously prized it open with his bare teeth. As he poked through it, he stared with eyes wide open, in astonishment at the score: worn and dog eared and well thumbed. How many years had it been since he had last clasped eyes on it? *Ten*? *Twenty*? It was the very special written copy of a musical composition which his mother and he had created together, all those years ago. He had completely forgotten that it even existed. He took it into the living room.

He placed it slowly, hesitantly and carefully onto the stand. He looked fixedly and engaged his fingers.

Being so ear-minded, Ben meticulously played the old score in the intensifying shade of the living room and something mysterious happened: all his key existential issues crystallised within his anguished mind and his ordinarily anaesthetized body experienced an unusual range of heightened emotions. He felt at once the extreme coldness of his tumultuous childhood. He felt the dejecting vast emptiness of the big old house. He felt the infinite impenetrable darkness of the ancient cellar. He felt the poignant sonority of the old Fazioli. He felt the white-knuckle ambivalence of his most primitive prepubescent sexual orientation. He felt the immensely disabling harrowing guilt of not really loving Jane in the way she so patently loved him. He felt the terrible insurmountable distance between him and his only child Ann. He felt the absolutely unmanageable pressure heaped on him by his cold unappeasable father. He felt the back-breaking load of his crucifying publisher's demands. He felt the grave dissatisfaction with his musical career. He felt the severe anxiety at not being able to create. He felt the paralysing fear of performing publicly. He felt the profound madness of inescapable ontological status. He felt the bitter loss of a once deep-seated and life-affirming Christian faith. But he felt most of all the indecipherable and overwhelming guilt surrounding his mother's death, all those years ago.

As he reached the pounding chest of the grand old piece, he could see blurry smoky pictures of the bitter, deeply held and lost lasting resentment in his mother's huge dark eyes. He could hear the muffled reverberations of pitched voices from a long ago childhood. He could perceive the faint odour of a reeking hysteria as his mother's life slowly ebbed away. He could taste the bitter tears of an irreconcilable loss. He only wished he could feel once more the irrepressible aftershocks of harsh beatings.

In the evocative closing moments, he remembered that it all had something to do with self-preservation. Vital self-preservation. And to do with revenge. Gut-wrenching revenge. And then it had something to do with the most devastating remorse. How strange that a single piece of music could play a thousand words!

When finally he had finished the ancient piece, he breathed laboriously. *Oh, mother*! he thought. *Dearest mother*! *What on earth became of us*? *Were we not once among the truly awesome*? A helpless tear streamed down his ruddy swarthy cheek. He hammered a giant cacophonous chord. *Clash*.

I have to go back, he thought.

I rang Chase.

'*Ewok*!'

'I drove to the son's house.'

'Did you use the laser microphone?'

'I did, yes.'

'Who is he, then?'

'Ben.'

'And?'

'He has a violent temper.'

'In what way?'

'He lost something.'

'What did he lose?'

'A sheet of music.'

'And?'

'He felt deprived.'

'Why?'

'It belonged to him and his mother.'

'And?'

'He lost his mother?'

'Who?'

'Agatha.'

'How?'

'I don't know. He suspected his fiancée of throwing it away.'

'Who is his fiancée?'

'Jane.'

'Why would she have given it away?'

'No reason. She declared that she didn't.'

'Who might she have given it away to?'

'A friend?'

'Who?'

'I don't know, a female friend.'

'And?'

'The son was jealous of her.'

'Why would he be jealous of her?'

'I'm not sure.'

'Anything else?'

'He has a daughter.'

'Who is she?'

'Ann.'

'How old is she?'

'She's twelve.'

'Did he or his partner mention any other children?'

'No.'

'But they are a family.'

'Yes, it would sound so.'

'What about the girlfriend?'

'The partner mentioned the town and the street.'

'What was the town?'

'Keppochhill?'

'And the street?'

'Where is that?'

'Glasgow.'

'Who is she?'

'I don't know.'

'The son never said?'

'No, nor his partner.'

'But?'

'He would have been seven years old, making it highly unlikely.'

'You will check out the friend. And you will bring your married son with children to check out the family.'

CHAPTER TWENTY-FIVE

Day Three; 7 am; The Niece's Viper Nest

The almighty bang was becoming customary. The mobile was on the bedside table, bucking and clacking around, kicking my keys about. RATTA TATTA TATTA TATTA...

'*Ewok*!'

I gasped. 'Chase. Which window did you use this time?'

'One of the spare bedroom's.'

'I see. So I've to investigate the friend.'

'My niece. Exactly. Well done.'

I stifled a cough. 'What if she's guilty?'

'My innocent nephew Nicholas would obviously take precedence.'

'How is your nephew?'

'One moment. Do you wish to speak to Ewok, Nicholas?'

I smiled with exhaustion. I was perceiving a side to Chase I could appreciate.

A very young voice seemed to evaluate. 'Has he worked it out yet?'

I prodded. 'I'm getting there,' I said.

'Ewok's getting there, Nicholas. He's a bit slow.'

'Did the bullet reach him?' said Nicholas.

'Not exactly, but it's getting closer.'

I was at the breakfast table again. I scratched my head. My daughter Lilly had watched the nephew, my son Martin had seduced the nephew, I had listened in on the conversation with the nephew and his uncle. I had listened in on the talented son of the disgruntled client. I was now to listen in on the friend.

I drove to Keppochhill. I knew Ferguslie in Paisley to be the most deprived area in Glasgow, Possil the second and Keppochhill to be the third. As I had felt my Mercedes to be too shabby to be in Thorntonhall, conversely I found it too risky to be in Keppochhill. I parked the vehicle some distance away from the house.

Richie did not so much as snore as snuffle. He sprawled about the ramshackle Murphy bed. He was parallel to a small child with attention deficit hyperactivity disorder. He was unable to concentrate on anything. The only things that emanated from him were instinctive, unsophisticated and unsavoury deportments.

These were lewd and libidinous postures, grunting, blaspheming and belling. He was comatose and semi-conscious.

The bed was permanently unfolded. It had a broken frame, barely supported a raggedy mattress that had no sheet on it, was covered by a mangy duvet with no cover. He clutched a pillow with no slip to the side of his head.

Susie had long given up making up his bed for him. Richie always found a drunken way to muddle it up in a flash.

As he sniffed, he thought about the feeling he was perceiving. It was intense, it was as though he was making his own music, but it was not quite poppers. No, poppers were brain-sapping lethal but ineffable things. He had learned *a posteriori*; that is to say, deriving knowledge from experience: reasoning from observed facts or events back to their causes. A sniff didn't last long, tens of seconds at most, but they transported you into a world of delight, had you in seventh heaven, on cloud nine. He believed he had tried or at least been given poppers at least once. It was eight years ago. He had been twenty-one, studying German Law at the Johannes Gutenberg Universitat. He had been on a tram at the time. He had left Munsterplatz to Schillerplatz in Mainz in south-west Germany to another. A lad with a woman's good looks had met his glance, had gazed at him, beamed and winked. He had perceived an overwhelming feeling of euphoria. It had actually made him fall in love with him. This was weird since he was brutally heterosexual. He had never thought about a man or a boy in that way, not even once. It had vexed him for years. Why had he felt like that? How old had he been? Seventeen? Eighteen?

But it wasn't just twelve dozen red roses either. That was a pleasant smell but not really a euphoric sensation. He had bought Susie twelve dozen red roses before when he had asked her to marry him. They were in the Panda House.

'I guess all I need now is a rose bowl,' she had said.

'Already thought of it,' he had said.

He handed her a long empty tub of cheese and chive-flavoured Pringles.

Susie had sighed. 'Or at least a bud vase.'

Richie had smirked. 'Bud comes in bottles, cans even, not vases.'

Susie had smiled patiently.

No, the sensation he perceived was unfortunately not poppers, although faint memories of the *ad hominem* experience were there. That was what happened when you drank yourself silly on a beautiful woman. Cider was the poor man's heroine.

He sniffed like a man with more than a cold to contend with. He sniffed like a person with more than pneumonia for discomfort. He sniffed to clear the unsolicited blockages in his nasal passages. People who drank copious amounts of alcohol had a lot to irrigate; they had to snivel away the wet acrid tears.

He turned his mind to the Alpha and Omega; the staples of life.

He snorted. 'Shadows of flames?' *Bah*! It was something Susie had been working on; a story or something; a novella or something; something big and important; something that would catapult her- him- them to a higher level of social standing.

Whatever it was, it wasn't quite a novel. It wasn't long enough. Apparently a novel was a good thing; a better thing. Could he have penned one himself? He supposed not. No, nothing would have been good enough and once the guilt had gone the befuddlement would set in; plus, he had his legal career to develop.

Ritchie hadn't been sure of the integrity or even value of these stories. He had plenty of his own to tell. He could have painted quite a picture of misery.

As it had actually turned out it had been a parable Susie had scribed. She had spent weeks on end on it. It had meant a lot to her. She had barely looked up from her notepad. She had taken the time to explain it to Richie one evening; the difference between a short story, a novella, a fable and a parable. She had said that a fable was a very important thing. It was a story that taught a lesson. It was a short story with a moral, especially one in which the characters are animals. Ritchie used to like animals. They had a vulnerable quality which made them endearing. Susie was an ailurophile, a cat lover: somebody who loves cats. She doted on Shnoogles. Shnoogles was their cat. She was a domesticated cat but she was also Richie thought a witch's cat.

He called them Catty-pusses. That was his special name for our feline friends. She had explained that a parable was a moral or religious story. It was short simple story intended to illustrate a moral or religious lesson.

'Shadows of Flames' was not so much an oxymoron; that was to say, it was not so much an expression with contradictory words: a phrase in which two words of contradictory meaning are used together for special effect, e.g. "wise fool" or "legal murder", or even a contradiction in terms, as it was undiagnosed schizophrenia. It was the auto-da-fe that followed gross wrongdoing. Richie had been completely in the dark about his condition.

It was a bit like the chicken and the egg. Susie respected chickens. She respected them because they had nervous systems. Richie thought they were stupid, ugly and delicious. Susie felt it was unforgivably cruel to keep them locked up in tiny cages where they couldn't move. She felt it was an affront to animal rights. She felt that even organic hens had a rough deal. And she had absolutely nothing to do with their eggs. She felt that human beings had no right to deprive them of them even if they were unfertilized. She wouldn't let him eat eggs even though he adored them.

Which anteceded the other? Was it the shadows or the flames? Did the shadows cause the flames? Or did the flames cause the shadows? And what did they mean together? What had Susie meant when she wrote her parable? What were the shadows? Were the shadows his chronic alcoholism or her chain-smoking and their mutual autonomous consumption? Were the flames the crapulence and the penury?

Richie snuffled. He wheezed while he snored. An empty bottle of frosty jack lay abandoned in the corner. An air of staleness enveloped the room.

Susie roused. His breath smelled of a distillery. She grimaced. His thoughts were abandoned. His images were grotesque. His sensations were painful. They fulminated like ammonium nitrate inside Richie's utterly befuddled mind- that very rapidly disintegrating element of him that scarcely enabled him to be aware of his idiosyncratically chaotic world and his incalculably turbulent experiences- as he slept fitfully toward that preordained frenzied state of complete and drawn out bodily paralysis.

First, he thought: *You're carrying this animal rights thing far too far*! *Does that pugnacious wee bloodsucker really have to be on top of the world*? Evidently so; for Shnooglepuss (the cat or rather the critter) was clinging tightly on top of a mini-representation of the earth, which was twirling so rapidly that it made his blood-shot eyes and thumping skull do numerous circuits. Suddenly, the globe halted! Her huge gimlet eyes glinted with fury in the firelight. She engaged her razor-sharp fangs and claws and ripped the world to shreds. His eyes popped like a bayoneted bouncy castle.

Secondly, he thought: *The law is an ass*! *The Law Society of Scotland* and *The Scottish Legal Aid Board* crumpled like the *Twin Towers* as they were struck by massive jet-engines. He smelt the reeking hysteria of old Jan Macalister, the former *Legal Education and Training Manager*, and the hypothetically untouchable President of *the Board*, who were among his fiercest enemies, as they powerlessly evacuated the souvenir buildings.

Thirdly, he thought: *That pig-headed toffee-nosed bank manager is causing the infernal credit crunch by setting up a bank within a bank*! Sparks flew as forgotten millions zipped through wafer-thin wires. He could perceive the ear-splitting sounds of his own despairing implorations to have his paltry overdraft limit even infinitesimally increased.

Fourthly, he thought: *I'm the single most powerful man in the world*! George Bush, Gordon Brown and the rest of the 'oh-so-great' world leaders were genuflecting humbly. He could taste the greatest landslide victory in the ultimate popularity contest.

Fifthly, he thought: *Susie. Spill the beans about those scars*! *About your mother*! *About that Judas Tam!* Susie's belly was heavily engorged, Tam was grinning from ear to ear and a hideous apparition of Susie's dead mother was waggling savagely in the background. As he tried to push past them to get to Susie, he inadvertently ripped her delicate facial skin to the smallest of ribbons.

It was time for the ultimate datum, as later in the daisy chain things bounced from the abandoned to the unsmiling.

A cut-in. A fade-in. Ever so ear-grabbing. The first movement: *The Moonlight Sonata...*

The world went dark. A misty green garden. Flecked with steamy corollas.

A little pair of ghostly figures. One with a shock of foggy yellow. Muted singing. Stiff dancing.

Soft Laughter. Sardonic. Infiltrating the smoky air.

The air. Smelling of electricity.

Their ice-poles. Tasting of burning flesh.

Augmented singing. Looser dancing.

Inside. A clock ticking. Muffled screeches.

Outside. Louder singing. Now abandoned dancing. Time standing still...

Inside again. The clock *stopping.*

Then... Outside again...

Stopping too. The singing and the dancing.

Now... Pandemonium! Scuttling!

Then inside once again. *With the figures.* A new image: stomach-churning! *Through the sand with lime and soda!* Tears.

Then...

Primal screaming...

After the dreaded sleep paralysis was over, Richie roused with an almighty bang. He wheezed like a worn-out donkey as he mopped his clammy brow. He unlocked his bone-dry mouth and tasted raw meat. It certainly wasn't steak. It wasn't fillet, it wasn't sirloin, it wasn't rib-eye, it wasn't rump, and it wasn't even frying steak.

He peered through the dimness at the empty crumpled bottle of cider on the floor. He massaged his throbbing head. He climbed out of bed and lurched toward the bathroom.

Susie, who slept in the other bedroom, intercepted him in the hallway. Her nose was more concave than ever; upturned. It was characterised by a curve which depressed in the middle with a protruding tip, its inward arching caused by an overly bulky and bulbous tip. It was often a problem associated with Caucasian people. As it snouted, it revealed both her capacity to turn her nose up at other people but also her vulnerability to suppression. Her singing voice rose a trifle sarcastically, and she twisted her full lips which provoked so much resentment in relation to another aspect of her appearance and which declared her superiority over her husband, as she said, '*Another one*, my darling?'

Richie's sealed his blue deep set eyes, sniffed in his pug nose, and bowed his head, tightening his thin lips which had never justified his wife and gave away his mood of inadequacy, and said, 'Yep.'

'That's the third one this week. It must be getting to you.'

'What?'

'My mother's disappearance for starters.'

'What disappearance?'

'Exactly. You know she did things to me. You know he did

things to her. You know you did things to it. You know he's even better than you.'

'We all need taught lessons, my sweetness. If nothing in the exemplary manner of your father, you are the very image of your mother.'

Susie glared at her husband sarcastically. 'You mean I don't look like him. You mean I don't act like him. You mean I am her.'

'She,' my sweetness. 'As we know, we mean more when we say less.'

'Something's wrong, dearest. The old Frosty Jack's playing with your mind.'

'So?'

'I imagine my old friend would be more present than you.'

'Who was she?'

'I imagine she was someone who met a man even more suitable.'

'Compete with her, do you?'

'I imagine I already lost.'

'There you go, then.'

'So I've taken action.'

'What action?'

'I decided to do something with my writing.'

'What is your writing?'

'I emailed someone.'

'That daft machine that delivers nothing- that puts us out of business.'

'Indeed.'

'And?'

'They got back to me.'

'Who?'

'A publishing company.'

Ritchie goggled with disbelief. 'What?'

'A company that will help my book to work.'

'How?'

'I spoke to a senior publishing consultant.'

'And?'

'They enable you to gain access to a professional team.'

'What?'

'Professional, darling.'

'You mean fuss-pots?'

'No, not quite.'

'Who? Snobs? You write unequivocal pish, sweetness.'

'No,' said Susie, 'they turn an unripe manuscript into a professionally created title.'

Richie glared doubtingly. 'And?'

'My novel has passed content evaluation.'

'You mean they tolerated your incurable verbal diarrhoea. You must get that sorted out.'

Susie shook her head. 'No, Richie. It means my writing was good enough.'

Richie snorted. 'How can logorrhoea be good enough?'

'I know the word as well, Richie.'

'Only because I told you. What else?'

'I received an ISBN.'

'Is the queen involved?'

Susie wiggled her head. ''No, does she need to be?'

'If it's an official honour.'

'It's not an honour, Richie, it's more to do with access.'

'I do law.'

'Yes, sweetheart, I know.'

'Have you agreed to anything?'

'No, not as such, but I seem to be learning from you, darling. Apparently, now, this is the best time to go forward.'

'Why?'

'It's an opportunity.'

'Are you sure?'

'We can be more innovative and competitive.'

'You must achieve the best position.'

'I thought so, darling.'

'What next?'

'There are forms of publication and financial potential.'

'Yes?'

'With their skill they could even find me on-line.'

'And?'

'They could make my book known by everyone.'

'And?'

'They could even make my work better as to the type.'

'And?'

'They can even make my book popular.'

'How much does it cost?'

'A fraction of the cost of your liver, darling.'

'And how much in terms of those lungs, my sweetness?'

'It would cost more than your Frosty Jack, Richie.'

'More than your Pall Mall cigarettes.'

'Possibly.'

'Definitely.'

'What do they do?'

'They offer publishing services.'

'Such as?'

'I could have a big book, you know the one with the solid edges. You're just like my mother.'

'In what way?'

'You're very abusive.'

'Your mother was right, you require too much attention.'

'My father was right, you both needed rejected.'

Suddenly, Susie moaned. 'Oh, no,' she said.

'What's the matter?' said Richie.

'I feel deeply unwell.'

Ritchie grimaced. 'That makes two of us.'

'No, Ritchie,' she said, 'it's more than that.'

'What?'

'My brain is starving.'

'You need to eat. There's some bread in the kitchen.'

'No, it's more than that.'

'You need to go to sleep.'

'Someone's done this, Richie.'

'It wasn't me.'

Susie dizzied. 'Yes, I'm sure it wasn't.'

'What's happening?'

'My brain's suffocating.'

'It's probably those fags.'

'Yes, but I've always smoked.'

'Maybe you've smoked too much.'

'No, I'm no where near that stage.'

'Then, it's a bad packet.'

'You don't smoke, Ritchie.'

'No, but I can observe.'

'You think it's the cigarettes.'

'I know it is.'

'Who would have done this?'

'The company.'

'No, it's more than that.'

'Unless you think someone gave you a bad packet.'

'Yes, that seems likely.'

'In which case you'll have to stop.'

'I'll have to go to bed.'

'See you in the morning, then.'

'I'm not sure I'll make morning.'

'D' you want me to get someone?'

'My cousin.'

'Why?'

'He's capable of it.'

'It's far too late for that, Sooze.'

Susie mustered all the strength she could. 'Yes- yes it is.'

Susie collapsed to the ground. Richie gaped. His brain was swirling. He smiled pigeon-heartedly and proceeded to the bathroom. He stubbed his right big-toe on the door jamb and yelped. He stumbled forward and banged his scabby elbow on the steel towel rail, then cracked his fragile skull against the rigid wall.

He steadied himself. He squinted awkwardly at the splintered pint-sized mirror. His face was *eau de Nil.* He squeezed his bulging neck and dabbed his thinning scalp. He sighed. He turned the freezing cold tap on and vigorously scooped handfuls of clean water into his parched maw. He moistened his desquamated facial skin. As he peed into the toilet bowl, he suffered mild dsyaria and droplets of urine sprinkled onto his bare legs.

Life is like a dream, he thought. *A bad one.* He muttered expletives.

Richie aimed for Susie's mobile in her bedroom. Before he could dial 999, he crashed out and ricocheted off the nightmares...

I mobiled Chase.

'*Ewok*!'

'I have listened to your niece.'

'Did you use the laser microphone?'

'Yes.'

'And?'

'She has a husband.'

'Who?'

'Richie.'

'And?'

'She is very hard on him. She is also very sarcastic towards him.'

'Why?'

'She seems to consider him to be too weak.'

'Why?'

'He appears to be an habitual drunk, as well as mentally ill.'

'Why?'

'I consider he might have done something.'

'What?'

'I don't know, something terrible, something painful.'

'And?'

'He seems to pass out regularly.'

'What else?'

'She seems to compare him with another man.'

'Who?'

'Her friend's fiancée.'

'Ben? The talented son?'

'Yes.'

'Why?'

'I infer your niece considers that he gets her everything, that her husband gets her nothing.'

'And?'

'She possesses a cold indifference which makes her remorseless and ruthless.'

'Why might she have killed my brother and/or his wife?'

'I couldn't tell from the room conversation.'

'But?'

'She's angry with her mum.'

'Why?'

'According to your niece, she was 'abusive.''

'What about her father? My brother?'

'I think she loved him.'

'I want you to visit the second suspect.'

'Who?'

'The female whom the anonymous caller said was "used".'

'Is this absolutely necessary?'

'It is if you want to promote yourself to an accessory, rather than a murderer.'

'I'm not either.'

'You'll be able to prove that then.'

'How?'

'By meeting her.'

CHAPTER TWENTY-SIX

Day Four; 6: 45 am; The Second Suspect; Alana

The mobile screeched. I wakened. I slipped backwards upright in bed.

'Chase?'

'*Ewok*!'

'I want you to visit the second suspect.'

I rubbed my eyes. 'Where does she live?'

'Silverstream, Moor Road.'

'Where's that?'

'The north of Glasgow.'

'How do you know?'

'I received a telephone call.'

'From whom?'

'It was another anonymous caller.'

'The same one?'

'Yes, I think so.'

'What did they say?'

'He said: "*Remember me? He used her She lives at Silverstream, Moor Road.*"'

'When did you receive the call?'

'Last night.'

'Isn't that a bit of a coincidence, since you asked me to visit her earlier?'

'Not necessarily, I think someone's on to you.'

'How?'

'He obviously listened in on our conversation.'

'How?'

'It can be done with cars- as I said, I'll explain later.'

I huffed. 'Why don't you meet her?'

'I really think she would respond better to the presiding judge at the time, rather than the victim's brother and brother-in-law.'

'But I've never heard of her, whoever she is.'

'Then, as I said, you'll be able to prove that by meeting her.'

I hurtled towards the north of Scotland in the Mercedes, biting my chapped lip born of stress and cold in vexation at being assigned in this way, which compromised my driving control. I arrived outside the front gates of the house: Silverstream, Moor Road. The place was a sheer icon of effortless pulchritude: a towering baronial edifice with innovative ultramodern windows, gleaming hi-tech doors, and an expansive rich demesne, glazed with a thick brush of kaleidoscopic flora and inspissated by a great clump of emboldening evergreen. As I gazed out of the front left hand side window, I drank in the rippling glittering waters. A galaxy of morning sunbeams tripped the light fantastic on the dim cold sea. I sighed with humble appreciation. I conceived puttering up to the main front door but elected to savour the spectacle by ambling. I exited the Mercedes and hiked up the flush serpentine driveway. I reached the tall glinting French doors. There was a buzzer. I motioned to press the buzzer when the front door slipped open.

A surprisingly alluring woman, wearing a cotton dressing gown and dull-lit amber eyes greeted me.

I coughed politely. My name's Ewald.'

'Yes, my mother said you would come.'

I gawked slightly. 'She did?'

'Yes, she received a telephone call last night.'

'I see. May I enquire as to who made the call?'

The young woman revealed a toothpaste smile. 'He said his name was Chase.'

I nodded contently. 'May I ask your name?'

'Greer.'

I scratched the back of my head. 'Greer?'

'Yes.'

'I believe it means 'watchful' or 'vigilant.''

Greer cast me a complaisant smile. 'I presume so. Would you like to step in, I'll just fetch my mother. She's very phlegmatic.'

'Thank you, madam.'

'You're welcome.'

I stepped inside between the French doors, I saw that the house was as beautiful on the inside as it was on the outside. It was appointed with neo furniture, stylish carpeting, bright walls, and practical ceiling.

'Please, take a seat,' said Greer.

Greer traipsed upstairs. I could hear her voice. 'The man's arrived, mother!'

'Escort him to the kitchen, Greer,' said another voice.

Greer sashayed down the stairs. She beckoned me with a graceful hand. 'Please come to the kitchen, Sir.'

I smiled graciously. 'Very well, thank you.'

Greer lead me into the kitchen. 'My mother will be with you shortly. I must go.'

I stood against the inside wall. The kitchen was capacious, pristine and sophisticated. After a minute or so, the kitchen door opened and a middle-aged woman with amber eyes in a silk gown greeted me. 'Ewald?'

I swallowed. 'Yes, madam and your name?'

'Alana.'

I nodded respectfully. 'I believe that's a Scottish name meaning 'beautiful'.'

She revealed a surprising white mouth. 'I once was.'

I blushed slightly. 'I must say your house is simply spectatcular, madam.'

'Please, Ewald, call me Alana.' Yes, I believe I had to be.'

'Thank you, Alana.'

'You're welcome. Chase said you would come.'

'Yes, your daughter said he called you. May I ask how you know him?'

'I must confess I don't. He said someone had contacted him and that he was looking for some important information. He said he would arrange for someone to come over. I said that would be fine but that I would wish that my time not be wasted. How do you know Chase?'

'He attended my leaving do and asked me to run a few errands.'

'I see. Might I offer you a cup of tea or a mug of coffee? I have every hot beveridge in the cupboard, including hot chocolate.'

The airstreams of the cruel whips of the morning air lingered in my wishful throat. 'Coffee, thank you.'

As Alana prepared real coffee, she glinted at me. 'Tell me, Ewald, why are you here?'

I smiled sombrely. 'I'm afraid it's rather unfortunate.'

'Unfortunate?'

'Yes.'

'Why would that be?'

'He believes I might have killed his brother and his wife.'

Alana leaned back. 'Who were they?'

'Andrew and Susanna McLean.'

Alana shifted her head. 'Never heard of them. Why would he believe that?'

'He received a call.'

'What call?'

'An anonymous one.'

'What did the caller say?'

'"*Weapons...people killed in there...executions... He made her do it... The judge is retiring...*'

Alana's eyes squinted. 'I'm afraid that makes no sense to me. When did he get the call?'

'1995.'

Alana's amber eyes dilated. 'I'm surprised he remembered it.'

'Yes, I'm surprised as well. He believes I'm lying or I've forgotten.'

'Why would you lie?'

'He imagines in order to protect myself.'

'Why would you need to protect yourself?'

'That's what I don't understand.'

Alana smiled patiently. 'How would you forget?'

'He suggests I witnessed the incident, left the room and said nothing. He suggests I got drunk, or that I was distracted, or that I was hypnotised, or that I was treated.'

Alana nodded with interest. 'Did you get drunk?'

'Not that I remember, no. I don't drink.'

'And how would you have been distracted?'

'He suggests I was pulled out of the room before it happened.'

'May I ask, Ewald, were you treated?'

'Yes, I went into hospital for a while.'

'Why was that?'

'I had a heart attack.'

'I'm very sorry. How did you have a heart attack?'

'I had been smoking very heavily for years.'

'Do you still smoke?'

'Yes.'

'How old are you?'

'Seventy-eight.' I coughed politely. 'Chase believes that if I didn't kill his brother and his wife that you did.'

'Why would he believe that?'

'The anonymous specified a female and gave your address.'

'I see, but I've never heard of Andrew or Susanna McLean- not until you told me.'

'Yes, that's what I thought.'

'He sounds disturbed.'

'He's very persuasive.'

'You're not a police detective are you, Ewald?'

'No, I was a judge.'

'I see. Where did you work?'

'In the Asylum Division.'

'Where is that?'

'Glasgow.'

'So?'

'He believes I might have shouted at you and made you kill his brother and his wife.'

'But I don't even know you.'

'That's what I thought.'

'Why would you have shouted at me?'

'He considers I was used to verbally controlling people.'

'And are you?'

'Not to that extent. You don't remember me?'

'No, ought I to?'

'No, not really. Did you ever work for the court services?'

'No. Even if I had, how would I have done it?'

'According to the anonymous caller in 1995, it would have been with a weapon.'

'Which weapon?'

'I don't know.'

'You may check the house if you like, Ewald, sorry Sir but you won't find any weapons here.'

'What about in 1995?'

Alana gave a look of confusion. 'I didn't live here in 1995.'

'Where did you live?'

'I lived in the west end. I was bringing up my daughter.'

'Greer?'

'Yes.'

'You were a judge, right?'

'Yes.'

'Why would you have told me to kill them?'

'Chase imagines you were going to kill me.'

'If that had been the case, would it not have been self-defence?'

'It could have been. But if I had made you kill someone if you were going to kill me, the defence doesn't apply.'

'Why not?'

'It only applies in the first person, not the third person.'

'But in which case I would have been coerced.'

'Yes, that would have exculpated you but not me.'

'I see, and in the preposterous event you had issued the command?'

I sighed. 'It would make me an accessory to murder.'

'Why would I have responded.'

'Chase imagines you didn't care, that you had no ability to differentiate between right and wrong.'

'I have a daughter. I can tell you I do care.'

'You love Greer.'

'With every bone in my body.'

'May I ask, Alana how you came into possession of this property?'

'I saw a conveyancer. You understand that, don't you?'

'Yes, of course. What I mean is, how could you afford it?'

Alana shrugged. 'I was prepared to do things other people weren't.'

I lowered my head and peeked at Alana. 'What were you prepared to do?'

Alana smiled soberly. 'Anything for my daughter.'

I cowered at the thought of what that meant. 'May I ask why you decided to buy this property?'

'I had always dreamed of a waterfront property. There was Mill of Catter, Rhu Lodge, Burnbank House, Ardoch, Renagour, Pass of Aberfoyle, Breakwater House, Fife, Ferndene house, Argyll and Bute, Water's Close, Edinburgh.'

'These are all beech front properties?'

'Yes, but I decided I wanted to stay in Glasgow.'

'Why was that?'

'My daughter went to school in Glasgow; plus, I loved the house and the garden.'

I nodded with understanding. 'It seems you and I have nothing to reproach ourselves for.'

Alana nodded with agreement. 'I don't know about you Ewald, unless you did do it, or forced someone else to do it, but I certainly didn't.'

'No, and I have no memory of doing it myself.'

'You are seventy-seven?'

'Yes'

'And you have no history of mental health?'

'None whatsoever.'

'And you have no problems remembering?'

'No.'

'You don't have dementia?'

'No, I trust my abstinence has stood me in good stead.'

'Yes. Then perhaps the anonymous caller got it wrong and Chase is pursuing a false lead.'

'Yes, I think so.'

'And just so you know my opinion, Ewald, in terms of the female, this Susanna McLean, I think it's more likely poison was used. My daughter has a thing about mushrooms.'

'Why do you think that?'

Alana smiled wistfully. 'My bloom may have popped but no one likes spoiling a pretty face.'

I nodded intently. 'Thank you, Alana.'

'Not at all.'

There was a call from upstairs. 'That's my daughter, Ewald. I must tend to her.'

'Of course.'

'May I see you out.'

I smiled placidly. 'Thank you.'

'You've obviously had a very demanding life, Sir. I hope it gets less difficult.'

'Thank you, Alana.'

'You're very welcome.'

I mobiled Chase.

'*Ewok*!'

'I'm sorry to disappoint you but I didn't recognise your second suspect. Furthermore, she doesn't remember me.'

'What's her name?'

'Alana. She has a daughter Greer.'

'What did they say?'

'Greer said her mother was very phlegmatic.'

'And what did her mother say?'

'She said she never worked for the court services and that she couldn't see that she had done it.'

'I see, Ewok.' I want you to visit the overshadowed fiancée again tomorrow,'

CHAPTER TWENTY-SEVEN

Day Five; 6: 30 am; The Overshadowed Fiancée

The godawful bang went again. I wakened. Andrea stirred. The mobile sounded: Ratta-tatta-tatta-ta-CLANG CLANG CLANG, as it rattled up beside the gold-plated alarm clock trying to bully the digits.

'Ewok!'

'Chase. I take it you used another bedroom window.'

'Of course.'

'You shall visit the son.'

'Why?'

'I wish to know if he killed my brother and his wife.'

'Yes.'

'This time you shall bring your eldest son- the one who is married with children.'

'Why?'

'You must learn his view of family relationships.'

'Why?'

'Your ivory tower is too tall, it needs down-sized.'

I grumbled. 'I will call David. He will of course be forced to renounce his prior excogitations.'

'Good.'

I drove to my son David's house. He protested that he had work to go to. I persuaded him that he would only have work to go to if he came with me. He wanted to get Chase himself. I told him we were working with a professional criminal.

As we arrived at Park Drive in Thorntonhall, the morning sky was dark as slate and the icy north wind was blowing rain straight into the windscreen. Together we assembled the sounding equipment.

Ben was at home. He was sitting in the music room at the piano. He had spent not inconsiderable time on selecting it. He had considered the best options. He had considered the German (Hamburg) Steinway, Bosendorfers, Shigeru Kawais; Baldwins Mason and Hamlin's Mason and Hamlins Sauters, Seilers, Scimmels, Bechsteins, Grotrians, Heintzmans, countless Yamahas and Kawais, and Korean pianos. He had narrowed it down to the best four: Bosendorfer; Fazioli; Mason and Hamlin; Shigeru Kawai; Steinway Hamburg.

Eventually he had decided on the Fazioli.

It was a much thought-out room. In terms of the dynamics, the flat horizontal part of the room on which people walked (*if they dared*) far from being a thick heavy fabric to warm one's winter toes, was for acoustic reasons a cold arrangement of strips of wood; in fact the whole room was denudated.

Jane's eyes laughed good-naturedly. She sniffed the music room with her button nose, revealing her sensitivity and feeling of disapproval. Her plump lips twisted with a sheen of moisture on her upper lip. She anchored her attention on her fiancée. 'Must we dance on ice, sweetest?' Jane said. 'I mean, I'm sure a basic rug wouldn't interfere with your playing.'

'There's so much to consider.'

'There is?'

'Yes, lighting, audio, floor length, mic placement...'

'Mic placement.'

'Yes, the acoustics. Carpets deaden sounds.'

'They do?'

'So do curtains. People absorb sounds and their clothing. You want a moderate amount of reflection.'

'You've got the computer in here.'

'Yes, the webcam is plugged into the USB since I'm using an external camera.'

'And?'

'I've adjusted the output volume to maximum.'

Jane yawned. 'I see.'

'I have to do it differently now. Since January 2015, you have to use alternatives to webcam capture.'

'Yes?'

'I'm using software on my computer to record and save a webcam video to YouTube.'

'And it has to be be strips of wood,' he said. 'And they have to be *deplanate*.'

'They have to be what dearest?'

'Made level.'

'Oh, I see.'

'The notes come first.'

The vertical structures forming the inside partitions were high. This again had acoustic value. The moveable barrier used to open and close the entrance to the room was once a solid panel but after a number of temper tantrums was barely hinged to a frame. *You really must not disturb me when I'm composing, Anne*, he would think. The openings in the walls with inner frames of wood with glass fitted in them let in precious little light due to the eternally drawn curtains. Ben found darkness as opposed to light the more appropriate ambience for composition. And when they were opened they let in precious little air. The black rest marks on the scores were all the fresh air one needed. The moveable items in the room: the chairs, the desks, the cabinets, were not so much moveable as nailed to the floor, lest Ben's creative thought processes should be disrupted.

The focal point, the cynosure, of the room and eternal conversation piece was undoubtedly the baby grand. It was not as grand as the one way down in the dark and dingy cellar of the big old house had been. But it was more than functional. That part of the piano: the airway and digestive tract, between the mouth and both the oesophagus and the windpipe; that critical area between elongated and nimble fingers and the ivories, a piano whose strings were horizontally fixed behind the keyboard in a harp-shaped frame, sputtered its last dying chords. It drew up the fag end of a barren working week. Jane had been lucky enough to get in dozens of clients. Daft young lassies with pocket-mirrors for brains. Girls who only thought about the appreciations of handsome boys and men with money and elderly women considering the need for an eccentric blue rinse.

It was of course the room which was traditionally used for socialising. Down the ages, many a practical mind had lost itself entirely in such a room, when other people's thoughts and opinions, usually fuelled by alcohol, had thrown a cat among the pigeons by unsteadying old stalwart beliefs and long-held perceptions as to acceptable comportments. Indeed his father had often snapped at his maladroitness and unmusicality as the whiskey reached boiling point. 'Sorry, father,' he would say. 'I'll try to get it right next time.'

In addition, this mind-altering event occurred every last Saturday evening of every second month; typically, when Jane's ridiculous posse of dippy Beauty colleagues would come over for a night of mindless pampering. It made him think that it was perfectly acceptable to rabbit on and on; to butter people up until they succumbed to high cholesterol; to pour liquor into ashtrays; to drop ash onto the floorboards; to weep uncontrollably and to physically restrain your far more sober companions. Despite mental health principles to the contrary. Not that Jane was a chimney or a lush. She was quite the opposite. It was in fact her enduring abstemiousness that precipitated this occasional dramatic and uncouthly metamorphosis. These were the sorts of things men, especially aloof men, would never comprehend. Not that Ben was not prone to the odd 'Elton John' tantrum and tiara. But he liked to think he was more self-possessed. It was also the night Ben had to pretend that he had other things in his life. He had to pretend that he didn't need the baby grand, the solid and dependable texture of the keys, the heart-warming richness of the notes.

The living room had other traditional functions. It was the room where people usually relax but strangely it was the room where Ben got most of his work done. It was also the room where people usually entertain guests but the only other person around was Jane. And Anne was at school. It was also the room which was used for asserting one's independence: to think and to plan.

'What's the ESC again, honey?' said Jane.

Ben's eyes rolled skyward. 'It's the Eurovision Song Contest, my darling.'

Jane's clear eyes assented. She nodded her head complaisantly. 'Oh, yes. Do you plan on watching it this year dearest?'

'Not exactly.'

Jane gave her fiancé and exacting look. 'I wondered. Ann and I were left on our own that night.'

'You were?'

'Yes, I remember it distinctly.'

'You do?'

'We were weeping, eating chocolates, wondering where you were. I specifically remember it was a Thursday evening.'

'Thursday?'

'Yes. It was 7 am.'

'And?'

'And then it was Saturday.'

'I'm very sorry, my darling.'

'Where were you, dearest?'

'I was- I was...'

'In the pub?'

'No.'

'With someone else?'

'No.'

'Look me in the eye.'

'No.'

'Where?'

'I had to help out the gardener.'

'Frank?'

'Yes.'

'At that time.'

'I'm afraid so.'

'Twice.'

'Yes.'

'So?'

'I was rather thinking I might like to win it.'

'Win what my darling?'

'The trophy.'

'What trophy?'

'The one that's given to the winning songwriter.'

'That could be you.'

'You think so?'

'Yes, dear.'

'How did the United Kingdom do last year?'

'It didn't do as well as we felt it might.'

'No.'

'She sang her heart out and it was a lovely tune but it didn't seem to get appreciated.'

'Would I?'

'Of course you would my sweetness.'

'Why?'

'You're a genius.'

'I am.'

'Oh, yes. You have a lovely voice.'

'I do?'

'Yes, it's absolutely gorgeous.'

'It is?'

'Yes, and you play so well.'

'You think so?'

'Yes, my goodness if I tried that I would break a nail.'

Ben nodded sympathetically. 'That would hurt.'

'It certainly wouldn't do any good, Ben A girl has to look her best, you know.'

'Why?'

'To have the best man.'

'Yes.'

'How does it work again? This male PMT thing.'

'ESC. I would have to enter.'

'How?'

'I would have to contact the broadcasters.'

'And what would happen?'

'The participating broadcaster has the right to choose their entry in the format they choose. Sometimes entries are picked internally. In some cases the artists and the song are picked by the broadcaster while the public decide on the eventual representative. There is also a national selection.'

'So?'

'I must contact the Heads of Delegations.'

'Who are they?'

'They are the people responsible for the broadcaster's side for the Eurovision Song Contest. There is also the Broadcasting Union.'

'And what's that dear?'

'It's just called the EBU.'

'So you will watch it this time?'

'If I get- send it off there.

But Ben had barely been able to work out a first verse. Jane was polishing the lid of the grand.

He rose from his piano seat. 'Jane.'

Jane was innocently humming his last tune.

'*Jane*,' he said.

'What honey?'

'I'm trying to concentrate.'

'Oh, sorry my love! Am I incommoding you?'

'You remember that word?'

'Yes, of course, my sweet, you taught me it the other day.'

He grumbled. 'It's fine, don't worry about it.'

'Of course I worry about it. I worry my hat off about it. I wish for you to come up with something truly lovely.'

Ben glimpsed at his fiancée. 'I might need peace and quiet to do that.'

Jane glanced at him quizzically. 'Even when you're writing songs? I would have thought-' She wiggled her hips, 'Sounds would have helped.'

'I need more than just sounds, I need definite inspiration; a muse.'

'I see, you're not inspired, baby? Is something the matter?'

Ben breathed laboriously and said, 'It's nothing.'

Jane smiled disapprovingly. 'Come on! It must be something.'

'How so?'

'You've been at that prickly little tune almost a week now.'

'And?'

'You need fresh impetus.'

'Like you could do better.'

Jane's eyes dilated with surprise. 'I'm not a songwriter, sweetheart. I'm a beautician.'

'Well, there you go, then.'

'But I still have holes at the sides of my head.'

I think you mean in your head, thought Ben.

'What, you don't think it's any good?' he said.

'I don't know, it's not one of your better ones, honey. It sounds...I don't know, what's the word? 'Distracted.''

Ben nodded glumly and said, 'Yes, it does, doesn't it?'

'You're not worried about the dumb old police, are you?'

Ben scratched the back of his head with vexation. 'No, of course not.'

'Because if you are, you can stop. It's just a rumour- a malicious rumour, that's all. Somebody with nothing better to do with their time than to stir up trouble. It's probably that old bag-'

'The ear duster?-'

'Yes, her, the woman in the village outside where you once lived. She never did like your mother. What was it? Your mother's cakes were better baked? She's probably dying for her to have been killed. There's no truth in it.'

Ben stared at the floor, his nose twitched and he said, 'No.'

'I mean, who would have wanted to kill your mother? She was such a good person, wasn't she?'

Ben's eyes flickered and he said, 'Yes.'

'She played music. She went to church. She had a family. I can think of no one less likely to be the victim of murder.'

'Precisely.'

'So you can stop worrying.'

'It's easier said than done.'

'And to suggest that your father might have had something to do with it, it's outrageous.'

'Quite.'

'I mean, she was his dear wife after all. He must have loved the bones of her. I think there's a word for it.'

'Uxorious.'

'Yes, euphonious. It's downright insensitive, if you ask me. The poor old man lost his dearly beloved wife, the mother of his child, has had to live with the unimaginable grief for years, and then becomes accused of killing her. It isn't right. It isn't right at all.'

'They didn't accuse him.'

Jane gawped and said, 'Didn't they?'

'No.'

'Well, what did they do, sweetness?'

'They asked questions.'

'Frightful questions they were. The most impertinent sort. We should make a complaint.'

'Why?'

'Because they made you feel bad. Terribly bad.'

'And?'

'And it's affecting your music.'

'It is?'

'Most definitely. I mean, as if your father was in some way linked to her death.'

'He was just doing his job.'

'Your father?'

'No, the Chief Inspector.'

Jane frowned. 'Some job that is. Digging up filthy dirt.

Mud-raking. Casting aspersions over good honourable characters. We should make a complaint.'

Ben shrugged his shoulders and said, 'Who to?'

'I don't know. Somebody. Somebody with authority. Somebody that knows how to put lesser people in their proper place.'

'He was a Chief Inspector, honey.'

'Yes, but there's bound to be people in higher places. You know, who would sit him down, as he sat us down, and make him see how wrong his actions were.'

'And who is this?'

'I don't know. I don't know at all, but they must exist, surely. You can't have people without their betters.'

'People have betters?'

'Well, yes. Especially within business contexts.'

Ben's eyes darkened with sympathy. 'Am I your better, Jane?'

'You're my strength, sweetness. You're my rock. You make me feel strong, sorted, as though things will be okay.'

Ben bowed his head solemnly and said, 'I'm glad.'

'If it were not for you, my sweetness, I would have nothing else. Except Anne, of course. She's my other rock; my other strength.'

'You have your own strength, Jane.'

'I do?'

'Yes, you understand nature. The way things are.'

'I do?'

'Yes, you're always there. Always there to help. You're goodness, Jane. Sheer goodness!'

'Well, thank you, honey! Thank you, my sweet!'

Ben nodded patiently. 'You're welcome.'

'So we must make a complaint.'

'I don't know if I can be bothered with the complaints procedure right now. I've got far more important things to-'

'I mean, what next? They'll actually believe *you* killed her.'

Ben simpered. 'Silly, isn't it?'

Jane suppressed a pang of contrition. 'They might as well believe that I was capable of killing someone's mother.'

'Quite.'

'Yes. I mean she died. The poor woman just died. The way people do sometimes, when something inside is not quite right with them. There's nothing suspicious in it; nothing sinister.'

'It was a fire, Jane.'

'I know it was sweetheart. I do so hate to think of it like that. I hate to think of a person burning to death.'

'But the smoke would have gotten to her first.'

'Yes, of course. Thank goodness! And it's so unfair on you, too. You were her son. The last thing you needed was for the painful past to be raked up again.'

'I'm alright, really.'

'I don't think you are, baby. I think you're in shock.'

'I wouldn't go quite as far as that.'

'I would. It normally takes you five minutes to come up with a lovely tune, but it's now taking an eternity.'

'It's just writer's block.'

'It's more than that. It's post-traumatic stress disorder.'

'I think that's going a bit far.'

'It's not going nearly far enough. We should get the doctor, Ben.'

'I don't need the doctor, I need a melody.'

'Good melodies start with a free and happy mind.'

Ben glanced quizzically at Jane. 'You know this, do you?'

'Yes. The only time I can sing is when I'm happy.'

'But you always sing, my radiance?'

Jane's eyes lit up like a Christmas tree. '*Do I?*' she said.

'Yes.'

'I didn't know that. *Ooh*, are you sure? Yes, I suppose you're right. Silly me!'

Ben gave her a slightly patronising look. 'Happy you.'

Jane gave him a more directed look. 'I want you to be happy as well.'

'I will be. I will be. Just as soon as this damned tune is over.'

'You'll be happy when the chief of police comes over and apologises.'

'I don't want them to come over. I want them to leave me- *us*- alone.'

'In that case, I'll make sure they never bother us again.'

'How d' you plan to do that? Smother the house in perfume?'

'No, I'll do some detective work of myself. I'll prove it wasn't you.'

Ben coughed and said, '*You*?'

'Yes, me.'

'You'll prove it wasn't me?'

'Yes, why? D' you not think I can?'

'I think there's a lot of things you can do, my sweetness. Smile, laugh, augment, but refuting matricide suspicions isn't one of them.'

'I'm not as daft as I look, Ben.'

'I never said you looked daft.'

'Come off it! You think I belong in a bird cage.'

'I never said anything about bird cages.'

'You didn't have to. A girl can tell when their mind's not respected.'

'I have every respect for your mind.'

'That's my face you' re thinking of, dear. I know they're both close to the head but they perform two quite distinct functions.'

'Oh, yes?'

'The face is for seducing rich men and the mind is for banking the cheques afterward.'

'So you only want me for my money?'

'I want you for you, my sweetness. It's just your money makes you that good bit more desirable.'

Ben frowned. 'What if I was dirt poor? Would you still want me, then?'

'Of course I would. You would still have your music- and I love that.'

'What if I didn't have my music?'

'Then you would still have your sense of humour.'

'Does my sexual attractiveness even come in to this?'

'Why of course! You're the most handsome man alive.'

Ben beamed and said, 'You really think so? You're not just saying that?'

'No.'

Ben twirled his head with some element of pride and said, 'I am rather good looking am I not?'

'Well, maybe except for Brad Pitt.'

Ben's head fell.

'And maybe Jonny Depp.'

Ben's head fell still further.'

'And then there's of course, Tom Cruise. Although he's getting a bit older, isn't he?'

'Alright! Alright!'

'Sorry, honey! I didn't mean to dent your ego.'

'I think I'll live.'

'You'll do much more than that. You'll flourish.'

'You think so?'

'Yes, just as soon as you stop worrying about the dumb old police and let your brilliant fiancé handle the investigation.'

'Just as long as you know what you're doing.'

'I always know what I'm doing.'

Ben snorted.

'I do actually. I just pretend to be thick so you'll have someone to be above.'

'You think I need someone to be above?'

'Absolutely. You've been so used to clever-clogs like your mother and father and the people in the music industry, that you enjoy dumbing down.'

'Do I dumb down with you?'

'All the time, baby. Why, sometimes I'm not sure who you're speaking to, whether it's the cat or me.'

'You're about as cute.'

'Yes, but there's more to me than my good looks.'

'I didn't say there wasn't.'

'I think we're going round in circles, dear. Like you with that tune.'

'What d' you think I should do?'

'Well, since you asked, I think you should rip it up and start again.'

'And waste a whole week's work?'

'You're spending good money after bad.'

'I suppose you're right.'

'I'm always right, honey. In my own way.'

'I think I prefer it when you babble.'

'Of course you do. We've covered that.'

'Would you prefer it if I spoke up to you?'

'I would prefer if you just became happy.'

'Happiness is being with you, my dearest.'

'Happiness is a beautiful melody.'

'You're the inspiration for such a thing.'

'You'll be able to concentrate, now?'

'You try and stop me!'

'I thought I had.'

'At first but not now.'

'Glad to have been of some use.'

'You're always of use.'

He was going through the best songs he had ever heard. He had felt that Eurovision had produced a few numbers that could never be beaten. He had played 'Insieme' by Toto Cutugno, which had been won by Italy in 1990, 'Molitva' by Marija Serifovic, which had been won by Serbia in 2007, 'Goodbye to Yesterday' by Elina Born and Stig Rasta, which had been won by Estonia this year, and had tried to work out other greatest Eurovision songs.

It was a difficult business. There were the generations, there were the countries, there were the genres, there were the timings, and there were the best. He had accepted John Lennon's Imagine as a worthy winner. He felt that Michael Jackson's "Earth song" was a catchier tune but not as beautifully simple. He had accepted that the best of the boy bands had been 'Westlife', better than 'Take That' in the eighties. He had also felt a different nation's songs. He had tried to understand girl bands. He had tried to understand Disney.

He believed that Eurovision created better pop songs than conventional teams.

Eurovision 2015 had passed. Sweden had won with Heroes. The best Eurovision songs of all time was 'Molitva' by Serbia in 2007. The next best song was 'Insieme' by Italy in 1990. He remembered the best

The best power ballads were 'Take my breath away' by Berlin and 'Show me Heaven' by Maria McKee. The best song of all time was

Ben was processing the best modern tunes. Ben wasn't gay but he had come across 'Same love' and 'Take me to church.'

He was in the living room where the baby grand was situated.

Jane decorously departed the living room, leaving behind a gorgeous mist of sweet feminine fragrance. Ben checked his watch, assessed the light and got back to his song writing. In the space of an hour, he composed a delightful little tune about a very special girl, about love and about promise. She was damned clever as well as pretty.

The next day Ben awoke with a beam. 'Jane! Jane!' he cried.

Jane came round, wiped the smudges from her eyes, and said, 'What my dearest?'

'I've done it!'

Jane stared with wide eyes and said, 'Done what my sweetness?'

'I've come up with it.'

Jane's voice elevated with wonderful surprise and she said, 'Come up with it?'

'Yes, the new song.'

Jane gaped and said, 'You have?'

'Yes, I have. Shall I play it for you?'

Jane was transported and said, 'Okay! Okay! Go for it my sweetness.'

'Will you sing?'

'If you give me the words.'

'I'll give you the music first.'

They hurried out of the master bedroom and dashed downstairs and entered the living room.'

Ben played the tune. It was so simple, so very pretty and so wonderfully sentimental.

'I love it, my dear!'

'You do?'

'Yes. It's total ear candy.'

'You're not just saying that?'

'No, it's wonderful.'

'Should I call my dad?'

'Yes, indeed, my forever love! But first you should praise God.'

'Praise God?'

'Yes, by going to church. By playing and singing his own lovely songs as well.'

'I should?'

'Yes, *depardieux*.'

'Eh?'

'"In God's name; certainly".'

'But-

'No buts, my dearest. You must go tonight. But first put on your ecclesiastical attire.'

With ecclesiophobia, Ben grimaced and braced himself for an evening in the bloody buggery church.

I rang Chase.

'*Ewok*!'

'I am with my eldest son David outside Park Drive.'

'And?'

'The sound equipment was set up.'

'What did he think of that?'

'He found it odd, but he assented.'

'And?'

'We have listened to the son.'

'So?'

'The son is trying to win Eurovision, while his daughter is trying to win his affection.'

'What was your son's interpretation?'

'He didn't care for the son's treatment of his daughter.'

'No?'

'The son's trying to make his daughter something she's not.'
'What does that teach you?'
'I don't know.'
'That you have tried to make your son something he's not.'
'I didn't tell him to become a judge, if that's what you mean.'
'So detail, Ewok?'
'The son is a musician.'
'What sort of a musician?'
'A songwriter and a performer.'
'Is he any good?'
'Yes, very.'
'And?'
'He's entering Eurovision.'
Chase seemed to smile over the phone. 'And?'
'He intends to win it.'
'Is he gay?'
'No, not according to his partnership.'
'Might he be the talented son of my brother's client?'
'Yes, I consider he is.'
'Did he mention his father?'
'No, but his wife advised him to call him.'
'Who is his wife?'
'Jane.'
'And?'
'She's a beautician.'
'Might she have killed my brother and/or his wife.'
'I don't know.'

SIXTH INTERLUDE

Jaeger White Challenges Jack Dorcha

'You bite off more than you can chew,' said Jaeger White.

'If wasn't for me your family would be eating humble pie,' said Jack Dorcha.

'How so?'

'You have made a fortune out of food and beverages.'

'So?'

'I got your whiskey, salmon, lamb and beef accepted world-wide.'

'My whiskey was perfect.'

'Perhaps, but your capacity to market it wasn't. As for your salmon, not everyone was prepared to accept inferior overcrowded fish-farming.'

'My salmon is as good as any naturally caught.'

'Once I had cleaned-up your operation. As for your lamb and beef, not everyone was prepared to accept orf and mad cow-disease you were spreading.'

'That was never proven. They didn't even know what orf was.'

'Unfortunately, their doctors did. Fortunately, I did: an exanthematous disease caused by a parapox virus and occurring primarily in sheep and goats. It is also known as contagious pustular dermatitis, infectious labial dermatitis, ecthyma contagiosum, thistle disease and scabby mouth. Orf virus is zoonotic- it can also infect humans.'

'So?'

'I got your sheep farm exonerated and promoted. They ended up believing your lamb and beef was naturally free from these things.'

CHAPTER TWENTY-EIGHT

Day Six; 6: 15 am; Death's Kitchen: Mother, Mushroom and Murder

There was a bang. I roused. Andrea wriggled. The mobile which I had strategically placed in the corner of the room went: 'vzzzzzzt.' I crawled out of bed, picked it up, and placed it to my ear.

'*Ewok*!'

'Chase. You must be running out of bedroom windows.'

'I used your living room.'

'You do realise it's going to cost me a fortune to repair them all.'

'It will cost you a greater fortune not to repair my problem.'

'The friend's mother?'

'Exactly.'

I drove to Hyndland. I parked my car outside the house and got out. I could hear murmurings outside the kitchen window. I set up the sounding equipment. The niece and her mother were inside the kitchen.

Judith White moued her fat lips, confessing years of shovelling salmon, beef and lamb down her gullet and vaunting her feeling of justified satiation. She was busy stuffing prawn vol-au-vents into her gaping mouth. She garbaged down. She licked her fingers. 'How's Ben?'

Jane squeaked. 'He's entering Eurovision.'

Judith White's faded azure lace eyes squinted, revealing her age and hominess. 'What ever is that dear?'

Jane frowned. 'It's a song contest.'

Judith White licked her fingers again. 'A what?'

'A song contest. He's trying to come up with the best tune.'

Judith White's affluent face gawked. 'He is?'

Jane pointed her diffident eyes at her mother. 'You remember, mother that he is a singer-songwriter, as well as a pianist.'

Judith White gobbled. 'What was his last song?'

Jane sighed. ''If only'.'

Judith White grunted. 'And how's that ghastly man of a father of his?'

Jane swallowed. 'You mean Mr Sharp.'

'Yes.'

Judith White smiled tolerantly at her daughter. 'I think he did something, Jane.'

Jane flustered. 'What might that be mother?'

'I'm not sure.'

'Why would you think that?'

'You were unhappy after you were around him.'

'Unhappy?'

'Yes, unnatural.'

'So?'

'I slaved for him for years and he paid me buttons.'

Jane simpered. 'I'm afraid that's the way it is with the better half.'

Judith White waved her head defiantly. 'I was the better half.'

Jane knit her brows. 'You were?'

'You know I saw a lawyer once?'

'Which lawyer?'

'Andrew McLean- your friend's father.'

'When?'

'Over twenty years ago.'

'And what happened?'

Judith White snorted. 'Nothing.'

'Nothing?'

'He lost the case. The judge decided Sharp had paid me my dues.'

'Why?'

'His ridiculous lawyer was much better. He managed to convince the judge that I had frequently been benighted and laggard and that my work had been slow and sloppy. He even accused me of raiding his fridge and helping myself to his drinks cabinet.'

'And had you, mother?'

'I had to drop you off at school and pick you up and bring you back. Mr Sharp never cleaned up after himself and the house itself was massive; it took ages to correct his mistakes.'

'And what about the food and drinks?'

'It was the occasional light snack to keep my strength up and the odd aperitif was a hard-earned reward.'

'Mother!'

'Honestly, Jane, the man was a bully.'

'Why did you agree to work for him?'

'Your father ran off with my father's money.'

'What did grandfather do again?'

'He owned a food company: 'White Foods'. I'll never forgive him for that.'

'Why would dad do that?'

'He was a thief and a con-merchant.'

'Did he love me?'

'The only thing he loved was the art of deception. So, working for Hugh Sharp was all I could do to enable us to survive.'

'There were no other jobs?'

'It was not the same in our day- women simply did not have any opportunities. Anyway, I think there's another reason he doesn't like you.'

'Oh?'

'Yes, I- he thinks you might have done something.'

Jane gulped. 'Oh, yes.'

'His son should pay me, you know.'

'Ben can't afford to pay you, mother.'

'His house and location say otherwise.'

'That's because I work as well.'

'You make a pittance, Jane- just as I did.' Judith White scoffed another vol-au-vent. How's Ann?'

'She's perfect.'

'Pity she didn't get our looks.'

'I think she's beautiful.'

'And if nothing else, your fiancé's rather handsome. She must take after your fiancé's mother.'

'Agatha?'

'Yes.'

'Was she plain?'

'She had the hardest face imaginable, I'm surprised even Mr Sharp went for her.'

'Why did she?'

'She was brilliant, I'll give her that.'

'Yes, in what way?'

'You know a maestro, a virtuoso. That mattered to him.'

'Am I brilliant?'

'You are many things, my dear Jane, but brilliant isn't one of them.'

Jane sunk slightly.

Mrs White looked sternly at her daughter. 'I still know what happened, Jane.'

'Mother?'

'I taught you everything about mushrooms.'

'You did?'

'Of course. From the big brown ones to the tiny little white ones. You still remember the story.'

Jane's flawless face wrinkled. 'What story?'

'The story of the mushroom man.'

'Vaguely. I remember he was very poor. I remember he was

very honest. He had a kind wife and a beautiful daughter. He also had a nice young boy helping him.'

'That's correct. They were so poor that they couldn't afford to eat. But he had a secret.'

'What was the secret again?'

'He knew how to turn mushrooms into soup.

'Where did they grow again?'

'They grew in the meadows beyond the kingdom- under the beech trees and the oaks.'

'And what was it he did again?'

'He would keep gathering up the mushrooms in the king's outlands and feed his family.'

'So why did he do it?'

'He needed them for soup- to feed himself and his family.'

'And he was caught out wasn't he?'

'Yes, one of the king's less-travelled servants caught him doing this and reported the mushroom man to the king.'

'Why would the servant do this?'

'To make himself more popular with the king.'

'Yes, and what happened?'

'The king took great exception.'

'Why?'

'He wanted to know why he was stealing his mushrooms. He told his servant to bring the mushroom man to him. When the mushroom man arrived, he explained that he was able to turn them into soup in order to feed himself and his family. The mushroom man argued that the mushrooms were for everyone and not just for the king.'

'And what did the king say?'

'He said he owned the lands and so he owned the mushrooms upon them. He said the mushroom man was stealing his mushrooms. The king said he would kill the mushroom man.'

'He was evil.'

'Yes.'

'And what happened?'

'The mushroom man begged the king to spare his life.'

'And did he?'

'Out of pity, the king relented. He ordered the mushroom man to turn some mushrooms in to soup for him. The king was so delighted by the taste of the soup that he asked the mushroom man to collect as many mushrooms as he could and turn them in to soup for him. The king said he would reward him handsomely.'

'So?'

'The mushroom man was very honest at first. He said he couldn't possibly take the king's money. He said he would rather just feed his family. The king said he either turned the mushrooms into soup or he would be killed.'

'So?'

'The mushroom man got to work. He gathered up all the mushrooms every day, every week, every year. The king got very greedy. He wanted to keep all the mushrooms to himself. Over time, the mushroom man became very rich. Inevitably, he said to the king that he no longer needed to make mushroom soup for him. The king got very angry and said he would kill the mushroom man if he did not keep making him mushroom soup.'

'What did the mushroom man do?'

'The mushroom man said he could do that but that the king would go mad. The king asked why this was. The mushroom man explained the mushrooms could alter his feelings. The king ignored this and ordered the mushroom man to keep making him soup.'

'What happened?'

'The mushroom man made the king magic mushroom soup. The king was starting to go mad. The king kept insisting on more soup. Eventually, however, the lands ran out of mushrooms. The mushroom man apologised to the king that it was no longer possible for him to make him the soup.'

'And what happened?'

'In his mad state, the king killed his queen. As the king grew madder and madder, he worked the mushroom man harder and harder. He ordered the mushroom man to give up his daughter as his wife.'

'Was she beautiful?'

'Very. Anyway, the mushroom man's daughter refused to marry the king.'

'Why was that?'

'She loved the mushroom boy who had helped his dad. Plus, the king was too old and having eaten all the soup he was too fat. The king decided he would kill the mushroom man for his daughter's refusal. The mushroom man got scared. He scoured high and low to find more mushrooms. Farther away, he found some. He said to the king that he could make him more soup if the king didn't kill his daughter. The king relented. Unfortunately, the mushroom man couldn't find any more mushrooms.'

'So what did he do?'

'He resolved to kill the king.'

'How?'

'By poisoning him with the soup. He used toadstools instead. He made him a bowl of mushroom soup with lethal mushroom.'

'And?'

'The servant made the mushroom man a bowl of soup with lethal mushroom.'

'In the end, the evil king died. The mushroom man died as well. The mushroom man's daughter became queen and the mushroom boy became king.'

'And what about the mushrooms?'

'The new king planted more mushrooms and the whole kingdom enjoyed mushroom soup together.'

Jane smiled wistfully. 'That's a bitter/sweet story, mother.'

Judith White nodded. 'Yes, and very telling.'

Jane scratched her puzzled head. 'The mushroom man obviously started off very poor and honest but he became spoiled.. The less-travelled servant exacted his revenge. The mushroom boy retained his innocence. Why did you recount this story?'

Judith White's slanting eyes drooped downwards, exhibiting her pessimism. 'I know what you did Jane, you acted out the story.'

I mobiled Chase. '*Chase*?'

'*Ewok*!'

'I used the microphone laser.'

'Good.'

'I've listened in on the friend's mother Judith White- she was with your niece's friend, her daughter.'

'And?'

'She worked for your brother's client.'

'And?'

'She sued the disgruntled client Hugh Sharp.'

'And?'

'He didn't win.'

'And might she have killed my brother?'

'Possibly.'

Suddenly, there was a scream. 'Chase, I have to hang up.'

The scream continued. 'Jane! Jane!'

Jane stirred in her bed. 'Mother?' she murmured.

'Help me, Jane!'

Tired-eyed, Jane got up out of her bed.

Suddenly, there was a bang. Thick black smoke funnelled up through the floorboards.

'Jane! Jane!' Judith White screamed. There was smoke everywhere. Jane sprung out of bed, darted along the hallway. She tried to push open the door but it wouldn't budge.

'The door's jammed!' said Jane.

'Hurry, Jane!'

'I'm going to have to break it down.'

'There's an axe in the shed, Jane.'

Jane shot downstairs. She entered the burning kitchen. She opened the sink cupboard and grabbed a towel. She spun the cold tap and soaked the towel with water. She placed the wet towel over the chip pan. The furnace extinguished. She turned the cooker off. She filled the basin in the sink up with water. She threw the basin of water up into the burning ceiling. There was a hissing sound as part of the fire snuffed out. She filled up another basin of water and launched it at the ceiling. She could still hear her mother crying: 'Jane! Jane! There's fire up here.' She bolted out of the kitchen and dived towards the shed. She found the axe hanging from the wall. She plucked it from the wall and raced back into the kitchen and ran upstairs. She lofted the axe into the air and brought it crashing into the door. The wood split and a chunk fell to the floor. She swung again. A second chunk fell to the floor. She then swung again and again. Eventually the axe went through the door. She aimed for the lock. The axe clinked as it hit the metal. She struck the lock again and again and again, making a clashing sound.

The door released with a clangour. Jane threw the axe down and pushed the door open.

'Mother!' Jane cried.

Judith White was on all fours coughing, fighting for breath.

Jane pull the duvet cover off the bed. She clawed the sheet from the mattress. She wrapped the sheet over her mother. She rolled her over the floor. Jane carried her mother out of the bedroom downstairs into the garden.

Judith White was snivelling.

'What happened mother?' said Jane.

'The kitchen went on fire.'

'How did that happen?'

'I was making chips. I left the kitchen for a few seconds and when I returned it was on fire. I tried to get to you but the bedroom door was locked.'

Jane sighed. 'Yes.'

'This has never happened before. I have never ever made a mistake with cooking. I'm always so careful.'

There was the squeak of the garden gate opening.

I mobiled Chase. 'Chase?'

'Ewok.'

'The kitchen went on fire.'

'How?'

'It seems to have been caused by a chip pan.'

'Seems?'

'I saw someone running from the house.'

'Who?'

'I don't know. The person was wrapped in a cloak with a hood over their head and a mask.'

'Where did the person run to?'

'They ran along the pavement and disappeared into the shadows.'

'Do you think this person started the fire.'

'It's very possible.'

'Tomorrow, it's my niece's husband.'

I sighed. 'Yes, Chase.'

CHAPTER TWENTY-NINE

Day Seven; 6 am; The Henpecked Husband

The bang came again. I woke up.

'*Ewok*!'

'Chase. Which window did you use this time?'

'The kitchen. It was rather unclean.'

'I know, for some reason my wife hasn't been in the mood for polishing.'

'No? Re-visit my niece and that husband. I wish to know more about their capacity to have murdered my brother and his wife.'

I drove to Keppochill. I set up the recording equipment.

There were shadows in the living room. They were elongated and crepuscular. They were like the shadows of last night's Frosty Jack-fuelled nightmares. They smouldered in the rising electric fan-heat of the evening. They shrivelled, as Richie quaffed three litres of the gut rot straight from the neck. As these shadows diminished, the fear, too- that overwhelming indecipherable fear, the one he had harboured for so many, many years, something to do with heat, pain and Susie- began to submit to allaying de-recrudescence. He some how felt more relaxed.

His favourite songs were playing. He had a broken list of them. They were the songs he and Susie had compiled together in the weeks running up to their marriage. They were reporting from their personal hi-fi. It was virtually the only conversation piece they had, apart from a withering Amaryllis. It included 'Bat out of hell' by Meatloaf and 'The speed of night' by Bonie Tyler and finished with 'Take my breath away' by Berlin: pure ear candy and also earworms. They were particularly a nuisance when you were trying to get off to sleep. Richie tended to notice them less when he passed out in spite of them.

His anaesthetized thoughts shimmered like a gorgeous early evening sun on the *River Clyde*. His mind and his heart drifted...

Hadn't weird and wonderful things happened? he thought. *Hadn't Tony Blair, his amazing former Prime Minister, sung the song he had written about him live on the box? Hadn't George Bush, the President of the United States of America, the most powerful man in the world, condescended to smoke a fag and paid homage to his greatness? Again from the comfort of his own front room?*

Suddenly, the tape tripped. The sun in his mind went down. *But hadn't the judge, the man he had so desperately wanted to be, also upbraided him? Reminded him that although career éclat relied naturally on serious levels of education and training and that it induced a certain drunken smugness later, that it was also extremely hard work? Hadn't the little black child soldiers in Zimbabwe been firing guns? Hadn't they raised excruciating questions of cultural relativism? Hadn't he seen the darker side to global appraisal? If only she believed. If only she didn't make him so afraid to suspend his disbelief.*

He swayed like a battered metronome as he sat down onto the cold bare splintered floorboards of the living room. He swiped the desparpled junk: last week's *Carlsbergs*, crumpled manuscripts, quarter-eaten snack-boxes, delicatessen food wrappers and pungent miscellaneous socks. His thoughts, predictably abnormal, were now whining: *Fuck you, Susie! Fuck off, Susie! Get to fuck, fucking Susie! One, seventeen, one hundred and three...*

Susie, who had her back to him as she brushed the last of the dust into the shovel, swivelled round. 'You know my brain went, Richie.'

'Yes, it happens to me all the time, get used to it.'

Susie shook her head. 'No, it's not the same. Your brain powers up and then shuts down automatically, my brain went completely.'

'I told you, it's those fags you smoke.'

'But I always smoked.'

'There you go then.'

'I know someone did that.'

'Who?'

'I don't know.'

'But?'

'I think they wanted to get me back.'

'What for?'

'Betraying them.'

Richie smiled tolerantly. 'How's your brain now?'

'It's fine now.'

'There you go then.'

Susie nodded disappointedly. 'We really have to do something about that creosote,' she muttered.

'Yes, your lungs must be black by now.'

Susie was back in some form. 'And your sweet defining vocabulary.'

'What?'

Susie jutted her head out and giggled and said, '*Two million and six*?'

Richie dauded the floorboards with his fist and said, 'How the hell did you know?'

Susie smiled. 'Just a guess,' she said.

'It's genius,' he said.

Susie shook her head and said, 'Not to me it isn't.'

'You always seem to know what I think,' said Richie.

'You always seem to tell me,' said Susie.

The house suddenly went dark. 'Christ!' said Richie, 'What now?'

Susie clenched her jaw and said, ’The card’s run out. And the shop’s shut.’

‘Why didn’t you buy a frigging spare, you dopey bitch?!’ he said.

Susie bit her lower lip and said, ‘I should have, shouldn’t I?’ She put down her brush and shovel and went over to the window. She went to unbolt the curtains, to let some light. She went to open the window to de-smog the place.

Ritchie snapped: ’Leave it!’

‘Okay, okay,’ said Susie.

‘I like it black,’ said Richie, ‘It’s like our supposedly rich Somerfield coffee these days.’

‘I don’t,‘ she said, ‘It’s like your rear end.’ She retreated from the window. Richie bent forwards and picked up an empty of piece of sweet corn. He threw it in her direction. Susie dodged out the way. ‘My end’s like a snowman’s,’ he said.

‘Yes,’ she said, ’Where the sun don’t shine- but just enough to move the coal-face downward.’

Susie dug her nails into her apron pocket and scraped out her second pack of twenty *Richmond*. She lit up a fag.

‘Another blooming fag?’ he said, ‘You need nicotinamide. You already have dyspnoea. Is that how your father went?’

‘Not quite Sweetheart.’

Susie blew the smoke serenely out of her mouth and said, ‘I suppose I’ve got a claim as well,’ she said.

Richie lifted his head proudly and said, ‘”If it is reasonably foreseeable,’ he said, ’as a reasonable and probable consequence of the defender’s breach of his duty of care that the pursuer would sustain harm, then the defender is liable to pay damages in delict.’

‘Well learned,’ said Susie, ’And what’s the next legal conjecture?’

‘You follow civil procedure,’ said Richie.

‘Which is?’ said Susie.

Richie gestured at an impenetrable manual which was lying in a cardboard box in the corner of the room. ’It’s all in there,’ he said.

Susie looked at him contemptuously and said, 'Not in your head, then?'

'Doesn't need to be,' he said.

'Still need our crib sheet?'

Richie glared indignantly. 'No, I certainly do not.'

'Still got no desire to know?'

'Not any more?'

'A double negative. Not ever. Anyway, I was cumbered.'

Susie sneered. 'You mean Cu-cumbered?' Susie sighed. 'You're nowhere near to being a D.C.L.'

'A what?'

'A doctor of Civil Law.'

He hated his ignorance. He hated the way the *real* lawyers knew the things he didn't. He thumped the floorboards again. 'What the hell is this all about?!' he said.

'Mental illness, my darling!' Susie said.

'What the hell causes it?'

Susie smirked and said, 'Fresh oranges.'

Richie looked hopeful. '*Really*?' he said.

'No, the drink.'

'When in God's name did I start?' he said.

Susie inhaled the smoke in her mouth, breathed out and said, 'A long time ago.'

Richie flopped his head and said, 'How long?'

'About twenty years ago. You were nine.'

'I see. Above the age of criminal consent.'

'According to whom?'

'Not "whom" but 'Hume'.'

'Who's he?'

'Why my dear, he was one of the institutional writers.'

'I do write, my darling.'

'Yes, my freak of a wife, but not institutionally.'

'And what does that mean?'

'It means your linguistics are way behind...'

'Behind?'

'You know, the great works.' Richie coughed importantly. 'So I was nine.'

'Yes.'

'Why did I start at nine?'

'You did something, Richie.'

'What?'

'Something terrible.'

'How would you know?'

'It was the same time my mother...'

Richie wiggled his head assumingly. 'She was a pure goddess, the woman. Big pendulous breasts, wavy blond hair, perfect blue eyes- the kindness to match-'

'No, she wasn't, Richie, she was a total bitch.'

'In what way?'

'She physically abused me. And she cheated on dad.'

'I'm surprised you speak up for him.'

'Why?'

'You're nothing like he was.'

'How?'

'He was nice. He knew how to speak to people. He never lost his temper. He was always fair. And by the way, you bear no physical resemblance to him whatsoever.'

'I thought you resented him for rejecting you from the house.'

'He was just following your mother's orders.'

'But you told your parents and they went mental.'

'They over-reacted to him. I remember he was nice the way he put it.'

'How did he put it?'

'He said it wasn't my fault, that it was only fair to me that I got to stay away. Remember your dad asked you what happened to you.'

Susie nodded.

'You refused to talk about it. Your dad confronted your mother. She said a paedophile was responsible. Did the paedophile get to you, Susie.'

Susie grimaced. 'They got to both of us.'

Richie squinted. 'There were two paedophiles?'

Susie shook her head. 'I don't want to talk about it. All I know is that my mother was a bitch.'

'Come now, my sweetness. We can't blame our mother for everything. Plus, you should never speak ill of the dead. I love my mother.'

'You do?'

'Yes.'

'Why?'

'She beats everyone.'

'In what way?'

'She knows she had me, she knows she's better, she knows how to put everyone in their place.'

'My darling, I lost my mother in July 1995.'

'How?'

'She- they weren't- still aren't sure. She was presumed dead.'

'After seven years.'

'Yes.'

'And what was I drinking?'

'Your folks' supermarket beer. You pinched it from the lounge cupboard.'

Richie angled his head haughtily and said, 'The word is *purloined*, my dear. And why was I doing this?'

She threw the fag into the sweet corn tin. She glowered at him and said, 'You tell me.'

'A distant relative must have interfered with me. I was pretty tasty at one point. Blond hair, blue eyes-'

'Shut up, sweetheart!' she said. 'Don't be so earth bred.'

'Either that or the kids at school must have been bullying me. They never did like my cut-glass accent.'

Susie twisted her head and puckered her lips; and said, 'Hmm.'

'No?' he said.

Susie twitched her head.

'And then what happened.'

'You went onto the hard stuff.'

'Whiskey?'

'Whiskey, vodka, gin, rum...'

'...And never stopped?'

'Well, not until recently. I suspect that's cider, isn't it?'

Richie scrunched up his face. 'Yes,' he said. After a brief cessation he had another strident thought. 'It can't have been good for my health.'

'No, you were vomiting a lot. Generally suffering. You even chipped your crown.'

'How did I do that?'

'You fell onto the stairs.'

'Fuck me!'

Susie peeked at his mammoth stubble which was very far from designer and her stomach turned; she felt like truncating her husband's manhood. She said, 'If it's all the same to you, I'd rather not.'

'Why was I doing that?'

Susie gnarled at Richie. 'You did something terrible.'

'What?'

'You're so drunk you can't remember.'

'Gorgeous, am I?'

'Hardly. The whole house needs cleaned up. Susie smiled and said, 'Nor is your condition. And it's getting worse. Panic disorder now; auditory and visual hallucinations.'

'It was murder,' he said, 'There was colours- yellow and green- faces, screeching, and then I was thrown up into the ceiling'

Susie gulped and nodded. 'Is it 'Californication?''

'The Red Chilli Peppers?'

'Too hot for you?'

'Too hot for anyone. Still, that's expensive drink for you. Damn those real ales, fancy wines and sparkling champagnes! Just as well I'm back on the nasty stuff.'

'It's a bit late, though.'

'What d' you mean? Health wise? I won't recover?'

'No, money wise.'

Richie's jaw slipped. 'Charming!' he said. He recovered. 'But that's what dole money's for. To drink yourself to death with.'

Susie tilted her head and said, 'And the overdraft?'

'To bring you back to life.'

Susie titled her head still further and said, 'And the increases?'

'To drink like there's no tomorrow.'

Susie nodded.

'That stuck-up mule of a Bank Manager will soon realize the error of his ways.'

Susie smiled and said, 'And breach the banking code?'

'Judicial discretion has it covered.'

Susie sustained her glare for a few more seconds and then relented. She sighed and said, 'If only my book was selling?'

Richie grunted. 'Why isn't it?'

Susie shrugged. 'I guess the cumulative audience isn't big enough.'

Richie belched. 'The what?'

'Everyone who sees or hears the advertisement.'

'Where d' you advertise?'

'Publications, broadcast programs.'

'What was it called again?'

Susie frowned and said, 'Can you not even remember that?'

'I can.'

'So?'

'So, the rusted cogs of my imagination can't be actualized.'

'I know they can't. You just have to do some groundwork.'

'Yes?'

'Some oleganenous research- and then harness your spiritual energy.'

'Yes, Richie?'

'The novel wont write itself, although they've been said to do.'

'In other words?'

'You have to write it.'

'I have?

'Yes.'

'You have to get your thoughts together and put them into words.'

'Perhaps I lack the life experience, the know-how or the imagination but-'

'But I do possess the desire.'

'Why am I not writing?'

'How this quite legitimate and innocuous question offends your vanity.'

'It does?'

'Yes.

'I've got so many things to remember. When the off license opens, when it shuts-'

'-"Beyond the waterfall."'

'Lovely title, bitch! What was it about?'

Susie sighed again and said, 'Two young guys from different social backgrounds who got drunk and fell in love.'

'I thought you hated drink.'

'I do. But audiences much prefer to see characters have flaws. It gives them something to relate to. It even makes them feel better about themselves.'

Richie grimaced. 'Like being a rotten queer.'

Susie waved her head and said, 'Being gay is not a flaw, my darling. In point of fact, it's a major selling point as far as writing goes. It makes the person different; interesting.'

'Na, the drink and the bent both just make the reasonable hypothetical man on the Clapham Omnibus want to vomit. And why's it 'Beyond' the waterfall anyway?'

'They had nowhere to go after that. They could only regret.'

'You mean they fell out?'

'Yes.'

'Why?'

'Because of the worst thing.'

'Which was?'

'Agony.'

Richie bobbed his head in a silly knowing way and said, 'I see. Sounds good.'

'You're sure?'

'Yes, blooming lovely!' Richie said. 'Just like your boyfriend Tam.'

Susie puckered her brow and said, 'Tam isn't my boyfriend, sweetheart. He's supposed to be yours.'

'Then how come *we* never sleep together?'

'It was a tent, Richie. What was I supposed to do? Sleep out in the rain?'

'I had to.'

'Yes, but I didn't drink the entire loch.'

'You drank more than Madge, anyway.' At least she bothered to look for me.'

'You weren't that difficult to find. I've heard quieter outboards.'

'I've heard far more convincing stories. I'm not surprised you don't sell.'

'Thanks.'

'You'll have to write another one.'

Susie cast her eye over the room. There were empty cans, polystyrene boxes, plastic bags, refuse sacks and scattered paperwork. 'What with?' she said.

'I thought you writers were supposed to have imagination. See the toilet bowl, there's clogs of sh-'

'-yes, thank you-'

'-and the walls are still sort of yellowy-white. You could even use one of your foul fag ends as a quill if you don't fancy your fingers. Just don't touch my bottle-opener!'

'Look! It's your filth that is cupreous. Your alcohol costs more than my nicotine. Plus, I get twenty out of the fiver, you only get eight.'

'Yes, but it's quality not quantity that counts.'

'Frosty Jack's not quality, sweetheart. It's cut-rate crap. It's dynamic pricing gone badly wrong. And three litres does count.'

'It helps to ease the pain.'

Susie glowered at him again and said, '*Yes*. What pain?'

'The pain of living with you.'

Susie scowled. 'You still don't remember, do you, you bastard?'

'Remember what?'

'I thought so. I'd be better asking the cat.'

'Why don't you, then? You seem to speak the same language anyway.'

'You mean the language of love, as opposed to...'

Richie yawned in agony. Susie exhaled noisily.

'We can't go on like this, dearest,' said Susie. 'We'll have to do something.'

'Isn't that a bit rash? The bottle's not dead yet.'

'No, I mean about the money.'

'But your parents left us thousands.'

'Yes, but we spent that.'

'What on?'

'Your addiction.'

'Our addictions.'

'Tell me about your mother.'

Susie dipped her head and said, 'She's not my mother, darling.'

'Well, who the hell is? Or was?'

'I don't want to talk about it.'

'You never do.'

Susie's eyes retraced their path to the serious problem. 'You do know we've already used half of it.'

'The money?'

'No, the alcohol fumes in the air.'

'Well, if you wouldn't insist on smoking we'd have more.'

Susie eyed Richie with a certain suspicion and said, 'More for alcohol, you mean?'

Richie looked away innocently and said, 'It's medicinal.'

'No, it's madness.'

'It helps- *really*.'

'What would be more helpful is if you got a job. We need earned income. We can't all be on the demand-side; society needs some supply.'

'I'm doing my best, woman! I've been to see some employers. It's not easy when the god-darned phone's disconnected. You're dad wouldn't help to get it back on?'

'My dad's gone, sweetheart.'

'He is?'

'Yes, he's been gone for years.'

'Where did he go?'

'I never knew.'

'So?'

'Why don't we beg *your* dad instead ?'

'No, dad-blamed, he's got nothing.'

'Well, it's time for a crisis loan, then.'

'There's no way a man in my position is filling out those stupid forms.'

'For goodness sake, sweetheart. Can you not even process a data element? I thought you were supposed to be a lawyer.'

'I am. I will be.'

'*When*?'

'When the stuck-up Senior Partners appreciate my brilliant education. When The Law Society stops meddling. When The Legal Aid Board finally recognises a case of need. When the credit crunch is over.'

'You got a third, darling; face it you have dysgnosia. And it's The Law Society's function to regulate. And you don't get SLAB Payments at trainee level. And the crunch doesn't exactly impede employment law.'

At this stage of the evening, four counterarguments were too much for him. His eyelids whirled and he said, 'I only got one third. And your subject was mince. Anyway, I got my completion certificate, didn't I?'

Susie smiled.

'God knows how!' said Richie.

'Yes, but you have to do more than that.'

Richie bobbed his head childishly.

Susie drilled Richie with her eyes. 'And if you don't, my sweetness...' She wiggled her wiry elongated figure, de-tangled her locks and tossed her long defluous golden hair, like one of Katy Perry's 'California Gurls.' '...I'll leave you.'

'Then we'll both have scars.'

Susie sobbed. 'I'm afraid of it, Richie.'

'Your appearance?'

'No, the thing we cook our meals with.'

'That's why I wanted to protect you. Mushrooms would have done.'

Susie suddenly sobbed, feeling desexed. 'Never mention my scar- or our mushrooms.'

Richie gulped. 'Sorry, Sooze.'

As Susie wiped the tears from her eyes, she said, 'I'll sort out the loan. You get help. *Or else*.'

I mobiled Chase.

'*Ewok*!'

'I'm at Keppochhill.'

'Did you use the laser microphone.'

'Yes.'

'How is my niece?'

'Revengeful as ever.'

'And?'

'She's still smoking, while he's still drinking.'

'When did he start drinking?'

'Your niece says he was nine.'

'Why?'

'He seems to have done something.'

'What did he do?'

'I don't know, something terrible.'

'And?'

'It does appear that she was being abused.'

'Why?'

'She didn't say.'

Chase exhaled with satisfaction. 'Good work, Ewok.'

I said: 'thanks', as if I needed his approval.

'You start again tomorrow. You are to investigate the friend and the older cousin.'

'Thorntonhall? Aberdeen?'

'No, Queens Park.'

'Queens Park?'

'Yes, the friend runs a boutique there- the older cousin has excogitated a visit.'

'How do you know, Chase?'

'I taped one of his mobile telephone conversations.'

'How?'

'I got his mobile number.'

'How?'

'I went through the mobile directory. I gave the man on the phone his name.'

'And what did he say?'

'He said: "I'll see her tomorrow".'

'Who was he talking to?'

'He was talking to his mother.'

I scratched my head. 'And I thought I was the sleuth.'

'Yes, but I control the sleuth.'

'You're not joking.'

'Night, Ewok.'

'Night, Chase.'

CHAPTER THIRTY

Day Eight; 5: 45 am; Boutique Break-in

Another fulmination. I woke up automatically.

'*Ewok*!'

'Chase. One of my three bathrooms windows?'

'I hadn't thought about that. No, the dining room window.'

'Just getting to know the place.'

'Exactly.'

'The friend and the older cousin?'

'Indeed.'

'The little bird is of course also early.'

'Too late is too little.

I drove to Victoria Road in the South Side of Glasgow. I parked the Mercedes outside the boutique. I sat outside an embarrassingly young and over trendy coffee shop- it was called 'Cool Cups, hot cups'- feeling more than a little displaced, in the duplicitous afternoon shade. I could presage a longer darker shadow. I was sipping very hot tea. Tea had never burned my mouth. I was too experienced. I considered myself to possess an asbestos mouth. As usual, I had a generous helping of semi-skimmed milk. Certainly, no sugar. I had bought a Caramel Wafer.

There was a profane clatter. It reminded me of Chase's

pot-shots. The front entrance of the boutique swung open. It did so like the chiasmic jaws of a great white shark. It was as if it had gotten a whiff of nothing but the irresistible ichor from an eviscerated corpse. The glass cracked like the hourglass in 'Topgun'. The frame battered against the inside plaster-board support column like the shark's tale end.

Jane shuddered. '*Ann*, my darling!' she exclaimed. '*Run*! *Ben*, help us!'

Jane turned to see the lacerated countenance of a man who looked exceedingly angry.

'Hello,' he said with a rictus which paraded a golden front tooth, 'my old friend.'

Jane squeaked. 'Who are you?'

'Mickey.'

'Why are you here?'

'My father was murdered.'

Jane eyed the man demurely. 'He was?'

'Yes.'

'By whom?'

'By a man who had neglected his wife.'

'Why would he kill your father?'

'My father knocked sense into his wife.'

'Why?'

'She had betrayed him.'

'How?'

'She didn't help him with the cause.'

'What cause?'

'The Irish catholic cause.'

'When was he killed?'

'1995.'

'Where?'

'Dublin.'

'How do you know?'

'I was there.'

'How did he do it?'

'I don't know.'

'So?'

'It's your girlfriend's fault.'

'Sorry?'

'Your friend when you were growing up.'

'Who?'

'Susie.'

Jane cast her mind back into the past. 'Susie?'

'Yes.'

'I remember she was being hurt.'

'You do?'

'Yes, someone was hurting her.'

'Yes, you cared for her.'

'What do you mean?'

'It's the 'Same love' I believe.'

'It's what?'

'It's 'Macklemore'.

'What?'

'It's 't.A.T.u."

'I don't think you understand my business at all. I perform beauty therapeutic procedures, not tattoos.'

'"All the things she said."'

Jane nodded hesitantly. 'Yes, yes, I know the songs- Ann thinks they're coo-' Jane covered her mouth with her hand, realizing her mistake.

The man grinned. 'Ann, eh? So you have a daughter? Or is that your latest girlfriend?'

Jane shook her head fearfully.

'But you do know the song.'

'Yes, of course, Ben can play all the contemporaries-' She covered her mouth again.

'Ben?'

'My fiancé- I mean my very, very well-built fiancé.'

Mickey eyed her quizzically. 'You are betrothed to a man?'

'Yes, I certainly am. A very strong man. What of it?'

'I'm just surprised that's all.'

Jane glared. 'Surprised why?'

'I thought you would be into- you know- *other girls.*'

Jane stamped her high-heel. 'You thought what? Just who in God's name do you think you are?!' she demanded.

The man bore his teeth. 'Why, Jane my long lost darling, I'm your *confidante.*'

Jane's mind flashed back into the past. She squinted. 'Mickey?'

'Who else?'

'The only secret you kept was the abuse of my friend. How did you find me?'

'You advertised.'

'I did?'

'Yes, through Thomson's Directory: '"Looking Sharp." I take it that's your fiancée's surname.'

Jane waved her head. 'Why would you take that?'

'It wasn't your surname, it is White.'

'How do you know my fiancée?'

'He's the son of the friend of my my father's friend.'

'Who?'

'My father was Jarrod Fields. His friend was Albert Bennet. His friend was Hugh Sharp.'

'And?'

'I want paid.'

'What are you asking me?'

'I'm telling you to pay me back for what you did to me?'

'What did I do to you?'

'You tried to kill me.'

Jane shook her head indignantly. 'I tried nothing of the sort.'

'You forget.'

'No, you choose to ignore. I also want to know where your friend is.'

Jane grimaced. 'Even if I did know, I wouldn't tell you. Now, would you kindly please remove yourself from my premises this instance.'

Mickey flashed a nicotine-stained smile. 'No, honey I don't think I'll be doing that.'

'Then I shall surely call the police.'

'Yes, that would be a first-rate idea.'

'What d' you mean?'

'I remember you attempted my life.'

'I remember you hurt me.'

'You didn't like it?'

'No, of course I didn't.'

'Strange, I didn't either.'

'What d'you mean?'

'Your friend's father abused me.'

'Andrew McLean.'

'Yes.'

'Why would he abuse you?'

'He was a gay paedophile.'

'I find that very hard to believe. Mr McLean was a family man. He was also a lawyer.'

'Yes, he might have played the part but he preferred the young boys.'

'I really think you're wrong.'

'I could have you done for attempted murder. I could also tell people what you are.'

'What do you think I am?'

'A closet lesbian.'

'I'm nothing of the sort.'

'The police will lock you up.'

'I might have to go into hospital but the Mental Health Tribunal will see that I have regained my sanity, and then I'll be discharged. You on the other hand might not be so lucky...'

'Meaning?'

'You would either go down or this Ben of yours and your precious daughter Ann will suffer.'

'Meaning what?'

'I will kill them.'

'That alone gives me the reason to report you.'

'We made a deal remember?'

'We did?'

'Of course we did.'

'When?'

'Let's see, this is 2018- over twenty years ago.'

'And?'

'I agreed I wouldn't tell them what you tried. You agreed you wouldn't tell them what you thought I did.'

'So?'

'I think it's best you pay me and that I see your friend.'

'Why would you want to see her?'

'She owes me as well.'

'Why?'

'As I said, she betrayed my father.'

'Where do you live?'

'Silk Road. But I had to move. I had to move.'

'Where?'

'Silk Road 3.'

'You moved across the road.'

'Kind of. There is also Silk Road URL.'

'So I had to use Tor and an onion router'

'Excuse me?'

'It's a browser.'

'You're a reader.'

Mickey smirked. 'Yes. I had to set up VPN.'

'Which is?'

'Virtual Private Network.'

'It's called the deep web. It's called the Darknet. I have to use bitcoins.'

'What are bitcoins.'

'They are counterfeit coupons.'

Jane gawked. 'Pardon?'

'It's a crypto currency.'

'Which is?'

'A virtual currency. I have to create an account, select the required items, specify the quantity and pay using Bitcoin.'

'And what happens?'

'The item is shipped through snail-mail.'

'You know things I have no wish to know.'

'There is also Agora and Middle Earth. There is also N2 underworld.'

'What is it you want?'

'The same thing I wanted all those years ago.'

'Which was?'

'To appreciate what little this meaningless world has to offer.'

Jane's face wrinkled. 'Excuse me.'

'I wish to enhance my royal existence.'

'What does that mean?'

'It means I want to get high.'

'High?'

'You know when your body- well at least the mind exults.'

'Use your grubby hand then, you brutish fool.'

'You insult me.'

'You disgust me.'

'Anyway, I shall be requiring money- rather a lot in fact.'

'Well, get a job, then, you despicable lazy bully.'

'You wouldn't offer me one.'

Jane's voice modulated. 'Certainly not. I should never employ someone so disgraceful as you.'

'Just as well I don't need you to.'

'No?'

'No, I'm an employer.'

Jane looked at the man quizzically. 'You are?'

'Yes.'

'So why extort money from me?'

'Business is a bit slow at the moment.'

'Well, so is mine.'

'Yes, I caught you at the right time.'

'Pardon?'

'No one else was in.'

'You're mad.'

'Yes, but I didn't do what you did.'

'You have no proof. Anyway, you caused too much pain.'

'You have no proff of that.'

Jane stammered. 'I-'

'Now, in my generous state, I'm going to give you a bit of time.'

'Time for what?'

'Time for me to chase up my brother.'

'Who?'

'Sean.'

'Why?'

'He owes me as well.'

'What for?'

'Betraying my father.'

'How?'

'He fled Rathnew years ago.'

'Why?'

'He was too weak for the cause.

'Where is he? Your brother?'

'Under the northern lights.'

Jane shrugged.

'He's living on the streets.'

'I'm paying you nothing.'

'Oh, I think you will. The time I'm allowing you will afford you that luxury. We'll meet soon at the Buchanan in Glasgow.'

I mobiled Chase.

'*Ewok*!'

'I drove to the friend's workplace.'

'Did you go in?'

'Of course not.'

'Why not?'

'That would made my investigation too conspicous.'

'Good.'

'So?'

'What happened?'

'I might not have needed the laser microphone.'

'Why's that?'

'The conversation was pretty audible.'

'The older cousin turned up, then?'

'Yes? She was interrogating her.'

'And?'

'He demanded that she give him money.'

'Why?'

'He wants to enjoy himself.'

'In what way?'

'With drugs.'

'And?'

'They have holds over each other.'

'What holds?'

'He knows she tried to kill her, she knows he caused a lot of pain.'

'What pain?'

'I don't know.'

'Why not?'

'They never said explicitly.'

'And?'

'He's affording the friend some time, while he chases up his brother.'

'The younger cousin?'

'Yes.'

'Where is he?'

'I don't know.'

'It's just as well I know where he will be.'

'How?'

'I tapped his mobile telephone conversations.'

'How?'

'In the same way I did with the older cousin.'

'Yes?'

'I got his mobile telephone number through the mobile directory.'

'And?'

'He's painting pictures in the town square.'

'In which case, can you not just record his conversations.'

'Unfortunately not.'

'Why not?'

'His mobile broke.'

'How?'

'I think someone stamped on it.'

'What makes you think that?'

'As I was recording the mobile telephone conversation, the line cracked.'

'So I have to drive all the way up there myself?'

'Yes.'

'Where will he be?'

'In the town square.'

'And then I use the laser microphone?'

'You might not need it, you might just need voice recording.'

'Why?'

'You have no building to penetrate. You have no walls to get through. You just have to hear what he's saying. Seriously, Ewok, he'll be there all day, painting his pictures.'

'How d'you know?'

'He has no other way of surviving.'

'Where does he sleep?'

'He sleeps under a bridge.'

'How d'you know?'

'He said so in one of his last calls.'

'Who was it to?'

'The rivalrous uncle.'

'You mean they know each other?'

'Yes, they've met.'

'How?'

'The rivalrous uncle knew the younger cousin's father.'

'Jarrod Fields?'

'Yes.'

'And?'

'The rivalrous uncle has plans for the younger cousin.'

'What plans?'

'You'll see.'

CHAPTER THIRTY-ONE

Day Nine; 5: 30 am; Painting the Town Blood-red

I did not even have to wake up. I was conscious to the blast of another window shattering. My mobile bleeped.

'*Chase*!'

'You're in front, Ewok.'

'The downstairs bathroom?'

'Yes, I thought I would give you a break.'

'The younger cousin?'

'All the way to Aberdeen. Bring your youngest son. I want him to test the Irish traveller.'

I parked the Mercedes away from the front gates of the house and skulked my way to the outside of the house. I set up the sounding equipment outside the kitchen wall where there seemed to be some activity.

Alexander's gay dreams were like his bowels, his intestines, his colon. With the regular ease of a time-honoured solar system; with a salubrious, progressive and inexorable earthly graduation, like the dependable radiation emitted by the Earth's sun, falling irreversibly beneath the intricate and thought-provoking pattern of polygonal shapes made by the various features of the landscape, the woody, perennial and towering trees, the high rounded hills and walled and roofed buildings, against the sky, Alexander roused, like a heavenly angel descending to earth, from his idyllic young at heart dream-peppered slumber.

Crystaliferous vapour, moisture visible in the air as clouds, and the diffident inceptions of rivers, waterfalls, lakes, seas and oceans; and rollers upon which the human imagination, as well as the human body, surfed and which hung around the mixture of gases, expanding infinitely, condensing to form water, surrounding the earth, froze into ice crystals. These were solids containing internal patterns of molecules that were regular, repeated and geometrically arranged, like the priceless and glittering 24 carrot diamond of the human heart. In the case of others the heart was made of cubic zirconia.

They fell in drops like the most bitter human tears, from the visible masses of ice particles to the ground in the form of flakes. Small flat pieces, like fragments of the human soul, detached from the larger objects, the crystals, like a sweet smile from dismissive eyes. Just as soon as he had had the dream, he forgot it. Dreams were like snowflakes. Soft, beautiful but ephemeral.

He climbed out of his luxurious four-poster bed, deftly kicked on his flat lightweight *Snoopy* slippers, which dearest Aunt Doris had bought him long before her broken-hearted demise, shuffled over to the window, finely adjusted the craftily installed Venetian blinds, and sleepily beheld the infinite impenetrable niveous beauty. It was like a waking dream.

He tumbled down the ancient stairs, narrow and winding, crossed the lush rosy-carpeted hallway and entered the deluxe kitchen.

Uncle Albert's tired grey eyes bleeped. 'How did you sleep, son?'

'Like a log, uncle? You?'

Uncle Albert's crapulent mind had lost none of its age-old conservative definition. 'Like a section of a tree that has been chain-sawed and then halved by a log-splitter.'

Alexander smiled kindly. 'Not quite as well. Whatever can have happened, I wonder?'

Albert turned his head effeminately. 'I don't know what you mean.'

Alexander wiggled his head sarcastically. 'Of course not.'

Searching for a distraction, Albert said: 'Have you seen the snow?'

'Indeed I have yes, Uncle. It was the very first thing I saw. It's like the North Pole out there.'

Alexander gorged like a diminutive and emaciated African camel-prodder on his full English breakfast, perusing a few more pages from his now dried-out encyclopaedia, and thought about what he would do next. He donned a soft, warm, brushed and woolly fleece and ventured with temerity outside. He scrunched across the layer of fallen snow, which covered the small stony chips. He jinked like an adroit football winger between the gap in the hedge. The faithful old river was ice-capped in parts and the waterfall incorporated a monument of long drooping jagged ice, frozen in time. The small flat broken flakes dissolved in the river like dreams.

'Listen, Alex,' said uncle Albert

'Yes?' said Alexander.

'I need you to nip into town for me.'

'Town? Sure. Why?'

'We need one or two things.'

'We do?'

Albert nodded. 'Yes, look here, I have a list.'

Alexander took the list and scanned it. 'Irish potatoes...sybies... gammon-' He gazed at his uncle quizzically. '-Draft Guinness?' he said.

Albert coughed. 'Yes, I thought we could wash down the Kilcanan.'

Alexander gawked. 'The what?'

'It's ham with champ.'

Alexander dazed. 'Why on earth would we have...?'

Albert pretended to miss his nephew's confusion. 'I would also like you to buy a few paintings.'

Alexander glowered. 'Paintings?'

'Yes, I feel the walls need freshened up a little.'

'They do?'

'Yes, we've had the same old drab portraits for years.'

'But they're our ancestors.'

'Yes, but I was thinking more landscapes.'

'Landscapes?'

'Yes, for the drawing room.'

'Where would I find landscapes?'

Albert coughed. 'Funnily enough, there's a man in the town square that does them.'

'Which man?'

'I don't know his name.'

'You mean you've not met him.'

'I spoke to him very briefly but his name eludes me.'

'Very well,' said Alexander.

'Oh, and Alex?'

'Yes.'

'Have a shower first.'

'A sh-'

'And make sure you shave.'

'But it's only shopping.'

Albert winked. 'A young man must look his best when facing the public.'

Having shaved, showered and put on a pair of trendy jeans, a very smart shirt and some of his better clobber, Alexander exited the house and jumped into his ridiculous but gleaming latest registration BMW and sped precipitately towards town. He passed through the local village: the group of houses with their low-ceilinged walls and small roofs; and other buildings, such as the old primary school, the sacrosanct church and the signal village hall. There wasn't one house here he couldn't afford. When he reached town, he dumped Betsy, The Beast or Herby- he couldn't make up his mind what to call her- in the jam-packed supermarket car-park. He precoded to buy the items on his uncle's very strange list. Having done so, he aimed to locate the man in the town square whom his uncle had said sold the paintings. He parked the car in the vicinity, exited and ambled through the open four-sided town square, where the streets met and passed by the trees, grass and benches. He sat down on one of the benches and sipped his polystyrene cup of hot tea, which he had purchased from a small café called 'Meet and Eat.' It tasted so refreshing after a long brisk stroll.

CHAPTER THIRTY-TWO

Day Nine; 4 pm; The Object of Desire

I rang Chase.

'*Ewok*!'

'I'm just back from the house.'

'Fall's Hall?'

'Yes, the uncle sent the nephew out to go shopping.'

'You used the laser microphone?'

'Yes. It was rather a strange errand.'

'Strange?'

'The shopping list consisted of Irish food and drink, and landscape paintings. I can see from his shopping bags that he's finished buying the food and drink and now he's spotted the painter.'

'You're in the town square?'

'Yes.'

'Have you put on the voice recorder.'

'Yes.'

'Is the younger cousin there?'

'Yes, he's painting pictures by a monument in the centre.'

'And?'

'I think you're right.'

'Right?'

'Yes, I think the uncle has met the younger cousin before.'

'Yes, and?'

'I think he has arranged for his nephew to meet the younger cousin.'

'Yes, why do you think he would do that?'

'I'm not sure.'

'But?'

'I think the Uncle is trying to hide something or make his nephew happy.'

'Okay, Ewok. Hide behind the monument and listen in.'

Alexander was sitting on a black steel bench. He glimpsed a young male figure out of the crook of his eye. He looked very striking with his wavy blond hair, as well as comical with his flyblown painter's smock. He evacuated his seat and ambled towards him. He peered at him through the risings of the late afternoon mist. As he drew up to him he saw that he was quite tall and slim. He had green wide set eyes, telling of all sorts of adventure and unimaginable excitement; freedom and liberty; and he had an immensely cute boyish face. He wore discoloured jeans and lousy trainers. He leered at the painter, a mixture of feelings going through his heart. He surveyed the collection. The man acknowledged him with a winsome beam. He fanned his right hand. '*You like*?' he said.

Alexander smirked as he nodded.

The young man spoke in an American accent. 'Twenty bucks and you can kiss 'em.'

Alexander crouched down. He picked up a couple of the pictures.

'Go on!' said the man.

'I can't!' said Alexander.

'Why not?'

'I don't have twenty bucks.'

The painter looked daggers at him. He punched a hole in the canvas which fell over.

Alexander gulped. 'I'm sorry, what did I do wrong?'

The painter flashed a smile at him. 'I was joking my friend but to tell you the truth you can't just hold them, not kiss them, and not pay up.'

'Why is that?'

'It's the way it's done.'

'According to what?'

'A film called 'Roadhouse.'

'I see.' Alexander delved into his pocket. 'I could give you twenty pounds.'

The painter smiled at him again. He changed to an Irish accent. 'You're gay, aren't you?'

Alexander frowned. 'Pardon?'

The man smacked his plump rosy lips. 'I said you're gay.'

Alexander stammered. 'I- I...'

'You haven't come out yet, then?'

Alexander gawked. 'But I am out.'

'No, I mean: *out*.'

'What makes you say that?'

'You leered at me before you cast an eye over my paintings.'

'Are *you* gay?' said Alexander.

The man tilted his head. 'I could be.'

'What does that mean?'

'It means I can take it or leave it- either way.'

'So you're bisexual?'

'Possibly.'

'You don't give straight answers.'

'I could do that as well.'

'Please!'

'Very well,' he said. 'You use.'

'Pardon?'

'Yes, you use.'

'I don't use anyone.'

'No, but you're on something.'

'I don't take drugs.'

The man pinched his chin. 'Yes, they're prescription.'

'I don't take prescribed drugs either.'

'No?'

'Why would I lie?'

'Which means someone else has you on them.'

'What?'

'Tranquillizers.'

'I think I would know.'

'Yes, you would think, but it's just as well I do.'

'How do you know?'

'My brother knows everything about drugs and I can read people's behaviours.'

'What d' you mean?'

'Despite your young age and your excellent looks-

Alexander blushed. Thank you-'

'If you were clean, and even if you were gay, you'd either be smoking, drinking or working very hard, and you certainly wouldn't look at another man like that.'

Alexander frowned. 'I am clean and I do work hard but I don't need to drink or smoke- and I would hardly say I was looking at you like that.'

'You must do education.'

'Of course.'

'And you don't qualify your statements.'

'Am I supposed to?'

'And you're assertive.'

'So?'

'I'm not on it, but I understand it and you're at risk of losing your academic propensity.'

'How?'

'You see my family wasn't on it. My father was a very angry man and my mother is a very anxious woman. I was nervous- still am- so was my brother.'

'Yes?'

'My brother was put on it.'

'Tranquillizers?'

'Yes.'

'And?'

'He was being relaxed for sexual abuse.'

Alexander glowered. 'That's terrible. How old was he?'

'Fourteen.'

'And?'

'He was being popped.'

'What does that mean?'

The man pushed out his lips. 'I'll show you.'

Alexander waved his head. 'No, I don't think you will.'

'The man flashed his irresistible smile again. 'Please.'

'Yes, close your eyes a second.'

'If this is dangerous I'm not doing it.'

'No, you won't come to any harm, trust me.'

Alexander quailed back.

'Pretty please?'

'Very well.'

Alexander closed his eyes.

'Now, sniff!'

Alexander did so. Instantaneously, his feelings went from their original calmness to happiness, to excitement, to euphoria.'

The man delicately placed his hands around his face and kissed him. As he was exalting, Alexander worked his lips against him.

After about thirty seconds it was over. 'What was that?' said Alexander.

'That was poppers.'

'It felt incredible.'

'Yes, it does. That's how he did it.'

'Who?'

'The man that sexually abused my brother and I.'

'I wouldn't call your kissing me sexual abuse.'

'That's because you're an adult and also I didn't take it any further.'

'No. What did this man do to you?'

'He raped my brother and he touched me all over.'

'How old were you?'

'I was five.'

'That's opprobrious.'

'Yes, it is.'

'Who did it to you?'

'I think it was my dad's brother-in-law.'

'Why would he do that?'

'Because he was a paedophile.'

'I see.'

'Yes.'

'So drugs are very powerful things.'

Alexander sighed. 'Yes, bang goes my career.'

'No, your career will be fine so long as you understand.'

'What have I to understand- apart from being popped?'

'You've to understand what you're already on.'

'Which is?'

'*Valium.*'

'But I told you. I'm not on anything.'

'Well, you're very relaxed for someone who showed sexual interest in a strange man.'

'I won't dignify that with a response.'

'No, but you need a response from someone who understands.'

'Why?'

'Because if they take you off that stuff, you won't be half as clever.'

'Nonsense, a person's intelligence has nothing to do with Valium- if anything that would make you stupid.'

'No, it's the other way around- and you my friend are hooked. And furthermore, if the poppers I had given you had been mushrooms, you would be hallucinating auditorily and visually, as well as later vomiting profusely and developing an all-over body cramp.'

'Then, perhaps I won't take any interest in your paintings- if you're going to accuse me of something I'm not doing.'

'No, I'd like you to stay, there's still time to get through to you. Now, what d' you think of my humble collection of watercolours?'

CHAPTER THIRTY-THREE

Day Nine; 5 pm; The Tête-à-tête

I set up the sounding equipment some metres from the monument in order to hear the conversation.

'I like them,' said Alexander.

'Yes?'

'Yes, they're like dreams.'

The man cast Alexander a quizzical look. 'Dreams?'

'A mixture of real and imaginary people and places.'

The man glanced at him and smiled. Alexander's senses; his spine, too, became echinate in character: bristly, prickly. Alexander turned to his accent. It was brogue; regional.

'Which part of Ireland do you come from?'

'Dublin.'

'The capital.'

'Yes, although my grandfather came from Doolin.'

'Doolin?'

'Yes, it's a coastal village in County Clare.'

'I see. When did you come over?'

'A few months ago. I took the ferry from Dublin to Cairnryan.'

'Yes?'

'Yes, it took over seven hours.'

'What made you come over?'

'I wanted to know what happened to my father.'

'Who was your father?'

'Jarrod.'

'Yes?'

'Yes, I have a harrowing memory of killing him, although I was really hoping it was someone else.'

'Why would you have killed him?'

'As I said, I was sexually abused.'

'"Popped?"'

'No, I didn't need to be.'

'Why?'

'I was five.'

'When?'

'1995.'

'You're twenty-five.'

'Yes, you're a bit younger, I think.'

'Twenty-two.'

The man nodded.

Alexander gulped. 'How would you have killed him?'

'I seem to remember a knife.'

'Anything else?'

'Yes, a pool of blood.'

'Where did the remembered killing take place?'

'At home.'

'Dublin.'

'Yes.'

'Who else could have killed him?'

'My uncle-in-law. My father's employee.'

'Why?'

'They might have sexually abused me.'

'You don't know who did it.'

'I think it was my father and that's why I killed him but I'm not one hundred percent sure. Do you see one you like?'

'The paintings?'

'Yes.'

'And?'

'I like them all.'

The man smiled sweetly. 'You do?'

'Yes, except perhaps for that one.' He pointed at the small picture of an old man walking a dog.

The man nodded matter-of-factly and looked un-offended. 'No, it's not one of my better ones. It's just a croquis.'

'Pardon?'

'A sketch.'

Alexander frowned. 'Of course. But the rest are good.'

The man pushed out his lips. 'Good?'

'You know, well done.'

'Well done?'

'You know, pleasing to the eye.'

The man glanced again at him and smiled. 'I see you have an eye for places.'

Alexander already knew he had an eye for law, for reasoning. *But for places as well*? he thought.

'What's your name?' Alexander said.

'Sean.' Sean nodded respectfully at Alexander. He extended his hand, loosing the slip of his pullover, revealing a long narrow but muscular wrist and an expensive looking watch.

Alexander marvelled for a moment and said, 'Where did you get the watch?'

'I won it.'

Alexander's petite azure eyes rolled about in their sockets. 'You won it? How?'

Sean grinned. 'In a hand. In a lucky hand of poker.'

'It must be worth a fair bob or two.'

Sean tilted his head. 'Perhaps. But it's worth more on my hand.'

Alexander offered benignantly: 'One in the hand is worth more than two in the bush.'

'Exactly. Hey, what's your name?'

'Alexander.'

'After the great Scottish queens-' Sean spluttered. '-I mean kings.'

Alexander gave an indignant stare. 'You're Irish,' he said.

'Oh, to be sure, Jesus! Is my accent that strong?'

'No, it's just that most people around here have a Scottish accent. It stands out. Which part of Ireland are you from?'

'Southern.'

Alexander could have guessed that. 'And where about in the south? What is your demonym?'

'My what?'

'The name used for the place you come from.'

He doffed his war bonnet theatrically and said, 'City and capital of the Republic of Ireland. It is situated on the Liffey in east central Ireland, at the head of Dublin Bay on the Irish Sea.'

'You define, do you?'

Sean rolled his head. 'At least once, maybe more if the pressure's really on.'

'I define all the time.'

Sean cast him a quizzical look. 'You do? Why?'

'It helps with understanding.'

Sean yawned. 'It does? How's that, my friend?'

'By giving meaning to your word.'

Sean sized Alexander up. 'And that's important?'

'It is if you want to progress in this life.'

'And what is progressing?'

'Getting a degree. Demonstrating an exceptional capacity for learning.'

Sean gave him a disingenuous enquiring look. 'What if you don't get a degree?'

'I can't afford to think like that.'

Sean nodded dizzily. 'I think SLAB Payment's your concept.'

'My concept?'

'You know, your desiderata.'

'And what is that, exactly?'

'Wanted things.'

Alexander frowned. 'Obviously. I mean SLAB Payment.'

'You're studying to be a lawyer and you don't even know what that is?'

'No, should I?'

'If you want a big house and a fancy car, then definitely, yes.'

Alexander gave a puzzled look. 'But I already have a big house. A mansion, in fact. Well, at least my Uncle Albert does. It'll be mine one day. And I definitely have a big car. A BMW actually.'

Sean cast him an incredulous glance. 'You do? Crony capitalism, is it?'

Alexander was too vain to let his ignorance show; plus, he could work out the meaning from the context. 'Something like that,' he said.

'But I thought students were supposed to be dirt poor.'

Alexander smiled. 'They usually are, I suppose, but not me.'

'Is that so? How come?'

'My great aunt and uncle left me some money. And my Uncle will, too.'

'You're joshing, surely.'

'No.'

'So why study law, then?'

Alexander knit his brows and puckered his lips. 'What d' you mean?'

'Well, the only reason- to my infinitesimal microscopic excuse for a brain, at least- you would study is so you can get a better job. A business, even. But it seems you already have what these offer: big money.'

'Yes, but I want to do more than that.'

Sean gawked. 'You do?'

'Yes.'

'Such as what?'

'I want to regulate the actions of people. And impose penalties if they contravene the established law.'

Sean gawped. 'Why?'

'Because that's what law's about?'

'It is, is it?'

'Well, yes.'

'How d' you know?'

'Oxford says so.'

Sean's deep green eyes dehisced. 'You go to Oxford?'

'No, I mean the dictionary.'

Sean composed himself. 'Oh, I see. And is the dictionary always right?'

'It's received at least.'

Sean grinned and said, 'What, as a malicious birthday present?'

Alexander laughed. 'No, I mean that people generally accept it.'

'They do, do they? Would that not dehumanise you?'

'In what sense?'

'In the sense, would it not divest you of your individuality.'

Alexander smiled with equanimity and said, 'Yes, I suppose it might. I'd never thought of that. So you don't have much truck with the dictionary?'

'Well, I don't have Oxford, if that's what you mean?'

'I could buy you one if you like. A desk dictionary at least, maybe?'

Sean stifled a splutter with his hand. 'No, thanks. I think I'll pass. I'm no craw-thumper.'

'A what?'

'It's Irish.'

'Oh, I see. But it might help you.'

Sean smothered a second cough. 'Help me?'

'Yes.'

'In what way?'

'With your painting.'

'How on God's beloved earth would a dictionary help me with my painting?'

Alexander picked up his brains, allowed a furrow, and said, 'Well, painting takes skill and skill is a word and a word has meaning.'

'Yes?..'

'So if you know what the word means, you can satisfy the criteria.'

'And what is the criteria?'

'Well, it depends what the word is; what it means.'

'I see.'

'For example, intelligence is the ability to acquire and apply knowledge and skills-'

'Can we not just call it thoughts and leave it at that?'

'We could but to pass exams you need the right answers.'

Sean exhaled noisily. 'You are one boring individual, virtually have me crib-biting.'

'Eh?'

'It's something horses do when they're bored.'

Alexander frolicsomely flipped off Sean's war bonnet. 'I'm not boring, I'm intellectual.'

Sean smiled and picked his bonnet off the cobblestones. 'Then it's the judge's job you need.'

Alexander gazed sentimentally into the future. 'Maybe one day.'

Sean searched for a conversation-regenerator. 'Where do you live, anyway?'

'I live at Fall's Hall.'

Sean smiled wryly. 'Fall's Hall? Sounds like a show. A circus even. Never heard of it.'

Alexander nodded, unsurprised. 'No, you wouldn't have. It's not very well known. And it's extremely well-hidden. Within the dip and among the foliage.'

'Is it a farmhouse?'

'No, it's a mansion.'

'You live in a mansion?'

'You find that surprising?'

'Not really.'

'It comes from spirit.'

'Yes?'

'It was forged from years of border-struggle.'

'Between the Scots and the English.'

'Yes.'

'And?'

'Edinburgh castle is the most recognizable.'

'Yes?'

'Notable Scottish castles include Craigmillar castle, Duart castle.'

'The might of Caelaverock is fascinating.'

'Dunnotar castle is spectacular.'

'Where do you live?'

'Here and there.'

Alexander's eyes widened. 'Here and there? You have no fixed abode?'

'No, I'm a D.P.'

'Excuse me?'

'In Social Welfare terms, it means a displaced person.'

'So where are you living at the moment?'

'Here.'

Alexander looked casually at him. 'What, in the town?'

'Yes.'

'Are you staying with relatives?'

'No.'

Alexander nodded. 'With friends?'

'Not exactly.'

'In a hotel?'

'I wish.'

'In a hostel?'

'No.'

'Where then?'

'Does it matter?'

'I suppose not. But you must live somewhere, surely?'

For the very first time since their inaugural acquaintance, there was a simmering resentment in Sean's Irish timbre. 'Look! I don't know who you are, where you come from or what you do to pass the time. But I live under the bright lights of the sky.'

Alexander gave a concerned look. 'But you do know all these things.'

'Huh?'

'You know that I'm Alexander, that I come from Fall's Hall and that I study the law.'

Sean calmed down a bit. 'I do?'

'Yes. It's quite obvious that you're homeless.'

Sean smiled in a pacifying way. 'I suppose you could call me that.'

'So what d' you do if it's cold. If it rains? Snows even?'

'Camp out under a bridge.'

'Under a bridge?' Alexander gasped.

'Or a tree. I have a thick jacket and an even thicker skin.'

'And how d' you keep yourself clean?'

'The public convenience.'

'And what if it's shut?'

'A stream, a river, a lake- anything I can find.'

'That's no way to live. Can you not get, what do they call them?...'

Sean glared somewhat condescendingly. 'Benefits?'

'Yes.'

'I suppose I could if I had a fecking bank account, although I don't fancy the dependency culture.'

Alexander cocked a brow in surprise. 'You don't even have a bank account?'

'No. Look, what's with all the questions?'

'I'm just shocked, that's all. I could never live like that.'

'Maybe you never had to.'

'You had to?'

'Since my daddy- I mean my old man...died, yes.'

Alexander nodded empathetically. 'My dad died as well.'

A flicker of doubt passed across Sean's very green eyes. 'He did?'

'Yes, a long time ago.'

'But then I bet your mum looks after you?'

'No, she's dead as well.'

'So what do you do?'

'I live off my inheritance. Like I said.'

'It's alright for some.'

Alexander procrastinated for a moment and said, 'I could give you some money. If you're really stretched.'

'Now, why would you want to do that?'

'Perhaps you need it. Perhaps I feel sorry for you.'

Sean winced. 'I don't need your money, thank you. Or your pity.'

'Why not?'

'A man has some pride.'

Alexander grimaced. 'Pride won't keep you warm at night.'

'I make my own money.'

'Well, at least let me buy one of your paintings. I can't have them de-contextualised.'

At that, Sean winked at him. 'Now, that, I can readily accept.'

Alexander cast another eye over the collection. 'I'll have the big one. The one with the streets- the trees, grass and benches.'

'You mean the town square?'

'Yes. How much is that one?'

Sean tottered his head as he considered. 'Call it a fiver.'

Alexander gaped. 'Just a fiver. Come on, my old son! It must be worth at least twenty. If not fifty.'

Sean's eyes smiled gratefully. 'No, a fiver will do.'

'You're a stubborn old thing. And I'll have the other one as well.'

'Which other one?'

'The one with all the buildings.'

Sean's face crinkled. 'You mean the townscape.'

'Yes, that one. How much is that one?'

'Three-fifty.'

'Okay, I'll have that. And I'll have that small one as well.'

'Which small one?'

'The one with the old man walking his dog.'

Sean cast him a distrustful look. 'The crayon? But I thought you didn't like that one.'

'It's grown on me.'

'Very well. If you insist. That'll be one fifty.'

'And I'll have all those other ones as well.'

Sean huffed. 'You're just extracting the urine, now.'

'Not at all. They'll look smashing on our drawing room wall. Next to the mounts.'

'Whose drawing room wall?'

'My Uncle and mine.'

Sean's expression simulated the manipulations of a heavily punched calculator. 'Alright, that'll be, let's see... that'll be sixteen pounds.'

'Call it twenty.'

Sean wheezed. 'No, sixteen. I think you could use a Cuisenaire.'

Alexander ignored the word he presumed to be trivial.

'And let me buy that war bonnet. It looks expensive. Real wool, is it?'

'I got it from the army.'

'The best kind.'

Sean cast him a derisory look. 'No, Alex. I need that.'

Alexander smiled abashedly. 'Of course, you do. Silly me.'

'Will that be all, kind Sir.'

'I could always wait for you to paint another one. Perhaps I could be the depicted object.'

'No, I don't think so.'

'I don't mind. Really. I've got time.'

'It's six a clock.'

'And?'

'I'm badly lit.'

'You can't paint in twilight?'

'I can but then it would be demi-tint.'

'And that's a problem?'

'No, but my medium is light.'

'Then let me buy you a coffee, at least.'

'I told you. I make my own money.'

'Then you buy me one. You can afford it now.'

'Oh, alright, then. But not a coffee. A cold Guinness.'

Alex frowned.

'What's the matter?'

'I don't really drink.'

'Why not?'

'It clouds the mind.'

'You need a clear mind?'

'Well, for learning, yes.'

'But I would have thought the colleges would be closed by now.'

'I think you mean the university.'

'There's a difference?'

'A quicker multi-conceptual difference.'

'Snob!'

'Invert! Anyway, I can't afford to relax.'

'Why not?'

'I might fail.'

'And that's significant?'

'It is after three years.'

'Three years well spent?'

'Spent at least.'

'And what happens later?'

'I'll cross that bridge if and when I come to it.'

'I've already seen that bridge.'

'Over troubled waters?'

'Over my head, anyway. Come on, let's go!'

Suddenly, there was a hollering. A young slim dark-haired figure loped across the square. He wrapped his arm around Alexander and pulled him closely.

Alexander gazed into Martin's green eyes. He beamed. '*Martin*!'

CHAPTER THIRTY-FOUR

Day Nine; 6 pm; The Pub-brawl

The late afternoon sun showered over Martin's face like a mirror ball, irradiating a vision of young dark male handsomeness.

'Yes, Alexander,' said Martin.

Alexander's youthful ingenuous green eyes spangled with elation. 'You've surprised me.'

Martin winked at Alexander. 'I promised you I would.' Martin kissed him firmly on the lips.

Sean coughed into his fist. Martin turned to face the other man. Sean flashed him a superior smile. 'You're Martin.'

As Martin regarded the other man, he apprehended the adorable looks and quivered. He lapsed into a trance. He glanced at his sweet-looking boyfriend and then peered into the allure of a magnoliid dicot genus. He swallowed slightly. 'Yes.'

Sean waved his long golden hair. He scratched the back of his head. 'So was it an English law promise?'

Martin squinted tentatively at Sean. 'A what?'

'I mean does it require consideration?' said Sean.

Martin frowned. 'You know of legal promises?'

Alexander ricocheted from Martin's reappearance with a giant beam. 'Sean, here, is quite the knowledge font.'

Martin leaned back. 'Yes.'

Sean smiled neutrally. 'All I know is that a promise can take you to another part of the world.'

'Oh?' said Martin. 'In what way?'

'I promised my mother I would find the man who killed my father.'

Martin glazed. 'Your father was killed?'

'That's my memory,' said Sean.

'How old were you?' said Martin.

'I was five when I thought he was killed,' said Sean.

Martin scoffed. 'Thought?'

'Yes, he returned to the house one evening when I was thirteen.'

'What happened?'

'Someone killed him.'

'Why?' said Alexander.

'I don't know,' said Sean.

'Are you sure you didn't kill him?' said Martin.

'I sometimes think I did,' said Sean.

'Why?'

'I went for him with a putty knife.'

'Why?'

'I thought he had abused me.'

'And?'

'My mother said it wasn't me.'

'Who d' you think it was?'

'I think it was one of the members of the families,' said Sean.

'Which families?'

'The families which resented him.'

'How did you get here?' said Alexander.

'My dad drove me up,' said Martin.

'The judge?'

'Retired judge,' said Martin.

'Why, we do move in fast circles.'

'We had to work for it,' said Martin.

'You came all the way from Newton Mearns?' said Alexander.

'Yes.'

'Newton Mearns?' said Sean. 'That's Glasgow, isn't it.'

'Approximately, yes.'

'Why?'

'Yes, why would that be?' said Sean.

Martin glanced at Sean. 'He's checking something out.'

'What's he checking out?' said Alexander.

'Two people went missing,' said Martin. They were presumed dead after seven years. My father's trying to work out what happened.'

Sean nodded knowingly. 'You mean they were killed as well?'

Martin glared at Sean. 'Yes, it would appear so.'

'Why would your dad do that?' said Alexander.

'He's been put under pressure from someone else,' said Martin.

'You mean the family objected,' said Sean.

'Something like that,' said Martin.

'Who?' said Alexander.

'One of the relatives,' said Martin.

'Which relative?' said Alexander.

'The brother,' said Martin.

'What's his name?' said Alexander.

'Chase McLean.'

Sean yawned. 'Sounds like an alias.'

'You think so?' said Alexander.

'Definitely,' said Sean. 'Chase isn't an obvious name.'

Martin glowered at Sean. 'And what is your real name?'

'I told you: Sean,' said Sean.

'Really?' said Martin.

'Is that so hard to believe?' said Sean.

'Your genuineness is,' said Martin.

'Oh?' said Sean. 'Why would that be?'

'You don't seem to be in a position to pay for things,' said Martin.

'I'm in a position to understand things,' said Sean. 'You guys know each other, then.'

Martin stared at Sean. 'No,' said Martin, 'we are together.'

Alexander smiled. 'Yes, that's right.'

Martin frowned. 'This guy's not your type, Alexander.'

Sean glimpsed at Martin. 'Oh?'

'Yes,' said Martin, 'You're using him.'

'You judge a book by its cover?' said Sean.

Martin glowered at Sean. 'No, I judge a very short story by its meagre content.'

Sean smiled accommodatingly. 'And how d' you know it's a short story? How d' you know its content?'

'A short story with a flashy cover wears very thin and has nothing underneath,' said Martin.

Sean shrugged. 'Perhaps it's a full novel with a sense of style and a lot of depth.'

'I very much doubt it's a series,' said Martin.

'You think it's a one-off,' said Sean.

'I think it's a write-off,' said Martin.

'You know,' said Sean, 'Perhaps it has insurance.'

'No, I don't think so,' said Martin, 'only false promises.'

Alexander sighed. 'You two don't seem to like each other much.'

'I like you,' said Sean.

'Yes,' said Martin, 'but I love him.'

Alexander smiled happily. 'I love you, too.'

'For now,' said Sean.

'For always,' said Martin.

'I could use a drink,' said Sean.

I'm sure you do,' said Martin.

'I don't drink,' said Alexander.

'No, he doesn't,' said Martin.

'But you do,' said Sean.

'I only drink what I need to,' said Martin.

'Me too,' said Sean.

'I don't mind paying for it,' said Alexander.

'I do,' said Martin.

'I'll pay for it,' said Sean.

'Very well,' said Martin.

I rang Chase.

'*Ewok*!'

'The younger cousin is confused.'

'Confused?'

'He seems to think he might have killed his father.'

'And?'

'He's focussing on the nephew.'

'Why?'

'I can't be sure but I suspect it's financial. I think he wants a roof over his head.'

'What else?'

'My younger son has met up with them. Martin doesn't like the younger cousin.'

'Why not?'

'Martin thinks the younger cousin's after the nephew's money.'

'Why would that bother your son?'

'To my sheer disappointment, Martin seems to like Alexander.'

'Like? You mean fancy?'

I sighed. 'Something like that.'

'Anything else?'

'I agree with you, Chase. I think the Uncle planned for the nephew to meet the younger cousin.'

'Why?'

'As I said, I think he was trying to hidec something or to assist in his love life.'

'So what's happening.'

'They're off to a pub.'

'Follow them, record their conversation.'

'Yes, Chase.'

The nephew, the younger cousin and my younger son wended their way together, like three unaligned spirits, two soldered by the gentle fairy-liquid hands of providence and communal benevolence, and one born of concupiscence and protection, out of the bustling rush-hour town square, beyond the tall woody perennial sycamore trees, newly shaved grass and black steel benches, over the road, along the street and crossed the threshold of a pub named *Paddy's*. It served food as well but neither of them were hungry.

'What will you be having, Sean?' said Alexander.

'Here, let me get it,' said Sean. 'What d' you fancy?'

'I'll have an orange juice,' said Alexander.

'What about you, Martin?' said Sean.

'Since we're in an Irish pub,' said Martin, 'I'll have a cold Guinness.'

The bar manager smiled at Sean. 'And for you?'

'I'll have a cold Guinness and a craythur,' said Sean.

After drinks were placed on the bar, the three young men picked up their drinks and isolated a table. Alexander and Martin nestled beside each other. Sean sat opposite.

'Go on, Sean,' said Martin, 'Tell us about your mother.'

'She misses my dad, she blames a man for it.'

'Which man?'

'She doesn't know, she wasn't in the room when he died.'

'So how come you blame yourself?' said Martin.

'I remember going for him,' said Sean.

'You were five, then thirteen,' said Martin, 'You went for him twice.'

'Yes,' said Sean.

'Why?' said Martin.

Sean sighed. 'I think the first time I thought he had abused me,' said Sean, 'the second time I thought he had neglected me.'

'What did your father do?' said Martin.

'He worked in textiles to begin with. His father, my grandfather, Aiden Fields owned his own textiles business.'

Martin's eyes widened. 'Really? What was it called?'

'Fields Textiles.'

'And when he was gone?'

'He worked in mechanical engineering.'

'Did you love him?' said Alexander.

'It's hard to say. I was five. I remember being angry with him.'

'Because you thought he had abused you.'

'Partly,' said Sean, 'There was also the fighting.'

'What fighting?' said Alexander.

'The fighting between the Catholics and the Protestants.'

'Your father was Catholic?' said Martin.

'My whole family was. That's the south of Ireland for you. There was also the fracas between the nationalists and the unionists.'

'What were you? said Alexander.

'I was brought up to me a nationalist,' said Sean.

'And where were you born?' said Alexander.

Sean shrugged. 'In a hospital,' he said.

Martin thumped down his Guinness. 'You see, Alexander, you won't get straight answers.'

Sean bore his teeth. 'My answers are as straight as your certainty.'

Martin smiled sarcastically back at Sean. 'I just like to know my boyfriend isn't being lied to.'

Alexander wiggled his head. 'I'm sure he's not. I mean, Sean, which town.'

'Cork,' said Sean. He glared at Martin. 'So there.'

'And where did you grow up?' said Alexander.

'In the countryside,' said Sean.

'See?' said Martin

'You lived in a farm house,' said Alexander.

'Yes,' said Sean, 'I used to paint the lands.'

Martin sneered. 'Of course he did, just before he tried to colour your opinion.'

'Actually,' said Sean. 'Our family moved to Dublin.'

'Are you sure that's your real accent,' said Martin.

'Quite sure,' said Sean, 'We lived in Rathnew.'

'Never heard of it,' said Martin.

'Then that's your ignorance,' said Sean, 'Not mine. Anyway, my father got a new job.'

'I thought he was dead,' said Martin.

'He is,' said Sean, 'but we moved first.'

'Do you have any brother and sisters?' said Alexander.

'Yes, one.'

'A made-up family?' said Martin.

'No, a real one,' said Sean.

'Do you have a girlfriend?' said Alexander.

'Not really,' said Sean. 'Does it matter?'

'He's not gay, Alexander,' said Martin, 'But he wants you to think he is.'

'Oh?' said Sean. 'And why would I want that?'

'So he pays you for your interest,' said Martin.

'Are you gay?' said Alexander.

'Around you, yes,'- he glared at Martin- 'but not around him.'

'Only because I know what you're doing,' said Martin.

'Anyway,' said Sean, 'I have a brother.'

'What's his name?' said Martin.

'Michael,' said Sean, 'we call him Mickey. Have you ever had a girlfriend, Alex?'

Martin loured. 'His name is Alexander,' said Martin.

Alexander smiled in pacification. 'I don't mind,' he said, 'I had one.'

'How long ago was that?' said Sean.

'It wasn't a proper girlfriend, was it,' said Martin.

'Well,' said Alexander, 'Unfortunately, I didn't quite feel the same way about her as she did about me.'

'He knows all about that,' said Martin, 'Don't you, Sean.'

'Alexander didn't say he fancied me,' said Sean.

Alexander flushed. 'I am with Martin.'

'There you go, jealous guy,' said Sean. 'What was she like?'

'She was very sweet,' said Alexander.

Sean smiled wryly. 'Sweet?'

'Yes,' said Alexander, 'and very headstrong.'

'So what happened to her?' said Sean.

'She ran off to be a dancer,' said Alexander.

Sean chortled. 'Hopefully not a dancing girl.'

'See,' said Martin, 'he's got a dirty mind.'

'I was being facetious,' said Sean.

'Sure you can spell that?' said Martin.

'Let's think,' said Sean, 'I know it begins with a ph.'

Martin gave an exasperated look. 'It probably does in your vocabulary.'

Sean ignored Martin. 'And is there anyone else in your life, Alexander?'

'No, not really- just my Uncle Albert,' said Alexander. 'My mum and dad died when I was six.'

'What caused the defiliation?' said Martin.

Sean blinked. 'The what?'

Alexander smiled non-judgementally at Sean. 'The abstraction from my parents.'

'Yes, you like abstracts, Sean' said Martin, 'much more important than actually doing something.'

'So what do you do?' said Sean.

'Same as Alexander,' said Martin, 'I study law.'

'And your law is practical is it?' said Sean.

'More practical than your art work,' said Martin.

'Oh?' said Sean, 'In what way?'

Martin hugged Alexander's shoulder. 'My law- our law will regulate actions and impose penalties.'

'Where as my art work,' said Sean, 'has already moved Alexander to invest and has invoked your admonition.'

Alexander flushed again. 'I think both subjects possess validity.'

'Thank you, Alex,' said Sean. Sean simpered at Martin. 'Sorry, *Alexander*.'

'No, Alexander,' said Martin, 'Our law is paramount, it regulates everyone. All art does is indulge the inebriated and indolent.'

'I've heard that in Scotland the welfare of the child is paramount,' said Sean.

Alexander smiled contently. 'Yes, that's right.'

'Another trinket from your font of knowledge,' said Martin. 'Or did Alexander have to tell you?'

Alexander wiggled his head. 'No, I didn't.'

'It was actually my cousin who told me,' said Sean.

'How would he know?' said Martin.

'It's a she- and her husband's a lawyer,' said Sean.

'What stage is he at?' said Alexander.

'I believe he has his degree,' said Sean.

'Believe?' said Martin.

'Unless my cousin has to lie about basic education,' said Sean.

'An LLB is not basic,' said Martin.

'Well,' said Sean, 'it hardly comes with a wife, children, car and a mortgage. It's a bachelor's degree, is it not?'

'Some of us already have a car,' said Martin, 'as for your dabbling, it hardly delivers the rest.'

'I thought you didn't want me to be gay,' said Sean.

'You can be as gay as you like to pretend,' said Martin, 'Just not around my boyfriend.'

Alexander cringed but said nothing.

'Your wife's very aggressive, Alexander,' said Sean. 'Tell me, Martin, is your husband allowed an opinion?'

Alexander giggled.

Martin glowered. 'His *obiter dicta* are very authoritative,' said Martin.

'Of course, like your snide- I mean passing remarks,' said Sean.

Alexander sighed.

'So what happened to your parents?' said Sean.

'They died in a car accident,' said Alexander.

'That's terrible,' said Martin.

'Yes, it is,' said Sean. 'How did it happen?'

'We think my dad had been driving too fast,' said Alexander. 'They flew off a cliff.'

'We?' said Sean.

'My uncle Albert and I,' said Alexander.

'So it was a common calamity,' said Martin.

'And not a problem with the car?' said Sean.

'Alexander just said,' said Martin.

'What was your dad like?' said Sean.

Alexander's dad, from what he could still remember of him- those smoky white blurring pictures, those wraith-like dimming voices- had been a very good man- wonderfully kind.

'I remember,' said Alexander, 'he took me to the seaside once. As a small boy, I witnessed at first hand the spectacular splendour and the peerless puissance of the great north east sea.'

'Do you remember anything else?' said Sean.

'Yes,' said Alexander, 'he had been very poor. He worked hard though. He was a carpenter.'

'Do you remember anything he said to you?' said Sean.

'Yes,' said Alexander, 'He said once: "You have to understand, son. Now that we have laid the rug, we must tack it."

'And what did you say?' said Sean.

'I said,' said Alexander, '"But that could hurt our fingers, daddy,"' he had said.

'And then what did your dad say?' said Sean.

'He said,' said Alexander, '"Not if we're careful, son.'

'Does your uncle have a wife?' said Sean.

Alexander smiled pensively. 'He did, Aunt Doris.'

'What happened to her?' said Sean.

'She died,' said Alexander.

'How did she die?' said Sean.

'She was found dead in our garden pond,' said Alexander.

'You lost your aunt as well,' said Sean, 'That's very sad.'

'Of course it is,' said Martin, 'he doesn't need reminded.'

'What did your aunt she say to you?' said Sean.

'She said once,' said Alexander, '"You're a simply adorable boy. A sweet precious love." She wasn't my mum, though.'

'And what did your girlfriend say to you?' said Sean.

'She said,' said Alex, '"Alex, you're a genius! A true whiz. But, you know, you don't quite understand girls.'

'And what did you say?' said Sean.

'I just repeated the word "girls". She said: "Yes. We girls need a bit of encouragement. "Encouragement?" I said. And she said. "Yes. Eyes. Responsive and piercing eyes. Whether blue, green or brown. We need smiles. We need interest. We need...why are we here again?'

'We're here again,' said Martin, 'because your con merchant keeps asking invasive questions.'

'Or simply displaying an interest in someone,' said Sean.

'Someone?' said Martin. 'It might as well be the quiz master's banker.'

Sean fumbled inside his jeans pocket for some change. He

flashed his winsome smile at Alexander. You wouldn't happen to have any more dead presidents on you, would you Alexander?'

'You mean cash?' said Alexander.

'Just a fiver perhaps,' said Sean.

'Oh, just,' said Martin. 'There you go, Alexander, I told you.'

Alexander smiled placidly. 'Yes, of course I do, but it's just I thought you didn't like taking money from people.'

Martin grunted. 'As if,' he said.

'No, I don't. Not usually, anyway. But I'm afraid I've spent it all on refreshments.'

'Then, it's your own fault,' said Martin.

Alexander gazed at him benevolently. 'Here, have twenty!'

Martin grimaced. 'No, Alexander,' he said, 'don't give that to him. That's why he's being nice to you.'

'I do know how the world works, Martin,' said Sean.

'Yes, it revolves around you,' said Martin.

'I'm not the one owning someone else,' said Sean.

'I don't own him,' said Martin, 'I love him.'

'I am here, you know,' said Alexander. Alexander grimaced. 'At least I was, I must nip to the bathroom.'

When Alexander came back up the toilet stairs, he witnessed an affray.

'You don't even fancy him,' said Martin.

'No, but you fancy me,' said Sean.

Martin gaped. 'Excuse me.'

'I saw the way you looked at me in the town square,' said Sean.

'Why would I fancy you?' said Martin.

'Because I'm even better-looking than your good-looking boyfriend.'

Martin bristled. 'He's worth a trillion of you.'

'But not to you,' said Sean. 'Admit it now, you're that capricious you want me now, not him.'

Alexander frowned.

'I don't go for guys who go for money,' said Martin.

'Then you're lucky you don't have to,' said Sean.

'I'm not lucky, I worked at it,' said Martin.

'Yes, it helps when the judge can bankroll your education,' said Sean.

'You had your chance at school as well,' said Martin, 'it's a meritocratic system.'

'Not without a father,' said Sean. 'As I said I thought he was dead when I was five and then he actually was when I was thirteen.'

'Looking for more pity,' said Martin.

For the first time, Sean railed. 'You know, Martin you really are a heartless upper-middle-class bastard.'

'Alexander doesn't need a parasite like you,' said Martin.

'No, but you're hypocritical enough to prefer one,' said Sean.

'I don't fancy you, Sean,' said Martin.

'You don't fancy admitting it,' said Sean.

'You might be smooth and pretty, mate,' said Martin, 'but you're no man of law.'

'And you're no man of the world,' said Sean

'Leave my boyfriend alone,' said Martin.

Alexander re-joined the company. 'I'm fine really, Martin,' he said.

'I'm sure Alexander knows what he's saying,' said Sean.

'Oh, yes he does,' said Martin, ' but you don't.'

'I'm perfectly aware,' said Sean, 'that you've taken to me over him, but you'll lead second-best on anyway.'

Martin scowled at Sean. 'You bastard!' he said. He threw a punch at Sean which Sean caught. Sean brought his knee under Martin's stomach and brought his elbow down on his back. Martin wheezed on the pub floor. Sean vacated the pub, leaving an impishly scrawled note on the table. It was something of a cryptogram. '*Nice doing business with you*,' it read.

'Are you okay, Martin?' said Alexander.

Martin groaned. ''I'll live,' he said.

Suddenly, there was a tumult. Alexander lifted his head up and noticed another man who had skulked into the pub. He looked at bit like Sean, only fuller and not so handsome. He engaged his pierced lips and said, 'You haven't seen a young Irish man with wavy blond hair,' he said. 'Goes by the name of Sean.'

'Yes,' said Martin, 'the bastard's just left.'

'Where did he go?' said the man.

'Who cares?' said Martin.

'What about Susie?' said the man.

'Who?' said Alexander.

'His cousin,' said the man.

'No,' said Alexander, 'we've never met her.'

The man clenched his teeth. 'Well, if you do see either of them, tell them Mickey wants to see them.'

Alexander nodded gingerly.

The man stormed out of the pub.

'What now?' said Alexander.

'I have to get back to my dad,' said Martin.

'Where is he?'

'He's in the vicinity.'

'When will I see you again?'

'Soon.'

'I have to say I don't necessarily agree with everything you said tonight but I still love you.'

Martin smiled sadly. 'I love you as well. Goodnight, Alexander!'

'Goodnight, Martin!'

They left the pub and parted ways.

I rang Chase.

'*Ewok*!'

'What happened?'

'They went to a pub.'

'And they exchanged basic histories.'

'And?'

'There was a bust-up.'

'Yes?'

'He assaulted my son.'

'Why?'

'My son was angry with him for trying to steal the person he liked and for assuming his own admiration of him.'

'What else?'

'The older brother stormed into the pub.'

'The younger cousin?'

'Yes, the intruder at the wife's boutique.'

'Was he looking for his brother?'

'Yes.'

'And?'

'The younger brother left the pub.'

'Why?'

'I suspect he was trying to avoid his older brother.'

'Follow him!'

'Why?'

'I want to know more.'

I sighed. 'As you wish.'

As per his uncle's initial instructions, Alexander drove to the Supermarket. He bought the ingredients his uncle had requested. He drove home. He rang the door bell.

'Alex?' said Albert.

'Yes, uncle,' said Alexander.

'Well?'

'I got the things you were looking for.'

Albert smiled contentedly. 'Good. Come in! You'll be tired after your drive.'

Alexander sighed. 'Yes.'

Alexander lay supine in his luxury four-poster bed, long, lean and bent arms clasped underneath his weary buzzing head. He wondered if Sean was in fact gay. He wondered if Martin liked Sean more than he liked him. He wondered if he himself might prefer Sean. There was definitely something about Sean. Something strange- subtle and alluring. He was astonishingly handsome. He was funny, talented, street wise and charming. Martin was very different. He wore his heart on his sleeve. He was natural, angry and direct. Alexander heaved a heavy sigh. He dipped into his pocket and took out the note Sean had left him. In a scary way, he somehow wanted him to re-enter his life.

CHAPTER THIRTY-FIVE

Day Nine; 7 pm; The Hotel

Sean inserted several pound coins into the Hotel phone.

'Mother?'

Catherine Fields gasped. '*Sean*?'

'Yes.'

'Where are you?'

'I'm in Aberdeen.'

'The north of Scotland.'

'Yes.'

'Where in Aberdeen exactly?'

'A hotel.'

'Which hotel?'

'Hilton Garden Inn.'

'What ever are you doing there?'

'Apparently it got a good trip advisor rating.'

'A what?'

'A man in the town centre told me.'

'How on earth did you end up there?'

'After I took the ferry from Dublin to Cairnryan, I made my way up north.'

'And?'

'I met a man who knows the person who might have killed Dad.'

'Who was the man?'

'He said his name was Albert.'

'How would he know?'

'He said he knew my father.'

'The only Albert who met your father was Albert Bennet.'

'Who?'

'The man who was in our house when you were five. It was 1995.'

'I don't remember him.'

'He was in our house in 2003. You were thirteen.'

'Perhaps it's the same man.'

'I think it must be. What did he say?'

'He said he would help.'

'Help how?'

'He said he would give me money but in return I had to befriend his nephew.'

'Who?'

'Alexander.'

'Wait a minute, Albert Bennet had a young nephew in the house in 2003- the night your father died.'

'It must be him then.'

'Yes, it must. Why would he want you to befriend his nephew?'

'He's gay.'

Catherine choked. '*Gay*!'

'Yes, it's quite common mother. And he's young and lonely.'

'But you're not gay are you, Sean?'

'Of course not.'

'So?'

'I don't mind pretending if it means getting paid and finding the person who killed dad.'

'What about Cinnia?'

'What about her?'

'You must not cheat on her.'

'Don't be silly.'

'What d'you mean?'

'I mean it wouldn't mean anything.'

'No?'

'No, I wasn't planning to sleep with him.'

'Good.'

'You're sure?'

'Yes.'

'Who does he think killed your dad?'

'He said it was probably the man who had his music insulted?'

'Who?'

'He said his name was Hugh.'

'Yes, there was a Hugh Sharp in our house in 2003.'

'Well, maybe Albert's right.'

'We don't know, it was dark, we couldn't see anything.'

'I'm also hunting down the man who abused Mickey and I.'

'There's no point, Sean, he's dead. It was your father's brother-in-law.'

'Uncle Andrew?'

'Only in law.'

'How do you know?'

'You told me, so did your brother.'

'I don't remember that.'

'It was 1995. You were only five.'

'What did Uncle Andrew say?'

'He denied it.'

'So?'

'As your mother, I was inclined to believe you and your brother.'

'Was Mickey absolutely sure?'

'Not everyone that night was but your brother was adamant. You claimed your dad beat you. You went for him with a putty knife. You also hated your uncle-in-law.'

'Why?'

'He told you off.'

'What for?'

'Taking money from my purse.'

'Why would I have done that?'

'To buy chocolates, to impress the girl you liked.'

'What did Mickey say?'

'He said Andrew had been touching him.'

'So?'

'So the man you're hunting down is dead. He went missing in 1995 and his body was never recovered.'

'I don't think it was Uncle Andrew.'

'Why not?'

'I remember dad beating me but I don't remember Uncle Andrew touching me. Anyway, Mickey was a mad teenager. He said all sorts of things. Plus, he's been on drugs for years- he wouldn't remember a thing.'

'Because of what Andrew did to him.'

'No, mother, because dad beat him.'

'Your dad would never have laid a finger on your brother- or you Sean.'

'No, dad was very angry. He wanted to get the protestants back. He didn't agree with the unionists. He believed in a Republic of Ireland.'

'Your dad believed in his family. Your dad was a good man, Sean. He was no child batterer.'

'He felt he had been treated very badly. He was being made to do things he didn't agree with.'

'So who were the other men?'

'What other men?'

'The men that were there at the house that night.'

'What night?'

'The night dad was killed- before it went dark.'

'2003?'

'Of course.

'Well, your father's employer had brought his son.'

'Who was he?'

'Hugh Sharp.'

'And?'

'Another man was his acquaintance. He had his nephew with him.'

'That would be Albert.'

'Yes.'

'So?'

'So your dad thought one of the men might have been his father.'

'Who?'

'Ewald Wren.'

'Who was he?'

'A lawyer, I think.'

'But Grampa Aiden was dad's father.'

Catherine Fields sighed. 'I'm not so sure, Sean. Your dad's mother was definitely Alainn but as for your dad's father, it could have been anyone.'

'Who?

'Patrick Fields, Ewald Wren, Hugh Sharp...'

'How?'

'They all had sexual intercourse with your grandmother Alainn.'

'How do you know?'

'They told me. As for your Auntie Susanna, I'm not sure at all that she was Grampa Aiden Field's son.'

'Why not?'

'Alainn said so.'

'What did she say?'

'She said: "I'm sorry, Aiden, I don't think Susanna's yours".'

'When was this?'

'1962.'

'At home?'

'Yes. Patrick left Ireland for the Congo in 1962.'

'And?'

'He never made it back.'

'So?'

'Your father was six.'

'So?'

'Your father overheard a conversation between your grandmother Alainn and Aiden.'

'And?'

'Ewald Wren confessed that he had slept with your grandmother Alainn in 1962.'

'So?'

'Your Auntie Susanna was twenty-two in 1995. She wasn't born until 1972.'

'So?'

'She would have had to have been thirty two to be this man's daughter.'

'So Ewald Wren was not Susanna's father.'

'It's still possible.'

'How?'

'Your father wrote to Ewald Wren.'

'And?'

'Your father wanted to know if he was his real father- and his sister Susanna.'

'So what happened?'

'Ewald Wren came back to the house in 1972. He admitted he had slept with Alainn.'

'How d'you know?'

'He told your father.'

'Was my dad definitely my dad?'

'Yes, son. There's no doubt there.'

'My father was sixteen when my Auntie Susanna was born?'

'Your half-Auntie, yes.'

'What else?'

'It's remotely possible another man killed your father.'

'Who?'

'Your half cousin's husband's father.'

'Susanna's husband's father?'

'Yes.'

'Who was her husband?'

'Richie Reid.'

'And who was his father?'

'Doctor Taylor Reid.'

'What makes you think he could have killed my dad?'

'His wife called me?'

'Who?'

'Angela Reid.'

'And?'

'She told me what had happened.'

'And what had happened?'

'She thought she knew who might have killed Susanna.'

'Who?'

'She wouldn't say.'

'Why not?'

'She said her husband had confronted this man and that he he had threatened him.'

'Who was the man?'

'Hugh Sharp.'

'Hugh Sharp threatened Doctor Taylor Reid?'

'Yes.'

'When was this?'

'1995.'

'And?'

'Doctor Taylor Reid's wife Angela warned me he might try to kill your father, that he might try to use mushrooms.'

'Why would Hugh Sharp wish to kill my dad?'

'I don't know.'

'Why would Doctor Taylor Reid try to kill dad?'

'His sister Susanna and her husband Andrew threatened him.'

'Why?'

'They had banned his son from their house.'

'So?'

'Susanna contacted her brother and told your dad that Doctor Taylor Reid was threatening to section them.'

'And?'

'Your dad said he would sort the Doctor out.'

'When was this?'

'1995.'

'So?'

'So if you're looking for your father's killer I suggest you include Doctor Taylor Reid.'

'How would I find him?'

'You know where your half-cousin lives.'

'Yes, Keppochill

'You will be careful, Sean.'

'Yes, of course.'

'Angela Taylor warned me that a man might try to kill your father. Make sure you get some proper food- and avoid the mushrooms.'

'I will do, mam.'

'I love you, son.'

'And I love you.'

I mobiled Chase.

'*Ewok*!'

'The younger cousin's in the Hilton garden hotel.'

'How did he get there?'

'He walked.'

'And?'

'I tailed him with the Mercedes.'

'And?'

'He phoned his mother.'

'And?'

'I listened in.'

'How?'

'I had the call traced.'

'Who is she?'

'I don't know.'

'Why might she have killed my brother and/or his wife?'

'I don't know.'

'Keep tabs on him.'

CHAPTER THIRTY-SIX

Day Nine; 8 pm; The Hotel Dining Room

Sean planted down the receiver. He vacated the plastic hooded booth, ambled across the gangway and entered the dining area. He sat down at a table next to the window. He gazed pensively out at the bitter night sky with lachrymose homesick eyes. He saw the moon, which seemed dimmer than the one he remembered as a boy. He remembered a strong stale smell. He remembered a low voice. He could feel fingers trickling down his stomach and reaching down below. He shed a tear. '*No,*' he said in his mind. He shivered. He could hear the bustle of the traffic outside. He peered up at the stars. They, too, seemed dimmer than they had been.

Suddenly, there was music. It was 'Dying To Try' by Brendan Murray. He recognised it because he had stayed up one night with his mother to watch Eurovision; it was Ireland's entry. It didn't win but it was a pleasing enough tune. As he watched the Aberdeen city world go by, he lapsed into a faint solitary trance. The nonchalant music passed through his senses and a soporific haze of memories infiltrated his weary mind. He thought of home, of Rathnew, of years ago, of his mother and his older brother.

As he sat there, the left hand side of his face resting on his left hand propped up by his elbow and the table, gazing out of the window, he could smell the food his mother used to make. He remembered a conversation with his mother one morning before he left the cottage door for school, his mother said: 'You've forgotten your breakfast roll, Sean?'

'What is it?' he said.

'It's a bread roll,' his brother Mickey said.

'Which elephants does it have today?' he said.

'Elements,' said his brother Mickey.

'It's egg and bacon with pudding,' said his mother.

'Is it Drisheen or white pudding?' Mickey said.

'It's white pudding,' said his mother.

He frowned. 'I don't want that one. I want the one with all the blood.'

'I think he means black pudding, mam,' said Mickey.

'Yes,' he said, 'How many elephants does that have?'

'It's sausage, Sean,' said his mother. It's made from cooked pig's blood.'

'Yes, I want that one.'

'It's also made from pork fat, pork rind, pork shoulder, pork liver, oats, onion, rusk (wheat starch, salt), water, salt, pimento, and seasoning (rusk, spices).'

'I want that one.'

'No, Sean,' said his mother. 'I don't want you staining your clothes.'

'Why does it stain your clothes?'

His mother pressed her lips. 'Because it contains pork meat and fat, suet, bread, and oatmeal formed into a large sausage shape.'

That was of course during the week. On the Saturday morning, his mother would alter the menu slightly. She would cook a full breakfast: bacon sausages and eggs. Sometimes she included fried bread, which was bread fried in bacon fat.

Sean's mind maundered. He remembered being in secondary school. His mum would make him a packed lunch. It included pastie. He remembered it being a round battered pie of minced pork, onion, potato and seasoning. His girlfriend said to him once,

'You always have pastie for lunch, Sean. Have you left any room for me.'

He beamed amiably at Cinnia. 'I always have room for you.'

In the evenings, his mother might concoct anything. He recalled one evening when they were at the dinner table.

'What're we having tonight, mam?' said Mickey.

His mother nodded at her older son. She winked at Sean. 'See if you can guess.'

'It's not the old Irish stew, is it?' said Mickey.

'Not tonight, son,' said his mother.

'What is Irish stew?' he said.

'It's meat,' said Mickey.

'Yes, Mickey, but do you know which meat, Sean?' said his mother.

'Sheep.'

'Yes, that's pretty close, Sean,' said his mother. 'It's a traditional stew of lamb, or mutton, potatoes, carrots, onion and parsley.'

'Is that what we're having?' said Mickey. 'It's not skirts and kidneys again, mam, is it?'

'No, not tonight,' said his mother.'

'I'm tired of meat,' he said.

'D'you even know, Sean what's in skirts and kidneys?'

'Clothes and bones,' he said.

'That's not what skirts mean,' said Mickey. 'And kidneys are organs, not bones.'

'Yes,' said his mother, 'it comes from the pig. It includes the kidneys, the bladder and the liver.'

'Is it coddle then, mam?'

'It might be.'

'What is coddle?' he said.

'It's the pig again. It's layers of roughly sliced pork sausages bacon, usually thinly sliced, somewhat fatty back bacon, with sliced potato and onions.'

'It's not cottage pie, is it, mam?' said Mickey.

'We can't eat our house can we,' he said.

His mother laughed. 'No,' she said. 'It's a beef and vegetable mixture with gravy topped with mashed potato.'

'Anything to go with it?' said Mickey.

His mother tilted her head. 'You never know.'

'Champ?' said Mickey.

'That's when you win things,' he said.

'No,' said Mickey. 'That's when you eat your spuds. They're called Poundies.'

'Yes, Sean,' said his mother, 'It's mashed potatoes with chopped scallions.'

'What are scallions?' he said.

'Spring onions with butter and milk,' said his mother.

'Do they bounce up and down?' he said.

'Only in your stomach,' said his mother.

'So we're persevering with the potato diet, mam?' said Mickey.

'I thought you like Colcannon, Mickey,' said his mother.

'What is that?' he said.

'It's mashed potato with kale or cabbage,' said Mickey.

His mother nodded. 'There's also bacon and cabbage.'

'What's that?' he said.

'It's unsliced back bacon boiled together with cabbage and potatoes. I also make mashed potato. I prepare it by mashing freshly boiled potatoes with a potato masher, a fork, a ricer, or food mill, or I whip them with a hand beater. Sometimes I add butter and milk.'

His older brother levelled with him. 'She also makes boxty.'

'Is that the stuff adults drink?'

'No, Sean,' his mother said. 'You're thinking of boxed tea.'

'So?' he said.

'It's finely grated raw potato and mashed potato, mixed together with flour, baking soda, buttermilk and occasionally egg, then cooked like a pancake on a griddle pan.'

'We're not having Limerick ham, mam,' said Mickey.

'No, Mickey,' said his mother.

'A Limerick is a poem,' he said.

'Good, Sean,' said his mother.'

He smiled.

'It's also special way of preparing a joint of bacon,' said his mother.

During the holiday periods, his mother would make a range of bread. He remembered one time he had been cycling all morning with his friend Jim. He remembered having no energy to turn the wheels.

'We're starving, mam,' he said.

'Starving?'

'Yes.'

'I see boys,' said his mother. 'Try this, Jim!'

'What is it, Mrs Fields?' said Jim.

'It's barmbrack.'

My mother gave Jim a slice.

Jim gobbled it up. 'It tastes very sweet.'

'Yes, it is,' said his mother. 'That's because it has sultanas and raisins.'

'Yes, Mrs Fields,' said Jim, 'I can see them.'

'Barmbrack is also leavened.'

'What does that mean, mam?' he said.

'It means the bread has been fermented and risen,' said his mother.

'Try this one, Jim,' said his mother.

'What is it, Mrs Fields?'

'It's potato bread.'

'It's a bit plainer.'

'Yes, it's a flat bread made from potato bread. It's fried dry.'

'You mean you didn't use any oil?'

His mother rubbed her forehead. 'No, that's correct. It was a key component of the Ulster Fry.'

'Try this one, Jim.'

'What is it?' said Jim.

'Farl.'

'It almost looks like a triangle.'

'Yes, it's a traditional quick bread. Oh, try this one, Jim.'

'What is it Mrs Fields?' said Jim.

'It's soda bread.'

'It's a bit sweeter.'

'Yes, I added raisins.'

'What's the difference, Mrs Fields?' said Jim.

'I added sodium bicarbonate, otherwise known as baking soda instead of yeast.'

His mother could also do the third course. He remembered his birthday. He and some of his school friends were sitting round the kitchen table.

'Now, boys, this is Goody,' his mother said.

I remembered the chanting. He and his friends were all saying 'Goody' again and again.

'It's a dessert dish made by boiling bread in milk with sugar and spices. And this boys is Gur cake.'

He remembered the chanting starting again. 'Gur cake, Gur cake, Gur cake...'

'It's a pastry confection associated with Dublin,' his mother said.

On special occasions, his mother made Irish Seafood Chowder. It was Mickey's birthday.

'What is this, mam?' said Mickey.

'It's a particular method of preparing a seafood soup, often served with milk or creal.'

'It's absolutely delicious,' said Mickey.

'Well, it is your birthday,' said his mother.

One Christmas his mother concocted something very special.

'What is this, mam?' Mickey said.

'What is that?' he said.

'It's a cured and salty joint of rump steak or silver side beef.'

'Which one is it?' said Mickey.

'It's the steak,' said his mother.

'Too bad dad isn't here,' said Mickey.

'He'll always be with us, son,' said his mother, 'in our hearts.'

'Dad's inside us,'

'Yes, Sean,' said Mickey. 'Not inside our bodies, but inside our hearts.'

His mother smiled sadly. 'Yes, that's right.'

He remembered one Halloween, his mother had made something weird.

'What is this?' Mickey had said.

'They're called crubeens.'

'What is that?'

'Boiled pigs feet.'

He had giggled.

He remembered turning eighteen. He had gone out for a night on the town with his friends. After copious pints of Guinness they became hungry.

'I could use a spice bag,' his friend Jim said.

'Yes, me too,' he said.

They entered a fast food joint. 'We would like to have a spice bag,' said Jim.

'Do you know what that is?' he said.

'Certainly,' said the man behind the counter. 'It consists of deep-fried chips, chicken balls or strips, red and green peppers and a variety of spices.'

Suddenly, the music in the dining area of the Hilton hotel stopped. He awoke from his trance. He glazed at a man who smiled kindly at him.

'Sorry to disturb you, Sir,' he said. 'Are you okay?'

Sean exhaled deeply. 'Yes- yes I'm fine.'

'May I bring you anything, Sir?'

'Do you have anything Irish?'

'Of course we do, Sir. We have whiskey.'

'Ah, the water of life.'

'We also have Guinness.'

'A pint of plain.'

'We have other beers as well.'

'A wide variety.'

'We have cider, too.'

'A cold drink in summer, a hot one in winter.'

'There is also cream liquor.'

'Not just a "girlie drink".'

'We have mead.'

'Traditional but rare.'

'We have Poitin.'

'Now also available in legal.'

'We have Irish coffee.'

'Yes, it warms the cockles.'

'We have wine.'

'Imports rule.'

'And finally we have alcopops.'

'The teenager's choice for getting plastered.'

'Yes, I suppose so, Sir.

'I think I'll just have a pint of the plain.'

'As you wish, Sir. And would Sir care to dine with us?'

'Yes, I am rather hungry. You wouldn't happen to have spiced beef.'

'Spiced beef?'

'Yes, my mother used to make it on special occasions. It's a joint of rump steak or silverside beer- cured and salty.'

'Chef does do steak but it's fillet or sirloin, rather than rump.'

He nodded with appreciation. 'Sirloin is a better cut.'

'Indeed, and fillet is the premium steak.'

'Yes, why not, I'll have the fillet. I don't suppose I could have it with poundies.'

The waiter's face wrinkled. 'Excuse me, Sir?'

'You know, champ.'

'Champ, Sir?'

'It's mashed potatoes with chopped scallions.'

'Yes, I know scallions. They are spring onions with butter and milk.'

'Indeed.'

'Chef usually does roast potatoes, but permit me to have a word with him.'

'That's very kind, thank you.'

'Not at all.'

'And would Sir care for a glass of wine with his meal.'

'Yes, why not, I'll have *Lusca*.'

The waiter looked with impression. 'Very well, Sir.'

As he waited for his meal, he remembered the local restaurant back home in Rathnew. He had taken Cinnia there after their first date at the local cinema. He had been thirteen.

Sean yawned in agony after his meal. The waiter approached him. 'There was a man looking for you, Sir,' he said.

'Oh, yes?' said Sean.

'Yes, Sir.'

'Who was that?'

'I don't know but he looked rather like you, only older.'

'Like me?'

'Yes, he had your teeth.'

'My teeth?'

'Yes, your mouths are exactly the same.'

'What did he say?'

'He said he wanted to speak to you.'

'What about?'

'I apologise, Sir but he was very uptight. He claimed you had disgraced the family.'

'How?'

'He didn't specify.'

'What else did he say?'

'He said he was looking for his wee brother.'

Sean nodded. 'What happened?'

'We had to ask him to leave, we felt he was being too disruptive.'

Sean smiled with agitation. 'I see. I'm afraid I must retire. Might I have a bottle of Jameson.'

'Of course, Sir,' said the waiter. 'Would you prefer that I brought it up to your room?'

'No, I'll carry it myself, perhaps some ice.'

The waiter brought Sean the bottle with a bucket of ice and a quaich.

'Thank you,' he said. He left the table and wobbled to his room.

CHAPTER THIRTY-SEVEN

Day Nine; 9 pm; The Hotel Bedroom

Having made it from the town square to the pub to the hotel, and having called his mother, and having wined and dined, he drank Jameson into the night, listening to YouTube on the wide flat-screen television on the opposite side of the wall to the bed, smoking a packet of Pall Mall cigarettes. He eventually crashed out.

A few hours later, he woke up. The back of his head jagged. When he climbed out of bed, his brain was not there. He ghosted to the dressing table mirror. His sight was there. He peered into the mirror. There was nothing there. He could not feel happy, he could feel sad and he could not feel indifferent. His brain had gone. He could still think. He thought himself to be a hundred year old woman with long thin white hair. He thought about requesting an ambulance but with no brain-sensation he did not have the will to do so. Instead he alternated from the couch to the bed. He was not sure if he had had a stroke. He did not know if he was going to die. Eventually after hours, he drifted off to sleep. The following morning he felt better. He exited the hotel bedroom, walked along the corridor and tumbled down the stairs. He passed reception. A middle-aged man behind the reception desk stirred.

His voice pitched. 'Are you okay, Mr Fields?'

The younger cousin faced him. 'Not really, no.'

The man was middle-aged. He smiled kindly at him. 'We knocked on your door a few times yesterday but you wouldn't answer.'

Sean shook his head. 'No, not really.'

'You paid up front for a week's stay so we had no occasion to open your door.'

'My brain suffocated.'

The man nodded his head tentatively. 'Are you being sarcastic, young Sir?'

Sean sniffed. 'No.'

The man smiled sadly. 'I can see that. I'm not quite sure what to say. I'm deeply sorry, Sir. What happened?'

'I'm not sure.'

'I assure you the bedrooms are continually ventilated. This has never happened to one of our guests before.'

'I think it might have been the wasp spray.'

'But we don't keep wasp spray in the bedrooms.'

'No, I had some in my hold-all.'

'I see, and how much of the spray did you use?'

'I'm not sure, lots.'

'May I ask if you were drinking, Sir.'

'Yes, lots.'

'Were you smoking?'

'Yes.'

'I'm sorry, Sir but we don't usually permit smoking in the bedrooms. But I can see it's not important enough in this case.'

Sean smiled plaintively. 'No.'

'As for someone putting a pillow over your head, they would have needed the keys to gain entry to your bedroom. Th door locks automatically when closed. And I'm the only one in the hotel in charge of a spare set. In fact, it's over-' The man gaped as he noticed the set was missing. 'You're right enough, Sir. The spare set seems to have gone amiss. I'll try to find out what's happened there. This needs reported.'

Sean nodded.

'Would Sir care for a glass of water?'

'I'm going to the shops. Perhaps when I come back.'

'Of course, Sir.' The kind good-looking middle-aged man's eyes bleated at Sean. 'I am sorry.'

Sean returned to the hotel.

'Hello again, Sir.'

'Please call me Sean.'

'Sean, then. I'm still trying to locate the missing keys. I have phoned the police and reported your event. Is there anything I can do for you?'

'Yes, I would appreciate a bottle of champagne.'

The man smiled seriously at him. 'Certainly, we will pay for that ourselves.'

Sean smiled at the man without speaking.

Sean alternated from the bar where he gulped champagne to the hotel back garden where he smoked his cigarettes. He felt better than he did but he was still not right. He suffered *genuine* paranoid schizophrenia. It was a very numismatic experience. Alarm bells echoed in his mind and high sharp thoughts attacked his mind. The thoughts became quicker and louder. The thoughts went: '*Sean Fields you have paranoid schizophrenia, Sean Fields you have paranoid Schizophrenia, Sean Fields you have paranoid schizophrenia...*'

The waiter stepped out into the garden. 'Are you okay, Sir?'

Sean waved his head desperately. 'I'm actually very ill.'

'Will I call a doctor?'

'No, I think I'll have a lie down.'

Sean took himself back into his hotel bedroom. He was smoking cigarettes and drinking whiskey. He was having an imaginary conversation with Cinnia. All his brain-strength had returned. He was singing. He decided he would use the money Albert Bennet had given him to stay longer at the hotel.

I rang Chase.

'*Ewok*!'

'The younger cousin's brain suffocated.'

Chase gasped. 'God Almighty! How?'

I swallowed. 'I'm not sure. There are three possibilities. Either he smoked a bad packet of cigarettes, or he inadvertently applied insecticide to his brain or someone smothered him with a pillow.'

'Is he still alive?'

'Yes, he eventually fell asleep.'

'How is he?'

I groaned. 'He was alternating between the hotel bar and the back court. He has been going through an almost religious paranoid schizophrenia. He has returned to his bedroom. I can actually hear him singing.'

'Yes, why d' you think that?'

'He must be on coke.'

'I don't think it's soft drinks, he ordered a bottle of whiskey

'No, I mean cocaine.'

'How would he have cocaine?'

'It's obviously being transmitted through his cigarettes.'

'The tobacco companies can do that?'

'They can do anything, they're called lines.'

'What does that mean?'

'It means his tobacco company are encouraging one of their customers.'

'Encouraging?'

'Controlling.'

'I see. What next?'

'You may drive home.'

I drove back to Newton Mearns.

CHAPTER THIRTY-EIGHT

Day Ten; 5: 15 am; Taylor-made for Murder

There was another bang. My mobile bleeped. It screeched through my unconscious.

'Chase?'

'*Ewok*!'

I bolted upright. 'One of the bedroom windows surely.'

'Of course.'

'The father of the husband?'

'Exactly.

Sean ambled by the hotel reception desk. The kind old man at the reception desk stirred. 'How are you feeling today, young Sir?'

Sean smiled defiantly. 'Well enough to leave and to travel.'

The man smiled at him happily. 'Excellent, Sir. Where will you go, Sir?'

'To the man who may understand a suffocated brain.'

'A doctor, Sir?'

'Yes.'

'Good luck, Sir!'

'Thank you.'

Sean trudged to Aberdeen Train Station. With what was left of the money Albert had given him he got the train to Glasgow

Central Station. Upon arrival, he took the underground towards Hyndland on the west line.

I drove from Keppochill to Hyndland. Is set up the sounding equipment I heard murmurings outside the living room window. Inside, a heated argument was fomenting.

Angela Reid was tearing strips out of her head. 'Our son is coming over, Taylor.'

Doctor Taylor narrowed his eyes at his wife. 'He is?'

'Yes.'

'Why?'

'I insisted that he come over.'

Doctor Reid pinched his brows. 'Why?'

'Because we have to do something.'

'What?'

'We have to help our son.'

'Why?'

'He's drinking himself into oblivion.'

'How do you know?'

'Susie phoned.'

'And?'

'She said he was out of control.'

'And?'

'He needs our help.'

Doctor Reid dizzied his head. 'He's obviously mentally ill, Angela.'

'You always say that, but you do precisely nothing to help him.'

'So?'

'That becomes our fault.'

Doctor Reid waved his head. 'No, it doesn't. We have paid that boy a fortune over the years.'

Angela Reid's hardened blue eyes pricked tears. 'Yes, but he doesn't need more money, he needs proper help.'

'Why?'

'He's hurting.'

'No, he's not, he's patronising everything.'

Angela Reid glared at her husband. 'Including his own pain.'

'The boy's very far away from pain.'

'No, Taylor, he's suffered all of it because of you.'

Dr Reid grimaced. 'You're spouting absolute garbage, Angela.'

'No, I'm not. All you ever cared about, Taylor was your job, your career, your reputation, your importance, you never cared about him.'

'It was a lot more than that. I didn't need to drink to empathise in order to provide.'

'Yes, but now it's different.'

'Different in which way?'

'He might just do something terribly stupid or die.'

'While you just condescend to him as a stone.'

'*Excuse me*?'

'You drink all the time, Angela. You always have.'

Angela Reid scowled. 'How dare you!'

'What d'you mean?'

'A lot of people hate you.'

'Who?'

'Susanna's daughter, her two cousins, Hugh Sharp, his son, Albert Bennet...'

'Why?'

'You threatened to section Susie's mother, you failed to warn the cousins' father what he would do, you threatened to tell his wife of his infidelity and abuse, his son whose father's reputation was on the line, you threatened to expose Albert Bennet's secret, the list goes on Taylor.'

'No, how dare *you*! You need to understand, Angela.'

'What?'

'You haven't worked for years, love.'

'How dare you say that! I have worked hard all my life.'

Taylor Reid shrugged. 'So you say.'

'You're obscenely spoiled by your job.'

'All you mean is that I keep on working, while you entertain yourself.'

'Yes, but you must be aware what I had to give up for your job.'

Doctor Reid waggled his head. 'It's just his age. The boy will grow out of it. I used to do the same.'

Angela Reid heaved a heavy sigh. 'Our son is already a man, he is thirty-one, Taylor.'

'Our son is a married man and he's trying to make it as a lawyer.'

Angela Reid's face furrowed with frantic worry. 'No, Taylor, something's wrong.'

'Which is?'

'Susie's doing something to him.'

'Who?'

'See, you can't even remember his wife.'

'Of course I know his wife. So?'

'I don't know but she's making his life a misery.'

Doctor Taylor Reid sighed. 'I know the feeling.'

'Please don't be sarcastic with me, Taylor. Maybe he's-' Angela Reid wiggled her finger in the air. 'Gay.'

'Crap, Angela, my son has always fancied girls.'

'Well, what then?'

'The poor boy lost his girlfriend's mother when he was nine.'

The anguish in Angela Reid's eyes abated a fraction. 'Yes.'

'And he was rejected from his girlfriend's house.'

'Yes.'

'We know it wasn't him.'

'Yes, only because I dragged it out of him. There was nothing there.'

'So he couldn't have done it.'

'No, that's right.'

'It was Susanna McLean's fault. She was behaving totally irresponsibly.'

'No, it was that horrible man's fault.'

'Yes, Andrew McLean was totally arrogant.'

'That's not who I mean.'

'Who do you mean?'

'That other man.'

'You mean that man who threatened me and threatened to get Susanna McLean's husband.'

'Yes, that's why I telephoned Susanna's sister-in-law. We knew he planned to kill her brother.'

'Jarrod Fields?'

'Yes.'

'You told her what you were worried about. Plus, he made me go over to Dublin.'

'Do you remember why you did that?'

'Of course, I wasn't having my nine year old son accused of something we know he didn't do.'

'You have to speak to him.'

'Yes?'

'You have to work out why he's mentally ill.'

'He'll be here any moment. In fact, there's the doorbell now.'

Richie stumbled into his parents' house. He wobbled into the living room.

'Son?' he said.

'Father?' said Doctor Reid.

'You asked me to come over.'

'Your mother did, yes.'

'What is it?'

'Your mother says you're unwell and by the look of you, you are.'

'What's that supposed to mean?'

'You're mentally ill.'

Richie glared indignantly. 'Don't be ridiculous. I'm hardly mentally ill. You're just putting words to people.'

'No.'

'You're a bully, it's a financial concept. They pay you far too much.'

Doctor Reid waved his head. 'No.'

'What then?'

'It's your health.'

Richie shook his head. 'My health is fine, it's a financial concept.'

'No.'

Ritchie blazed at his father. 'In that case you are purely and simply: evil.'

His father waved his head.

'You're not even the slightest bit prepared to listen.'

His father waved his head again.

'Why not?'

'No, because it's crap.'

'You're just grumpy because you drink.'

His father nodded.

'You stink, son.'

'You're being obnoxious.'

'No, your behaviour isn't good enough.'

'You don't get paid for that.'

'No.'

'Yes, but they pay you.'

'No, son. I turn up. I always have.'

'You have it all given to you.'

His father ignored him.

Richie flailed. 'They pay you to do nothing.'

'You need help. And by the way, son, I know what you did.'

'What?'

'You caused pain.'

'What pain?'

'Pain you don't remember.'

'What?'

'I didn't kill my wife's mother.'

'No, you didn't prepare or serve the mushrooms, but I do know you were involved. Anyway, that's not what I meant.'

'What did you mean?'

'It's better you don't know.'

There was a knock on the door. Doctor Reid grumbled before going to answer it. He opened the door. There was a soaked bedraggled figure standing outside.

'Yes?' said Doctor Reid.

'Are you Doctor Reid?'

'Yes, who are you exactly?'

'I'd rather not say.'

'What can I do for you?'

'I believe a man was killed.'

Doctor Reid tensed. 'Are you here to threaten me?'

The figure was non-committal.

'No, Sir.'

'May I ask who was killed?'

'I believe Jarrod Fields had his life taken.'

Doctor Reid furrowed his brows. 'Jarrod Fields?'

'Yes.'

Doctor Reid nodded his head understandingly. 'You better come in then.'

Doctor Reid escorted the visitor to the living room.

'We have a guest, son,' said Doctor Reid.

'Yes,' said Richie. He waved out a hand. 'Hello.'

'I believe you knew the victim,' said the visitor.

'If you mean Jarrod Fields, then yes.'

Richie stirred. 'That would have been my wife's great uncle.'

The visitor nodded. 'Yes.'

'I was fifteen.'

'Yes,' said the visitor.

'It happened in 2003 at Rathnew.'

'Yes.'

'Who are you?' said Richie.

'I'd rather not say.'

'You'd better say something,' said Doctor Reid.

'Well, then, you might have killed Jarrod Fields.'

Richie scoffed. He flicked his head at his father. 'Knowing him, he probably did.'

'Why would I have killed him?' said Doctor Reid.

The visitor winked at Richie. 'Because your son was rejected from his girlfriend's house.'

'That's hardly a reason to kill a man.'

'You were invited over, you were warned that a man was planning to kill him.'

'Why would that be?'

The visitor gesticulated at Richie again. 'Since your wife Angela told you to look after your son's girlfriend's uncle.'

'You mean Jarrod Fields?'

'Yes

'Why would she ask me to do that?'

'Since a man named Hugh Sharp threatened you. He warned you he would kill Jarrod Fields.'

'Why would he do that?'

'Since Jarrod Fields threatened to expose him.'

'Expose him?'

'He knew what he was doing to his sister.'

'Well, perhaps he did then, I certainly didn't.'

'I think you might have used a surgeon's scalpel.'

'You're as bad as my son,' said Doctor Reid. 'I'm a doctor, not a surgeon.'

'No, but you could easily have accessed one.'

'Maybe your visitor is correct,' said Richie.

'No, the pair of you are delusional. I don't think you follow what happened.'

'The lights had gone dark, we couldn't see anything. We don't know who did it.'

'That's not good enough.'

'Well, it's all your getting. Now, if you don't mind, I'd like you to leave my house.'

'What?' said Richie. 'In the same way I was made to leave the house.'

'No,' said Doctor Reid, 'this person is mistaken, you are mentally ill.'

'I'm not mentally ill,' said Richie.

'You stink of alcohol, son,' said Doctor Reid.

The visitor glowered at Doctor Reid. 'Do you understand ether?'

'Of course I do.'

'Chloroform?'

'Well, yes.'

The visitor put a cloth to Doctor Reid's face. He sank to the floor.

I mobiled Chase.

'Chase?'

'*Ewok*!'

'I'm right outside the house of the henpecked husband's father.'

'You used the laser microphone.'

'Yes.'

'The arrogant doctor has been knocked out.'

'How?'

'With chloroform.'

'Is he still alive?'

'Yes, I think so, I can hear breathing.'

'Who knocked him out?'

'I don't know.'

'Surely, you would know.'

'No, the visitor was very discrete. So what next?'

'You will return to the disgruntled client's house.'

'Why?'

'The talented son's coming over.'

'Why?'

'He has announcement to make.'

'What announcement?'

'His fiancée is pregnant.'

'How do you know?'

'I tapped his mobile telephone.'

'Could not just tap the disgruntled client's mobile telephone?'

'Yes.'

'So?'

'He won't be using it tomorrow- and we wouldn't hear the full story.'

'How d'you know he won't be using it tomorrow?'

'The talented son said to his publisher: 'I'm away on other business tomorrow, I'm seeing my father. Jane's got the mobile and my father's mobile has broken down.'

'Could his publisher not just call his father's landline?'

'Yes, but that would be a conversation between the talented son and his publisher, not between the son and the father.'

I sighed. 'I see.'

CHAPTER THIRTY-NINE

Day Eleven; 5 am; The Disgruntled Client

The mobile bleeped.

'Chase?'

'*Ewok*!'

'The second bedroom window?'

'Of course.'

'The disgruntled client?'

'You will drive to Aberdeen.'

As I puttered along the country lane in the Mercedes, approaching the front gates of Music Hall I could espy two figures moving closely together. I was going to have to be careful to avoid being detected. I parked the car some distance from the gates. I set up the voice recorder outside the gates. I

Ben had been returning to the family home for years, his old stomping ground. He had always felt like a defeated dissonant chord rather than a victorious major chord. His grandfather Frank Sharp had been as rich as a Croesus. The house was originally called 'Well Manored.' It was a fair witticism made by some old proprietor. His grandfather had the name change to 'Music Hall.' It had been an intricate business, involving chunky fees and high-octane lawyers. Music Hall was a most decorated shed; a palace almost. It was endowed with an exceptionally large declive plot of ground, even for a once distinguished conductor. Plants, such as fruit, vegetables and flowers were grown.

On this occasion, he harboured some very important news. His uniquely fertile imagination debulliated with weird and wonderful arrangements of pop, rock and folk, and classical music, as well as the news.

As they strolled side by side in the cold afternoon drizzle, his father singled out all the plants. He described them in tedious but impressive detail. Ben bowed and swallowed during this observance of actions and procedures in a set, ordered and ceremonial way.

The aged fermented grain in his father's relaxed degage veins took affect. To Ben's father it was a victory march. Redolent of the days when he would walk before the big audiences in London after an encore and take a bow. It was a victory, not just over his son, but over almost everyone with a house and an accomplishment for status. To Ben it was an inevitable recurring walk of shame. He felt like a battery chicken in the vast open plains of the Serengeti. Not so much liberated as dropped right in it.

His father briefly tilted up his sturdy eyeglasses and peeked at him. He smiled superciliously and said, 'Take a look, son!' He signalled with his hands. 'Go on! Take a look!'

Ben cast yet another diffident eye over the place, over the edifice, large and impressive, over the rolling gardens, over the purling rivulet, over the water feature, over the endless exquisite beauty. He smiled humbly and nodded resignedly.

'What d' you think?' his father said.

Ben courteously smothered a cough and said, 'Yes, father, it's very nice.'

His father's pitch black eyes bulged and he said, 'You think so?'

'Yes. It's very big.'

'And what d' you think of the gardens?'

'They're big as well, father.'

A smile creased his father's lips. 'You're not too disappointed?'

Ben glanced incredulously at his father and said, 'What's there to be disappointed about?'

'Sometimes sons, especially very good sons, such as yourself, have high expectations of their fathers.'

Ben smiled ruefully. He knew he was being patronised.

Ben's father bowed his head and said, 'My dad, your grandfather, son, did so much better than I.'

Ben's eyes flickered and he said, 'He did?'

'Yes, the house was bigger.'

Ben stared open-mouthed and said, 'Bigger than this?'

'Yes, much.'

'I'm surprised.'

'And the garden was rosier.'

'There's quite a prodigious number of plants here.'

'Yes, but his garden was fit for the public. They would pay money just to see it. And the people...they were...*happier*.'

'You're not happy, father?'

Ben's father smiled wistfully and said, 'I try to be, son. I try to be.'

'What stops you?'

His father nodded contemplatively. 'Your mother.'

Ben nodded gently and said, 'Of course.'

'You miss her too, son, don't you?'

'Yes. She couldn't have had a worse ending.'

His father coughed in to his right fist. 'No, as I have often said before, the smoke would have gotten to her first.'

Ben smiled uneasily.

As the grain strengthened, a ripple of good humour went through his father's body. 'My father once said to me that a father should impress his son.'

'Peter Sharp?'

'Yes.'

'He owned the top music company in Scotland.'

'Yes.'

Ben nodded tentatively and said, 'Well, you have imprseed me, father.'

'I have?'

Ben nodded.

'Yes, but I sense something's wrong.'

'Wrong?'

'Yes, an unease.'

Oh, how perceptive! he thought. He had never been less awkward.

Ben sighed. 'You do.'

'Yes. Almost an unwarranted jealousy.'

Ben bit his lower lip. 'I know the point, father.'

His father's eyes stirred. 'You do?'

Ben nodded. 'Yes. Health and happiness.'

Ben's father tottered his head.

Ben glanced cautiously at his father. 'Jane and I are both well. And content.'

'The woman is as useless now as she was as a girl.'

'Jane wasn't useless, she was poor.'

'Her mother ought to have been better.'

'Mrs White worked very hard for you.'

'You mean I let a lower class female in to my upper-class house.'

'No, father, you paid her buttons for slave labour.'

'I don't see how you could be content.'

'Why?'

'She has always battened on to your talent.'

'Jane runs her own business.'

'You could easily do without it.'

'Perhaps, but she couldn't.'

'No?'

'No, she needs her independence.'

'Then leave her to it.'

'She loves me.'

'So?'

'I love her.'

'Why?'

'She is a lovely person.'

'Pretty you mean?'

'No, lovely.'

'So?'

'She doesn't need to subjugate to survive.'

'She hasn't worked hard enough to live in Thorntonhall.'

'Where as you have, I suppose.'

'I have worked harder.'

'Yes.'

'Yes, and for years.'

'She is trying.'

'Never mind her, what about you?'

'What do you mean?'

'You haven't had a single thing published for- what is it now- over a year.'

'I have a daughter to look after.'

'Yes, she is hideous.'

'I thought you didn't regard looks. Anyway, she's beautiful.'

'No, son, she is exceptionally plain. God knows how with her parental looks!'

'She'll grow out of whatever you find unappealing.'

'She would have to die first.'

'Why do you hate my daughter?'

'He or she was supposed to be great.'

'Why?'

'My father was great, I am great-'

'And me?'

'You are but fair.'

'Really?'

'Yes.'

'Why would that be?'

'Because your plebeian whore has dragged you down.'

'You can't call her that.'

'No, son. She has undone all the years of hard work your mother and I put into you.'

'You mean the lectures.'

'You see, son, it takes a lot more than you are doing to have all this.'

'You're sure.'

The old man father pursed his lips. 'Yes, you have to get up early. Very early in the morning without exception. Even if the lark is splashing a note. You have to force yourself into the hub. You have to organize lots of people and perform a myriad of tasks.'

'But you were a composer, father.'

'Yes, and among the very best of my generation.'

'So?'

'My music was exceptional, son.'

'And mine?'

'It's pithy.'

'Excuse me?'

'Don't think I haven't noticed son. I've heard you. You've descended into pop music- Eurovision even.'

'What's wrong with that?'

'It's cheap and easy.'

'So?'

'You need wisdom, skill, comprehension, intellectuality. But most of all perspiration. Discipline.'

Ben dipped his head and sighed. 'I can't control a publisher's random and excessive demands.'

'No, but you can make them think. Take you seriously. With competence and industriousness.' Ben's father winked cheekily at him. 'It's hard work you're comparing yourself to. Take it from me, it was that which was *quod erat demonstrandum*.'

'Yes.'

'Yes?'

Ben sighed. 'That which was to be shown or demonstrated'.'

'Maybe there's still some hope for you yet.'

'You make me sound at the end of things.'

Hugh Sharp stared into space. 'It was all about mushrooms. They got to her in the end.' His stare became a lost gaze. 'No, he wasn't doing a very good job. He cost me a fortune. I wanted to kill him. Just as well I know what the other man did. We would never have recovered. She had infinite beauty, shame her husband was too academic to fully appreciate it. She was almost worth it in the end.'

Ben frowned.

They entered the large stately house together. His father with hauteur, Ben with feelings of inadequacy. The house was similar in a way to the one he first grew up in, the house he and Jane had recently revisited. They were both big and posh but the main difference between the two houses was that this one was not burned to a crisp on the inside. It was not so replete with frightful memories.

Jane was with him. She was upstairs in one of the big luxury *en suite* bathrooms. Probably trying to make sense of her ordinarily prepossessing appearance which took a dent in less clement weather conditions. Anne was with him as well. She was outside in the garden, in-line skating on the concrete slabs.

After long periods of pussyfooting, Ben finally broached the question of the pregnancy. 'I have some news, father,' he said.

His father, who was scowling out the living room window, turned round and said, 'News?'

'Yes.'

'Good, I trust.'

'Yes, as far as Jane and me are concerned.'

Ben's father's voice modulated and his mood switched from scorn to hope. 'You're no longer desponsated?'

'No, father.'

'Well, what then?'

'Jane's pregnant.'

Ben's father spluttered and said, '*Pregnant*?'

'Yes.'

Ben's father sneered as he said, 'As if one mutant child in the family wasn't enough.'

'Anne's not a mutant, father. She's your granddaughter.'

'Well, half mutant.'

'She isn't that either. She's performing very well at school. The teachers have said so.'

His father shook his head and muttered and said, 'So you're pregnant again?'

Ben raised his head and said, 'Either that or Jane's been eating her cosmetics.'

Ben's father grunted and said, 'I wouldn't put it past her.'

Ben cast his father a disapproving look and said, '*Father*.'

'Well, you know, son?'

'*What*?'

'She's not exactly a damsel?'

'A what father?'

'A young woman originally of noble birth.'

'Maybe not b-;

'And she's hardly Carol Vorderman, is she?'

Ben's furrowed his brows and puckered his lips and said, 'Who's Carol Vorderman?'

'I forget, my lad, you were never allowed to watch the old box, except for current events. It was chewing gum for the eyes.'

Ben saw his long-awaited chance and said, 'Hypocrite.'

'No, privileges, son. Privileges of the meritocracy.'

'Not quite the aristocracy, then?'

'I never said we were on Debrett's Peerage.'

'On what?'

'Not you, too! The list of the British aristocracy. And, anyway, she's the woman who does, or at least *did*, countdown.'

Ben stuck out his tongue and said, 'What's countdown?'

Ben's father sighed and said, 'A words and numbers programme.'

'You're obviously very retired now.'

'Not so. I get a lot done. In the house. In the garden. On the boat.'

Yes, *the boat*, Ben thought. *How outstripped was a son supposed to be? Perhaps his father could kneel down as the queen tapped his shoulder with a sword.*

'Anyway,' continued his father, 'I've seen pre-fives with a better command of English and Maths.'

'What even better than Carol Vorderman?'

His father's eyes boiled. 'No, you idiot! Better than your Jane.'

'She's kind, that's all that matters.'

'You could do so much better for yourself.'

'Like you did.'

'I was young. Young and foolish.'

'So like father like son.'

The malt was now surging through his father's bloodstream. 'You have a long way to go to be like me, son.'

'I write music, don't I?'

'Yes, but I was a world-class musician.'

'Pity you didn't stay that way.'

'I would have done- if it hadn't been for that infernal bimbo, Samantha. That's why I don't want you making the same mistake.'

'It's too late for that. We're already engaged.'

'Yes, but you could still call it off. I'm sure she could find someone else. She is a looker. I'll give her that.'

'And why would I want to do that?'

'So that you have the very best chance of succeeding.'

'And what is succeeding?'

'Creating and performing true masterpieces.'

'And who decides what constitutes "true masterpieces?" *You*?'

'Well, yes, the past and present virtuosos.'

'And what do they know? All they understand is tedious classical music. It's not everyone's cup of tea. And anyway, I thought you were a conductor.'

'I had many strings to my bow. And we're not everyone. We're the Sharps.'

Ben breathed laboriously.

'By the way,' said his father, 'how're things going with the recital? Are you ready to weave magic?'

'They're going okay. And I hope so.'

'Just okay? You only hope so? But this is your big night. The one you've been preparing for. For weeks. Months. Your whole life, really.'

Ben rubbed his throbbing forehead. 'It's just a recital. It's not the Queen's Speech.'

'It's more than that. It's a chance to show the whole world what you're made of.'

'I'm made of flesh and blood, father.'

'You have to be made of more than that; you have to be made of steel. If you muck this up, you might never get another chance.'

'I'm not convinced I want another chance.'

'That's not the attitude. Your poor mother died so you could have this opportunity.'

'Nothing like piling on the pressure, is there?'

'Has that feather-brain Jane been putting you off.'

'No. And she's not a feather-brain, father. She's a clever cookie. She just lacks the confidence of independent thought.'

'She lacks everything: talent, skill and definitely brilliance.'

'We can't all be virtuosos. It doesn't make you a bad person.'

'It makes you a lesser person, with no right to impede your betters.'

'Jane's a good person. A very, very good person.'

'She's an imbecile.'

'She's not. She's gentle and kind.'

'Dippy you mean? If it wasn't for her looks, she would automatically qualify for a Council Tax exemption.'

'Why so?'

'Severe impairment of intelligence and/or social functioning.'

'How would you know about that?'

'Owners of mansions have a strong command of property issues.'

Ben nodded tentatively and said, 'Jane's fantastic. She can doll up anyone. Even a two hundred year old dead red Indian dwarf. And she's able to draw them in, in the first place.'

His father waggled his head.

I rang chase. '*Chase*?'

'*Ewok*!'

'I set up the voice recorder outside the front gates.'

'And?'

'I listened in on the conversation between the disgruntled client and the talented son.'

'What did you find out?'

'The father possesses far more than his son. The son's father wanted to impress him. He is disappointed in him. The son feels inadequate. The grandfather was inordinately wealthy. They talked about his mother and his wife.'

'And?'

'The disgruntled client re-assured the talented son that the smoke would have killed his mother.'

'And not the fire itself?'

'Yes.'

'What else?'

'The disgruntled client knows all about flora, especially mushrooms. He quaffs whiskey. He has rejected his granddaughter. He resents his son's fiancée. He feels she has spoiled his investment in his son. She is pregnant. He maintains the house, tends to the garden and operates a boat.'

'And?'

'I think he knows a secret.'

'What secret?'

'I don't know.'

'But?'

'I think he has been manipulating it.'

'I see. Why might the disgruntled client have killed my brother and/or his wife?'

'There could be several reasons.'

'Oh?'

'Yes, revenge, survial, greed.'

'What about revenge?'

'I think the disgruntled client was less than happy with your brother's work.'

'How do you know it was my brother's work?'

'You told me outside his mansion that you brother was a lawyer and that he was not in the habit of giving away his clients' names, although he did tell you a few things.'

'So?'

'The disgruntled client may have killed your brother as revenge for, as he might have seen it, negligently representing him.'

'What about greed?'

'According to his conversation with his son, he may have had intimate feelings for someone.'

'What makes you think that?'

'The disgruntled client said that she was almost worth it.'

'So?'

'I think that was your brother's wife.'

'Why?'

'Something else he said.'

'Which was?'

'"She had infinite beauty, shame her husband was too academic to fully appreciate it."'

'I see. So?'

'The disgruntled client might have killed your brother's wife out of obsession.'

'More about greed.'

'I think the disgruntled client might well have been jealous of your brother.'

'Jealous? You mean romantically?'

'Yes, and sexually. What exactly did your brother say about this man?'

'He said: "*This man's mad, Chase. He lost his wife a long time ago.*"'

'And?'

'My brother got the distinct impression there was more to it than that.'

'He told you?'

'Yes.'

'And?'

'My brother wondered if she might have been killed.'

'Why?'

'I don't know.'

'But?'

'My brother told me that his client felt so guilty.'

'Why?'

'I don't know.'

'And?'

'He talked about a feeling.'

'What feeling?'

'I don't know, but he made it clear to my brother that it was unlike any other.'

'I see. How did you find me, Chase?'

'You were in the paper.'

'Yes?'

'The Herald.'

'I see.'

'The article said you were retiring and that you were having a do. It said you would be present that night at the Premier Inn.'

'What else?'

'I want you to stay in Aberdeen.'

'You mean overnight?'

'Yes.'

'Why?'

'The aggrieved mother is coming over.'

'She is?'

'Yes,I want you to listen to her conversation with the residents of Music Hall.'

I breathed laboriously. 'Very well, I'll stay at the Hilton Hotel.'

'Good.'

CHAPTER FORTY

Day Twelve: 4: 45 am; Judith White Visits Music Hall

I drove the Mercedes from the hotel towards Music Hall. I was driving very conservatively in order to make sure I did not arrive before the suspects, which would have me detected. A taxi cab overtook me on the b-road before it turned right onto the country lane which lead up to the house. I spotted two people in the back of the cab. I presumed it was Judith White and her daughter. After affording them enough time to get to the house, again I parked the car some distance from the front gates.

I actuated the laser microphone and aimed it at the front door.

Inside, Hugh Sharp and his son Ben were alerted to the hushing sound of falling rain. Hugh brushed towards the drawing room window. He peered outside. 'Yes, it's a very wet day,' he said. There was a rap on the door. As he tinkled his glass, he turned his head and gestured at his son Ben. Ben sighed and answered the door. His fiancée and her mother were dangling outside, rain bouncing off their wet clothes.

Ben smiled submissively at his fiancée. 'Hello, Jane.'

'Hi, honey.'

Ben was always nervous around Jane's mother. His fiancée's

mother disapproved of him almost as much as his father disapproved of her daughter.

Ben blushed. 'Hello, Mrs White.'

Mrs White's facial expression did not contort. 'Benjamin.'

Ben whispered. He gesticulated with his hands. 'Please, come in.' Ben escorted Susie and her mother into the drawing room.

Ben stood by with open arms as Jane stepped in first, her mother eyeballed him before assenting to walk in.

Hugh Sharp bowed at Mrs White. 'Judith,' he said.

'Mr Sharp,' she said.

'To what do we owe this unexpected pleasure.'

Judith White grit her teeth. 'I would like you to pay me.'

Jane wiggled her head. 'What my mother means is we're here to see the family.'

Ben winked at his fiancée. 'Of course.'

Hugh Sharp lowered at Judith White. 'I know we sorted that out years ago, Mrs White.'

'Yes, but I never said I had forgotten, Mr Sharp.'

Hugh sharp shifted his head. 'I still believe we can entertain you. Would you like a beverage or would you prefer to take one yourself?'

'Perhaps I could clean up the mess first on the floor, before I wash the glasses.'

'That is if you could take another break from our fridge.'

'That is if the fridge is clean enough.'

Hugh Sharp pointed his finger in the air. 'Son, please fetch Mrs White her favourite beverage. And while you're at it I'm sure your conscientious fiancée would appreciate some lemon tea.'

Together they sat around the coffee table.

'Do you remember your mother at all, Benjamin?'

Ben smiled grimly. 'Parts of her.'

'And which parts do you remember?'

'She was brilliant but hard.'

'In what way was she hard?'

'She made me play piano all of the time.'

'Why did she do that?'

'She expected me to be brilliant as well.'

Hugh Sharp's beetle-brows tweaked a fraction. 'What are you?' He snorted. ' A cub reporter?'

Judith White glared at Hugh Sharp. 'No, a witness.'

'She died in a fire. In an horrendous fire. Everyone knows that.'

'Yes, I always thought about that.'

'And?'

'I think her death was deeply suspicious.'

'Mother!'

Ben's father's voice rose indignantly. 'Suspicious?'

'You remember the old post-mortem, Mr Sharp?'

'No, I don't. How on earth would you?'

'Jean Reid told me.'

'That old harridan. What did she tell you?'

'There were bruises on her neck.'

Hugh Sharp scoffed. 'How would she know?'

'Her son was a doctor- Taylor Reid- still is- he found out through a colleague.'

'Which colleague?'

'A colleague in the mortuary.'

Ben huffed. 'That is easily explained.'

Jane gawped. 'It is dear?'

'Yes, she wore a necklace,' said Ben. 'A tight-fitting necklace.'

Judith White frowned. 'I did see a couple of things.'

'What did you see?' said Hugh.

'I saw a cigar burning.'

'What cigar?' said Ben.

'It was burning away in an ashtray in the basement where the piano was. I also saw a piece of wire.'

'What wire?' said Hugh.

'I couldn't tell but it was lying next to her.'

'It's quite straightforward- sad but straight forward: she died in a fire.'

'I am not all sure she did.'

Judith White brought her head down firmly. She gazed at Ben. 'What did you think of your mother?'

'She was very accomplished,' said Ben

'Of course she was,' said Hugh.

'She was also very strict.'

'She was a pianist- a concert pianist. All such people are firm with their children.'

'Yes, but they don't all beat their sons.'

'Ben?' said Jane.

'It didn't happen all the time, anyway I was being unruly.'

'She shouldn't have beaten you at all,' said Jane.

'It was no more than I required. Successful pianists require diligent teachers.'

Jane frowned slightly. 'You're sometimes too diligent with Ann, dear.'

'Nonsense, Jane. Ann would not be able to strike a note, were it not for me.'

'I don't think you're firm enough with her,' said Hugh.

'Child abuse is still a crime in this country,' said Judith White.

'I would hardly call it child abuse,' said Ben.

'Oh?' said Judith White. 'What would you call it.'

'Instruction.'

'No, it's done out of greed.

'Are you trying to suggest some sort of *cui bono?'*

'I have no idea what that term means, Mr Sharp,' said Judith White.

Hugh Sharp squeezed his brow. 'Now why did I think you would.'

'What does it mean?' said Jane.

'It's a legal principle,' said Ben.

'Yes, it's the legal principle that somebody who would gain something from a particular action or event is probably responsible for it.'

'In that case,' said Judith White, 'Your mother stood to gain a successful son. You stand to gain a successful daughter.'

'Ben would have been successful anyway. Ann is already successful.'

'Your daughter is nothing of the sort,' said Hugh.

'Father!' said Ben.

'She has a problem with numbers, that's all,' said Jane.

'And with letters,' said Hugh.

'You abused your son,' said Judith White.

'It was not all the time,' said Ben.

'Often enough,' said Judith.

'Like you have never physically chastised your child,' said Hugh.

'I have never laid a finger on my daughter,' said Judith White. 'Unlike you.'

Jane nodded assertively at her mother. 'No, you haven't.'

'I assure you, Judith,' said Hugh Sharp, 'I did not beat my son.'

'Perhaps not, but you beat you wife.'

'That's outrageous!' said Hugh.

'Come now, Mr Sharp!' said Judith White. 'I oversaw your physical mistreatment of her on several occasions.'

'Father?' said Ben.

'Your fiancée's mother is delusional,' said Hugh Sharp.

'I'm nothing of the sort,' said Judith White. 'Your marital problems were considerable.'

'It was not my spouse who ran off with my money. Anyway, quarrelling is part of the contract.'

'You just don't know when your beaten, Mrs White.'

'No, it is that your wife was beaten and your granddaughter is being beaten.'

'You believe, Mrs White that you can rival our family with diamond store criminal psychology.'

'Why should I wish to rival your family?' said Judith White.

'We still have the wealth that you lost, Judith,' said Hugh. 'And we have the talent your family has never had. I consider that you feel the need to punish your betters.'

'I only live in a semi-detached house, father,' said Ben.

'Exactly!' said Judith White.

'Our house is a palace,' said Jane.

'My daughter has done extremely well for herself.'

'You mean my son has done it all for her,' said Hugh.

'I run my own business, Mr Sharp,' said Jane.

'Yes, she does,' said Judith White.

'My son can command a whole industry,' said Hugh.

'My daughter tells me it's been ages since his last success,' said Judith White.

'It's just writer's block,' said Jane.

'In any event,' said Hugh Sharp, 'it has to be earned.'

'And not all given to you by your father,' said Judith White.

'I have never taken any of my father's money,' said Ben.

'Are you trying to suggest you wouldn't have held on to your father's money, Judith?' said Hugh Sharp.

'What I'm declaring is that I could survive without it,' said Judith White.

'Then you won't be needing any more money from me,' said Hugh.

'It's not a question of needing it, Mr Sharp,' said Judith White, 'it is a question of being owed it.'

'That's not what the judge decided.'

Judith White smiled grimly. 'So you will not pay me my dues.'

'Certainly not. In fact, I might ask you to reimburse me for the food and beverages you appropriated.'

'I hardly think that's necessary, father,' said Ben.

'I'll pay for my mother's perks,' said Jane.

'You will do nothing of the sort, Jane,' said Judith White.

'Agreed,' said Ben.

'Then things remain the same,' said Hugh. 'Now, unless you have anything else to say, apart from accusing my son and I of murder, then I suggest you leave, Mrs White.'

'I will drive my fiancée and her mother back home,' said Ben.

'Would you mind, honey,' said Jane. 'I'm rather too flustered to drive myself.'

'As you wish, son,' said Hugh. 'Then it is goodbye, Mrs White.

Judith White, her daughter and the son made there way out of the house, climbed in to the car and drove south.

I mobiled Chase.

'*Ewok*!

'The friend and the mother have visited the house.'

'Did you use the laser microphone?'

'Yes, the friend's mother sought unpaid earnings from the disgruntled client.'

'And?'

'The disgruntled client refused to pay her. She also claimed the talented son's mother had abused him and that the disgruntled client resented his wife's inadequate instruction.'

'And?'

'I think she was hinting at the wife and the mother's death.'

'Anything else?'

'No.'

'You will visit the grandmother tomorrow.'

'Jean Reid.'

'Yes.'

'Why?'

'Her grandson's coming over.'

'Your niece's husband?'

'Yes.'

'How do you know?'

'I tapped the husband's mobile telephone conversation with her.'

'And?'

'I want you to listen in on their conversation. I want to understand why either might have killed my brother and/or his wife.'

CHAPTER FORTY-ONE

Day Thirteen: 4: 30 am; Grandmother's Graveyard

The mobile bleeped.

'Chase?'

'*Ewok*!'

'The bullet didn't need fired.'

'Yes.'

'The husband's grandmother?'

'Of course.'

I drove to Hyndland. There were murmurings outside the dining room. I set up the laser microphone.

Jean Reid and her grandson Richie were seated opposite each other at the dining table, which was covered with a very elaborate cloth. Richie clasped a giant mug of hot tea in his hands, which he sipped sporadically, while Jean Reid had a much smaller china cup of tea. After a ceremonial pause, Jean Reid looked up and cast her grandson a discerning look. 'So, Ritchie, you telephoned me and now you have come.'

Richie stiffened his back and did his best to adjust his acting. He coughed slightly before speaking. 'Yes, Gran.'

Jean Reid mouthed silently. 'And?'

Richie peeked at his grandmother's eyes. 'I'm all over the place.'

Jean Reid nodded with concentration. 'Yes, why is that?'

'I'm always feeling miserable.'

'What's making you feel that way?'

'I hesitate to say.'

'It's a bad concept.'

'Yes, I don't think you'd like it.'

'Is it to do with drugs?'

'No, I don't take drugs.'

'Good. Is it do with alcohol?'

'Partly, yes.'

'What are you drinking?'

'Cider mainly.'

'How often?'

'Every day.'

Jean Reid winced. 'Why?'

'It makes me feel better.'

'About what?'

'Susie.'

'Your wife.'

'Yes. She's horrible to me.'

'Why d'you think that is?'

'She blames me for something.'

'What?'

'I don't know.'

'Does she drink?'

'No, but she smokes.'

Jean Reid winced again. 'What does she smoke?'

'Cigarettes.'

'How many?'

'I don't know but she's always doing it.'

'It costs a fortune and is very bad for you. Tell me, does your mother drink?'

Richie shifted his head. 'I'd rather not say.'

'I infer that means yes.'

'I never said that.'

'No, but your reply was obvious. What about your father?'

'What about him?'

'Does he drink?'

'No comment.'

'You did law didn't you, Richie?'

'Yes, that's the other thing that's making me miserable.'

'How?'

'I can't find an employer.'

'What type of employer are you looking for?'

'A Senior Partner.'

'Which is?'

'Someone who owns a share of a law firm.'

'I see.'

'What about other employers.'

'I'm not interested, I really want to qualify.'

'What would that mean to you?'

'It would mean I had made it.'

'In what way?'

'Successful lawyers qualify.'

'What comes after that?'

'You become an assistant.'

'Then what?'

'I'm not sure. I get a bit lost there. My memory is so poor now.'

Jean Reid nodded knowingly. 'Then, I'm going to have to remind you how it was done.'

'And how was it done?'

'Keep sipping your tea. Many of life's problems come from poison.'

'Poison?'

'And in your case, it came from mushrooms.'

'What do you mean?'

'The friends went to the garden and picked chanterelles.'

'What are chanterelles?'

'Floral mushrooms. The friends went to the garden and picked chanterelles and cremini.'

'Cremini are mushrooms as well.'

'Indeed. The friends went to the garden and picked chanterelles, cremini and morels.'

'More mushrooms?'

Jean Reid nodded her head. The friends went to the garden and picked chanterelles, cremini, morels and buttons. Sip more tea. Now, you try it- add Portobellos.'

A relaxing feeling imbued Richie's senses. 'The friends went to the garden and picked chanterelles, cremini, morels, buttons and Portobellos.'

'Good, then what?'

'I'm afraid the only other mushroom I know of sounds very rude.'

'Not at all, they're meaty: and Shiitakes.'

Richie cringed.

'Say it anyway.'

'Very well. The friends went to the garden and picked chanterelles, cremini, morels, buttons, Portobellos and Shiitake.'

'Now, add enokis.'

'The friends went to the garden and picked chanterelles, cremini, morels, buttons, Portobellos, Shiitakes and enokis.'

'Good and oysters. Sip more tea.'

The relaxing feeling became more gratifying. 'The friends went to the garden and picked chanterelles, cremini, morels, buttons, Shittakes, enokis and oysters.'

'Excellent, you see your memory's coming back. Now add porcinis.'

Richie smiled contently. The friends went to the garden and picked chanterelles, cremini, morels, buttons, Portobellos, Shittakes, enokis, oysters and porcinis.'

'Now finish with hen of the woods. Sip more tea.'

'The friends went to the garden and picked chanterelles, creminis, morels, buttons, Portobellos, Shiitakes, enokis, oysters, porcinis and hens of the woods.'

'Perfect, your recall is total. How do you feel?'

Richie's eyes glazed over peacefully. 'I feel different, very relaxed. Is there whiskey in this tea.'

Jean Reid waved her head carefully. 'Just cinnamon. What about your miserable feeling?'

'It appears to have gone.'

Jean Reid nodded her head. 'Yes.'

'So?'

'It's about social conscience.'

'Social conscience?'

'Yes, when people use alcohol they feel guilty that they are not doing enough for others.'

'How do you know?'

'Experience.'

'What d'you mean?'

'Knowledge is the facts, feelings or experiences of a person or group.'

'So?'

'Experience is direct participation in an object or an event. I have been around the drunks.'

'And?'

'They get rejected, they get defeated.'

'Why?'

'They invested in their own feelings, rather than other people.'

'But you said knowledge was also feelings.'

'Yes, but information is better.'

'Why?'

'It is more reliable. Tell me, Richie. What information have you received?'

'I used to receive very good information.'

'Such as?'

'Home Office Reports.'

'Yes, good.'

'The US State Department reports.'

'Excellent.'

'The Amnesty International reports.'

'All very impressive.'

'So?'

'You have to keep improving your knowledge. What was the first thing I said to you in German.'

'You said: "*Wer bist du*"?'

'Yes, and what did you say?'

'I said: "*We haven't been taught that.*"'

'Yes, and what did I teach you?'

'To be more intelligent.'

'Yes, and that's what I taught your father, I made him clever.'

'I'm afraid, Gran I think that my father doesn't love you.'

Jean Reid sighed. 'What makes you say that?'

'He said.'

'And?'

'He doesn't listen.'

'No, he wouldn't.'

'Why not?'

'I taught him not to defer.'

'Why?'

'Those who defer are unable to control. I think that's what's happening with your wife. I think your drinking and unclear thinking has forced you to concede too easily. You see your father has been successful with a wife and children, but also with money and property.'

'How?'

'With perfect attendances and hard work.'

'So?'

'I could have killed them.'

'Who?'

'Your wife's father- and his wife.'

'Mr and Mrs McLean.'

'Yes.'

'Why?'

'Mr McLean threatened to sue your father.'

'Why?'

'He rejected you from their house. He also believed your father was responsible for his uncle-in-law's death.'

'Who was his uncle-in-law?'

'Jarrod Fields.'

'How did he know him?'

'He didn't really.'

'So?'

'Your father knew that a man was planning to kill him.'

'What man?'

'A Mr Hugh Sharp.'

'Who was/is he?'

'He was having extra-marital relations with your wife's mother.'

'Mrs McLean? Susanna?'

'Yes.'

'And?'

'Your father confronted him.'

'Mr Hugh Sharp.'

'Yes.'

'Why?'

'Your father was deeply unhappy with the way he was treating you.'

'Me?'

'Yes. Do you remember?'

'I remember a couple of men would come in to the house. I forget their names. Was Mr Sharp one of them?'

'Yes.'

'Who was the other?'

'Michael Fields.'

'How was he related to Jarrod Fields?'

'Michael was Jarrod's son.'

'And?'

'Your father threatened to section your girlfriend's mother?'

'Why?'

'She was on drugs, abusing her daughter.'

'That's what Susie said.'

'Exactly.'

'So?'

'He rejected you from the house.'

'Why?'

'He was being driven mad by his wife's unfaithfulness.'

'And what happened?'

'Your father threatened to have your girlfriend's father sectioned as well.'

'And?'

'Andrew McLean presumed to explain that the law was there to catch bad doctors out.'

'And?'

'Your father said good doctors were there to treat bad lawyers. Andrew McLean told your father that the law finished bad doctors. Your father said medicine released bad lawyers.

'So?'

'Mr McLean threatened to sue your father in defamation.'

'And?'

'Andrew McLean told your father that the knife of justice cut through the mushrooms.'

'And?'

'Your father told Andrew McLean that the stone of medicine disabled the knife and set the mushrooms free.'

'How do you know this?'

'Your father told me.'

'And?'

'I said I would kill Mr McLean if he ruined your father.'

'Why would you do that?'

'Your father was my life's work. I wasn't going to allow Mr McLean to wreck his career.'

'And?'

'Susie's father went missing.'

'Yes, I remember. 1995. You didn't actually kill him did you, Gran?'

His grandmother smiled without committing.

Richie was left uncertain what that expression meant.

'And what about his wife? Susie's mother? She went missing as well.'

'Yes, she was threatening to spoil your father's concept.'

'How?'

'She claimed he was a bad doctor, that he hadn't understood what she had been through.'

'And what had she been through?'

'She claimed she had abused.'

'By whom?'

'I have my suspicions.'

'And?'

'All I know is that other men were visiting her.'

'Which men?'

'One man had a disgusting Irish accent, while another man had filthy money.'

'How do you know?'

'Your father told me.'

'He did?'

'Yes.'

'How did he know?'

'You told him.'

'I did?'

'Yes, don't you remember, you were nine?'

'Why would I tell him?'

'You were there. Anyway, I could have killed her on moral grounds, never mind the other stuff.'

'What was the other stuff?'

'She slapped you across the face.'

'She did?'

'Yes.'

'Why?'

'She said if you blabbed to anyone, you wouldn't be allowed to see your girlfriend any more.'

'My wife?'

'Yes.'

'So?'

'You told your father. Your father told me. And I decided to get her back.'

'How?'

'By discrediting her.'

'I told her family and friends what I thought about her. I couldn't allow my son to be destroyed by an ignorant Irish Catholic.'

'So?'

'I know what matters, Richie.'

'And what matters?'

'The ending and the way to heaven.'

'So?'

'In the interim, the benefit drunks and drug-abusers have been trying to wreck your father's concept for years.'

'They have?'

'Yes.'

'Why?'

'They are jealous

'Perhaps they have a point.'

'No, they lost their point, as you lost yours with your wife, when you and they became intoxicated.'

As the full relaxing effect of the cinnamon filled Richie's senses he nodded his acceptance.

'Now,' said Jean Reid, 'if you want to think clearly again, you will have to respect your dad and stick to tea.'

'With cinnamon?'

'I will speak to your dad.'

'I'll be going then, Gran.'

'Yes, keep in touch.'

I mobiled Chase.

'*Ewok*!'

'I have listened in on the conversation between the grandmother and the husband.'

'Did you use the laser microphone?'

'Yes.'

'What were they talking about?'

'The husband's health, his drinking, his career, his memory...'

'Why might the husband's grandmother have killed my brother and/or his wife?'

'We talked about this outside the club.'

'Cosmo, yes I remember: love, lust, lucre and loathing. You explained the motives for murder.'

'Yes, it might be to with lucre and loathing.

'Okay. I want you to go to the bitter rival's house tomorrow.'

'Albert Bennet.'

'Yes.'

'Fall's Hall.'

'Yes.'

'Why?'

'It's the anniversary of his dead wife.'

'How do you know that?'

'I tapped his room conversation through his mobile telephone.'

'Whom was he speaking to?'

'His nephew.'

'So?'

'I want you to understand his memories, they might reveal something.'

'Such as?'

'Why he might have killed my brother and/or his wife.'

CHAPTER FORTY-TWO

Day Fourteen; 4: 15 am; Fall's Hall Collapses

The mobile warbled.

'Chase.'

'*Ewok*!'

'The disgruntled client's bitter rival?'

'Yes.'

I drove up north towards Fall's Hall. I parked the Mercedes some distance outside the front gates. I aimed the laser microphone in all directions until I isolated the attic for sound.

Albert had been executing the same rite for eight years on the trot now. He had been venturing sky-high up into the vaults of Fall's Hall; into the lesser explored clouds of the ancient crumbling mansion. They were dark, dank and dusty. He would commemorate the cherished memory of his beloved wife of over sixty years Doris. They had gotten married at sixteen.

One very, very sad, still cold grey morning in December 2009, he had discovered his wife's nude body lifeless in their burbling purling garden pond.

He could re-picture the catastrophe as though it were yesterday. The back door to the capacious open-plan kitchen had clanged as it swung on its hinges and clattered against the inside wall. His exuberant but sensitive thirteen year-old nephew Alexander had burst in, extreme anguish embossing his youthful ingenuous face, bitter irrepressible tears gushing down it.

His silver eyes had darkled. 'What ever is the matter, Alex?'

Alexander had jactitated violently, like a miniature rodent during its death throes, as he sobbed uncontrollably. He had stuttered. 'It's- it's- it's Aunt Doris.'

His heart had lap-danced out of his chest. 'What about her?'

His young adolescent nephew had whimpered. 'She's- she's dead uncle Albert.'

He had gaped. 'How can she be dead?'

His nephew convulsed again. 'She's lying frozen in the pond.'

Immediately, he had tossed his slightly dry biscuits, which had been warmed up, doused in milk and sprinkled with sugar into the kitchen basket. He had thrown down his over-sized coffee stoup, which had clinked as it shattered on the hard unforgiving tiles. He had waved his arms away as he had stormed out of the back door to the kitchen. He had slewed around the outside of the house. He had spilled over on the wet grass. He had clambered to his feet. He had loped across the front garden towards the pond in the centre. He had sail-planed on his heels as he had reached the pond. He had tottered backwards as he had beheld the dehumanising sight of his dearly beloved wife's body lifeless in the water.

He had covered his mouth which had been warm from the biscuits, creating vapour with his trembling right hand. His heart had plumped. '*Oh, no,*' he had said.

He had trampled into the murky icy pond, creating giant splotching sounds. He had clutched her static body, had wrapped his arms around her back, had pulled her towards him and had carted it from the pond, and had held her body down on the frosty wet grass. As he had held her with his left arm, he had dabbed her blue milky cheeks with his right hand. 'Wake up, Doris, my darling! It's morning. We must have breakfast.'

His warm hand seemed to fizzle as his veined wrinkly fingers patted her wan countenance. Her once plump red lips were thin and blue.

He had heard Alexander's chuffing as he had come racing towards him. He had glanced over his shoulder. He had laid his wife's body down on the sodden grass. His nephew Alexander had thrown his arms around him, lachrymosity effusing from his decimating heart. He had gripped Alexander tightly and rubbed his shoulder. Together in the still cold light of the morning sun, cruel air gnawing at their faces, he and his nephew had stood, interminably waiting, uttering no words, gaping at Doris's opaque inanimate body, staring at a scene of unimaginable horror, gazing into a horrible surreality, peering into a cold world which made no sense.

He had been seventy-five when he had discovered her dead. He was eighty-four now.

Every single year since that cold grey December morning, he would climb high up into the ancient gantry and fondly reminisce. He would go to the small rectangular window, a rusty skylight which admitted very cool dim light. He would unbolt the latch and push the window outwards.

'Let us take some air, Doris, my darling,' he would say.

He would gaze up expectantly at the mute vaporous moon which he could feel was her, winking wryly back at him. He would smile nostalgically into the star-studded gloom. He would go to an old trunk which languished in a damp corner of the room. He would prize it open and take out some clothes. He would remove his present attire and change into the same suit he wore at their wedding. He would go to an old cupboard and take out the shoe polish and assiduously burnish the shoes which he had worn at their wedding party. He would go to the sink unit and scrub his face. He would shave first and then apply the same aftershave he had worn. He would wrap around his neck the cravat he had worn. He would go to the drinks cabinet and fetch out a Kavalan Solist Pork Cask 2009. It was the most expensive whiskey in its range for the time. He had bought it the day he had found Doris dead. He had needed something to anaesthetise the pain. He would fetch out an old quaich. He would rinse it meticulously in the sink bowl. He would prepare himself the same dram he had enjoyed on the night of their wedding. He would also prepare the same gin and tonic his wife had had that evening. He would then go to a small stack containing vinyls. He would light a small fire. He would go to the gramophone. He would retrieve an old record which was stored in a mahogany escritoire which remained locked. The key to the drawer was kept in an old envelope which was kept underneath the water tank. The song was called 'Mona Lisa (Nat King Cole song)'. It had reached number one on July 15 1950.

They had been sixteen when they got married. They had waltzed to the song after the wedding.

Every year since he had found his wife dead in the garden pond, he would waltz alone in the gantry, pretending she was still there. 'I'm so sure you exist, my darling. Your mother said you're very special. I'm so sorry."'

Suddenly, towards the very end of the song, there was a creek followed by a crash. The roof caved in. The timbers came crashing down and the slates fell from the roof.

Alexander stirred in his bed. '*What*?' he murmured. He licked his dry lips. There was moaning. He roused. He sprung up. He wiped his tired eyes. He got out of bed, flipped on his slippers, left the room, made his way up the stairs, and climbed in to the attic.

There was the eerie sound of old music playing. He could hear moaning.

'Uncle?' he said.

I mobiled Chase.

'Chase?'

'*Ewok*!'

'I'm outside the uncle's attic.'

'Did you use the laser?'

'Yes I did, and part of the roof has just caved in.'

'How?'

'The timbers gave way.'

'Is the bitter rival still alive?'

'Yes, I think so. I can hear breathing.'

'So?'

'I consider it might have been done on purpose.'

'Why?'

'I don't know.'

'And?'

'All I could make out is that someone was coming over tomorrow to teach her a lesson.'

I sighed. 'Very well.'

CHAPTER FORTY-THREE

Day Fifteen; 4 am; The Old Bat

The mobile was angry, rattling up beside the gold-plated alarm clock trying to bully the digits. Ratta-tatta-tatta-ta-CLANG CLANG CLANG.

'Chase?'

'*Ewok*!'

'The henpecked husband's bitter and twisted grandmother?'

'Who else?'

I drove towards Hyndland. I parked the car outside the front gates. I waited until a masked figure with a holdall entered the house.

Before comfortably ensconcing herself in her favourite mustard armchair, Jane Reid reposed a cup of tea by her side on an occasional table. 'Ah!' she gasped, 'Vintage Narcissus.' She hoisted the cup aloft, meticulously making sure no drops were spilled. She crossed herself. 'To the family, father,' she said, before supping.

The tea was extremely rare, it was a type of Oolong tea. It was named after Narcissus, a Greek mythological figure. It seemed to blend with her character. It was harvested in the Wuyi Mountains, and was fired once in two years, which helped the extra moisture to dry out. It was one of the most exquisite Chinese teas, it was oxidised to about 60 per cent. She purred as the wooden, floral and chocolaty flavour profile infused her gustatory senses. Vintage

Narcissus was one of the most expensive teas in the world, it came with a price tag of $6,500 per kg. She ordered it every so often on line. She might have been old-fashioned but she understood modern technology. Just like vintage wine, her favourite taste improved with age. She pierced the silver foil of an unopened packet of 2mg diazepam tablets with her short thumb-nail and chucked back three tablets. She swallowed some more tea. She prized open a box of Harrods Dark Chocolate and Roasted Hazelnut Biscuits, tweased out a single specimen and winced as swarms of crumbs cascaded on to the plush carpet. She picked up the remote and channelled 'Songs of Praise' with her pointer.

Suddenly, there was a terrific smashing sound followed by a dull clanging sound. She could hear footsteps pounding on the floor. An intruder entered the living room wearing a mask.

'Jean Reid!' a voice muffled.

Jane Reid shuddered. 'Yes?'

The voice gnarled. 'You are a deeply vicious old woman.'

Jean Reid recoiled, her hands taped to her breast. 'How dare you break in to my house, stride towards me and deprecate me!' She gingerly eyeballed the intruder's baseball bat. 'What on earth do you plan to do with that? Smash up my very circumspect house?'

The intruder waved his cloaked head. 'No, my place easily matches yours and so I have a healthy respect for property.'

Jean Reid nodded emphatically. 'Good, glad to hear it. You'll be paying for the pane and the lock then.'

'No, but I will break a bone.'

Jean Reid blazed at the intruder with her red-grey eyes. 'You intend to strike me with that thing.'

'Yes.'

'Why?'

'For destroying my family.'

'I don't follow.'

'You poisoned all of us against each other.'

'Perhaps your family ought not to have attacked my father.'

'Your father, Jean Reid, Peter Reid put everyone in horrendous pain.'

Jane Reid's fleshy face mazed. 'How conceivably would he have done that?'

'He owned the top pharmaceutical company in Scotland.'

'Yes, so?'

'He spiked everyone.'

Jean Reid stamped her foot down. 'No, he was precisely the opposite. He alleviated so much pain.'

The muffled voice growled. 'In which case you would have learned.'

'Learned what?'

'Not to cause it yourself.'

'You're utterly mistaken.'

'No, I'm afraid not.'

'So?'

'You will forfeit your jaw bone.'

The intruder took in a deep breath and whacked Jean Reid full in the mouth with the baseball bat. Her jaw bone ringed as it cracked. She crumpled to the carpet, clutching her mouth. The intruder kicked her head, spat on her face and stormed out.

I saw the masked figure return from the house.

I mobiled Chase.

'*Ewok*!'

'I have listened in on the grandmother.'

'And?'

'She was gloating out loud.'

'What was she saying?'

'Everything.'

'And?'

'I saw someone in disguise with a mask and a couple of weapons break in to her house.'

'How did they do that?'

'They shattered the pane of glass in the door with a baseball bat and shattered the lock with a hammer.'

'And?'

'A while later, I saw the same person bolt from her house.'

'So?'

'They have disabled her jaw.'

'Who?'

'I don't know because of the disguise, but unless the female was groaning it was likely to be a male.'

'How did the intruder break her jaw?'

'With the baseball bat.'

Chase gasped. 'Why would they do this?'

I exhaled sadly. 'I understand they felt she had caused to much unnecessary pain.'

'How?'

'It seems she poisoned all the families.'

'Which families?'

I exhaled loudly. 'Your McLean family, our Wren family, the Fields family, the Sharp family and the Bennet family.'

As I listened to Chase over the mobile telephone, he almost seemed to snivel. To my not inconsiderable trepidation, I suspected he was being artful. 'This is where I leave you, Ewok.'

I faltered slightly. I even found myself squeezing by brow and weeping. I choked slightly. 'Leave me?'

'Yes.'

'Why?'

I heard a supercilious chortle. 'No offence, Ewok, you have certainly investigated the suspects but you haven't the most diminutive iota of who did it yet.'

I wheezed. I felt I had to impress Chase. I stuttered. 'No, but I will, I mean I can.'

'And you're nowhere near ready to punish them yet.'

'Well, no.'

'There you go then.'

'Yes, but that's because I haven't had the time or the opportunity.'

'Exactly. I'm giving you a break.'

'A break?'

'Yes, I want you to analyse everything you've learned.'

'I suppose you mean the data?'

'Quite.'

'You mean process the evidence?'

'Indeed.'

'So?'

'So, after you have processed the information, I expect you to formulate your deductions.'

I groaned. 'Or what?'

'I will purify my ultimatum. I will have you ruined or worse still killed, or even worse, I will have your whole family killed. Does that make sense?'

'To a psychopath yes.'

'I thought you would have learned by now but description is beaten by beyond description.'

'In what way?'

'The language defers to the pain.'

PART D

Data Analysis; Processing the Information

CHAPTER FORTY-FOUR

Revision

Several days had elapsed. Chase had not mobiled me once. I had realised gradually throughout the course of the squeezed investigation that he had been calling me fifteen minutes earlier every morning, as if twisting the couteau a champignon, or mushroom knife, which he had originally detained and marshalled me with upon the late evening of my leaving do. I had luxuriated in sleep, bordering on slumbers, which I had never had before, even when I was on holiday from the court. Chase's last three pregnant words filtered through my mind: "... *formulate your deductions*." I was in my study. It was a mixture of paperwork, computer work and reading. It looked elegant enough and I was spending increasingly more time in it. In some ways, the placement reminded me of being in the court. I was going over the minutia of an old case. It was an asylum case. A young lawyer by the name of Andrew McLean had argued that in the case of his client the Secretary of State's decision was not in accordance with the immigration rules, not in accordance with the law, and not in accordance with wider social policy considerations. He argued that he had a well-founded fear of persecution for a convention reason, namely his social membership. He belonged to a group of financiers. Andrew McLean argued that the group of financiers had lawfully helped a man named Jack Dorcha to take over several companies. This was in 1966. I saw that I had decided to reject the application for asylum.

Adrian was away at her sister's house, she would be back early tomorrow morning. Lilly was in her bedroom sleeping. Before the escapade began, Belay had evaluated my brand of criminal justice as too ruthless and too short-term. I had not had merest notion of what he meant. Consequently, notwithstanding that I had been seventy-seven, he had retired me. In all the years I had known Belay, I had realised I didn't know his second name. I remembered however how we had met.

'You want to be judge?' Belay had said.

'Yes, very much,' I had replied.

'What does justice mean to you?'

'It means that those who are good enjoy its protection, while those who have been bad suffer its penalty.'

'What if they are mad?'

'They go to the psychiatric hospital.'

'What if they are sad?'

'They suffer social rejections.'

'Okay, you've got the job. You are to call me only by my first name. Understood.'

'Sure.'

On the close of the evening of my farewell bash, I had had a mushroom knife, or as it had later been adverted to a *couteau a champignon* pinned against my throat. The assailant, who revealed his name as Chase confronted me with his suspicion that I had killed his brother and his wife. Chase believed via an anonymous call that I had been presiding at the time they had gone missing: 1995. He believed I was far closer to the murder victims than I might have imagined. Subsequently, he had issued me with an ultimatum. Either I satisfied him that all those who were involved in the suspected killings of his brother and his wife, his nephew's parents were probed and castigated, or I would be ruined, or face imprisonment or worse still, I and/or my immediate family would be forfeited. Left with no choice and steered by my conscience, I had carried out my own investigation.

Chase had demanded a two-week turnaround in terms of the investigation. I realised it had taken fifteen days.

We had visited the addresses of all his suspects, except his second suspect. Most houses were wealthy, although one house was very poor indeed. Chase had expounded his theories, while I had explicated the criminal law of Scotland.

Having done so, and at the exhortations of Chase, I had investigated all the suspects, including the second suspect.

On day one, I had driven to Fall's Hall in Aberdeen. I had investigated the nephew of the disgruntled client, the third suspect's bitter rival. From the nephew's soliloquy it was evident that he had lost both of his parents in a tragic car accident. I had learned that he had been six at the time. My younger daughter Lilly had romanced him and then my younger son Martin had seduced him, much to my disdain. Later the same day, I had investigated the fourth suspect, the bitter rival. I had learned that he harboured a very important secret, which he had kept from his nephew ever since he took him in after his parents' deaths.

On day Two, I had driven to the most affluent street in Glasgow: Park Drive, Thorntonhall where the talented son of the third suspect resided. I had discovered that he had the most foul temper imaginable. He had been deeply suspicious of his fiancée's relationship with one of her childhood female friends. His mother was dead. He had a daughter. The son was competing in Eurovision. He was mistreating his daughter.

On day three, I had driven to the battered niece's house. She was Chase's niece. She had a drunk partner whom she disdained. She was a heavy smoker who possessed a cold indifference. It appeared that she had been physically abused by her mother and sexually abused by someone else. She would have been nine at the time. I got to thinking about her scar. It made me think of the Glasgow Smiler.

On day four, I had driven to the north of Glasgow, Silverstream, Moor Raod. I met the daughter Greer and then the second suspect, the mother Alana. She had had no knowledge of Andrew or Susanna McLean. She had said she had not worked for the court services.

On day five, I had driven back to Park Drive, Thorntonhall, to the niece's friend's house, the overshadowed fiancée's house, the fiancée of the talented son.

On day six, I had driven to Hyndland, to the niece's friend's and fiancée's mother's house. She had appeared to have known that her daughter had done something. Her lawyer had lost her case.

On day seven, I had driven to Keppochhill, to the henpecked husband's house. He appeared to have done something terrible in his early youth. He was a man of the law. He knew that his wife had been abused by her mother.

On day eight, I had driven to Victoria Road in the South side of Glasgow, to the niece's friend, the overshadowed fiancée, to the habituated older cousin.

On day nine, I drove to Aberdeen, to the innocent nephew and troubled younger cousin. He had been sent by his mother to track down the man who killed his father.

On day ten, I had driven to Hyndland, to the henpecked husband's father.

On day eleven, I had driven to Music Hall in Aberdeen, to the disgruntled client. He had known all about flora, imbibed whiskey, looked down on his son, resented his fiancée, hated his granddaughter. He felt his son's partner was spoiling his own investment, he worked on the house, on the garden and on the boat.

On day twelve, I had driven back to Music Hall. The friend and her mother had visited the house. Judith White had sought to recover unpaid earnings from the disgruntled client.

On day thirteen, I had driven to Hyndland, to the bitter and twisted grandmother.

On day fourteen, I had driven to Fall's Hall in Aberdeen. Part of the roof had collapsed on top of him.

On day fifteen, I had driven back to Hyndland, to the husband's bitter and twisted grandmother. She had had her jaw disabled with a baseball bat. She had gotten members of the family to reject others. I had suspected it would have taken a violent psychopath, most likely Glasson Dorcha.

As well as visiting the suspects with Chase and investigating the suspects myself by listening in to their conversation with Chase's covert listening devices, I had come across three unexplained deaths. There was the death of the talented son's mother Agathe, the death of the habituated and troubled cousins' father Jarrod Fields, and of course the death of the bitter rivals wife Doris.

It became apparent to me that I had further work to carry out than just to probe two suspected murders. It seemed that I had to account for three mysterious deaths. I also had explain several suspected attempted murders.

CHAPTER-FORTY-FIVE

The Fungus Factor

As I replaced my old well-thumbed dog-eared determination in its attendant file, the low false goose-necked angle-poise light of the elegant study strained my silver eyes, which became more perplexed than wise, I considered another factor. I realised that 'mushrooms' were important in terms of the investigation. To me they had always been plain ordinary vegetables, the sorts of things you would have with your meat and mash. My wife Andrea had always reminded me that I liked them. However, I believed they harboured a more sinister significance. Mushrooms seemed to have cropped up consistently as a point of conversation among the suspects. All the suspects seemed to attach significant weight to them. They all knew about them: the quixotic nephew, the rivalrous uncle, the talented son, the overshadowed fiancée, the battered niece, the anonymous caller's older beauty, the aggrieved mother, the henpecked husband, the habituated cousin, the younger cousin, the home-loving mother, the arrogant doctor, the disgruntled client; and the bitter and twisted grandmother.

The quixotic nephew had said: "*Mushrooms killed the reckless. You must never attempt to eat them. Still, I wish I could share the magic you conceal with someone.*"

The rivalrous uncle had said: "*All I might say is that he is as dangerous and as poisonous as the mushrooms in the surrounding lands of which I warned you when you first came here.*"

The talented son had said: "*You picked mushrooms together, right?*"

The overshadowed fiancée had said: "*I have never even tried mushroom soup.*"

The battered niece had said: "*Never mention that- or mushrooms.*"

The anonymous caller's older beauty had said: "*And just so you know my opinion, Ewald, in terms of the female, this Susanna McLean, I think it's more likely poison was used. My daughter has a thing about mushrooms... My bloom may have popped but no one likes spoiling a pretty face.*"

The aggrieved mother had said: "*And Jane, your mother knows what happened. She knows you acted out the story.*"

The henpecked husband had said: "*I wanted to protect you. Mushrooms would have done.*"

The habituated cousin had said: "*I know what she tried to do with the mushrooms, so I passed them on.*"

The troubled cousin had said: "*And furthermore, if the poppers I had given you had been mushrooms, you would already be dead.*"

The home-loving mother had said: "*Angela Taylor warned me that a man might try to kill your father. Make sure you get some proper food- and avoid the mushrooms.*"

The arrogant doctor had said: "*You need help. And by the way son, I know you didn't prepare or serve the mushrooms, but I do know you were involved.*"

The disgruntled client had said: ""*It was all about mushrooms. They got to her in the end.*"

The bitter and twisted grandmother had said: "*Andrew McLean told your father that the knife of justice cuts through the mushrooms. Your father told Andrew McLean the stone of medicine disabled the knife set the mushrooms free.*"

It was too much of a coincidence that all the suspects would mention mushrooms. They had to be the means of Andrew McLean's death or his wife's Susanna's death, or perhaps both.

The disgruntled client's knowledge of mushrooms seemed to be the most comprehensive.

He had been a collector. He had possessed all the relevant equipment. He had worn a photographer's vest and carried a backpack with multiple compartments. He had had a notebook and pen for writing down finds. He had also had GPS which had represented an even better solution. He had had a magnifying glass- a 10x folding loupe in his pocket. He had had a mesh bag. He had had wax paper bags. He had had utility scissors, a garden trowel, a hatchet, a bug repellent and hat. He had had water. He had had footwear and gloves. Most significantly, he had had a mushroom knife.

I recalled his conversation with his son.

'Do you remember this, son?' he had said.

'You mean collecting mushrooms, father?'

'Yes.'

'Of course. We were at the old house. We were in the meadows. We were under the trees- the beeches and the oaks.'

'Yes. And do you remember why we collected them?'

'They were very special.'

'Yes, that's right. Tell me son, why were they very special?'

'They could be used for soup.'

'Yes.

'Yes, what else?'

'They could kill a man.'

'Yes, what else?'

'They could drive a man mad.'

'So you see what I'm doing?'

'You're still respecting them.'

'Indeed.'

'What do you plan to do with them?'

'There is a threat to our way of life.'

'What is our way of life?'

'You have lived in the suburbs for too long.'

'What is your fascination with mushrooms father?'

'They have been many a man's ruin.'

'You're saying mushrooms are important, father.'

'I'm saying that mushrooms have been very important.'

'In what sense?'

'If it were not for mushrooms, your half-sister and her husband would still be alive.'

Ben gaped. 'My half-sister?'

'Yes,

'Who is she?'

'Time will reveal all.'

'Tell me father, is that why you go mad?'

'I have many reasons to go mad, son but mushrooms aren't one of them.'

In addition to the events of the investigation, I remembered in technicolour the evening I had been retired. Belay had wandered in to the room. He had asked if I was hungry. I had said I would eat when I got home. Before retiring me, he placed a polystyrene cup in front of me.

'What is it?' I had asked.

'Soup,' he had said.

'Which kind?'

'Mushroom.'

By and by, I perceived a strange but gratifying feeling.

Both had begun as words to me. That had changed. I knew this because I had undergone something very different. It happened that afternoon in the courtroom before Belay had let me go.

'It is a secret family recipe,' he had said.

'Which recipe?' I said.

'The recipe which makes you feel and think.'

'Who owns it?'

'Perhaps I do, or perhaps someone in your own family does.'

'But I only have Andrea and the four kids.'

'Perhaps it was someone else.'

'Whom did you first sleep with?'

'Alainn.'

'And whom was her daughter?'

'Susanna?'

'And whom was her granddaughter.'

'Susie.'

'And who was her friend?'

'Jane.'

I realised now what Belay had done that early evening in the courtroom. He had served me magic mushrooms. Perhaps he thought it was funny but it was more likely he was teaching me a lesson. I had never once imbibed alcohol, nor had I ever taken illicit drugs but I had been put on something else. I had been involuntarily intoxicated. I considered why he had done it. I considered he had thought of a memorable way to reject me, to retire me, to expel me from the court, in a way I would forget and find hard to explain.

I considered the younger generation. I knew the quixotic nephew had learned about mushrooms from his rivalrous uncle. I knew the talented son had learned about mushrooms from his disgruntled father. I knew the overshadowed fiancée had learned about mushrooms from her aggrieved mother. I suspected the battered niece had learned from her friend's mother. I suspected Greer had learned about mushrooms from her mother Alana. I suspected the henpecked husband had learned from his childhood girlfriend, her friend, or his arrogant father Doctor Reid. I suspected the habituated cousin and the troubled cousin had learned about mushrooms from their mother.

As the false dim light illuminated the darkest corners of my mind, I suddenly realised that I had heard of all the families. My memory seeped into a lake of understanding....

CHAPTER FORTY-SIX

Family Conflicts

It was 1957. I was fifteen. I knew I was fifteen because my father had allowed me an early 'sweet sixteen.' A sweet sixteen was a coming of age party. It could also be celebrated by boys, not just the girls. We were in the capacious greyish open stone-bricked front room in Doolin, Fisher street. My father was pacing up and down the large-grained carpet, almost wearing a crevasse in its mire, clutching his jaw.

'What's wrong, dad?' I said.

My father exhaled loudly. He grimaced. 'I've got a few things to sort out.'

I glinted at my father. 'What have you got to sort out?'

He smiled worriedly at me. 'I'll tell you later, son- once I find out.'

I flinched. 'You mean you're coming back?'

My father nodded aimlessly. 'Yes, but don't worry, son. I won't cramp your style. I'll give you plenty of time.'

I peeked at my father. 'How much time?'

'I'll be back before midnight.'

I smiled contently.

'And I'll arrange for your friends' taxis. Now, with alcohol, son, be careful. It's one or two, it's not the whole bottle.'

'I don't drink, dad.'

His father nodded with understanding. 'No, son, but your

friends might. And might I politely invite you not to leave a spray of blood on the walls?'

'No, I won't dad.'

'And just remember, son, if you're trying to be a lawyer, you have to be very, very good.'

'I know dad.'

I remember my father shambled out of the house. Later, my friends arrived. On that night, my friend Patrick took the whiskey bottle, got drunk, ventured upstairs and slept with Alainn. As Alainn was reporting to her girlfriends, Patrick boasted about his conquest to me. I thought I would sleep with her as well. She was drunk enough to consent. I remember I slept with her again in 1962 when I was twenty-two. This was before my friend Patrick was dispatched to the Congo. Patrick's presumed brother would have been six. I recalled Jarrod Fields saying that he remembered a conversation between Alainn and Aiden Fields. He asked if I might be his father. I had told him it was possible. He also asked me if I might be his sister's father. I had asked him how old his sister was. I said for his sister Susanna to have been her age at the time, I would have to have slept with Alainn in 1972. I had no memory of doing that.

There was another reason I knew it was 1957. Aspiring towards law, I had learned that criminally insane prisoners had been transferred from the criminal lunatic department at HM Prison Perth to the State Institution for Mental Defectives at Carstairs which became the State Mental Hospital.

There was a rap on the door. It was a quarter to midnight.

'Okay, guys,' said my father. 'It's time to get you lot home.'

Alainn slurred. 'Just one more drink.'

My father waved his head firmly. 'No, dear. You and your friends are getting a taxi.'

'Come on,' said Patrick.

'No, Patrick,' said my father, 'You've had your fun, it's time to go home.'

Patrick belched. 'My dad wouldn't mind.'

'Aiden would mind.'

My father telephoned the local taxi firm and gave the driver the money. We were in the front room.

'I see my whiskey was almost finished.'

'I haven't touched a drop,' I said.

'Yes, I can see that, good for you, son.'

I smiled placidly. 'Where did you go, dad?'

'I went to the pub.'

'What did you have to drink?'

My father squeezed his brow. 'I didn't, I had a few soft drinks.'

'What's wrong, dad?'

My father grimaced. 'Everything.'

I glinted at him quizzically. 'Everything?'

My father suspired. 'Yes, we're in trouble son.'

'Why?'

'The families are at war.'

I gaped. 'At war?'

'Yes.'

'You mean Patrick's family.'

'No, son, I mean all the families.'

'Which families?'

'I mean the Fields family, the Sharp family, the Bennet family, the McLean family, the White family, the Reid family, and the Dorcha family.'

'Why are they at war, dad?'

'The patriarchs believe they are bewraying each other. It's internecine.'

My father had given me an excellent vocabulary. 'The heads of the family? Betraying? Mutually destructive?'

'Yes.'

'So?'

'I have stopped providing business services to the families.'

I gawked. 'Why would you do that, dad?'

'Aiden Fields stopped supplying the textiles, which furbished my company, Frank Sharp stopped providing the music which amused my workforce, James Bennet stopped supplying the engineering which maintained my mechanical systems, Lewis

McLean stopped supplying the gas and oil which empowered my business, Jaeger White stopped supplying the food and beverages which fed and watered my staff, and Peter Reid stopped supplying the pharmaceuticals which kept a significant number of my employees happy.'

'I squinted at my father. 'Why would they do that?'

'It's a long story, son.'

'We have time dad.'

'It's nearly midnight- and it's my birthday.'

'Very well, son. Aiden Fields believed that I was low-balling the value of exquisite textiles to a smart, polished, and professional company. Frank Sharp believed I was under-reckoning the power of music to galvanise a workforce and enhance a business. James Bennet believed that his mechanical engineering, the nuts and bolts of industry, as he called it, wasn't being taken seriously enough. Lewis McLean believed that I took for granted the fuel for my company. Jaeger White believed that had disregarded a primary need, in terms of food and beverages. Peter Reid believed I had put business development ahead of health and functioning.'

'Why would they all believe that?'

'Jack Dorcha told them.'

'How do you know?'

'Jack Dorcha told me.'

'When?'

'Tonight.'

'In the pub?'

'No, before I went out.'

'Why would he do that?'

'He would do that in order to de-stabilise all the families' companies.'

'Why would he want to do that?'

'Because son, he wants to take them over.'

'You mean an acquisition?'

'Yes.'

'Why would he want to take them over?'

'He's usurious.'

'You mean he's a mercenary.'

'Yes.'

'And how would that work, dad?'

'With a total loss of key supplies, none of the families could afford to keep our companies going. We would be forced to sell them to the parent company.'

'Jack Dorcha owns the parent company?'

'Yes.'

'What's it called?'

'Dorcha enterprises.'

'I see. What else has happened?'

'Your friend Patrick's father Aiden Fields stopped supplying textiles to Frank Sharp.'

'Why would he do that?'

'Frank Sharp released satirical music which bemocked his textiles company.'

'What sort of music?'

'Anti-Irish music.'

'Why would he do that?'

'Jack Dorcha told him that Aiden Fields felt his music lacked materiality.'

'So Jack Dorcha put Aiden Fields off Frank Sharp.'

'Yes, and he also put Frank Sharp off Aiden Fields.'

'What else happened?'

'Aiden Fields stopped supplying textiles to James Bennet.'

'Why would he do that, dad?'

'James Bennet had been denigrating the mechanical engineering aspect of his textiles company.'

'Why would he do that?'

'Since Jack Dorcha told him that Aiden Fields didn't care for the way James Bennet underestimated the importance of recherché textiles to a business.'

'So he made Aiden Fields and James Bennet fall out.'

'Yes?'

'What else happened, dad?'

'Aiden Fields stopped supplying textiles to Lewis McLean.'

'Why would he do that?'

'Lewis McLean hiked up the prices of oil and gas supply to him.'

'Why would he do that?'

'Jack Dorcha told Aiden Fields that Lewis McLean was condescending to what he considered to be a tinpot and effeminate enterprise.'

'You mean he made Aiden Fields and Lewis McLean fall out as well.'

'Exactly, son.'

'What else happened?

'Aiden Fields stopped supplying textiles to Jaeger White.'

'Why would he do that?'

'Jaeger White had been supplying food which was not fit for human consumption.'

'Why would he do that?'

'Jack Dorcha told Aiden Fields that Jaeger White was fed up of the complaints coming from Aiden Field's tasteless ungrateful staff.'

'What did Aiden Fields say?'

'He said the food was exorbitant and vastly overrated. He said his workforce would be better off with the old Irish stew.'

'So there was another fall-out.'

'Yes.'

'Caused by Jack Dorcha?'

'Yes.'

'What else happened, dad?'

'Aiden Fields stopped supplying textiles to Peter Reid.'

'Why would he do that?'

'Peter Reid had been supplying impure chemicals to his labourers.'

'Why would he do that?'

'Jack Dorcha told Peter Reid that Aiden Fields did not care for the way his fabrics were being treated.'

'How were they being treated?'

'Jack Dorcha told Aiden Fields very disrespectfully.'

'In what way?'

'The textiles Aiden Fields had supplied were stubbed with tobacco and stained with all manner of spillages.'

'So Jack Dorcha made Aiden Fields and Peter Reid fall out as well.'

'Yes.'

'So apart from Patrick's family, what about the other families? What about the Sharp family?'

'The Sharp family aren't happy either.'

'Why not?'

'They've had their supplies cut off as well.'

'Why?'

'Well, Frank Sharp stopped supplying music to James Bennet?'

'Why would he do that, dad?'

'James Bennet had been ridiculing his music.'

'And why would James Bennet do that?'

'Since Scott Dorcha told James Bennet that Frank Sharp didn't care for his vulgar blue-collar work.'

'And what did James Bennet say?'

'He said that his music sounded like a squeaky bladder.'

'So Jack Dorcha made Frank Sharp fall out with James Bennet.'

'Yes.'

'What else happened?'

'Frank Sharp stopped supplying music to Lewis McLean.'

'Why would he do that, dad?'

'Lewis McLean withdrew his power supply to his music company, dis-enabling all his electrical instruments.'

'Why would he do that?'

'Since Jack Dorcha told Lewis McLean that Frank Sharp had cancelled the jingle for his advertisement and was fed up amusing what he called his mob of philistines.'

'And what did Lewis McLean say?'

'He said he was fed up empowering them to criticise his philistines.'

'So Jack Dorcha made Frank Sharp and Lewis McLean fall out.'

'Yes.'

'What else happened, dad?'

'Frank Sharp stopped supplying music to Jaeger White.'

'Why would he do that?'

'Frank Sharp claimed the food and beverages Jaeger White was supplying were incapacitating his maestros, that music was the food of love.'

'Did Jack Dorcha tell him that?'

'Yes.'

'And what did Jaeger White claim?'

'He claimed that the music being produced by Frank Sharp was not the food of love, but the invitation to starvation.'

'Jack Dorcha told him this?'

'Yes.'

'What else happened, dad?'

'Frank Sharp stopped supplying music to Peter Reid.'

'Why would he do that?'

'Peter Reid was denigrating music as a form of therapy. He considered it to be weak practice.'

'And?'

'He also stopped his supply of feel-good chemicals which weakened Frank Sharp's creative inspiration.'

'What about the other families? The Bennet family?'

'Apart from ceasing his supply of mechanical engineering to Aiden Fields and Frank Sharp, James Bennet also stopped supplying mechanical engineering to Lewis McLean.'

'Why would he do that, dad?'

'Lewis McLean didn't like the way his energy was being wasted to drive obsolete inefficient mechanical systems.'

'Jack Dorcha told him this?'

'Yes.'

'And what did James Bennet say?'

'He said that his energy supply was a deep-sea vent to real predators.'

'What else happened, dad?'

'James Bennet stopped supplying mechanical engineering to Peter Reid.'

'Why would he do that?'

'Peter Reid felt that he had underestimated the the health and functioning to impel mechanical engineering.'

'Jack Dorcha told him this.'

'Yes.'

'What about the McLean family?'

'Well, son, Lewis McLean stopped supplying energy to Aiden Fields.'

'Why would he do that?'

'Aiden Fields criticised Lewis McLean on the point that he was assuming powerful ideas rather than carefully crafted ideas.'

'You mean Lewis McLean was getting too powerful for Aiden Fields?'

'Yes, son.'

'And Jack Dorcha told him this?'

'Yes.'

'What else happened, dad?'

'Lewis McLean stopped supplying oil and gas to Frank Sharp.'

'Why would he do that?'

'Jack Dorcha told Lewis McLean that Frank Sharp felt that proper music was born of manual power, not stolen energy.'

'So Lewis McLean was offended?'

'Yes.'

'What else happened?'

'Lewis McLean stopped supplying energy to James Bennet.'

'Why?'

'James Bennet claimed that mechanical engineering for far more enhanced than basic energy supplies.'

'What else happened?'

'Lewis McLean stopped supplying power to Peter Reid.'

'Why would he do that, dad?'

'Peter Reid supplied impure pharmaceuticals that caused mistakes in his workforce.'

'Why would he do that?'

'To get Lewis McLean back for assuming power over health.'

'What about the other family? The White family?'

'Jaeger White ceased supplying food and beverages to Aiden Fields, Frank Sharp, James Bennet, Lewis McLean, Peter Reid and Jack Dorcha.'

'Why would he do that?'

'Aiden Fields claimed that the food and beverages he was supplying were damaging his textiles.'

'In what way?'

'Aiden Fields claimed his work force were so sick and intoxicated that they were patronising the textiles. They were positively ruining them.'

'Jack Dorcha told him this?'

'Yes.'

'What about Frank Sharp?'

'Frank Sharp claimed that the music his company was producing was being spolied by a sick stomach.'

'And Peter Reid?'

'Peter Reid claimed that his food was laced with bad chemicals.'

'Jack Dorcha told him this?'

'Yes.'

'And what did Jaeger White say?'

'He said he was the one supplying the lethal chemicals.'

'And, finally, dad, what about the Reid family?'

'Well, Peter Reid stopped supplying pharmaceuticals to all the families.'

'Why would he do that, dad?'

'They all kept complaining.'

'Why did they complain?'

'Aiden Fields claimed that Peter Reid's chemiclas had caused his work force to botch up the textiles. Frank Sharp claimed Peter Reid had intoxicated his maestros. James Bennet claimed Peter Reid had caused accidents within his company. Lewis McLean claimed that Peter Reid's chemicals had diespowered his energy company by incapacitating his staff. Jaeger White claimed that Peter Reid's chemicals had put them off their food.'

'Jack Dorcha told them this?'

'Yes.'

Having recalled all the families and their reasons for falling out with each other, I considered mushrooms in terms of the older generation. I imagined the rivalrous uncle had learned about mushrooms from his father Ealdahach Wren, who had been oversensitive to pain. I imagined the disgruntled client had learned about mushrooms from his father Frank Sharp, who had composed music about pain. I imagined the aggrieved mother had learned about mushrooms from her father Jaeger White, who had made a life out of food. I imagined Susanna McLean had learned about mushrooms from her mother Alainn Fields, whose husband Aiden fields had made money out of textiles. I conceived the older beauty Alana had learned about mushrooms from either or both of her parents. I imagined the late Jarrod Fields had learned about mushrooms from his father, which could have been Patrick, Aiden Fields or even me. I imagined the arrogant Doctor had learned about mushrooms from his mother Jean Reid. I imagined the bitter and twisted grandmother had learned about mushrooms from her father Peter Reid. I imagined the home-loving mother had learned about mushrooms from her her mother or father.

As well as the mushrooms, I sensed the *couteau a champignon*, the mushroom knife, was important. I recalled vividly how Chase had clutched me from behind and placed the knife to my throat. "*Do you remember this*?" he had said. I had waggled my head. "*You used it to initiate a blood brother*.' I remembered who he meant, he meant Patrick, who died in the Congo in 1962. I considered it could very well have been the weapon that killed the brother and/ or his wife.

In the low soporific light of the evening, I determined to work it all out. One day I would fathom who had murdered Andrew McLean and his wife Susanna. But for now I had to concede that I had other things to do. I had to get Lilly to school tomorrow. It was at that moment as I took another sip of my mushroom cup of soup that I perceived a change in feeling.

SEVENTH INTERLUDE

The End of Jack Dorcha

Jack Dorcha was tilting at the head of the refectory table on the Manhattan Sunseeker 50, knocking back more Macallan, his guests seated around him. He was beaming like a summer sun. There was an occasional table behind him with a Wi-Fi fax machine. He spun round and went to the fax machine. 'Ah,' he said. He collected a few print-outs. He grinned wildly.

'You look very pleased with yourself, Jack,' said Lewis McLean.

Jack Dorcha shrugged. 'Of course I am.'

Peter Reid arched a brow. 'Oh,' he said, 'Why would that be?'

'I've finally gotten shot of the fifth wheels in my life.'

'What does that mean?' said Frank Sharp.

'It means they have all been blown up.'

'Make more sense,' said Jaeger White.

'It means you are all redundant.'

Frank Sharp stomped his foot. 'What?' he said.

'Yes, I'm afraid so.'

'You can't do that,' said Frank Sharp.

'I'm afraid I already have. As of now, I own all your companies.'

Frank Sharp bridled. '"Sharp Music" is mine.'

Jack Dorcha smiled conceitedly. 'It was, yes.'

'Was?' said Peter Reid. 'And "."'

'And "White Food is mine,"' said Jaeger White.

'And "Fields Textiles" is mine,' said Aiden Fields.

'And "McLean Oil and Gas-fuelled equipment" is mine,' said Lewis McLean.

'And "Wren Business Services" is mine,' said Ealdahach Wren.

'And "Bennet Mechanical Engineering" is mine,' said James Bennet.

Jack Dorcha cackled beneath the boiling rays of the sun. 'And "Dorcha Enterprises" is now mine.'

'*What*?' said Frank Sharp.

'I mean I bought them all up.'

'But you can't have,' said Aiden Fields.

'I'm afraid I already have.'

'How?' said Peter Reid.

'My lawyer is very good.'

'How?'

'It's called company law.'

'And?' said Ealdahach Wren.

'I bought up all your companies

'How?'

'The law said I could.'

'We say you can't,' said Jaeger White.

James Bennet smiled disappointedly. 'Why, Jack?' he said.

'You lot have done nothing but batten off my over-generous investment.'

'How?' said Lewis McLean.

'You might have owned the commercial premises, the assets, have run the businesses, made your profits, but as the investor and the bigger company owner, I could buy you all out.'

'Not without our permission.'

'Your sweet companies have always been a part of my bigger business.'

'A merger?' An acquisition?'

'No, a takeover.'

'We can challenge that,' said Ealdahach Wren.

'You could but it wouldn't change anything.'

'Who says?'

Jack Dorcha lofted the legal documentation. 'These pages say.'

'You said you would never do that,' said Aiden Fields.

'I changed my mind.'

Frank Sharp snarled. 'You've gone too far this time, Jack.'

'Don't worry, Frank, you all still have the money in your accounts, it's just you don't own your companies.'

'So, Jack?' said Lewis McLean.

'So, I am obliged to inform you all that you are to vacate the premises as of now- when you get back.'

'In which case,' said James Bennet, 'you only have one choice.'

James Bennet interceded. He took Jack Dorcha by the shoulder. 'What's happened to you, Jack? You were helping us?'

Jack Dorcha stammered. '*You*- I...'

'Sorry, Jack,' said James Bennet. 'Tell me, what is your point?'

'I haven't lost it, James,' said Jack Dorcha. 'My point is that a point is a word.'

'Of course it is. And what is a word?'

'A word is a concept.'

'And what is a concept?'

'Description.'

'And what is description?'

'Description.'

'I see, description becomes-'

Ealdahach Wren filled in. 'Linguistics finalisation.'

'And tell me, Jack, what is *the* description?'

Jack Dorcha simpered. 'A war on concepts.'

'And what is a war on concepts?'

'With alcohol, it becomes a war on feelings.'

'And what is a war on feelings?'

'With anger, it becomes a war on people: race, religion, nationality, ethnicity, social membership and political conviction.'

'And with anger and the social taxonomical groups, what is a war on people?'

'A war on pain.'

'And what is a war on pain?'

'A war on justice.'

'And what is a war on justice?'

'A war on entitlement.'

'And what is a war on entitlement?'

'A war on reprisal.'

'And what is a war on reprisal?'

'A war that is understood.'

'And what is a war that is understood?'

'A war that is even.'

Peter Reid half-snored. 'Total crap!' he said.

'Fuck you, Peter!' said Jack Dorcha. 'I hope you choke on your own chemicals.'

'Yes, I'm sorry, Peter,' said James Bennet. 'The man is allowed to feel.'

'And what would you know, James?' said Jack Dorcha.

'More than you think, Jack' said Lewis McLean.

'You know, Lewis,' said Jack Dorcha. 'With all that power, with all the gas and oil equipment, I might expect your brain to work.'

'He can feel all he likes,' said Jaeger White. 'The man's weak and pathetic.'

'You're a fucking kitchen hand, Jaeger,' said Jack Dorcha. 'You don't deliver all the top exports.'

Aiden Fields shrugged. 'Maybe he didn't need to'.

'Like you're intelligent enough, Aiden to clothe all the babies,' said Jack Dorcha.

'They weren't your babies,' said Ealdahach Wren

'Like ET could IT them,' said Jack Dorcha. 'I do admit you might have conceived them, but I brought them up.'

'Your company is abusive. You are a terrible parent.'

'My parent company has been nothing but responsible.'

'Is Mr Dorcha okay?' said Olivia McLean.

Lewis McLean's lips twisted. 'Not really, darling. He's being poisoned.'

Jack Dorcha recoiled. '*What*?'

'I'm afraid so, Jack,' said Lewis McLean.

'*How*?' said Jack Dorcha.

'Let's just say, your salmon, lamb and beef were a wee bit different to ours.'

Jack Dorcha winced. '*Different*?' said Jack Dorcha.

'Yes,' said Peter Reid, 'They contained some of my apparently now defunct chemicals.'

'So, Jack, it's the big launch?' said Frank Sharp.

Jack Dorcha gurgled. 'It was supposed to be.'

Lethal fire blazed from Frank Sharp's hard cruel eyes. 'Then let's christen this bastard ship of exquisite mercenary.'

Jack Dorcha flinched. 'Let's what?'

Frank Sharp smashed the bottle against the deck floor, instantaneously creating a gigantic long narrow saw-toothed glass dagger.

Jack Dorcha fended Frank Sharp away with his hands. 'Careful with that, Frank,' said Jack Dorcha.

'Oh, I will be. I know what I'm doing.'

Frank Sharp strode towards Jack Dorcha, drove the long glass dagger into Jack Dorcha's chest. Jack Dorcha clutched his aching chest, rivulets of scarlet blood cascading down his suspended body, and crumpled to the deck floor. Jack Dorcha gurgled. '*I- I...*'

'Sore is it, Jack?' said Frank Sharp.

'You're fucking right it is,' said Jack Dorcha.

'What now, then?' said Aiden Fields.

'You like being above, Jack don't you?' said Lewis McLean.

Jack Dorcha gagged. 'I- I like being able to move.'

Peter Reid glowered. 'Let's move you higher, then. Everyone grab an oar!'

'Yes, I'll take his hand,' said Jaeger White.

'Make sure it's the right one,' said Frank Sharp.

'Will do,' said Ealdahach Wren, 'Even if

'I'll take his other hand,' said Aiden Fields.

'I'll take his leg,' said Lewis McLean.

'I'll take his other leg,' said James Bennet.

The guests swung Jack Dorcha to and fro.

'What's happening dad?' said Olivia McLean.

'We're putting the Loch Ness Monster where he belongs.'

'In the sea?'

'In the sea.'

CHAPTER FORTY-SEVEN

The Glasgow Smiler Intrudes

Suddenly, everything changed. I dropped my cup of mushroom soup which spilled all over the desk and scolded my hands. The study which had been illuminated by a false dim light bit which had still been clear and still became blurred and ambulant. The mountain of papers swept up from the desk and circulated round the room. The laptop snapped shut. My pen snapped in half. The overhead light guttered and perished. I perceived an incision in my neck. I rubbed my neck and saw blood on my pointer and middle-finger.

There was a voice. Someone was singing. The voice was high and scary.

Verse 1:

Smile
Smile
Take a look at yourself
Just now

Smile
Just smile
Be thankful for the looks
You have
They can look so bad
They can look like

A hulk in the dark

Your smile will break your heart
Your smile will break your heart

Plaid Foul

Verse 2:

Mush
Mush
Mushrooms have power
To slight

Mush
Mushrooms
They can blind your eyes

They can hurt
Like a knife in the heart

Your smile will break your heart
Your smile will break your heart

Plaid Foul

Chorus:

Smile
And the look you were looking for
Becomes a kind of dinosaur
With fangs and claws and open pores
The vision of an eyesore
You're looking like a child

Smile
And the yes you were pining for
Becomes a mass of general nos
From boys and girls and older folks
You're feeling like a fright

Dnias Dirk

Verse 3:

Knife
Knife
Feel the sharpness within
Tonight

Knife
Just knife
Be fearful of
The slit
So sad

It can cut so bad
It can feel like
A stab in the sack

Your smile will break your heart
Your smile will break your heart

Plaid Foul

Chorus:

Smile
And the look you were looking for
Becomes a kind of dinosaur
With fangs and claws and open pores
The vision of an eyesore
You're looking like a child

Smile
And the yes you were pining for
Becomes a mass of general nos
From boys and girls and older folks
You're feeling like a fright

Verse 4:

Smiles, mushrooms and knives
Can engender a paradise

Or crush your mind

The difference
Will be clear
In a while
It's the Glasgow smile

Chorus:

Smile
And the look you were looking for
Becomes a kind of dinosaur
With fangs and claws and open pores
The vision of an eyesore
You're looking like a child

Smile
And the yes you were pining for
Becomes a mass of general nos
From boys and girls and older folks
You're feeling like a fright

When the voice finished it's song, I stretched my neck and glinted backwards. 'Chase?'

'No.'

'Then who?'

'Your adversary.'

'Who?'

'The man who lost his grandfather to your father.'

'How do you know my father?'

'Mr grandfather knew your father. He told my father about him.'

'Ealdahach?'

'Indeed.'

'And who was your grandfather?'

'Jack Dorcha.'

'Yes, I've heard of him. You're not Scot Dorcha's son, are you?'

'Yes. Your father helped kill my grandfather.'

I squinted. 'Why would you imagine he would do that?'

'I'm not imagining. Your father felt that my grandfather had manipulated and betrayed him.'

'Yes, your grandfather sabotaged all his supplies, de-stabilised his company, and stole his business.'

'My grandfather rescued a company that was going to the wall.'

'No, your grandfather propelled my father's company into the wall.'

'Your father was ineffectual at business.'

'No, you're wrong there, my father was very astute at business, he owned Scotland's top business services company.'

'Are you sure you know what business services are?'

'I certainly do, I consider whether you do.'

'It's a general term.'

'At least.'

'It describes work that supports a business.'

'Yes, what else?'

'It does not produce a tangible commodity.'

'No, for example?'

'Information technology.'

'Explain Information Technology.'

'It supports many other business services.'

'Yes, such as.'

'Procurement, shipping and finance.'

'Yes.'

'Indeed a good business service aligns IT assets with the needs of a company's employees and customers and supports business goals, facilitating the ability of the company to be profitable.'

'Yes, what else?'

'Documenting the value that an IT company provides to the business often involves an audit of IT infrastructure processes, the creation or updating of an IT service catalogue and/or the provisioning of an employee self-service portal to improve communication.'

'Yes, I can accept you understand business services. But that scarcely means that my father assisted in the killing of your grandfather.'

'But my father told me he did.'

'Your father?'

'Yes, Scott Dorcha.'

'Yes, I met him.'

'Where?'

'Rathnew, Dublin. It was 2003. What did he do?'

'Everything.'

'Meaning?'

'Business services, textiles, music, mechanical engineering, oil and gas, food and beverages, chemicals ans pharmaceuticals, you name it...'

'So?'

'I'm getting your family back.'

'Why me?'

'Because you're next in line.'

'How?'

'You're Ealdahach Wren's son.

'You plan to kill me?'

'I plan to do something far less less flattering.'

I grimaced. 'What?

'You'll see. By the way, I already know who did it?'

'You already implied my father aided and abetted the other families.'

'No, I don't mean that.'

I knit my brows. 'What do you mean?'

'I mean I already know who killed your friend's brother and sister-in-law.'

'How would you know my friend?'

'Let's just say he paid for me to be punished.'

'You're not Glasson Dorcha are you?'

'Yes, and you put me away.'

'If I remember correctly, you were taking all manner or narcotics and harming people.'

'No, you don't understand.'

'What have I to understand? Was it you who killed Andrew and Susanna McLean?'

'I'm hardly going to admit it, but no.'

'So?'

'People who kill people are often the last to know.'

'What's that supposed to mean?'

'I mean you did it.'

'How would you know? Did Chase tell you this?'

'Not exactly.'

'Well?'

'My father knew Lewis McLean.'

'The brother's father?'

'Yes.'

'Go on.'

'He told my father that you resented Andrew and Susanna.'

'Why would he tell your father that?'

'Lewis McLean was not happy with you.'

'Why would he be unhappy with me?'

'Since your father damaged his gas and oil supplies.'

'So Lewis McLean said it out of spite. In which case, you didn't know Lewis McLean at all. Lewis McLean was a very pleasant unassuming man.'

'No, he said it because it was true.'

'How would Lewis McLean know? I don't even know myself. All I know is that I didn't do it.'

'Lewis McLean lost his son and he and his brother knew he was attending court the day he went missing.'

'How would they know that?'

'He left a message on the kitchen table.'

'Yes, but that doesn't mean I killed him or his wife.'

'It means you had the opportunity.'

'Possibly, but what about the motive and the means?'

'I think you wanted the wife out the way.'

'Why would I want that?'

'I think you realised who she was, the damage it would cause to your family.'

'I afraid I have no idea what you mean.'

'And as far for the brother, I think you killed him because he was aware of what was happening in the court.'

'I cannot have done something of which I have no memory.'

'Not necessarily. Now, I suppose you've waited long enough.'

'So?'

'I'm going to re-configure you.'

'What does that mean?'

'It means I'm going to give you a smile.'

'I really wish you would, your knife around my throat is depressing me. You would at least have to look at me.'

'No, you would have to look at yourself.'

'What do you mean?'

'I'm going to give you a special smile.'

I trembled. 'Oh, yes?'

'Yes, it's called a Glasgow Smile.'

'What does that do?'

'It turns a spoiled academic into someone who understands the school of hard knocks.'

'You mean to disfigure me?'

'As I said, "re-configure".'

'Why?'

'You put me away, judge. And as for the the man you respect, his father helped kill my grandfather. Plus, your legal and judicial description must subordinate to beyond description.'

'I have been in pain.'

'What pain?'

'I have a wife, four children and I made judge.'

'Yes, lucky you.'

My assailant, Glasson Dorcha drew the mushroom knife from the corner of my right mouth up to the base of my ear. I winced in agony as my face burned. Blood poured down my face on to the cream study carpet. I held the side of my face in horror. My right hand was now soaked in blood.

'Now I'm sure you won't forget me,' said Glasson.

The pressure on my neck was gone. There was stamping. The

study door slammed shut. I froze in my seat. I lingered there for what seemed like an eternity.

Eventually, I evacuated my seat, lurched to the study door, scrabbled for the handle, abandoned the study, staggered along the hallway and stumbled into the bathroom. As I scuffed along the floor, I toppled backwards and crashed on to the floor, cracking my head against the tiles. The dull ache in my skull lanced through my body. As I lay supine, I peered up in to the ceiling. The bathroom light was psychedelic. It became a mirror ball, casting multi-coloured shafts all over the room and my body. After a few minutes, I surmounted the strength to pull myself off the floor. My ageing bones crackled like twig-lets in a fire. Once upright, I sidled towards the window holding on to the bath tub. I laid my hands on the frozen glass, streaking noises becoming judders of steel. The window became a disco of other lights. The sodium vapour lamps turned every shade of orange. The house lights likewise. I peered up in to the sky. A constellation of twinkling stars vibrated in the alternating blackness. The crescent moon revolved, as it enlarged and shrivelled, luminescent in colour. I pushed myself from the window pane, wobbling as I centred. I glinted left at the toilet. The smell of bleach became a night jungle of intoxicating flora. I tried to pee. The yellow became a deeper shade of orange. The droplets hit the tiles like bullets. I pushed the flushing button. The sound of running water became a boisterous ocean. The toilet seat lid snapped shut like the jaws of an alligator. I turned the other way. Something which resembled a sink became a Greek mythological figure beckoning me. I shuffled forwards. Through the delirium of the mushroom soup, I descried something which resembled a mirror. I saw the semblance of a face. It was a monster's face; a death mask, bulbous eyes leaping out from their dead sockets, something which resembled a nose elongating and twisting, a mouth grinning like a crocodile, ears wiggling like a distressed elephant's. I saw on the right side of this mask a giant crevasse. It was circular and deep. It was encrusted with mountains of copper. It was a canyon on Mars. Residual Zeppelins of blood leaked snowballs of red which plummeted to the floor, fulminating on the tiles.

I saw the figure of a human being who had been mutilated. My stinging eyes pricked with saline tears and I sobbed, my sobs becoming screams inside the mushroom nightmare.

'Andrea,' I cried. 'Help me.'

No one came. I was alone, mad and frightened. I eventually collapsed to the floor and passed out.

Later, I awoke to find blood and glass all around me. I searched my brain for a memory. All I could recall was sipping a cup of soup, the world going crazy; colours going chayotant; sounds going cacophonous; smells going horrible; tastes going piquant; touches going ragged; thoughts going electric; feelings going hysterical; actions going insane; images going warped; and sensations going torturous.

It was then that I resolved to catch the man. I resolved to catch Glasson Dorcha, the Glasgow Smiler, the man I had put away years ago. I wasn't sure what I would say to my wife Andrea, how I would explain the savage wound.

CHAPTER FORTY-EIGHT

Cliff-hanger

Within the pit of my stomach, I felt that I simply had to flee. I could never allow Andrea or my children to witness me in this grotesque condition. I left Andrea a short note on the kitchen table. It said: '*Mother's dying. Must see her. Will be away a few days- maybe longer. Tell Lilly not to worry. Make sure she doesn't miss her drama class.*'

I jumped into the Mercedes and careened towards a hotel. Later, I peered at myself in the suite mirror. My eyes were still silver but they were round rather than small since I was in a state of shock and deeply unnerved. They were also vacant; haunted; puffy, and ringed with red. I tried feebly not to fixate on my eye colour. I knew the colour of a person's eyes, an accused's eyes did not tell you whether they were kind or cruel, whether they were an optimist or a pessimist. I looked at my eye area. There were bags underneath them, revealing my anxiety and distress.

I spent the night in the hotel. First thing next morning, I got up and drove away to the coast. The early sun was thrashing through the windscreen. I picked out my phone from my jeans pocket. There was no point wearing a suit now. My former distinguished look had been lacerated. I rang chase.

'Chase?'

'*Ewok*!'

I stuttered as I trembled. 'I'm afraid- I'm afraid- I'm afraid I've had an unfortunate accident.'

'Oh, yes?'

'I've been brutally mutilated and viciously tortured.'

'I see. What happened?'

'Yes, the world went mad and I lost my face.'

'How?'

'I was in my study, preparing the deductions as you insisted that I do. I had a hot mug of mushroom soup.'

'Did you make it?'

'No, I thought Andrea had.'

'But?'

'My assailant had.'

'Who?'

'Glasson Dorcha.'

'I see, the Glasgow Smiler.'

'You know him?'

'Let's just say he didn't like the way you penalised him for drug-related pain.'

'How would you know that?'

'Glasson was one of my brother's clients.'

'Your brother told you about him?'

'Yes.'

'Did you say anything to him?'

'No, I think he just said it to you. So what happened?'

'I was at home- in the study. I had a few sips and...'

'And?'

'Everything changed.'

'I see. Where are you now?'

'On the edge.'

'Where?'

'The cliff's edge. I want to be left alone.'

'You feel sorry for yourself.'

'I feel entirely violated.'

Chase sighed mildly. 'So, you've lost your dignified looks, then.'

'Yes, I'll have to grow a beard.'

'Yes, I am aware of the trick. It might suit you.'

'I doubt it- but anything's better than a gaping hole.'

'Were you good-looking, Ewok?'

'I certainly wasn't disfigured if that's what you mean.'

'No. Then, I suppose you were seventy-eight.'

'I might as well be a hundred, a skull of a man.'

'You don't like your new look.'

'It makes me look like a hood.'

'Yes. So have you worked anything out?'

'Glasson Dorcha was avenging the death of his grandfather as well as getting me back for sentencing him.'

'How would his grandfather have been killed?'

'I have no way of knowing, although I suspect a mushroom knife.'

'Why?'

'It was your weapon of choice to detain me and all the families seemed to know about mushrooms.'

'Why would they know about mushrooms?'

'I think Jack Dorcha was probably poisoned with mushrooms and then had his throat slit.'

'Where?'

'I don't know.'

'What about my brother and his wife?'

'I think your brother might have had his throat slit.'

'Why?'

'It seems to be the obvious weapon among the families.'

'Who would have done it?'

'Any number of people, I don't know.'

'And what about his wife?'

'I consider she might have been poisoned.'

'Where?'

'I don't know, possibly at home.'

'Why?'

'If whoever it was couldn't have her, perhaps no one else could. You told me your brother said: "*She's betrayed me, I think it was him, Chase.*"

'So?'

'I consider it might have been the disgruntled client. What exactly did your brother say about this man?'

'" *This man's mad, Chase. He lost his wife a long time ago-* "'

'Who was his wife?'

'I don't know but-'

'But?'

'He said to my brother that she had died in a fire.'

'Yes, and?'

'My brother got the distinct impression there was more to it than that.'

'Meaning?'

'My brother wondered if she might have been killed.'

'Why?'

'I don't know.'

'And?'

'He felt so guilty.'

'Why?'

'I don't know.'

'And?'

'He talked about a feeling.'

'What feeling?'

'I don't know, but he made it clear to my brother that it was unlike any other.'

The very early evening September sky loured down down at me with Stygian brown eyes of abject disapproval, as if to say I had no place here. The co-coagulated sodium air was shuddery like a total obnobubiliation of mint and tea tree. The entire cavalry of uniformed clouds were leaking salty tears of disenchantment. I coaxed my thin veined hands together, as if attempting to ignite a couple of small bear twigs, desperately essaying to impart some warmth to my old chilling body.

As the last of the mushroom seemed to manducate at my senescent washed-out mind, I see-sawed in front of the terrifying precipice of the steep cliff.

I exclaimed into the void. 'I don't want to lose you, Andrea my darling.'

The dim unforgiving sky seemed to glare back. 'Obviously not,' it seemed to say harshly.

'And I don't want to lose my kids.'

The abysmal sky seemed to glower back again.

As I waddled back and forth, I tore out a large chunk of my grey hair. I obviously knew all to well that everything I had ever believed in or could possibly have stood for in this life was in deep jeopardy. My beloved wife of over fifty years Andrea and my four perfectly infeasible children could be killed. Their lives could be remorselessly forfeited if I did not precipitately unravel the two very mysterious unsolved murders. Chase had been monosemous about that in the Premier Inn at my retirement do, my farewell bash. I knew only too well I had to work out like thunder who had killed Chase's brother Andrew McLean and his sister-in-law Susanna. In the unthinkable event that I did not have those responsible not only investigated, as I had done so far, but also punished, I knew Chase would easily kill me. I was not especially worried for my own life, since my life at seventy-seven had enjoyed sufficient experience but I was positively delirious about the lives of my wife and children.

On a contiguous matter, I was also abundantly aware that my poisoner and dis-figurer/mutilator, the most ruthless gangster in Glasgow Glasson Dorcha himself could kill me himself. He seemed hell bent on getting me back for something my grandfather Ealdahach Wren had done, something his grandfather Jack Dorcha had gone through.

As my seventy-seven year old senescent mind fulminated beneath the bleak unforgiving sky, I was even beginning to excogitate that I myself had killed the brother and the sister-in-law. I certainly did not possess any visual memory of that. I recalled my former employer Belay saying to me that I was responsible for executions in the court.

I cast my discombobulated mind over all the things that had happened since Chase had forced me to investigate all suspects..

I thought about Alainn. I had loved her more than the older man ever could have.

I was starting to lose the plot. I was tearing strips out of my hair. I felt if I killed myself, threw myself over the cliff, Chase and Glasson Dorcha might leave Andrea and the kids alone. I was in a trap. Not being able to work out definitively who killed Andrew and Susanna McLean, I prepared for launch.

'Sorry, Andrea,' I exclaimed, 'Sorry kids, this is the best I can do.'

I motioned to propel myself into oblivion, I jumped in to the air when a force pulled me back.

A voice cried out. '*Ewald, no*!'

I swung down on to the ground. I was flailing, my hands splaying on the grass. I peered up at a forgotten sky. A face smiled at me.

'Belay?' I said.

'Yes, my friend.'

'I- I don't understand.'

'I might have retired you, Ewald.' I didn't mean to finish you.'

Belay picked me up and carted me to an outcrop. He sat me down. 'What's wrong with you, Ewald?'

I flustered. 'I'm in trouble, Belay.'

Belay smiled kindly. 'Yes, I can see that. We will go somewhere else.'

I nodded.

CHAPTER FORTY-NINE

The Reunion

Belay drove me to the nearest restaurant. I was stumbling. 'This restaurant is in...'

Belay was smirking. 'Saudi Arabia.'

I smiled half-heartedly. 'Sir, believes.'

'Yes, he does.'

I tried to be customary. 'The restaurant serves...'

'Dogs ears and cauliflower.'

There was a group of tourists at the adjacent table. I tried to acknowledge them. 'How often do you go to this restaurant?'

'First time,' said one of the group.

I then realised how inane my question was. I was obviously not on form. Belay picked up the menu. 'The food looks good,' he said.

I nursed my paunch. 'Yes- it probably does.'

'Probably?'

'I'm not sure I have the stomach for it.'

'No?'

'I have been queasy for days.'

'So no starter then?'

'No, I don't think so.'

'What about something easy on the bread-basket?'

'Yes?'

'The prawn cocktail.'

'Fish, no I don't think so.'

'What about the mushroom soup?'

I remembered my interloper. 'Not on your life.'

'Why don't you have a cigarette?'

'I'm not allowed.'

'No?'

I sighed. 'It's a public place, Belay.'

'So?'

'You have to go outside.'

'Yes?'

'Yes, it's the law.'

'You're sticking to that.'

'Of course I'm sticking to that, I was a judge. What's the matter with you, Belay?'

Belay sighed. 'It's nothing, it's meaningless.'

'If I remember, with you nothing means everything.'

Belay shrugged. 'Well, I guess something's happened, then.'

'Yes, what's happened?'

Belay waved his head. 'I've done something stupid.'

'Have you gotten involved with more of Glasgow's gangsters?'

'No, it's more than that.'

'Are you dying?'

'No.'

'Then what?'

Belay gazed into the air. 'I've fallen in love.'

'You have?'

'Yes?'

'With whom?'

He smiled sadly. 'James.'

I winced again at my former employer's homosexuality. I tried to hide my disgust. 'Oh, yes?'

'Yes.'

I gawked. 'How?'

'He was different.'

I suspired. You mean he smokes grass.'

Belay tottered his head. 'Well, yes.'

I tried my best to work with him. 'Where did you meet him?'

'Rutherglen.'

'What were you doing in Rutherglen?'

'I was having a night out.'

'And?'

'I went back to a friend's house and met him.'

'And?'

'I was going to leave but he stopped me. He asked if he could kiss me. I consented. He stuck his tongue down my throat.'

I nearly threw up.

'I'm afraid I want him, Ewald.'

'Why?'

'He made me feel.'

'How?'

Belay smiled defiantly. 'He made me hard.'

I was at breaking point. 'And?'

'After I left, I was in tears. I cried for days. All I could think about was him, all I could feel was him, I even fantasised about him.' Belay gazed at me vacantly. 'D'you think I'm insane?'

I levelled at Belay. 'You've always been insane, Belay.'

Belay nodded. 'Mad enough to employ you.'

'Mad enough to retire me.'

'You think I was unfair.'

'I think you could use a law of equity remedial.'

'Is that all that matters to you, Ewald: law?'

'It's important, Belay.'

'You've been on drugs, Ewald.'

'A drug. And it was involuntary intoxication.'

'It's still a breach of the Misuse of Drugs Act 1988.'

'No, it isn't, he put me on it.'

'Liability is strict.'

'So?'

'It doesn't require proof of negligence.'

'I was hardly negligent.'

'Anyway, since you've had a penalty above the law, what do you think of the concept?'

'It still regulates actions, still imposes penalties. The Human rights act provides for the right to thought.'

'But?'

'The Mental Health Scotland Act is an exception.'

'Yes?'

'If a doctor thinks you have a mental disorder and the Mental Health Officer agrees, a person may be sectioned.'

'And what of things said.'

'Again the Human Rights Act provides for the fundamental freedom of expression.'

'But?'

'It is qualified by the defamation law.'

'What if the law operates to persecute the individual?'

'Sectioning is not persecution, it's necessary care and treatment. Prosecution is not persecution.'

'What if the sectioners and the prosecutors represent the state.'

'Well, of course they do.'

'What if their activities cause fear?'

I sighed. 'Yes, Belay.' I told him all the things I had learned.

CHAPTER FIFTY

A Holiday

Belay beckoned me with a flick of his head to enter the taxi. We climbed into the back.

'Where are we going, Belay,' I said.

Belay smiled jocundly at me. 'We're going to the seaside.'

I glanced at my watch. I glinted at Belay quizzically. 'At this time of night?'

Belay nodded passively. 'Yes.'

I sighed. 'Where about exactly?'

'Inch Moan.'

I groaned. 'How are we going to get to Inch Moan?'

Belay spoke methodically. 'I've arranged for a man to skipper us there.'

'Which man?'

'He was a lawyer to begin with and then he took up the art of boating.'

'Do I know him?'

'I suspect you've heard of him, but I doubt you'd recognise him.'

I didn't bother to ask the name. 'Why are we going there?'

'We need a break.'

I groaned again. 'Really, Belay I'd much rather go home.'

Belay shook his head. 'No, we need a place where we can talk freely. The restaurant obviously wasn't private enough.'

I sighed. I had gotten used to taking orders.

We rode the rest of the way in silence to Balmaha. Belay paid the driver a thousand pounds.

'Keep the change, driver,' he said.

'That's very generous, Sir.'

'Not at all,' said Belay, 'You earned it.'

Sure enough, there was a boat waiting for us at the pontoon. The skipper piloted us to Inch Moan. We climbed out of the boat and stepped into a dinghy. As the vaporous moon shimmered on the dark waters, Belay paddled us peacefully to the shore. With the aid of powerful industrial lamps we were able to set up tent.

We were both inside our sleeping bags, lying head to toe.

I yawned in agony. 'You know, I've never slept with a man before.'

Belay smiled. 'No? I've never slept with a woman.'

'Just before I fall asleep, remind me, Belay, why did you make me redundant?'

'Your brand of justice was too ruthless and too short term.'

'It's funny, I don't remember it being like that.'

'No, I suppose not. Good night, Ewald.'

'Good night,' Belay.

I woke up. I felt disorientated. I peered into a strip of light. The front zip of the tent was open. I could hear Belay pottering about outside.

'Coffee, Ewald?' said Belay.

I rubbed my eyes. 'Yes, black please.'

'Are you hungry?'

'I could manage a roll.'

'Coming up.'

Belay and I sat around the camp fire, toasting our extremities.

'So, Ewald,' said Belay, 'summarise.'

I frowned at Belay. 'I thought I had already done that in the restaurant.'

'Yes, I remember.'

'Glasson was listening in on our conversation.'

'He was?'

'Yes.'

'So?'

'So I fell asleep.'

'You mean I was talking to a brick wall.'

Belay wiggled his head. 'More or less, yes.'

'But I thought you were paying attention.'

'It might have looked that way but no.'

'So?'

'So you retired me, Belay.'

Belay stared through me. 'I'm not sorry about that.'

I exhaled with exasperation. 'Anyway, it was my farewell bash.'

'Yes, and remind me again of what happened?'

'I was held up at knife-point.'

'Is this a sea story?'

I groaned. 'You have always been the most sarcastic man I have ever met.'

'So who held you up?'

'Chase McLean.'

'Who?

'An unknown assailant.'

'And?'

'He accused me of murdering his brother and his brother's wife.'

'Really?'

'Yes, he told me his brother and his sister-in-law went missing in July 1995 and were presumed dead seven years later.'

'What were their names?'

'Andrew McLean and Susanna McLean, formerly known as Fields.'

'Why would he accuse you?'

CHAPTER FIFTY-ONE

Camp Fire

As the bitter knife-like light of the early morning gradually descended into the chilling blunt light of the late afternoon, Belay and I remained crouched down opposite each other, rubbing our hands together around the small stubborn camp fire; it fizzled in a melancholic mizzle which slowly enveloped the inch. Belay had been knocking back large cans of cheap lager for hours, eructating intermittently, while I had been gulping inordinate amounts of strong black coffee and crunching endless fags. We had been watching each other closely, like two familiar strangers, counting each other's doubts. I told Belay about the other crimes I had come across.

Belay hunched his shoulders. 'So, Ewald,' said Belay, 'what about the Criminal Law of Scotland in all of this.'

I coggled my head slowly back and forth. 'As you are very well aware, Belay, prosecution is carried out by the Procurator Fiscal.'

'Who do you plan to have prosecuted?'

I waved my head. 'No one.'

'No?'

'My assignment was to probe and castigate the suspects, not necessarily to induce a prosecution.' I smiled disappointedly. 'I'm a sleuth, now, Belay, not a judge.'

Belay nodded. 'You do remember though, Ewald, that the police could easily be informed.'

I nodded with concession. 'Yes of course, but I won't be doing that.'

Belay gawked slightly. 'Why not?'

I maintained Belay's gaze. 'As I say, my role has changed.'

Belay opened his arms disingenuously. 'What about the crimes?'

I could present little resistance. 'Yes.'

Belay persisted. 'The murders of the brother and his wife?'

I smiled disappointedly. 'Yes.'

'Well?'

'

Belay intensified his squint. 'And what about the person who might have suffocated the brain of the niece with a malign packet of cigarettes? The habituated cousin possibly? What about the person who attempted to burn the aggrieved mother to death? The battered niece possibly? What about the person who might have attempted to smother the troubled cousin with a pillow? The habituated cousin possibly? What about the person who attempted to put down the arrogant doctor? The troubled cousin? What about the person who might have attempted to crush the rivalrous uncle to death by collapsing his roof?' The disgruntled client possibly? What about the person that might have attempted to poison the bitter and twisted grandmother? Again the battered niece possibly?'

I exhaled deeply. 'Except for the chloroform incident, they are all *mights*.

Belay arched his brows. 'And what if they were *weres*.'

I tilted my head at Belay in a placating way. 'Well theoretically, as you know, less serious crimes are prosecuted in the Justice of the Peace Court.'

Belay stiffened his mouth. 'These potential crimes are more serious.'

I nodded my head patiently. 'Yes, and as you know, with more serious crimes, they are prosecuted in the Sheriff Court.'

Belay cast me a incredulous look. 'These potential crimes would be the most serious.'

I dizzied my eyes. 'And, as you know of course, the most serious crimes would be prosecuted in the High Court.'

'So?'

'As a sleuth, I need to take a different approach.'

'Why?'

'The high court is for rape, the high court is for murder. The high court is not really for the most brutalising tortures that have ever obtained.'

'Why not?'

'They are beyond the scope of our standard penalties.'

'Yes, I see that, Ewald, but could you not at least have the multiple suspects arrested.'

I smiled thoughtfully. 'Naturally I could. Under the existing rules, naturally I could.'

'And they could be arrested without their being detained first.'

'Of course. The police could also detain them for up to twelve hours.'

'Yes, and in which circumstances?'

'If they have reasonable grounds for suspecting they have committed or are committing an offence.'

'In which case, you really should facilitate that.'

I waved my head. 'It's not worth detaining them yet.'

'Why not?'

'Many of the suspects have suffered more than the penalties would make them suffer.'

'I understand most painful experiences.'

'Yes, but you're a sad hypocrite, Belay.'

Belay glinted at me indignantly. 'I didn't ingest magic mushrooms.'

'That was involuntary. And it was your fault.'

'Liability can be strict.'

'Liability yes, not culpability.'

'And say the suspect or suspects did get detained?'

'Well, of course they would be entitled to legal advice and a lawyer.'

'Yes, and?'

'Bail would have to be requested, and if granted, it would require the accused to adhere to certain rules.'

'What about the jury?'

'As you know, all trials in the High Court are heard before a jury.'

'So?'

'In this case, I am the jury.'

Belay nodded with understanding. 'What is your verdict?'

'Guilty? Not guilty? Not proven?'

'Yes?'

'So your verdict is not proven?'

'Precisely.'

'So they would be acquitted?'

I sighed. 'Yes.'

'So they are acquitted.'

'For the moment.'

'So no sentence?'

'No. It is of course usually the Sheriff or Judge to sentence the accuse if convicted.'

'But?'

'In this case, I have to decide. The High Court, as you know, has unlimited sentencing powers, while the maximum custodial sentence imposed by a Sheriff Court is currently 5 years.'

'So?'

'The penalties in these case have to be higher.'

Belay's eyes bulged. 'How high?'

'As high as they can go.'

'So not the acceptable concepts, then?'

'No, the necessary concepts.' I bumbled for a few moments. I spoke like an unhopeful child. 'Belay?'

'Yes.'

'Can I have my job back?'

Belay suspired through his nose. 'How intelligent are you, Ewald?'

'I'm as intelligent as I always was, but as you know, I have smoked my whole life.'

'Are you mentally ill?'

I smiled guiltily. 'No.'

'And why is that?'

'I always worked, still work after a fashion and I didn't drink.'

Belay nodded.

'How intelligent are you, Belay?'

Belay smiled with despondence. 'I'm as intelligent as I feel.'

I gazed at Belay inquisitively. 'And how do you feel?'

'Very conceptual.'

I already knew the answer. 'Are you mentally ill?'

'Yes.'

'I see. Racing thoughts, loud thoughts, no brain power.'

'More or less. Does it come back?'

'You never smoked.'

'Not really, no. So?'

'I think it's about even.'

Belay smiled plainly. 'Do you still remember your girl?'

I smiled wistfully. 'Of course I do.'

'And?'

'I think she probably had a lucky escape.'

'Why would that be, Ewald?'

'I suppose men of law were meant for academic women, not women of spirit and adventure.'

'Andrea has no spirit, no adventure?'

I sighed. 'Only because I denied her it.'

'I see.'

I breathed laboriously. 'My life, Belay has been one long struggle with law and justice. I think I would have bored her to the point of strangulation. My recent, less empirical experiences have taught me that there is another side to life.'

Belay cast me a quizzical glance. 'There is?'

I exhaled nervously. 'Yes, an exciting, but much more dangerous side. In fact in another life I might have been James Bond.'

Belay tilted his head. 'Which do you prefer?'

I drew in my lips. 'They're different.'

CHAPTER FIFTY-TWO

My Self-discovery

'Different how?' said Belay.

I braced myself for a lengthy explanation. 'My legal life taught me regulations and penalties, my new life has taught me exceptions and freedoms. The regulations and penalties gave me safety and the feelings of safety, while the exceptions and freedoms have given me danger and the feelings of danger. I lived seventy-eight years of my life in my mind, I now live my life with emotions. The teachers gave me knowledge and understanding, the trainers gave me behaviour and skill, the employers gave me survival and security, while the outlaws like Chase McLean and Glasson Dorcha have given me risks and rewards.'

'And what are the risks and the rewards?'

'The risks are threats, abduction, torture, mutilation and murder, not only in relation to myself but more importantly in relation to my family, my wife and children, and friends, as well as vulnerable others, while the rewards are gateways, journey, frisson, healing and life. I could go back, if you would let me, but I'm not sure I want to. I would rather work out who killed the brother and his wife, who has attempted lives and who may be next to die and who may be responsible. I realise I have done all I can as a lawyer and a judge, but I have much to do as detective- as a sleuth, I suppose. A lawyer lives off his technical competence and financial aspiration, a judge lives off his fairness and his decision, while a sleuth lives off his curiosity and solution. I can see that skill and money and that attitude and opinion subordinate to passion and completeness. It is one thing to impress, another thing to control and another again to finish.'

Belay cast me a thoughtful look. 'You plan to finish the guilty?'

I shrugged. 'I have no choice, now. If they are punished, they may regenerate, where as if they are eliminated, it will be over.'

Belay nodded knowingly. 'So you plan to kill them?'

I shook my head. 'No, of course not, but I strongly feel someone will.'

Belay gawked slightly. 'What makes you feel that?'

Again I sighed. 'Whether it is Chase McLean as the instigator of the investigation and punishment, or Glasson Dorcha as the overarching threat, or someone else, it will not be enough that the guilty go to prison, since the stakes are so high; the victims will want an ending. If my own torture and mutilation is insufficient, then the only conceivable outcome is death.'

Belay opened up his hands slightly. 'You could always argue your own innocence.'

I waved my head. 'That will not satisfy the victims, although I will essay to prove that it would have been impossible for my to have had been responsible.'

Belay tilted his head. 'And what if you cannot prove your innocence to them?'

I smiled forlornly. 'Then I think it will be the end for me, too.'

Belay nodded. 'You have a lot of work to do then.'

'Yes.'

'What will you do exactly?'

'I will find more evidence.'

'Since you cannot prove just yet?'

'No, the evidence is too weak, too speculative. I do not have confessions, nor do I have beyond reasonable doubt. I have so many reasons but too few motives.'

'How long will it take?'

'As long as it needs to, as long as I can stay alive.'

'When will you start again?'

'After I have recovered.'

'Where will you start again?'

'Wherever the suspects are.'

'You want to go home?'

'Yes, Belay. I am old and I am tired and I need to sleep. It has been an exhausting escapade.'

Belay nodded.

'What will you do?' I said.

'I will return to work tomorrow.'

As the last of the sun's orange rays caressed the lands, bacterial pockets of darkness multiplied and became a complete umbrella. I turned to Belay and said: 'Belay, what is your second name?'

Belay spread out his lips. 'No, Ewald, we made a deal at your interview.'

'I could always work it out, you know- if I really wanted to?'

Belay shook his head. 'No, you wouldn't be able to.'

I glanced at Belay quizzically. 'I couldn't ask one of your associates?'

Belay tilted his head. 'You could but they wouldn't know.'

'You couldn't have kept your surname from everyone surely.'

'Yes.'

'You mean to say it is not on the birth certificate? The passport? The driving license? The Electoral Register? Your correspondence?'

'Oh, it is.'

'There you go then.'

'But it's not the name you will be looking for.'

I peered at Belay quizzically. I continued. 'You have been using a false name since birth?'

'Yes.'

'Why?'

'It was my father's idea, he wanted me not to be too obvious.'

'And who is/was your father?'

Belay swayed his head. 'Lewis.'

'And what did he do?'

'He empowered me.'

'He gave you your dominant personality?'

'And the rest.'

'And your mother?'

'What about her?'

'Who is/was she?'

'She was spontaneous, impulsive. She lived life in the fast lane, always willing to take risks.'

I suddenly realised that our roles had been reversed. For once I was asking the questions, taking an interest in Belay's life, his family, his history, his nature.

'Did she die in the fast lane?'

'Yes, she did extreme sports.'

'And back to your father?'

'He committed suicide.'

'Why?'

'He knew he couldn't live with what he had done.'

'And what had he done?'

'He had assumed lives.'

'Was he bad?'

'He was imperfect, but he knew the limits of his own justification.'

'Is that why you are always intoxicated, always damaged.'

'I suppose so.'

'Is there anything that would turn things around for you?'

'Yes, there is.'

'And?'

'The one who annihilates those who have hurt me.'

'Does that make you smile?'

'No, it doesn't.'

CHAPTER FIFTY-THREE

Belay's in Love

As Belay straggled away from me, grappling in the emaciated air for a sea-rail that was not there, in the moribund orange light, beneath the resplendent moon which sprayed cartridge silver across the canvass-white waters of the sea, towards the bracken-lands, a lost lands, I called out to him, '*You're wrong, Belay*!'

Belay arrested. He turned on his heels, making dents in the sand. He shouted back. 'How am I wrong?!'

I hollered into the proliferating gang of shadows. 'It's the one you want!'

Belay fanned the air. 'What does that mean?!'

I shrilled. 'The man that does it for you!'

Belay shouted back again. 'What do you mean? I'm the employer, Ewald- I employ torture judges- I employed you.'

'Where are you going then?'

'Some where I don't need to listen to you- or the bastards.'

My heart pounded. I screamed for my friend. 'I'm not talking about your work life here, Belay!'

Belay whined. 'What are you talking about?'

'I'm talking about the man who made you feel.'

'Who?'

'The man you told me about first in the house.'

'It was a good house.'

'Yes it was, so?'

'*James.*'

Belay grumbled. 'Okay, so I remember him.'

I railed. 'Is that all? You remember him? You fell in love, Belay.'

'No, I didn't.'

'Yes, you did.'

Belay shrugged. 'So?'

'So it's more than that. The reason you're always drunk, Belay, even to you, if it is conceptually, the reason you're always so unhappy, the reason you're such a morass, the reason you exercise power, the reason you over-compensate, is that you wanted someone- and you want him.'

Belay threw his hands in the mounting sodium air. 'Yes, perhaps but I don't need him.'

I pitched my voice again. 'No, Belay, come back just a moment.'

Belay tumbled back. 'That's basically what he was doing to me.'

'Where?'

'In the kitchen.'

'In the good house?'

'Yes.'

I looked up at Belay. 'He was obviously trying to help you.'

To my great relief, Belay re-manifested from the shadows. 'That's better,' I said, 'No, you do, you do need him.'

Belay palmed me away. 'He wouldn't be interested.'

I opened up my arms. 'Why not?'

'He likes 'Pink Floyd.'

'And?'

'He was total genius with it.'

'And?'

'He told me the complete story.'

'So?'

'I couldn't keep up with him- I couldn't remember everything he said.'

'And what? It made you feel humble.'

Belay stammered slightly. 'It- it made me feel inadequate.'

'Inadequate how?'

'He said it was a one-off. I must respect that.' Belay smiled congenially. 'He prefers women anyway, he always has, in fact he told me whom he loved, that he has loved her for ages- I love her as well.'

'Whom?'

'I can't say that.'

'Did he say?'

'Yes.'

'So?'

'I can't say.'

My eyes narrowed on Belay. 'In the same way?'

'No.'

'Why not?'

'I'm not bisexual.'

I nodded emphatically. 'And you're not straight.'

'No.'

'No, I know I love her- I have told her I love her, that I will always love her- but I am not in love with her-' Belay scratched his head- 'I don't know- I sometimes felt I was- think I am- but I'm getting weaker.'

'Exactly, but it came naturally with him.'

Belay looked quizzically at himself. 'If you call the major part of Russian Standard Vodka, three Jaeger bombs, two Schnapps, four beers natural, then I suppose. And anyway, it's too patronising.'

I was still pleading Belay with my silver eyes. 'No, it isn't my friend. I have been with Andrea virtually my whole life. And I'm still in love with her.'

Belay waved his head. 'It's different.'

'And we sometimes still do it.'

'Then it's completely different.'

'How?'

'They spoiled that aspect of me years ago, Ewald. That would be a disgust concept.'

This time I threw my hands in the air. 'To him?! To you?!'

'To both.'

'On whose side.'

'No, on both.'

I begged to differ. 'It's a fear of intimacy.'

'Yes, it is, but my brain itself is going.'

I probed Belay somewhat. 'Have you had a scan?'

'No.'

'Why not?'

'I don't know.'

'Then you can't know.'

'I can.'

'What d'you mean?'

'It's happened to me because of smoking; it's happening to you for a different reason. Anyway, what about kissing? Just the front part?'

'I'm too faint to try.'

'Exactly. You are lucky, you know, Belay. You have only done bottles with drugs. You have not smoked yourself into an absolutely conceptual oblivion, you haven't become a mime, which I know I have. Remember when he kissed you...'

Belay's smile wrinkled. 'Yes, I remember.'

'You did tongues.'

'Yes, I know.'

'Yes, in the kitchen.'

'Yes.'

'Yes, he made you hard.'

A wry smile creased Belay's lips.

I smiled defiantly. 'You're in love, my friend.'

Belay waved his head. 'Only because I had been drinking all day and throughout the night.'

I grappled for something to say. 'You're insulting the man, now, you love him.'

'The thought makes me tremble.'

I opened up my hands. 'There you go then. That's the heart speaking.'

Belay shook his head. 'No, that is called a faint heart, it *is* different. You see the way you feel with Andrea has been built up carefully over years. My love for him is conceptual, only believable because I had imbibed enough, only conceivable after a trillion units, but never practicable.'

'Are you disgusted by him?'

'No.'

'Do you like him?'

'Of course I do, very much.'

'How d' you know he's perfect? Are you not expecting too much of his own self-esteem and his self-evaluation.'

'Yes, I suppose.'

'Well, then.'

'I would disgust him if it went too far, and I didn't want to do that.'

'He flattered you, then, he made you feel desirable, as well as lovable, something you hadn't been able to feel in years.'

'Remember how you felt later in the morning?'

'Yes, after I walked home, I was in tears later in the morning.'

'All you could think about was him, all you could feel was him. You even fantasised about him. You had to drink more and fall asleep.'

For the first time in his life, my former employer of torture judges whimpered like a frightened child. He stared disconsolately at me. 'Ewald, my brain suffocated months ago, my mind developed full-blown schizophrenia, I went up high.'

'Frisson?'

'No, depersonalised fear.'

'Perhaps he might understand that.'

Belay threw his hand at me. 'Ewald, my brain collapsed years ago.'

I nodded at Belay. 'Does James know this?'

'I don't know. Perhaps she told him.'

'The woman he loved.'

'I am very faint, very weak.'

'I need to drink copiously to feel convincing, even for a moment.'

I gazed at him with imploring eyes. 'But you love him.'

'Yes.'

'Would it help to do what he does? I have met men that say that it saves the mind.'

Belay hunched his shoulders. 'I don't know, obviously I've tried it. All I know is that his brain is considerably better than mine. All I know is I'm becoming demented- my brain developed so many thought problems, so many emotional problems, so many functioning problems.'

'All because of him.'

'Not quite, but yes.'

I smiled at Belay. 'He might find that funny, men like that.'

Belay smiled sadly. 'Perhaps, but I don't. He's- he's more intelligent than me.'

'You're jealous of his intelligence?'

'No, I am jealous of my lack of intelligence for him.'

'Who says he needs that. It can't always be feelings-intelligence, Belay. There are other ways to be intelligent.'

'Not at my stage. The brain is numb, the heart is faint. I'm being beaten by the reasonable hypothetical man on the Clapham Omnibus.'

'But this is no hypothetical man. This is *James*.'

'Yes, James Aitchison.'

'This man obviously understands.'

'Yes, but not completely. Not in every way.'

'But you are in love with him.'

Belay smiled with defeat. 'Yes.'

'Well, he did his job then. It was you who backed out.'

'Yes.'

'Why?'

'I was too tired, and I knew the final push wouldn't be worth it.'

'In what way?'

'He would discover parts of me that would put him off.'

'Why?'

'He would see me, he would discard me.'

'What about now?'

'No, but you are right, when I am ready he must know that I love him.'

'You love, James?'

'Yes.'

'But you know a secret she might not know.'

'Yes.'

'And what makes you smile?'

'James- James Aitchison.'

'You love him.'

'Yes.'

'Does he make you smile?'

'He makes me smile.'

There was a roaring sound of metal grinding through water.

CHAPTER FIFTY-FOUR

Glasson Returns

Belay's disintegrated mind vibrated with the rolls of thunder as the early evening tide water lapped up on the beach, assibilating angrily. The waterways of Scotland ran through Belay's mind. For a moment, the basins of the River Tweed on the east coast and the Solway Firth in the west coast seemed somehow to tump over in his head. The North Sea and the Atlantic ocean seemed to fulminate like a galaxy of water-stars, as a Mexican wave of thunder rent the sky and a kaleidoscope of boiling lightning jabbed the land and the sea. The land was a cornucopia of mosses, sedums and sempervivums. There were flares of yellow as creeping jenny scattered the island. The scent of creeping thyme was pervasive.

The gnarling sound of metal grinding through water became more intense until an imposing shadow on a jet ski licked towards the beach. As the jet ski ground to a halt in the sand, the momentum of the ride sent the figure skating towards us.

'Hello, gentleman!' said a voice.

'Glasson!' said Belay.

'Yes,' said Glasson.

I gasped. '*Dorcha*?'

'Yes, judge,' said Glasson.

'What are you doing here?' I said.

'I thought we might have some tea,' said Glasson.

I gawked. 'Tea?'

'Yes, I didn't think you liked alcohol.'

I nodded contentedly. 'No, I don't.'

'I don't drink tea,' said Belay.

'I can always put whiskey in it,' said Glasson.

Belay shrugged. 'Very well.'

Glasson returned to the arrested jet ski and opened up the cool box. He took out a portable stove, a box of Tetley tea bags, a two-litre bottle of Asda water, a small carton of semi-skimmed milk, a jar of sugar and a small carton of sweeteners, a bottle of Jura whiskey and three mugs. 'I have the provisions.'

'So I see,' I said.

Glasson laid out all the items on the sand. He embedded the portable stove in the sand. He ignited the portable stove with a lighter. He placed the teapot onto the stove. After a few minutes the tea pot was whistling.

'Sounds ready,' I said.

'Yes,' said Glasson. 'How do you take your tea, judge?'

'Milk, two sweeteners,' I said.

'And you Belay?'

Belay smiled congenially. 'I'll have the Jura in mine.'

'So how did you get here, Dorcha?' I said.

'I sailed.'

'How?' I said.

'With my grandfather's boat,' said Glasson.

'The Sunseeker Manhattan 50?' I said.

'Yes.'

'She's yours?'

'I believe she will become mine.'

'When?'

'When my father dies.'

'Scot?'

'Yes.'

'What is it you want with us, Glasson?' I said.

'I want justice.'

I sipped my tea gingerly. 'I gave you justice.'

'No,' said Glasson, 'you gave me punishment.'

I smiled patiently at Glasson. 'Punishment is justice.'

Glasson waved his head. 'No, justice is fairness.'

Belay smiled awkwardly. 'It depends.'

'I gave you a very clement sentence,' I said.

'Fair!' said Glasson. 'Look at my face, it's like ribbons.'

'Who did it to you?' said Belay.

'A thug of a man.'

'Who?' I said.

'John McLaughlin.'

'Who was he?'

'He was my boyfriend.'

'If he was your boyfriend, why would he do that to you, then?'

'Because he was jealous.'

'What was he jealous of?'

'My pretty boy looks.'

'He was gay?' I said.

'No,' said Glasson, 'he was a brutal homophobe.'

'So?'

'He fancied females.'

'So?'

'He liked me at first.'

'Why would he like another man?'

'Glasson's transexual,' said Belay.

'So this John McLaughlin thought you were a woman?'

Glasson glared at me indignantly. 'I am a woman.'

I squinted. 'You are?'

'Yes.'

'So?' I said.

'He knew I loved another man.'

'Who?'

'David.'

'And?'

'He felt I had betrayed him.'

'Betrayed him?'

'Yes.'

'So?'

'He took everything from me: my looks, my desirability and my self-worth.'

'So he just took a knife to you?' I said.

'Yes.' said Glasson. 'And the rest.'

'What else did he do?' said Belay.

'He slipped me a pain pill,' said Glasson. 'He had me raped and sexually tortured. I went blind.'

'Yes,' said Belay, 'I know this one.'

I loured. 'For a blind man, you make excellent tea.'

Glasson tilted his head. 'It was long drawn-out but it was temporary.'

'Yes,' I said. 'I had considered all of that.'

'You had?'

'Yes, that's why I gave you a considerably lesser sentence,' I said.

'I was inside for two whole years,' said Glasson.

'It would have been twelve-eighteen years without the mitigation,' I said. 'And lest we forget, look at my face. You gave me the Glasgow Smile.'

Glasson grimaced. 'Your apology won't bring back my looks, my grandfather or my wasted years.'

'And your lust for revenge,' I said, 'wont bring back my obvious social acceptance.'

Glasson sneered. 'What does a man plummeting toward eighty need looks for?'

'It might surprise you to know that even at our age group we still have a certain pride. We still have to face the world. We don't want to look like Neanderthals.'

'Then you should understand,' said Glasson.

'What should I understand?' I said.

'The highest penalties,' said Glasson.

'The highest penalty is life imprisonment.'

'No,' said Glasson, 'the highest penalty is the most extreme form of torture.'

I leaned back slightly. 'That is a relative argument, not a legal penalty- at least not in terms of the law of Scotland. And the right to life comes before the fundamental freedom of torture in terms of the Human Rights Act.'

Glasson frowned. 'That might be logical in theory but it is sophistic in practice.'

'You know intelligent words?'

'I know meaningful words.'

'So?'

'It is obviously far worse that a man is tortured within an inch of his life, than for his life to be quickly and painlessly taken.'

Belay cast his mind back on his pain. 'I have to agree with Glasson.'

'I don't, I said, 'Murder is still a higher crime.'

'No,' said Glasson, 'murder is the younger sibling of torture.'

'So?' I said.

'I wish you to understand that.'

'Why?'

'You had no place imprisoning me,' said Glasson.

'Why not?'

'You had not gone through any of it.'

'So?' I said.

'I wish you to understand the experiences that will force you to realise that.'

'So?'

'Let's start with sleep deprivation.'

'Yes, Glasson,' I said, 'I remember it. Your lawyer used that in court.'

'Who was his lawyer?' said Belay.

'The brother,' said Glasson.

'No,' I said. 'Glasson gets it Belay, 'you don't.'

'Why would I not get it?' said Belay.'

'You're not an academic,' I said.

'I'm not either,' said Glasson.

'There you go then,' said Belay.

'No,' I said, 'There's more to it, Belay.'

'What more?' said Belay.

'Something you aren't able to rationalise within your feeling.'

'I can feel, I've always felt,' said Belay.

'Yes,' I said, 'and he knows that.'

'I'm no where near what you're talking about,' said Glasson.

'Yes,' I said, 'in that case you've come off it.'

'I don't need to be on it,' said Glasson, 'I still hate you.'

'Yes,' I said, 'the difference between you, Belay and I is that you're embittered by the successful one who had been using, Belay has never really remembered the successful one who has been using, where as I always remember the one who is using.'

'And who is using?' said Belay.

Glasson stared at me. 'You,' he said.

'So?' I said.

'You never understood feelings,' said Glasson.

'No?'

'No,' said Belay, 'You've always been concepts.'

I stared back at Glasson. 'So?' I said.

'I could make you understand what you're above.'

'How?' I said.

'By sleep-depriving you- for one thing,' said Glasson.

'How?' said Belay.

'By bombarding your tent with unbearable sound.'

'I was sleep-deprived,' said Belay.

'Yes?' I said.

'Yes,' said Glasson.

'Who by?' said Belay.

'My mother.'

'Explain,' I said.

'She would stay up into the small hours every night during my adolescence watching her films and listening to her music.'

'And?' I said

'I would never get any sleep, I would wake up feeling painfully exhausted. I fell asleep in class.'

'Perhaps your mother was unwell,' I said.

'She was obviously on coke,' said Belay.

'Why d'you say that, Belay?' said Glasson.

'Most drunks fall asleep pretty quickly,' said Belay, 'it's the drunks with lines in their cigarettes that make the noise later

'So you want me to understand sleep deprivation?' I said.

'I want you to understand a lot worse,' said Glasson.

'Such as?' I said.

'Electric staples.'

'Yes, I've heard of them,' said Belay.

'Go on!' I said. 'What are electric staples?'

'These are things you are forced to swallow and electrical pain lances through the inside of your body.'

'How do you know that?' I said.

'Because I went through them,' said Glasson.

'Who did that to you?' I said. 'Your father?'

'No, a woman,' said Glasson.

'Which woman?' I said.

'A woman I asked to annihilate everyone else for me.'

'Why would you ask her to do that?' I said.

'I wanted someone who could beat everyone.'

'Why?' I said.

Glasson smiled ruefully. 'I guess I was trying to be on top.'

'And?' I said.

'She annihilated me first,' said Glasson.

'So what happened?' I said.

Glasson snivelled. 'She drove the electric staples into my skull.'

'And?'

'She made me swallow a few staples.'

'And?' I said.

'And for five seconds my head was being electrocuted.'

Belay peered into an semiopaque past that was confounding him. 'Yes, I remember that.'

'Of course he knows it,' I said, 'but he doesn't know that he knows that he knows it.'

'Eh?' said Belay.

'What do you mean?' said Glasson.

'I know what you did, Glasson,' I said.

'What did I do?' said Glasson.

'Yes,' said Belay, 'what did he do?'

'Don't listen to this, Belay,' I said.

'So what happened next?' said Belay.

'When I went home, I was drinking beer-'

'Which beer?' said Belay.

'Stella Artois.'

'And?' said Belay.

'I didn't know what was happening at the time but the insides of my body were being made up of electric sensations.'

I decided to push Glasson to reinforce my point. 'You're making this up.'

Glasson's face burned up.

Belay flinched slightly. 'I don't think he is, Ewald.'

I kept pushing. 'Yes, he is. He's confabulating.'

Glasson snarled. 'What the hell does that mean?'

'Exactly,' I said, 'you can't remember.'

'Of course I remember,' said Glasson. 'I really want you to feel it- and all the other events.'

'Why?' I said.

'In order that you understand,' said Glasson.

'I can understand, Glasson,' I said. 'I don't need to be subjected to mammoth pain in order to accomplish that.'

Glasson fortified his stare. 'Of course you do.'

'Why?' I said.

Glasson cast me an exasperated look. 'You wouldn't be justified.'

'Why do I need justified?' I said.

'Because,' said Glasson, 'you weren't able to make the decisions you made.'

'It doesn't take pain to make decisions, Glasson,' I said.

Glasson smiled indignantly. 'No, that's correct. It doesn't take pain to make the decisions you made, but it does take pain to justify the decisions you made.'

'Yes,' said Belay, 'I think Glasson has a point.'

I levelled at Glasson. 'Well, put it this way, Glasson, I'm not going through it.'

'Why not?' said Glasson.

'It's stupid and completely unnecessary,' I said.

Glasson gazed at me derisorily. 'What you mean is that you're too cowardly to go through it.'

'No, I could go through it,' I said, 'but what would it achieve? I mean really?'

'It would achieve parity.'

'And this was done to you?' I said.

'Of course it was,' said Glasson.

'Where?'

'I don't need your countermining analysis.'

'No, but you do have to prove the point,' I said, 'you can't just make claims.'

'That's not difficult for me, judge,' said Glasson. 'I am well-defined.'

'You want me to feel the way you did?' I said.

'I want you understand why you couldn't afford to judge me,' said Glasson.

I waved my head slowly. 'I had all the concepts for it.'

'Yes, I can believe that,' said Glasson, 'but you didn't have any of the experiences.'

'I don't need tortured, Glasson,' I said, 'to dechiper the difference between murder and torture.' I stomped my foot. 'Anything else?'

Glasson signalled at various objects. 'You see these things?'

'Yes,' I said, 'that's a teapot, those are teabags, and that's a portable stove.'

'Yes,' said Glasson, 'I will put them on.'

Belay was still re-composing himself.

'Are we having tea, Glasson, 'I said.

'I don't usually drink tea,' said Belay.

'No, you're not to drink the tea,' said Glasson.

'What then?' I said.

'You are to feel it,' said Glasson

'How can you feel tea?' said Belay.

'Oh, there is a way,' said Glasson.

Glasson Dorcha lit the portable stove with a match and placed it in the sand. After a few minutes the kettle was whistling.

'What now?' I said.

Glasson scowled at me. 'I could pour it slowly over your head.'

I peeked at Glasson. 'If you were cruel or mad yes.'

'Or inimical?' said Belay.

Glasson nodded at Belay. 'Resentful, yes.'

'And why would you do that?' I said.

'Again, to teach you a lesson,' said Glasson.

I gaped. 'In what?'

'Pain and justification,' said Glasson.

I squinted at Belay. 'Why would I need that?'

'Because you've caused and presumed so much of it,' said Glasson.

'How have I caused it?' I said. 'How have I presumed it?'

'You have shouted at people for years-' said Glasson.

'That's called an admonition,' I said.

'I know what it is-' said Glasson.

'And you have stolen their money, and-' said Glasson

'Just how have I stolen their money?' I said.

'You have had so many illegal transactions,' said Glasson, 'You have billed clients for work not undertaken, you have billed rich clients on behalf of poor clients, you have broken so many contracts and kept the money, you-'

'You can't possibly prove any of that Glasson,' I said.

Belay leaned back slightly, his eyes whirling. 'Can you prove that, Glasson?

'Yes, I can,' said Glasson.

'How?' I said.

'The dead man said so,' said Glasson.

I gawked at Glasson. 'Who?'

'The brother,' said Glasson.

'You mean Andrew McLean?' I said.

Glasson smiled superiorly. 'Yes.'

'Even if I had, Glasson,' I said, 'it would have been in the name of justice and the social order.'

Glasson gnarled. 'It is in the name of ignorance and academic presumption.'

'So what exactly would happen, Glasson,' I said, 'if you poured that tea pot slowly over my head,' I said.

'You would squeal, whimper,' said Glasson. 'Tears would roll down your face.'

'And then what?' I said.

'Your right to punish would go,' said Glasson.

'What else?' I said.

'You see this?' said Glasson.

'Yes,' said Belay, 'it's a pen.'

'Have you any idea how painful it is to be struck with one?'

'No,' I said. 'Do you?'

'You recoil violently,' said Belay.

'How would you know, Belay?' I said.

Once again, Belay seemed to peer into a semi-opaque past, alcoves of memories opening up. 'I seem to remember an electric shock pen,' said Belay.

Glasson pulled out a small pouch from his pocket containing white powder.

I flinched slightly. 'What is that?'

Glasson glowered. 'It's coke.'

I squinted at Glasson. 'Why's it not a dark liquid pouch, then?'

Belay sighed with exasperation. 'He means cocaine.'

I gasped. 'That's illegal.'

'I want you to take it,' said Glasson.

I shrunk back slightly. 'What will that do to me?'

Glasson sneered at me. 'You see, you don't know everything.'

'So?' I said.

'It will make you feel powerful,' said Glasson.

'I don't need to be powerful, Glasson,' I said, 'I need to be fair.'

'You don't need to be fair now,
you need to be inquisitive.'

'Well, be fair enough to smoke this joint.'

'He's got a point,' said Belay.

I sighed. 'Very well.'

I smoked the joint. After a few draws I felt an irresistible energy sweep through my body. The moments passed...

'What's happening, Ewald?' said Belay.

I swirled. 'I feel amazing.'

I saw a man grinning at me. 'Yes, you do.'

Suddenly, I snapped. 'You were never good enough to employ me.'

'Here we go again.'

Eventually, I emerged from my phantasmagoria.

'How do you feel now?' said Glasson.

I gulped. 'I feel desperate.'

Glasson shook his head meanly. 'No, you don't.'

'What do you mean?' I said.

'You've smoked your whole life, cocaine doesn't cause a crash at your stage.'

'How would you know?' I said.

'I've watched people,' said Glasson.

'And?'

'You felt very powerful but you didn't crash.'

'Why?' I said.

'You're a clog.'

'Meaning?'

'Your brain doesn't respond the same way.'

'I think he's right,' said Belay.

'No, I'm not,' I said. 'My brain might clog, but it unwinds itself.'

Glasson grabbed a cup and poured a liquid into it.

'What is that?' I said.

'That is called mushroom soup,' said Glasson.

'We've done that before,' I said.

'Fair enough,' said Glasson. 'You remember it though?'

'Of course I remember it,' I said, 'it was the single most painful experience of my life.'

'What happens again?' said Belay.

'You hallucinate auditorial and visually,' said Glasson. 'You have petrifying diarrhoea. You vomit profusely. Your whole body cramps.'

Belay was still in a mist. 'Yes, I think that happened to me as well.'

'And you see this?' said Glasson.

'Yes, it's a tablet. What is it?'

'It is a giant pain pill.'

'It's obviously illegal,' I said. 'What would happen?'

'You would see in six dimensions, the room would swirl around you, you would scream for an ambulance, you would feel unimaginable sick. You would go blind and boil.'

'How do you know this?' I said.

Belay smiled compassionately. 'It was obviously done to him,' said Belay.

Glasson Dorcha stared at me with scorn. 'You are a very, very old man, Wren. You look like a cryogenic.'

'I am hardly a frozen corpse, Glasson,' I said.

'You put me away.'

I sighed. 'Yes, I did and I know why I did it.'

'Why?' said Glasson.

'You were taking all manner of illegal drugs,' I said.

'But it's okay for him to take them.'

I scowled at Belay. 'I have never approved of your drug-taking.'

Glasson Dorcha spat. 'You were threatened by your own prejudice.'

'He's worse than you, Belay,' I said.

Glasson frowned. 'At least this second fiddle man gets some of the in-between.'

'Are you trying to say my friend is homosexual, Glasson?' I said.

'No, he doesn't need to. You are a putrefying monster, Wren. But you're still too ignorant to see it.'

'What do you mean?'

'Your eccentric friend obviously wants to get you back for assuming his brobdinagian ineluctable pain.'

'Belay?' I said.

'Yes,' said Ewald, 'You are very selfish.'

'In what way?' I said.

'You assume privilege and pain,' said Belay.

'Yes, he does,' said Glasson, 'And he assumes upholstery.'

'I have had my face slashed thanks to this man,' I said.

'Perhaps you needed to learn.'

'You mean I worked hard,' I said.

Glasson seared Ewald Wren with his smile. 'Accepted old man. And not disrespected.'

'There you go then.'

Glasson Dorcha unleashed his blood-shot eyes on Belay. 'As for you the omnipotent torture-judge employer, do you wish to wear the smile?'

'No, I don't,' said Belay, 'But I am very ready to respect yours.'

'Respect it, do you?'

'You're a convulsive pederast, Glasson.'

'I have never touched boys in my life,' said Glasson.

'That's not what we concluded,' I said.

'Who's we?' said Glasson.

'The jury. I just gave directions.'

'So you feel the decision was wrong?' I said.

'It wasn't wrong,' said Glasson, 'it was opprobrious.'

'What are you, then Glasson?' I said.

'He's a transexual,' said Belay.

Glasson Dorcha launched spit into my eyes. 'Fuck off, Wren!'

'Why do you speak to me like that?'

'I love males as well, but I don't fucking think I need an innocent wee boy or a pleasing looking young man. Do you?'

'No he doesn't,' said Belay.

'I suspect you need a commensurate woman who crawls all over you, although I consider time has passed.'

'We did evolve, Glasson,' I said.

'You decayed.'

'So what are you saying?'

'You are a pair of merciless upper-middle class cunts.'

'How are we that?' I said.

'One of you will do all the judging and the other will pay for it.'

Belay smiled wistfully. 'In that case, it's the ending.'

My eyelids whirled. 'What ending?'

Belay half-snored. 'He means Nembutal.'

I mopped my brow. 'What is that?'

'It's the drug that puts you to sleep,' said Glasson.

'Belay?' I said.

Belay smiled uneasily. 'Yes, it is, Ewald.'

'In any event,' said Glasson, 'it's the understanding first, girls.'

'Which is?' I said.

Glasson snarled. 'You're both unimaginable cunts gentlemen.'

I nearly fainted. 'Pardon?'

Belay leaned forwards. 'Yes, in what way?'

'I was in the court as well,' said Glasson.

'When?'

'That afternoon.'

'In 1995?' said Belay.

Glasson smirked konwingly. 'I know what happened, Belay- and so do you.'

'No, you don't,' said Belay, 'You're claiming it.'

'Yes,' I said, 'I don't even remember you being there.'

Glasson flared. 'You wanted to remunerate people that decided the timing of the departure and the manner of the ending for other people.'

'You know nothing, Glasson,' said Belay.

'You see, Ewald,' said Glasson, 'Even I know you're guilty.'

I glared indignantly. 'How could you possibly know, Glasson?'

'I listened in on your conversation with Chase,' said Glasson.

'And?' I said

'He said you were guilty,' said Glasson.

I muttered. 'Chase says a lot of things.'

Glasson switched his eyes to Belay. 'That's not what he knows.'

'I have never told you anything, Glasson,' said Belay.

'Even if he had, then he is mistaken,' said Ewald.

Glasson conceded a nod. 'I will admit that he is better than you, but you're both horrible bullies.'

'How?'

'You want to feel it all as power, Belay,' said Glasson, 'pay people to kill, where as you Ewald want to judge and hide behind academia.'

'Why are you confronting me?' said Belay.

'So?' said Glasson.

Glasson scowled at Belay. 'The reason you love a man who is nothing-'

'He's not nothing,' said Belay.

'Yes, he loves him,' I said.

'What you accept him now?' said Glasson.

'I fully admit,' I said, 'that I have had to get my head around alternative orientation,' I said.

'Does he look good, Belay?' said Glasson.

'I thought he did,' said Belay.

'He's on grass, Belay,' said Glasson.

'He's better than that,' said Belay.

'No,' said Glasson, 'He has two things working for him: the grass and the controlling chemical.'

'How would you know?' said Belay.

'Again Chase said,' said Glasson.

'Where is this going, Glasson?' I said.

'Retribution,' said Glasson.

CHAPTER FIFTY-FIVE

Retribution

Glasson looked daggers at Belay and I. 'You do realise what you two are?'

My eyes glazed over. 'Go on then, Glasson,' I said, 'What are we?'

Glasson loured at us. 'You're spoiled brats.'

Belay promulgated a look of exasperation. He glared quizzically at Glasson. 'I'm not spoiled, Glasson. I might have some useful resources but I assure you, my life's been inordinately torturous.'

'No more painful than mine,' said Glasson.

I nodded with assurance. 'Belay's right,' I said, 'He prides himself on pain, not privilege.'

Belay smiled reprovingly at Glasson. 'If anything, Glasson, you have all the stupid money.'

Glasson glared ignominiously. 'My grandfather earned it.'

'Your grandfather was utterly usurious,' I said.

Glasson smiled despondently. 'No, he was considerably more intelligent. In any case, the money means nothing to me.'

'Which surely makes you the spoiled brat,' I said.

'It's the person that counts,' said Glasson.

'Well, it would,' I said.

Glasson sniffed. 'Money buys objects, it doesn't buy people.'

I offered Glasson an understanding smile. 'And which people did you want?'

Glasson coggled his head. 'In the beginning?'

'Okay, in the beginning,' I said.

'One or two boys at school.'

'Who?'

'Craig and David.'

I dipped my head. 'I see. And what happened?'

'I loved Craig for two years but he didn't seem to notice,' said Glasson.

'Why not?'

'I guess he felt differently,' said Glasson, 'maybe he didn't expect it.'

'And what about David?'

'He said he didn't fancy me,' said Glasson.

'Why didn't he fancy you?' I said.

'He said he liked girls.'

'And what did you say?'

'I said I was a girl.'

'And what did he say?' I said.

'He said I didn't look like a real one.'

'And what did you say?' I said.

'I said I wanted to be his real one.'

'Glasson, I have to ask,' said Belay, 'in what universe am I spoiled?'

'You have reputation, laurels. You have influence, sway, clout. You get to control so many things- so many people.'

Belay smiled plainly at Glasson. 'I had to earn that, Glasson.'

'As an upper-middle-class brat.'

'No, through pain and understanding.'

A smile creased my lips. 'And how am I a spoiled brat?'

Glasson sighed. 'You've been given absolutely everything, judge.'

'Oh, yes,' I said, 'What is everything?'

'The wife, the children, the grandchildren, the money, the property, the respect, the importance, the health.'

I smiled sympathetically at Glasson. 'These things appeal to you.'

Glasson shrugged. 'They could have done.'

'Surely,' I said, 'You could have had these things if you had wanted them.'

'No, I couldn't.'

'Why not?'

'Your selfish plastic eugenical club rejected me.'

'How did we reject you?' said Belay.

'You were the high-earning heterosexual snobs.'

'And?' I said.

'You sided with the highest common denominators.'

'What?' said Belay.

'You went with your alpha males,' said Glasson, 'You take and take all the time.'

Belay levelled at Glasson. 'I'm sorry, Ewald, I tend to agree with you, Glasson.'

'No, Belay,' I said, 'the man's obviously insane.'

'He's not insane,' said Belay, 'She's very hurt.'

'What would you know, Belay?' said Glasson.

'I know what Belay doesn't know,' I said.

'What would you know?' said Glasson.

'I wouldn't push it, Glasson,' I said, 'Or Belay.'

'No?' said Glasson.

'No,' I said. 'And if it was revenge, you've already achieved that.'

Glasson scoffed. 'You went through one instance of poisoning, so what?'

'You put language and attitude before equitableness.'

'You're saying I'm selfish.'

'Incorrigibly so.'

'I have a wife and four children, Glasson,' I said, 'I'm used to sharing.'

'Only because you had the opportunity and capacity to share.'

'That comes from hard work.'

'That comes from fluke and over-piviledge.'

'I was clever, Glasson,' I said, 'and I studied hard.'

'Beyond description beats description.'

'So?'

'Glasson is correct, Ewald. 'How is he correct?'

'Actions speak louder than words.'

'Just a minute Glasson, you have money.'

'Yes, but nothing else.'

'What do you mean?'

'You have had a whole life of people and importance.'

'You are very unwell, Glasson,' I said, 'Your vices have gone to your brain.'

'Tell me this, Belay,' said Glasson. 'Do you fancy me?'

'I can see,' said Belay, 'that you you were a very handsome man.'

'I was a girl.'

'How did you know that?' I said.

'My feelings.'

'And what did your feelings tell you?' I said.

'They told me outwards I was a boy, but inwards I was a girl.'

'That must have been very confusing,' said Belay.

'Not to me it wasn't. What about with this smile?' said Glasson.

'It wouldn't have a made a difference to me,' said Belay.

'Why not?' said Glasson.

'I'm gay- I prefer men,' said Belay.

'So you would only have liked me with my original looks?' said Glasson.

'In essence, yes,' said Belay.

'What about you, Wren?' said Glasson.

'With or without the smile,' I said, 'I wouldn't have been attracted to you.'

'Yes,' said Belay, 'you can't blame the straight men or the gay men for your transexuality.'

'I've gone to a lot of trouble.'

'You mean you came all this way?' I said.

'No,' said Glasson, 'I mean I got everything done.'

'Everything done?' I said. 'He- I mean she means she's had the operation.'

'So?' I said.

'So,' said Glasson, 'I can only get what I needed from a transexual woman.'

'Explain that to me,' I said.

'A transexual male is built like a male but the thoughts and feelings are feminine.'

'Yes, so?' I said.

'Because I am built like a man, even the gay man sees him as a man.'

'I can see you as a woman, if you like Glasson,' said Belay.

'Go on then!'

'What d'you want exactly?' said Belay. 'A kiss?'

'No, I want fucked!' said Glasson.

'Gay as I am,' said Belay, 'I have never actually had that type of intercourse. I could kiss you, but I couldn't fuck you.'

'Nor could I,' I said. 'You're mad, Glasson.'

'I'm not mad,' said Glasson, I'm real.'

Belay shook his head. 'I have never slept with a woman before.'

'I could sleep with you,' said Glasson.

'Yes,' said Belay, 'that's because you're a woman now- or always have been.'

'Yes,' I offered, 'He would have to fancy you first.'

'I'm not a bigot, Glasson,' said Belay.

'No?' said Glasson.

'If anything,' I said, 'Belay's far too permissive.'

'In what way?' said Glasson.

'In terms of the social norms,' I said.

'What d'you mean?' said Glasson.

'He punishes the straight men,' I said.

'No, I don't, Ewald,' said Belay, 'I make them face their assumption.'

'Yes, but you don't have a face like this,' I said.

'I would have been prepared to bed you,' I said, 'if I wasn't a happiy married man.'

'It didn't stop you sleeping with Aileen,' said Glasson.

'How do you know that?' I said.

'Chase said,' said Glasson.

'Did he?' I said.

'Yes.'

'That was different.'

'How?'

'I was twenty.'

'Where as now you are?..' said Glasson.

'Seventy-eight,' I said.

'I thought you wouldn't have liked age discrimination,' said Glasson.

'No, I don't,' I said.

'Especially as a judge,' said Glasson.

'What do you know?' I said.

'I know you were forced into retirement. What matters to you, judge?'

'The important things,' I said.

'What would they be?'

'My wife and kids, of course.'

'And you, Belay?' said Glasson.

'The same. My father- and my nephew.'

'I never knew you had a nephew, Belay,' I said.

'You never asked, Ewald,' said Belay.

'Now,' said Glasson, 'I'm going to have to get you both back.'

'Back?' I said. 'What for?'

'You falsely imprisoned me.'

'It was the jury that did that,' I said, 'I merely decided sentence.'

'Your sentence was too harsh,' said Glasson.

'And what did I do?' said Belay.

'You paid the man who imprisoned me.'

'I was just doing my job,' said Belay.

Belay shook his head with irritation. 'And it's not just that.'

'No?'

'My grandfather was murdered.'

'So?' I said.

'Since I'm clearly neither a judge,' said Glasson, 'nor the the employer of one, I can hardly have you imprisoned, or pay to have you imprisoned.'

'Yes, and?' I said.

'I decided I would have you confined instead.'

'Confined how?'

'I thought I would take you to one of the forgotten parts of the Island and leave you stranded.'

'How?' I said.

Glasson gazed into the distance. ' Ah, there he is!'

'Glasson!' a man hollered.

'Whos is he?' said Belay.

'He's my boyfriend.'

The brick-house figure went towards us. A colossus of a man stared through me. He had a gruff voice. 'Hello,' he said.

Belay squinched slightly. He waved his hand. 'Hello, Sir.'

'I understand you are the man who put my boyfriend away,' said the boyfriend.

'I'm afraid your boyfriend broke the law,' I said.

'He had his lovely face spoiled,' said the boyfriend.

'That was nothing to do with me,' I said.

He glowered at Belay. 'And I understand you are the man who paid him to do that.'

'I got people paid,' said Belay. 'I didn't decide sentence.'

'You're gay?' I said.

'Wrong,' said the virtual ogre. 'I'm heterosexual. My girlfriend's very sensitive.'

The man clutched me and put me in handcuffs. He did the same with Belay. He dragged us both by the collars along the sands, with Glasson following, and bound us both to a tree.

'Come on, Glasson,' said Belay, 'let us go, I've never done any wrong to you.'

'By the time anyone finds you,' said Glasson. 'You will either have frozen to death or you will have starved.'

Glasson and his giant boyfriend left us roped side by side several times round the waist to a tree. 'Sorry judge, sorry employer. We must be off. My boyfriend and I wish to spend some quality time together.'

'Yes,' said a gruff voice.

'But we'll freeze,' I said.

'You'll soon learn the value of fairness,' said Glasson.

'We'll learn the value of cruelty, Glasson,' I said.

'Belay?' I said.

'We're fucked, Ewald,' said Belay.

'Well,' said the burly man, 'you shouldn't have hurt my girlfriend.'

'And by the way,' said Glasson, 'this arrangement is fairer than you think.'

'How?' I said.

'Now, it will take you a while,' said Glasson, 'but these are knives and these are the keys.' Glasson slipped the keys inside our trouser pockets. He placed the knives into our hands. 'You won't be able to access the keys unless you've cut through the ropes. It might take you forever since your hands are cuffed and the knives are small, and remember not to drop them since you won't be able to bend down to pick them up again. If you get stuck here are two bottles of Nembutal.' He stuffed them into our top pockets.

'What's in these bottles?' I said.

'Enough to give you both a peaceful ending,' said Glasson.

There was the unmistakable whirring of rotating blades revolving above the wet sand.

'I think that's our whirlybird, my love,' said the boyfriend.

'Yes, I think that's our egg-beater,' said Glasson.

'Shall we go?' said the boyfirend.

'Yes, I think we shall. We have nothing more to do here.'

I winced. 'You can't just leave us here, Glasson.'

'Yes, be reasonable, Glasson,' said Belay.

'I thought I had been.'

The tenuous pallid actinic radiation of the algid barren inch crumpled into a biome of ceaseless murk, a federal agency of resist-less shadows, launching into the blazing furnaces of the tempestuous downfall and propelling into the infinite void all manner of disabling doubts in our anguished minds, inflicting fearsome tremulousness within our enfeebling bodies, evoking intense trepidations in our quivering hearts, and provoking serious doubts in our destroyed souls. My racing heart plumped and I could facilely perceive that Belay was relinquishing his heretofore consistent inured strength. The savage whipping squall deracinated great clumps of the thick wet shingle and sprayed a mist of detritus into the air. The entire conglomeration of flora on the island, including the leafy fern and the coarse bracken shimmered like an endless procession of an antagonised ant colony. The merciless inundation rocketed fierce bullets into the sodden earth. Glasson Dorcha and his behemoth of a boyfriend Alexander abandoned us, leaving us to whatever fate might befall us. The dismal vaults of heaven rent asunder, stentorian thunder clapping in a celestial claque of heartless glee and unpitying Schadenfreude. Boiling purple forks of lightning jabbed every corner of the forgotten soil. For a singular moment, Glasson and Alexander gazed deeply into each other's eyes, as if sharing something communal, something important, something meaningful- a knowledge, a joke, a secret-something only they knew. They enfolded tightly and warmly, desoculated and smirked together before forsaking us. I peeked at Belay. I had never seen my friend look so out of his comfort zone. His eyes were sunken and forlorn. He scraped his scalp and squeezed his chin. Enormous mental strain embossed his face. We watched aghast as the helicopter door swung open, ricocheting on its new-fangled hinges.

'Mr Dorcha,' a respectful voice said.

'Yes, captain,' said Glasson.

'Are you coming aboard, Mr Dorcha?'

'Yes, captain,' said Glasson, 'We are.'

The behemoth grinned at Glasson. 'I love you, Glasson Dorcha.'

'I love you as well,' said the behemoth.

Against the thrashing wind and lacing rain, Glasson and his boyfriend dipped inside the helicopter. Alexander slammed the door shut. The nimble air craft hoisted neatly from the ground and then coiled into the air in a manoeuvre of pre-engineered anomie and they whirled skywards and homewards, leaving my friend and I to our unimaginable doom.

PART E

Conclusions and Recommendations; Deductions

CHAPTER FIFTY-SIX

My Bench

It was late. Everyone had gone home. The security guards had been told they could leave. Belay had passed several hundreds of pounds in multi-coloured cash notes their way.

The male guard glimpsed at me. He seemed to leer. I flinched. I could not recognise him and he certainly did not remember me. He was obviously one of Belay's new recruits. He peeked at Belay. 'Are you sure, Sir?'

Belay smiled sternly. 'Yes, you are sure.'

The female guard nodded firmly at Belay. 'We return tomorrow, Sir?'

Belay smiled respectfully. 'Yes, madam, of course.'

'Thank you, Sir,' said the female guard.

Belay opened up his arms. 'This was your room, Ewald.'

I glinted at the moon outside, the stars above and smiled wistfully. 'Yes, it was, Belay.'

Belay pushed out his mouth. 'It was your favourite room.'

'Yes, it was.'

'And?'

'And what?'

Belay shrugged. 'How does it feel now?'

I heaved a heavy sigh. 'It's not quite the same.'

Belay arched his brows. 'No?'

'No.'

'Why is it not quite the same?'

I lowered my head. 'You ejected me from it.'

Belay nodded with understanding. 'And what did that do?'

I looked around plaintively. 'It has contaminated the atmosphere.'

Belay pressed his head. 'What was the atmosphere, Ewald?'

'It was one of importance, you used to be someone.'

'You don't feel important? You're not someone?'

'Not now, no.'

'What do you feel then?'

I sighed. 'Free.'

'Free?'

'Yes.'

'Why is that?'

'I was made to learn life rather than obligation.'

'Rather than duty?'

I waved my head. 'No, the duty's still there, it's just I don't need to do the things I used to do.'

'What do you have to do?'

'I have to satisfy Chase. I have to save my family.'

'Would he do it?'

'Yes, he would.'

'How do you know?'

'The man held me at knife-point, Belay. He had me going everywhere, doing everything.'

'So?'

'He made it perfectly clear what he would do.'

'So?'

'The trust has gone, Belay.'

Belay shrugged. 'Why has that happened?'

'You felt I had done things I hadn't done.'

'I did come back for you.'

'Yes, I realise that.'

'I rescued you from the edge.'

'Yes, I'm very grateful for that.'

'I was also with you when Glasson trapped us.'

'Of course.'

'We could have frozen to death.'

'Yes.'

'We could have starved.'

'Yes, but he gave us a way out, didn't he?'

'He gave us two ways out.'

'He put the bottles of Nembutal into our hands. We could have died together that evening.'

'Yes.'

'He also gave us a way of extricating ourselves.'

'Yes, he gave us the keys.'

'Yes.'

'He was giving us a choice.'

'Yes, we could either live or die.'

'He also arranged the way home.'

'Yes, once we had found the keys, a man arrived.'

'Yes.'

'He made sure a boat picked us up. He made sure the boat would take us back to the boat yard.'

'What do we do?'

'He's no angel but he has shown signs of fairness.'

'So?'

'So when I judged him, he had taken all manner of drugs.'

'Yes, I know. He was in our court. He was being represented by the brother.'

'So you will know he had disfigured people, many of the cunts in Glasgow.'

'Yes.'

'Why do you think he had done that?'

'To perpetuate his habit, to vaunt the transferred dominance of his father.'

'Scot Dorcha?'

'Yes.'

'Why would he need to do that?'

'Because his father gave him no credit.'

'And?'

'He wanted to show he could beat our blend of justice.'

'You mean the justice we shared?'

'What are you looking for, Belay? I was poisoned, Belay. I was tortured. I had my face slashed.'

'Yes, at seventy-eight.'

I returned Belay's question to him. 'How does it feel to you, now?'

Belay gazed out of the window and peered into the same pale vaparous moon that was slowly evanescing. 'It's not the same to me either.'

I smiled complaisantly. 'Why's it not the same?'

'It's not as affordable as it once was.'

'Why not?'

'They don't pay me the way they used to.'

'Who?'

'The banks.'

'Why not?'

'Because they think I am no longer entitled to pay for justice.'

'Why not?'

'They don't think I suffer enough now.'

'I see.'

'You do?'

'Yes, I actually know what happened to you.'

'And where do you think this sufferance came from?'

Belay shivered. 'Horrible men.'

I smiled knowingly.'

'Yes, Belay. I actually know what happened to you?'

Belay glared at me suspiciously. 'You have not the slightest conception of what happened to me.'

I coughed into my fist discretely. 'I beg to differ.'

'Oh?'

'Yes.'

'So?'

'You were sleep-deprived as an adolescent.'

Belay glinted at me quizically. 'Yes, that's correct.'

I smiled sadly. 'You also had electric stamples drilled into your head. You were forced to swallow some electric staples. The switch was flicked and you were elecrocuted from the insides.'

A memory of choler surged through Belay's tired mind. 'That's precisely what Glasson was claiming.'

'Yes.'

'So?'

'I know that happened to you as well.'

Belay regarded me with increasing incredulity. 'What else do you know?

'Yes, you toppled fully loaded kettles of boiling water over your head.'

'Again, that's what Glasson claimed. 'Why would I do that?'

'You were incredibly drunk, you were self-harming. You also tipped a kettle of boiling water onto your legs. You had been imbibing copiously.'

'And?'

'You bounced out of bed, danced unevenly in shock, and perceived incredible strength.'

Belay's hardened facial expression became more bemused.

'And you had contents of a kettle of boiling water trickled slowly over your head.'

'You know that as well?'

'Yes, you were squealing, whimpering.'

Belay's mind ghosted into the deep and distant past. Tears pricked his eyes.

'Yes, tears were rolling down your face.'

'Who would do that?'

'Someone who resented you.'

'What else?'

'You smoked a loaded joint of cocaine, perceived astonishing power, and endured a devestating crash, causing you acute feelings of despair.'

Belay smiled defererentially. 'You know more than I thought.'

'Yes. Now, you were also slipped a pain pill-'

'Which pain pill?'

'You think it was acid but you're not sure.'

'And?'

'The room around you whirled round and round. You descried a kaleidoscope of colours. You were opened up, raped and sexually tortured.'

'The tears which had been pricking Belay's eyes leaked and strolled down his face.'

'You went blind.'

Belay sniffed. 'Yes, for a long while.'

'You also perceived images of multi-coloured ghouls crawling and gibbering in and out of vision.'

'Yes, that was the worst experience.'

'What else do you know, Ewald?'

'You swallowed sixty-four tablets of paracetamol.'

'Why would I do that?'

'You had developed a massive nicotine craving and went mad.'

'Yes?'

'You sat down and waited to die. You thew everything up into the bath. You vomitted for several days continuously.'

'Anything else?'

'You had a violent collapse in your kitchen. The news was blaring out from the television and you crumpled to the floor.'

'Yes, it was five seconds.'

'Why did that happen?'

'You had been injected with alcohol.'

'Why did that happen?'

'Because somebody was killed.'

'What else?'

'You had a grass overdose and were poisoned with magic mushrooms. You suffered a a giant auditory and visual hallucination. You endured shocking diahorrea in a fit of shivers. You perceived feelings of pandemonium, you vomitted profusely, you had an all over body cramp, and you passed out in pain.'

'Yes, I remember.'

'You were also zapped with the electric shock pen. You recoiled violently and snapped at your perpretrator.'

'And?'

'You believe you had three heart attacks.'

'Yes, only one was diagnosed.'

'You were sectioned under the Mental Health Act and recovered in hospital for two months. When you came out, you came off the anti-psychotics for a period, you imbibed copious amounts of vodka, developed intense paranoid schizophrenia. You saw a sea of faces roar across your line of vision. Each time you closed your eyes, the images got worse. Eventually you were hurled up into the corner of the ceiling.'

'And?'

'After smoking coke for so long, you woke up one morning and the back of your brain went. You depersonalised and lost also your feelings, including your capacity for alcohol. This panicked you into researching Nemutal.'

'Then what?'

'You went back on it but...'

'But?'

'Your brain suffocated.'

'And what was that?'

'You had a stroke.'

Belay gazed at me as if I had lit upon points that had never been understood. 'I never told you any of this.'

'No.'

'So how do you know this?'

'The man you love told me.'

'Ecxuse me?'

'Yes.'

'James?'

'Yes, James.'

'You've met him.'

'Yes. He told me what you told him.'

'When did you meet him?'

'Shortly after we spoke in the restaurant.'

'How did you find him?'

'You told me where you met him, where the house was.'

'And?'

'He told me everything.'

'So?'

'I know what happened.'

'Which was?'

'Glasson transferred all his pain on to you.'

'Why would he do that?'

'Your father assisted in the murder of his grandfather.'

'My father?'

'Yes.'

Belay shook his head. 'You don't know who my father was, Ewald.'

'No.'

'You don't even know who I am.'

'No, I still don't know your second name.'

'So?'

'Someone else was on that boat.'

'How do you know?'

'Something Glasson said, when I was being poisoned in my study.'

'Which was?'

'He said: "*You put me away, judge. And as for the the man you respect, his father helped kill my grandfather.*"'

'What did he mean?'

'I infer he meant that your father, Belay helped kill Jack Dorcha.'

'Who did he mean?'

'I don't know. It could have been any of the men on that boat. Hell, it could have been my father.'

'You're trying to suggest we could be brothers?'

'Possibly half brothers, but I guess we would bear some resemblance.'

'How would Glasson have done this? Sleep-depriving me for example?'

'By intimidating your mother.'

'How?'

'By telling her what would happen to her son.'

'And what would happen?'

'She would lose you. 'As for the water, electrical, and chemical tortures, I think Glasson's associates did that.'

'I don't know whether to be impressed or deflated.'

I bobbed my head. 'No. You see, Belay. As much as you purported to understand me, I have learned to understand you as well.'

'And?'

I smiled sympathetically. 'I'm terribly sorry, Belay, you have been massively abused.'

Belay nodded his head sadly with understanding. He switched the subject. 'So who do you think did it, Ewald? Who do you think killed the brother and his wife?'

I paused for thought.

CHAPTER FIFTY-SEVEN

Obiter Dicta

Belay thrummed his fingers against the table. 'Well?'

'I'm not sure.'

'You mean you can't decide?'

I smiled feebly. 'I don't make decisions any more, Belay.'

'No?'

'No.'

'Why not?'

'You retired me.'

'So?'

'My role is different now.'

'How?'

I chuckled pigeon-heartedly. 'I'm a sleuth rather than a judge.'

'So?'

I squeezed my chin. 'The truth is I really don't know.'

'You don't?'

'Not for sure.'

'No.'

'But you must have some idea, surely.'

'Of course I do.'

'Who was the first the person you investigated?'

'The nephew.'

'And?'

'I observed that he enjoys freedom and craves romance.

I discovered that his mother and father had died in common calamity when he was a small child.'

'So?'

'I entertained the possibility that the brother and wife might have been responsible.'

'How?'

'I don't know.'

'But?'

'If they had been responsible, this might have provided the motive.'

'How would he have done it?'

'No idea.'

'But?'

'He was embarking upon his final year in law.'

'So?'

'He would have been twenty-one.'

'So?

'He wouldn't even have been born yet in 1995.'

Belay nodded his head attentively. 'Okay, so who was the next person you investigated?'

'The rivalrous uncle.'

'And?'

'I discovered he harboured a very important secret.'

'What secret?'

'I don't know. But whatever it was he had kept it from his quixotic nephew. Ever since he took him in after his parents' deaths.'

'When was that?'

'When he was six.'

'And?'

'I entertained the possibility the rivalrous uncle might have killed the brother and his wife.'

'Why?'

'In order to uphold the secret.'

'Why?'

'I imagined the secret might have destroyed the quixotic

nephew. I also imagined that the secret might have destroyed the relationship between the rivalrous uncle and his quixotic nephew.'

'Anything else?'

'Yes, I realised the rivalrous uncle was trying to buy affection from his quixotic nephew.'

'Why?'

'Out of guilt I suppose.'

'And?'

'I suspect the rivalrous uncle was being blackmailed over the secret.'

'What makes you suspect that?'

'Chase claimed that.'

'Why?'

'I'm not sure.'

'What else?'

'I discovered that the wife's brother Jarrod Fields knew the secret, whatever it was.'

'So?'

'Jarrod Fields might have told his sister.'

'So?'

'She might have told her husband, the brother. I conceived it was also possible that the disgruntled client had divulged the secret to the brother, his lawyer. I considered then that the brother had told his wife. And I entertained the notion that the rivalrous uncle knew about this.'

'How?'

'I can only speculate.'

'But thus?'

'Thus, the rivalrous uncle might have felt compelled to kill the brother.'

'To preserve the secret?'

'Indeed.'

'So?'

'The rivalrous uncle might have killed the brother and his wife.'

'To protect his quixotic nephew or himself.'

'Yes.'

'And?'

'And the disgruntled client revealed the address of his talented son.'

'Yes.'

'So what about the talented son?'

'When I investigated him, I formed the opinion that he had the most foul temper imaginable.'

'The temper for murder?'

'Yes, perhaps.'

'How?'

'He was overpowering his family, his daughter especially.'

'Why would the talented son have done it?'

'I thought it conceivable that he might have been getting the brother back for his father.'

'What had the brother done?'

'It was possible he had made a botch of his father's case.'

'What case?'

'A civil case.'

'And?'

'I suspect the brother had been trying to legalise his unusual capital gains.'

'Anything else?'

'Yes, the talented son had been deeply suspicious of his fiancée's relationship with one of her childhood female friends.'

'And?'

'His mother is dead. He has a daughter. He was competing in Eurovision. He was mistreating his daughter.'

'And?'

'The death of his mother had been put down to a fire.'

'But?'

'The aggrieved mother suspected that either the disgruntled client who had employed her to housekeep or his talented son had killed her.'

'Why?'

'She suggested this was because the disgruntled client's wife had given the talented son inadequate musical instruction, or that the talented son had given her brutal instruction and expelled his girlfriend from the house.'

Belay nodded again attentively. 'Who was most likely to have done it?'

I cringed. 'Apparently me.'

'Why would you have done it?'

'I ask myself the same question.'

'I told you about the executions.'

'And I told you, I had no recollection of that.'

'So who was most likely after that?'

'Alana was more likely first.'

'Why?'

'Chase believed so.'

'Why?'

'Because of an anonymous call, a tip-off.'

'And?'

'Having visited Alana, we both agreed that neither of us could be responsible.'

'But?'

'No buts, Belay. But what Alana did say is: "I did things other people weren't prepared to do".'

'Who else then? Who else might have killed the brother and his wife?'

'The overshadowed fiancée.'

'Why?'

'She had suffered.'

'How?'

'I don't know.'

'So?'

'She had done something because she was the battered niece's friend.'

'And?'

'I thought the brother and his wife's family might have rejected her.'

'Why?'

'I think she had become aware of abuse going on in the house.'

'What abuse?'

'Drugs, I think.'

'What else?'

'Extra-marital behaviour.'

'What extra-marital behaviour?'

'I'm not sure.'

'How would the overshadowed fiancée have done it?'

'I consider poisoning. Either that or bludgeoning.'

'What makes you suspect bludgeoning?'

'It would have been one of the few ways a young child could overpower an adult.'

'So?'

'Who next?'

'The battered niece.'

'And?'

'She was very sarcastic towards her husband. She demonstrated a cold indifference.'

'Why would she have done it?'

'I think the wife, her mother, was abusing her.'

'Why?'

'I'm not sure.'

'But?'

'I think she was on drugs.'

'How would she have done it?'

'Possibly poisoning again.'

'What with?'

'Mushrooms.'

'Anything else?'

'I think someone might have attempted to suffocate her brain.'

'Who?'

'I don't know.'

'But?'

'It might have been the habituated cousin.'

'How?'

'With a bad packet of cigarettes.'

'Who next?'

'There was also the aggrieved mother.'

'And?'

'I think she might have sought to help her daughter out or personally resented the brother and his wife.

'Why?

'The brother apart from rejecting her daughter, had been her lawyer. She had cleaned for the disgruntled client. Perhaps the brother lost her case.'

'Anything else?'

'She had insinuated that her former employer the disgruntled client or his son had killed their wife and mother.

'How might she have done it?'

'I think she could have poisoned them.'

''Who next?'

'There is the hen-pecked husband.'

'And?'

'He was hiding something. He might have sought to protect his girlfriend.'

'From what?'

'Abuse.'

'How old would he have been?'

'He would have been nine.'

'Who next?'

'The habituated cousin.'

'Why?'

'I don't know.'

'But.'

'I think he had done something to the overshadowed fiancée.'

'What?'

'I don't know.'

'But.'

'I discovered that he was attempting to blackmail her.'

'What else?'

'I discovered he was going to go after the quixotic nephew

for money. He was also after his younger brother, the troubled cousin.'

'Why would he have killed them?'

'I think he was on drugs, as well as sexually jealous of his aunt.'

'How would he have done it?'

'Probably with a lethal overdose.'

'Who next?'

'The troubled cousin.'

'Why?'

'I'm not sure.'

'But?'

'I think he believes the brother and his wife abused him.'

'How?'

'I don't know.'

'How old would he have been?'

'Five.'

'How would he have done it.'

'Possibly a putty knife.'

'Why a putty knife?'

'He is an artist.'

'And?'

'He thought he might have killed his father.'

'And?'

'He was planning to use the nephew for money by pretending to be gay and available. He had checked in to the Hilton hotel in Aberdeen.'

'Who next?'

'The home-loving mother.'

'Why?'

'I don't know.'

'But.'

'I consider she might have killed the wife for concealment.'

'For concealing what?'

'She believed the brother had molested her sons. She also believed that the brother might have killed her husband.'

'How might she have done it?"

'Given her family came from textiles, she might have smothered them.'

'Anything else?'

'Yes, she claimed that the brother's daughter was not his.'

'Susie.'

'Yes.'

'Who else?'

'The disgruntled client.'

'Well, it gets back to the third suspect.'

'I think the brother might have lost his case. I also think he might have been in love with the wife.'

'What else?'

'He knew all about mushrooms. He drank copious amounts of alcohol. He was disappointed by his his son-'

'The talented son?'

'Yes.'

'And he resented his son's partner. He abhorred his granddaughter. He felt that his son's fiancée was spoiling his investment in his son's musical career. He worked on his house, in the garden, and on the boat. He fell for a young woman called Samantha.'

'Why would he have killed them?'

'The brother was his lawyer. The brother may have messed up his attempts to legalise his unusual capital gains. I really think he was in love with the wife.'

'How would he have done it?'

'He would probably have used his gun cane.'

'And?'

'I formed the impression that he was not a very nice man, something of a persona non grata.'

'How?'

'And what about the wife?'

'I thought given that he knew so much about plants, and in particular mushrooms, he might have poisoned the wife.'

'Who next?'

'The arrogant doctor.'

'I think his son was rejected.'

'How?'

'From the brother and his wife's house.'

'And?'

'I think the brother threatened to sue him in defamation. I also think the wife threatened to report him.'

'How would he have done it?'

'I presume fatal medicine.'

'Who next?'

'The bitter and twisted grandmother.'

'Why?'

'I'm not sure.'

'But?'

'I think it could have been to do with family reputation.'

'In what sense?'

'I think the brother threatened to ruin her son's career'

'And?'

'The wife had rejected her grandson from their house.'

'Why?'

'I'm not sure.'

'But?'

'I think he had come across abuse.'

'What abuse?'

'Drug abuse and extra-marital behaviour.'

'How?'

'I don't know.'

'Anything else?'

'She had had her jaw disabled with a baseball bat.'

'Why?'

'She had gotten members of the family to reject each other.'

'Who would have done that?'

'I suspected it would have taken a violent psychopath, most likely Glasson Dorcha.'

'Anything else?'

'I considered there might have been other suspicious deaths.'

'Whose deaths?'

'The disgruntled client's wife, the rivarous uncle's wife, the quixotic nephew's parents and the home-loving mother's husband.'

'Who would have killed the disgruntled client's wife?'

'I don't know.'

'But.'

'Perhaps the disgruntled client himself or his talented son.'

'And the rivalrous uncle's wife?'

'Perhaps someone she had replaced.'

'And the quixotic nephew's parents?'

'I don't know.'

'But.'

'I think either rivalrous uncle did it or one of his associates.'

'And the wife's brother?'

'There had been several men there that night in Rathnew 2003, including myself.'

'And?'

'I don't know.'

'Anything else?'

'I think there were some attempted murders.'

'Whose?'

'The battered niece, the aggrieved mother, the troubled cousin, the arrogant doctor, the rivalrous uncle, and the bitter and twisted grandmother...'

'The battered niece?'

'I don't know.'

'But?'

'But either someone gave her a bad packet of cigarettes or insecticide was applied to brain, or someone smothered her.'

'Go on.'

'As I had listened in to her fierce exchange with her husband at their rundown home in Keppochill, it had seemed, if not clear to her exactly, then at least realistic to her that her cigarettes had been tampered with. Being a life-long heavy smoker myself, I had been aware that cigarettes could indeed starve the brain. She had seemed to believe that her older cousin Mickey had done it. If that had been the case, he certainly had not intended to kill her, merely perhaps to injure her. As my visit to the boutique had shown, he was and had been on drugs. He had bitterly resented her for not having helping his father.

'The aggrieved mother?'

'The aggrieved mother?'

'I don't know.'

'But?'

'Someone had obviously attempted to burn her to death. I recalled the figure bolting away from the house.'

'So?'

'I had considered that it might have been the niece. I considered that she might have believed that her friend's mother had killed her father Andrew McLean. He had been Judith White's lawyer. Andrew McLean had failed to win her case. She had sued for unpaid earnings.'

'The troubled cousin?'

'I don't know.'

'But?'

'I thought about the pub brawl. The crowd had been furiously unhappy that Celtic had beaten Aberdeen. I knew the older cousin had wound them up. He had shot his mouth off that the sheep-shaggers were insulting devout Irish Catholics.'

'And?'

I thought about the Hilton Hotel. The younger cousin's brain had suffocated. I had considered that perhaps someone had put a pillow over his head, or that he had sprayed himself with insecticide or that he had had a bad packet. If someone had attempted to kill him, I believed his older cousin would have done it. He would have done it to avenge his brother's abandonment of their father.'

'The arrogant doctor?'

'I don't know.'

'But?'

'I thought about the niece's husband's father Doctor Reid and his plush house in Hyndland. Someone had tried to kill him. I believed the younger cousin might have attempted this.'

'The rivalrous uncle?'

'I don't know.'

'But?'

'I thought about the first suspect's bitter rival Albert Bennet. As he was waltzing in the attic in memory of his late wife Doris, the roof had caved in. I had not believed at the time that it had been a *damnum fatale*. I had believed it had been engineered by someone who wished the Uncle dead. I considered that the first suspect Hugh Sharp had done it. In that case, he would have been trying to eliminate the man who had stolen his girlfriend Samantha.'

'The bitter and twisted grandmother?'

'I don't know.'

'But?'

'I considered this might have been the niece. In that case, it would have been because she believed Jean Reid had killed her father Andrew McLean. I considered that she might have used aconite in a plate of mushrooms. It came from the plant Monkshood. Also knows as wolfs-bane, aconite leaves only one post-mortem sign, that of asphyxia as it cause arrhythmic heart function which leads to suffocation. Indeed the emperor Claudius was said to have been poisoned by his wife. I also considered, given the degree of violence, the talented son or Glasson Dorcha.'

Chase heavede a sigh as he squeezed his chin. 'What about the notorious Jack Dorcha?'

I tilted my head. 'I believe he was murdered.'

'By whom?'

'I don't know.'

'But?'

'From what Glasson Dorcha said, I think he was poisoned.'

'Who would have poisoned him?'

'I can only imagine Jaeger White or-'

'Why Jaeger White?'

'He supplied the food and beverages.'

'But?'

'There was also Peter Reid.'

'So?'

'He supplied the chemicals.'

'And?'

'I think he was stabbed.'

'Why d'you think that?'

'Again, something Glasson Dorcha said.'

'Which was?'

'"My father said he went for him, he smashed the bottled and drove the glass dagger into his chest."'

'Then?'

'I think they threw him overboard

'I see.'

'Yes, I think that's enough for tonight, I think I'll go home.'

Belay smiled at me. 'Okay, Ewald, as you wish.'

'Thank you.'

'Would you mind locking the old cupboard, I just have to finish up.

'Certainly, Belay.'

CHAPTER FIFTY-EIGHT

The Anfractuosity

I steadfastly fastened the old sacral closet. So much draconian and newfangled apparatus of left and right-winged justice metaphysics had been so cautiously hived away. It had been done so in a capricious correctional zeitgeist of the time. I traipsed bunglingly down all four levels of steps, taking care, despite my disarray, not to tumble. I stumbled into the front glass doors, squashing my nose. My furrowed purple-veined hands splayed all over the glacial squeaking glass. I straggled out of the once long-familiar but now estranged convulsive courthouse. I felt like a chaffy pettifogger, was burbling like an antsy apprentice. It was adverted to as a trainee solicitor now, of course. I felt as though I had wafer-thin maritime law seabed-level indentures. I felt like an outlawed and ostracised jurist with pithy legal documents for accreditation. I felt as though I had junior legal validations, which had been grubbily-thumbed and dog-eared, and were now going plumbing fixture yellow in a spiral of magenta plumes and indigo hoops, and rank maudlin academic self-remembrance and self-congratulation. I felt like a man with eristic and polemical deficiency and prepubescent chicanery, like a man with low-level technical competence and buckled Scot's law promises, like a man who once believed he had done everything, but now like a man who had everything to prove and prove again.

Indeed, like a non-identifiable noun, scrabbling in the

labyrinthine wynds of a confabulated memory to find its germane adjective; like an ossified verb flailing in the Stygian pleo-nasticty of obligese to deracinate its corresponding adverb; like a subject splaying its befouled fingers along a prison wall of muddled syntax to grasp its subservient object; like Scots law forest-familating to hunt down the equiperation of English law 'consideration' it never warranted; like a small-town classless legal practice desperately trying to fabricate transactions; like justice trying to reunite itself with fairness and forgiveness; clemency; lenience; anything which could be legally conceptualised as commensurate with that which could be reasonably condign; like fundamentalistic religion proselytising toward the spaghettification of oblivion; and like belief systems beyond re-incarnation cerebrating about mystifying alternative realities.

Yes, in these mortifying diffident moments, as I humilitously peered up into a dark abandoned sky; perceived a dull rain-lashed night, my humiliated senescent body offered gymnastics to subsidise my wounded mind. A cloak of shadows enshrouded me, as artificial light bristled my weary silver eyes.

As I hobbled from the egress, a figure accosted me. His blood-shot gimlet eyes bore down at me like a twin of revolvers. He held aloft a menacing blade which glinted like fire, like an oligarchy of steel works in the hissing flames of the pale indigo moon.

'Hello, Ewok!' said a familiar voice.

I pirouetted on the downfall-pounded pavement. I beheld the figure of a man with the familiar beard. I peered at him in the freezing gloom. 'Chase?'

The man shrugged matter-of-factly. Who else?'

I stumbled slightly. 'I thought you had deserted me.'

'Yes.'

'So?'

'I also offered you a break.'

I swallowed duteously. 'Yes, so you did.'

Chase eye-balled me. 'So?'

'So what?'

'Now, you've had the time, I expected you to have analysed the data, all the secrets you had discovered.'

I quivered. 'Yes.'

'I also expected you to have formulated your deductions.'

I almost squealed. 'Or what?'

Chase squeezed his brutal knife irascibly. 'I will purify my ultimatum. I will have you ruined, imprisoned, or worse still killed, or even worse, I will have your whole family killed. Does that make sense, Ewok?'

I peeked at the mushroom knife and flinched. 'Potentially, to a psychopath yes.'

Chase bowed his head. 'You think I'm a psychopath?'

'Yes, I think you're deeply disturbed.'

'Then you haven't learned anything.'

I shrugged ingenuously. 'What was I supposed to learn?'

'You were supposed to have learned about the anomalies.'

'Which anomalies?'

'That hard work was sufficient, that intellectual usurpations were subsidiary, that description was spurious and sophistic, and that beyond description was a knock-down argument.'

'In other words?'

'The language, whether verbal or written, subjugates to pain.'

I waved my head. 'That's a grossly inebriated argument, Chase; an irrational person's reasoning.'

'It's very real to some people, Ewok. I thought you understood asylum law.'

'Of course I do, that was my job.'

'Then you should understand how torture begets justification.'

'Yes, I see. You desiderate emotional proof.'

'No, I demand proof of sufferance.'

I exhaled with exasperation. 'Then look at my face, Chase.'

Chase smiled tolerantly. 'Yes, you look differently.'

I scowled at Chase. 'Of course I do, I've had my face slashed to ribbons.'

Chase nodded contentedly. 'Yes, I'm impressed. How did it feel?'

'It was torture.'

'The nick itself?'

'No, the nick itself was bearable but the toxic condition was exquisitely painful.'

'You mean you were poisoned?'

'Yes.'

'Who poisoned you?'

'Glasson Dorcha.'

'And Glasson Dorcha would be?'

'A ruthless gangster.'

Chase wiggled his head with what seemed to be understanding. 'I see, Ewok. Do you remember the deal?'

'It was hardly a deal, Chase, it was an outright ultimatum.'

'So?'

'So?'

'Who did it? Who killed my brother? Who killed my wife? Who killed my nephew's dad? Who killed my nephew's mum?'

I exhaled with forlornness. 'The essential truth of the matter is that I don't know.'

'No?'

'No, not for certain.'

'Why not?'

'The evidence is too flimsy.'

Chase glowered at me. 'Why is the evidence too flimsy?'

'For so many reasons.'

'Why?'

'Any of the suspects might have killed your brother and his wife, and there are so many ways it might have been done, and there are so many places where it could have been done.'

'So?'

'I know I didn't do it'

'How do you know that?'

'I would have remembered. I would have remembered then, Chase and I would remember now.'

'And?'

'I'm pretty sure that your second suspect Alana hadn't done it.'

'Why not?'

'I met her.'

'And?'

'She was very candid and sensible.'

'So?'

'I think it's most likely that the disgruntled client did it, or the rivalrous uncle, or some of the other suspects did it.'

'I see.'

'Yes?'

'I'm sorry, Ewok, I might just have to let you go again.'

I sniffed slightly. 'Again?'

'Yes.'

'But?'

'You're losing more than me.'

I trembled. 'What do you mean?'

'I have another way of hurting you, Ewok.'

'How?'

'You're losing an in-law.'

I gawked slightly. 'An in-law?'

'Yes.'

'I don't know about you, Chase with your cut-throat knife and your incessant comminations, but of course I'm an in-law.'

'I'm not religious, Ewok. But of course?'

'Yes, my whole life, has been about learning and obeying, practising and upholding, and defending and exculpating the law-'

'Why would the law need defended and exculpated?'

'Because the law has been vitiated too many times.'

'By whom?'

'By the people who didn't understand it.'

'And what were they to understand?'

'Hard work, cleverness, diligence, honesty, controls, discipline.'

'You mean academia?'

'No, I mean fair practice.'

'And what not?'

'Well certainly not being alienated from the law, entirely not being ostracised from society.'

'That's not what I mean.'

'No?'

'No.'

'What do you mean?'

'We are related, Ewok.'

I yawned. 'Related?'

'Yes.'

'Yes, I suppose we are.'

'You suppose?'

'If you mean as former captor and captive, then yes.'

Chase waggled his head. 'That's not what I mean.'

'Then what do you mean?'

'We are related through marriage, Ewok.'

'Through Marriage?'

'Yes.'

'I married Andrea, Chase and as far as I understand, being homosexual, you never married.'

'No, that's correct.'

'What then?'

'You remember Alainn?'

I staggered. 'Alainn?'

'Yes.'

'How would you possibly know of Alainn?'

Chase smiled sadly. 'She was the mother of my brother's wife.'

'Are you trying to say that your brother's wife Susanna McLean or Fields was Alainn's daughter?'

'Yes.'

'How?'

'Someone slept with Alainn.'

'Who?'

'Quite a number of men.'

'Which men?'

'Aiden Fields, Patrick Fields, Hugh Sharp and also you, Ewok.'

'How would you possibly know that?'

'My father told me.'

'Lewis McLean?'

'Yes.'

'And how would he know that?'

'My father was acquainted with all these men.'

'So?'

'I know you had sexual intercourse with Alainn.'

'How would you know that?'

'My father told me.'

'He did?'

'Yes.'

'How would your father know?'

'Aiden Fields told him.'

'How would he know?'

'Alainn revealed it to him.'

'What did she say exactly?'

'She said: "I'm sorry, Aiden, I don't know what to say, I just know that Susanna isn't yours"'

'And what did he say?'

'He said: "Of course she is."'

'And?'

'Alainn said: "I'm so very, very sorry, Aiden."

I recovered. 'Back up a second, Chase. Your brother was twenty-five when he went missing?'

'Yes.'

'In 1995?'

'That's correct.'

'And how old was Susanna?'

'About the same age.'

I shook my head. 'Then you're completely wrong, Chase.'

'How?'

'What happened between Alainn and I happened in 1962- just before my friend Patrick left for the Congo.'

'It also happened in 1956. You were sixteen.'

'Yes, that's correct.'

'Your father told you this?'

'Yes.'

'That means your brother's wife couldn't possibly have been the same age in 1995. She would have to have been ten years older.'

'Yes, that's right.'

'So?'

'I think you slept with her again.'

'I think I would remember that.'

'Not necessarily.'

'What do you mean?'

'I think you got inebriated and forgot.'

'I don't drink, Chase- I never have.'

'No, but I think you were involuntarily intoxicated.'

'What makes you think that?'

'Something my father said.'

'Which was?'

'"She wanted to give him something back."'

'Meaning?'

'Alainn rejected you in 1962.'

I waved my head. 'No, no.'

'Yes. How old were you, Ewok? In 1962?'

'I was twenty-two.'

'And how old was Alainn?'

'She was seven years older. She was twenty-nine.'

'And what happened?'

'She said we couldn't be together. She said she was betrothed to someone else.'

'Who?'

'An older man.'

'How old was he?'

'The same age as Alainn: twenty-nine.'

'Yes, who was he?'

'I'm not sure.'

'He was the disgruntled client.'

'The man whose mansion we visited, the man I subsequently investigated.'

'Yes.'

'Okay, so what are you saying?'

'I'm saying you had another child.'

All my paternal memories came flooding back: David, Melissa, Martin, Lilly... 'Another child?'

'Yes.'

'The numbers don't stack up, Chase.'

'No, they wouldn't under that data analysis.'

'But?'

'I think you had sexual intercourse with her again?'

'When?'

'In 1972.'

I peeked at Chase. 'What are you trying to tell me, Chase.'

'I'm sorry, Ewok. My brother's wife was your daughter.'

I stuttered. My eyes pricked with tears. 'That- that's impossible.'

'No, I'm afraid it's true.'

'But I would have known.'

'I think you did know but you refused to believe it.'

I sniffed slightly. 'I was conscious of it as a possibility.'

'Yes, there you go then.'

'You're sure?'

'Yes.'

'You're saying I lost a daughter.'

'Yes.'

I could feel all the years of suppression welling up within me. I broke down. 'I loved my father.'

'Ealdahach Wren?'

'Yes.'

'I loved my father as well.'

'Lewis McLean?'

'Yes.'

Chase looked me in the eye and scrutinised my face.

'What does that smile mean to you, Ewok?'

I cringed. 'Mortification.'

Chase chuckled pigeon-heartedly. 'Anything else?'

I scratched my hoary head. 'I imagine it has multiple symbolic meanings.'

'Oh, yes?'

'Yes.'

'What would they be?'

'To me, it would obviously symbolise the assertion of male dominance, the emasculation of a rival male, the usurping of power, the exposition of mortality.'

'What else?'

'I think it also symbolises the forfeiture of sexual prowess; represents impotence.'

'Even at your age.'

'Especially at my age. I think it's also designed to foment obloquy and social expulsion. It also serves, I'm quite sure, as an ever-present reminder of peril.'

Chase nodded respectfully. 'Very deep, Ewok.'

'Thank you.'

Chase averted his gaze for a moment. 'So who's won, then?'

'Who's won?'

'Yes.'

'What do you mean?'

'Me; you; your former employer Belay; the Glasgow gangster Glasson Dorcha; the murderer or murderers' or one of the suspects?'

'It really depends on what you mean.'

'What would you mean?'

'I would say in terms of the focal point, the cynosure of this entire burlesque, the murderer has won.'

'Yes?'

'Yes.'

'Why?'

'Well, neither you, me, Belay, Glasson Dorcha, or one of the suspects seem to know for certainty who did it.'

'I told you, I think it was you.'

'Yes I know. You think it was me but you don't know that for a fact- and I don't even know that.'

'So you say?'

'So you think.'

'And?'

'Well, if the murderer hasn't won, one or other of the suspects have.'

'In what way?'

'Since they might have gained from the murders of the brother and his wife.'

'In what way might they have gained?'

'They all had so many motives, although none of the suspects seem to know for certain.'

'A bit like you.'

'No, Chase.'

'No?'

I coughed superiorly. 'If I had done it, if I had killed the brother and his wife, and didn't know that I had, that's different from one of suspects having done it, but not remembering.'

'In what way?'

'My mind has always been crystal clear, Chase. I have never imbibed alcohol. Still, having investigated all the suspects, their minds are either distracted or cloudy.'

'And?'

I leaked a tear. 'And Chase, if I had murdered my own daughter, a daughter I never even knew I might have had -'

'And her husband-'

'And her husband, that would make me an insane person, not a judge.'

'But you're not a judge, Ewok.'

'No?'

'No, you're a sleuth- and a very hit-and-run one at that.'

I squeezed my brow. 'Then, we'll just have to agree to disagree.'

'No, not quite.'

'No?'

'No you will revisit the suspects, re-investigate them, re-analyse the data, process the evidence, and re-formulate sturdier conclusions and healthier recommendations; you will make deductions.'

I shook my head. 'I'm not doing all that again twice, Chase.'

'That's correct, Ewok.'

I yawned satisfactorily. 'I'm glad you see that.'

'No, you'll be doing that more than twice.'

My inflamed silver eyes bulged. 'Excuse me?'

Chase smiled madly at me. 'Yes, you've only just started, Ewok.'

'Just started?'

'You're new to sleuthing, it takes time.'

'Well, do you know who did it, why they did it, how they did it, where they did it, and that it was definitely 1995?'

'I know more than you think.'

'What do you think?'

'I think I know all the answers.'

I frowned. 'Well, if you know all the answers, what's the bloody point in my researching the whole lampoon again.'

'Two points.'

'Yes?'

'The first point is you don't know who did it, why they did it, how they did it, where they did it- and yes it was definitely 1995.'

I leaned back. 'And the other point?'

Chase leaned forwards and teased the unscarred side of my face with his mushroom knife. '*This*.'

I gulped. 'Yes.'

'Yes.'

'Permission to breath, Chase.'

'With difficulty, yes.'

'If you already know it all, Chase, what possible satisfaction could you derive from my re-solving the unexplained murders.'

'There is a very good reason for it. The relevant person would be investigated and punished.'

I waved my head again. 'No, Chase, seriously, I have to stop you there. Don't get me wrong, I was a judge, and when I possessed sentencing powers, I I could have penalised them. But what is the value in a re-investigation you already comprehend and punishment you could inaugurate yourself.'

'There is a very signal point, Ewok. I might know who did it, I might know why it was done, I might know where it was done-'

'But?'

'But that doesn't mean that I know that you know these things, and that all of the relevant parties know.'

'And?'

'And far more significantly, it doesn't mean that I understand all the interlaced crimes and penalty points.'

'Why would that matter to you, Chase?'

'I want everyone surrounded by the killings of my brother and his wife, and my nephew's mum and dad perceiving the matters with contrition and regret; I want them probed and castigated.'

'You're mad chase!'

'No.'

'What about your smile, Chase? You don't even wear the Glasgow one?'

'My smile, Ewok is a smile of blanket justification, your smile is a smile of limited excuse; of extenuation or mitigation.'

I exhaled with exasperation. 'You don't sympathise with my gross disfigurement and violent poisoning?'

Chase tilted his head. 'No, I do.'

'Well?'

Chase smiled tolerantly. 'It's just you're at the lesser end of the torture victim's justification spectrum.'

I groaned, leaking a tear. 'What's next, then?'

'Heightened excruciation.'

As the whole ensemble of the age-old river city's most maleficent shadows banded together like the Scottish sequel to 'The Night of the long Knives', in the piping pea soup and scotch broth of the rising moon, I stomped my foot petulantly on the pavement, throwing up cascades of giant sploshes. 'That's poison, Chase!'

Chase laughed stoically into the furnace of the night, like a philosophical cacoademon. 'Yes, Ewok, I feel it would be.'

Lightning Source UK Ltd.
Milton Keynes UK
UKHW01f1940300718
326523UK00001B/147/P

9 781546 292357